CUTTING EDGE

CUTTING EDGE

A NOVEL OF SUSPENSE

ALLISON BRENNAN

THORNDIKE
WINDSOR
PARAGON

This Large Print edition is published by Thorndike Press, Waterville, Maine, USA and by BBC Audiobooks Ltd, Bath, England.
Thorndike Press, a part of Gale, Cengage Learning.
Copyright © 2009 by Allison Brennan.
The moral right of the author has been asserted.

The text of this Large Print edition is unabridged.
Other aspects of the book may vary from the original edition.
Set in 16 pt. Plantin.
Printed on permanent paper.

LIBRARY OF CONGRESS CATALOGING-IN-PUBLICATION DATA

Brennan, Allison.
   Cutting edge : a novel of suspense / by Allison Brennan.
     p. cm.
   ISBN-13: 978-1-4104-1908-8 (hardcover : alk. paper)
   ISBN-10: 1-4104-1908-8 (hardcover : alk. paper)
   1. Extremists—United States—Fiction. 2. Domestic terrorism—United States—Fiction. 3. United States. Federal Bureau of Investigation—Fiction. 4. Large type books. I. Title.
   PS3602.R4495C87 2009
   813'.6—dc22   2009028403

BRITISH LIBRARY CATALOGUING-IN-PUBLICATION DATA AVAILABLE

Published in 2009 in the U.S. by arrangement with The Ballantine Publishing Group, a division of Random House, Inc.
Published in 2010 in the U.K. by arrangement with Little, Brown Book Group.

U.K. Hardcover: 978 1 408 43131 3 (Windsor Large Print)
(Paragon Large Print)

Printed in the United States of America (LP)
1 2 3 4 5 6 7 13 12 11 10 09

For a wonderful storyteller,
a kindred spirit,
and a very wise woman.
ELAINE FLINN
1939–2008

ACKNOWLEDGMENTS

Terence Higgins, the wonderful firefighting husband of award-winning author Kristan Higgins; my brother-in-law Kevin Brennan, a wildlife biologist with the California Department of Fish and Game who has always been generous with his time and knowledge when I need it; my husband, Dan Brennan, who is always willing to answer any odd question I throw his way without blinking; Tammy Cravit, from the San Mateo Coroner's Office; CJ Lyons, who always seems to know the answers to the most arcane questions; Phelan Evans with the Sacramento County Coroner; retired FBI agent Max Noel; the Sacramento FBI special agents, especially the terrorism squad; Tom and Margie Lawson for online "flying lessons," and Margie for always being cheerful; Josh Rappaport for helping me understand genetic research and gene therapy; Elisa Warren with Avid ID Systems for her help in understanding microchip technology — and letting me take some liberties with my fictional prototype!

"Superagent" Kim Whalen and the Trident team, especially Lara Allen who does a magnificent job selling my foreign rights; my insightful editor, Charlotte Herscher, who really went above and beyond with this trilogy — the time difference worked to our advantage! Dana Isaacson, editor extraordinaire; Linda Marrow, Libby McGuire, Scott Shannon, Kim Hovey, Kate Collins, Kelli Fillingim, and the rest of the Ballantine team — *especially* the production department — this marks an even dozen. Thank you so much for your support and patience.

Friends are especially important when in deadline mode, and writers understand writers, even when we get loopy from lack of sleep. I particularly want to shout out to Toni McGee Causey for her humor, wisdom, loyalty, and brainstorming. Two thousand miles is nothing with the World Wide Web. And Roxanne St. Claire, a smart and supportive buddy who might not understand my hourglass analogy, but is still there to catch me if I fall. I miss you guys and can't wait for the next conference.

My kids deserve an extra-special acknowledgment because deadlines often interfere with fun time. Thanks gang for helping keep the house running smoothly and letting me disappear into my office or at Starbucks every night. And my mom, for being the surrogate driver when I was "in the zone," and trying to keep me organized.

PROLOGUE

Twenty Years Ago
I am going to die tonight.

It was a random thought, and should have been fleeting because Nora didn't believe she was in any *real* danger. As soon as they breached security, they'd be arrested, and then she'd be truly free.

But as soon as the dire prediction flitted into her mind, it hung heavily in the air as she drove with her mother, sister, and two men toward the Diablo Canyon Power Plant, nestled in the coastal mountains of Avila Beach. She had never been so close to a nuclear reactor in her life; fear flowed through her veins, riding on her blood cells, squeezing her until she could scarcely breathe. It was the situation that gave her fearsome thoughts, not that she was truly going to die.

Nora didn't want anyone to get hurt. She tried to be strong as they turned off the

Pacific Coast Highway and drove the winding roads into the mountains east of the power plant. Ten miles as the crow flies, and then they'd be at the end of the narrow road. They'd proceed the last mile on foot.

How her mother thought this plan was even remotely sane, Nora didn't know. When Cameron laid out the idea last month, she had laughed out loud and told him that the security at nuclear power plants was probably better than security for the president of the United States.

He'd slapped her. Lorraine hadn't even flinched. Nora wasn't surprised that her mother hadn't stood up for her, but it hurt deep down where Nora had thought she no longer cared how her mother felt about her.

Kenny used to work at Diablo Canyon, knew all the security protocols. He'd get them in, Cameron assured the group with complete confidence.

"Once we're in," Cameron said, "it doesn't really matter if we are able to cause a radiation leak. Getting *in* is the key. The press we get for penetrating their so-called security will be worth any trouble we have. The public will wake up, demand change. The revolution will start. And we'll be martyrs in a far greater movement."

Nora wasn't so sure. For years, her mother

had been involved in every kind of protest under the sun. They lived off the grid — Nora didn't even have a Social Security number or a driver's license or a birth certificate. She'd been born in a cabin in the woods. Had anything gone wrong, she would have died. She didn't think her mother would have cared.

Nora was exhausted. She'd be eighteen in October — her mother didn't remember her exact birthday — and had never had a real home. No formal education; her mother's friends taught her what they knew, which was heavy on creating fake IDs, making bombs that were rarely used, and stealing food. But she got by, and was giving her little sister an education that involved reading and math more than it did picking pockets.

Quin was smart. Nora couldn't let her grow up like she had. Her sister needed a permanent home, a real school, people who cared about her.

If Nora had even one small doubt that what she was doing was right, it disappeared when Cameron insisted on bringing Quin with them — and Lorraine didn't object. "She'll stay in the car," Cameron said. "No one is going to be left behind." And he stared at Nora. For a moment, she feared he knew. Then he went back to pontificating.

Last summer, Nora had contacted the FBI when Cameron and Lorraine attempted to burn down a housing development under construction in San Luis Obispo. The bomb fizzled, causing little damage, and the FBI said they didn't have enough evidence to arrest Cameron Lovitz. Since she hadn't been with them when the bomb was planted, her testimony would be hearsay and the U.S. attorney wouldn't prosecute unless he had an eighty percent chance of winning. But the FBI asked Nora to be an informant for them. They'd been watching Cameron Lovitz for a long time and believed an insider could give them the information to catch the radical activist red-handed.

Special Agent Andrew Keene was her handler. She'd been meeting him several times a week for the last eight months.

As Kenny drove the Jeep over the jagged, unpaved road, Nora shrank into herself and thought about Andy and what he'd said to her early this morning, before dawn.

She'd set up an emergency meeting behind the student union at Cal Poly to tell him about the bombs. Cameron was a lab assistant at the university, and Lorraine had moved Quin and Nora into his small faculty apartment last year. As much as Nora hated Cameron, the two-bedroom apartment was the closest thing they'd ever had to a home.

"Can you arrest him now?" Nora said as soon as she approached Andy.

"You're late — I thought you wouldn't make it." Concern marred his handsome face.

"I'm sorry," she mumbled. "I didn't want to take any chances." The truth was, Cameron scared her. She'd almost chickened out. But then she remembered the night Quin almost died when Cameron had her nine-year-old sister hanging banners off the freeway overpass, and she was empowered. This had to end.

"Andy, the bombs — did you get my message? Are they going to arrest him now?"

She knew the answer was *no* even before he spoke. She blinked back tears, wanting to be stronger than this.

"Don't," Andy murmured, and touched her cheek with the back of his hand. Her heart skipped a beat, her skin flushed. Nora had loved Andy almost from the day she met him. He'd promised her he would protect her and Quin, put Cameron and the others in prison, where they couldn't hurt anyone. He was her guardian angel and her link to the real world, all in one. He'd

15

shared stories about his large, fun-loving family, about the four-bedroom, one-bath house he'd grown up in, where he and his five brothers and sisters fought over who showered and when. But he said it with affection and wistfulness, and there was no doubt in Nora's mind that the Keenes had loved one another.

But Nora couldn't say anything about her feelings for him. Andy was twenty-five, she seventeen. When tonight was over, he'd go back to D.C. They had separate lives. He was a college graduate; she'd never had formal schooling. He was a federal cop; she'd broken so many laws she didn't know what was legal and what wasn't. He had a job; she would need to find one to provide a home for Quin. A place where her sister would feel safe and loved. A place she never had to leave, a place to keep her things and know they would be there when she returned.

But for now, for the next twenty-four hours, Agent Andrew Keene was her only hope for a real future — without Lorraine, without Cameron, without fear. She would be emancipated and her new life would begin.

If she survived tonight.

"I did everything I could, Nora. But in

the end, it wasn't a solid case. He burned the security map of the power plant, and he could argue that the bombs were for a lab project."

"But I'll testify! Tell the judge what they planned."

"Without physical proof, the U.S. attorney won't take it to court."

"That's not fair!"

"Shh." He hugged her and it felt right to be here like this. She wanted to enjoy his warmth and affection but she was too worried to relax.

Andy stepped back, tilted her chin up. "There is nothing they can do to damage the reactor or even create a small radiation leak, you know that, right?"

She hesitated, then nodded.

"Believe me, Nora. They won't even get inside the reactor building. Even if the FBI wasn't going to be crawling all over that place, there's no way they'd get past security. Lovitz's plan is pretty solid as far as getting past exterior security — and the plant will rectify that after tonight. But the rest is idiocy. The guy's a lunatic."

"He doesn't care about success. He wants to make a statement."

"And he could get you and everyone killed trying to make that damn statement." Andy

17

sounded more than a little angry. "No one wants a fatality tonight. We are optimistic that we can make the arrests without violence."

"Cameron isn't like the others — the other men my mother has been involved with. He's, I don't know. He doesn't seem quite . . . right. That sounds dumb."

Andy shook his head. "Not dumb. Our in-house shrinks suspect he's borderline schizophrenic. Paranoid, distrustful of anyone in authority. He could just as easily be targeting abortion clinics as nuclear power plants. Whatever he wraps his sick mind around. Remember that — this isn't about you, or even Lorraine, who is an enabler. This is about a violent, psychopathic criminal, and I will put him in prison. He'll never hurt you, Nora."

She believed Andy. He knew what he was doing; she could trust him.

"I think you should stay with Quin. We have his plan, and will —"

She shook her head. "I have to go. Cameron insisted. I don't think he trusts me. Not *this,* but in general. He's always watching me, it gives me the creeps."

"Make an excuse. Get sick. Can you make yourself throw up? They won't want some-

18

one with the stomach flu to slow them down."

Nora feared that if she pretended to be sick, Cameron would kill her. She evaded Andy's question and asked, "Is everything set for my emancipation and Quin?"

He nodded. "But we're keeping it confidential."

"She's all I have."

"That's not true."

Nora looked at him, hearing something different in his voice. Something like longing. But she had little experience with boys her own age, let alone men like Andy Keene.

He took her hand. Her stomach fluttered, her head felt light. "You have *you.* You're a strong, smart young woman with great instincts and boundless compassion. Never doubt yourself, ever." He looked nervous. "I — you have me, Nora. I'm not going to push you, I'm not going to crowd you. I know you'll have a lot of things to settle after tonight. But I hope you'll let me be part of your life, when you're ready."

She felt like Cinderella, being swept off her feet by a handsome prince as they battled her evil mother. But her life wasn't a fairy tale. It had been hard, cold, unforgiving, and ruthless.

Yet she still had hope. Maybe she *could*

19

have a future where she could make a real difference.

"I'd like that." Her voice sounded foreign. Had she even spoken?

Then he kissed her. It was short and light, but it was clear he was *kissing* her, his lips on hers, his hand pressing gently on her back. Kind, hopeful, supportive. But this wasn't friendship. Nora knew exactly what it meant.

I hope you'll let me be part of your life.

"You'll be safe, Nora," he whispered. "I promise I won't let anything happen to you."

Nora jumped when Cameron slapped her thigh hard enough to bring tears to her eyes. Gone were the memories of Andy kissing her, the warm feeling of being safe even for a moment. She was back in the Jeep, facing a half-deranged man.

"Pay attention, Nora!"

They had parked at the base of a mountain. Behind her were trees towering high into the sky — or so she imagined from the dense blackness on this moonless night. In front of them was two thousand feet of open space. A meadow blanketed with wildflowers — she remembered them from their earlier reconnaissance, bright and breezy. Now the grassy plain looked like a bottom-

20

less pit in front of an industrial complex that lit up the coast.

Quin had fallen asleep in the backseat; now she stirred. "Mom?"

"Stay here," Lorraine commanded.

"I want to go with you and Nora," she whined, her voice quavering with unshed tears. "It's dark."

Cameron turned and glared at Quin with his dark eyes narrowed, and she didn't say anything else, just pulled her blanket closer to her chest. Nora hated her mother then, for not protecting them. For bringing Quin into this.

"It'll be okay," Nora told her sister.

"I expect every detail to be handled with precision," said Cameron. "You'll have ten minutes to get out, then ten minutes to rendezvous back here after Ken and I set the charges. Ten minutes before the valves blow, releasing toxic radiation. If you don't move quickly you will die. It will be painful. Understand?"

Nora nodded and Quin stared with wide eyes, shaking. Nora reached over to console her, surprised at her steady hand. Maybe she'd gone on too many of these; she'd become jaded, complacent. The time her mother broke into a university research lab and released seventy rabbits, Nora had been lookout; she'd been nine like Quin was now. Or when Lorraine, pregnant with Quin, had staged a protest outside a slaughterhouse and gotten national news attention when she went into labor and gave birth in a nearby field. Nora had been the one to wrap her new sister in blankets and cut the umbilical cord because the ambulance hadn't arrived. She'd been eight. Or two years ago, when Lorraine first met Cameron Lovitz during an anti-nuclear-weapon rally, and they'd broken into a military museum and spray-painted obscenities and slogans all over the walls. That they'd gotten away amazed Nora; she thought for sure they'd all be caught and thrown in prison. The vandalism was all over the TV news for weeks.

But they were never caught, and soon thereafter Lorraine moved them off the streets of San Francisco to an apartment in San Luis Obispo and Nora thought she might have a home.

She'd been wrong.

After Nora turned informant, the FBI came up with a plan and brought in Special Agent Andrew Keene undercover at Cal Poly to handle her involvement. And now, eight months of secrecy, deception, and fear was nearly over.

Nora focused on breathing, on getting through each too-long minute. "Be brave," she told Quin. She handed Quin her small teddy bear, the one Nora had saved every time Lorraine uprooted them without warning. She mouthed *I love you,* and meant it. There was nothing she wouldn't do for her sister.

The air was cold at one in the morning, the salt-tinged breeze urging Nora to pull her windbreaker tighter around her thin body. She wore only a T-shirt and threadbare sweater under the windbreaker; Cameron insisted they all travel light.

They picked this time because shift change had been at midnight; it would be quiet, everyone would have settled into their routines, and the earlier shift would have left.

She saw Cameron's gun for the first time when they went through the weak link in the electric fence: a rarely used entrance. Why the powerplant didn't have a guard at the gate, and hadn't disabled the electronic code, she didn't know. Maybe this was what Andy meant earlier, that the FBI was letting them get through the gate first so they'd be caught red-handed with pipe bombs. No question what their plans were. But they'd already crossed over land that was closed to the public. What more did the FBI want?

The code Kenny had provided would disable the warning alarm so an employee could enter without the alarms going off. The main office would still be alerted, but because it was close enough to shift time, Kenny said no one would be suspicious.

They just needed to cross another two hundred feet of open space, and then they'd have cover up against an office building. The plan was to walk around the building, emerging only forty feet from the entrance to the reactors. The codes from Kenny would also work to get inside the building.

She hung back with her mother for a moment and whispered, "Lorraine." Her mother didn't like being called Mom. Nora couldn't remember calling her Mom, even as a child.

Lorraine turned to her, irritated. "Can it wait, Nora?"

"Cameron has a gun."

"It's okay."

Lorraine hated guns. How many times had Nora been dragged to a gun-control rally? Holding up signs and proclaiming at the top of her lungs that guns killed? But now her mother sounded like it was totally *normal* to have a gun. When had that changed? *Cameron.* He had charisma and charm to woo people into believing his bizarre philosophy, but he was also violent and unpredictable. He had turned her mother from a sixties hippie who would never hurt an animal, person, or plant into a terrorist.

But Lorraine had always been on the crazy side. She'd fallen in with bad groups before, but had gotten out before they went down or dropped out. Not this time. Not with Cameron leading the charge. Yet so much more was at stake. Her freedom and her life.

Then everything happened so fast Nora thought she was dreaming. But it was so vivid she knew she'd never forget.

"Change of plans," Cameron announced.

"What?" Nora exclaimed.

"Shut up or I'll kill you." He meant it. "We run low along the fence until we reach the cooling pools, then turn and move along the base of the north cliffs. It'll get us closer to our destination without increased risk."

Change of plans? What if the FBI didn't have people everywhere? What if they only covered the area where Nora had told Andy they would be? What if Andy was wrong and Cameron could get into the reactor and set off something that would kill not only them, but thousands of people?

Terrified, she followed. She had no choice.

It took nearly ten minutes to reach the

base of the cliffs. There were lights every-where, but Cameron was right. Running along this section of the fence, they re-mained just out of sight.

They paused only briefly before crossing a small open space to a warehouse. Nora saw a pair of maintenance workers, but they were heading in the opposite direction and didn't look their way. Nora glanced at Cam-eron; his hand was on his gun. She knew he'd kill. Her, Lorraine, strangers. His brutal determination was in his stance, in his eyes. Why didn't Lorraine see it? What was wrong with her mother?

"On three," Cameron said.

As soon as they moved from their hiding place, blinding floodlights snapped on and she couldn't see.

"FBI! Down!"

Nora dropped, just like Andy had in-structed her.

Cameron dove behind a stack of wooden crates only feet from her. Lorraine and Ken ran behind a large maintenance truck. Nora felt like she was in the middle of a war.

"Lovitz! Surrender. You can't get out," a voice boomed over loudspeakers. Nora couldn't tell where the sound was coming from.

She heard Cameron swearing, then he

called out, "Are you ready?"

"Yes," Lorraine said.

"Do it!"

Do it? Do *what?*

Lorraine moved from behind the truck and threw something over Nora's head. It rolled away from her.

It looked like a bomb. Just like the bombs Nora had helped her make. Oh, God, it was over. They were all going to die.

I'm going to die tonight.

"Cover!" Lorraine shouted at her.

Nora scrambled behind the crates closest to her. Seconds later, the bomb exploded.

"Run!" Cameron told her.

Nora didn't move. She had to stay here. She wasn't one of them, she didn't know if whoever was out there knew that she was helping, that she wasn't a terrorist. She didn't want to die. If she just stayed here, she'd be okay. Don't move. Don't breathe. Where was Andy? Did he know where she was? Would he come for her?

Cameron grabbed her arm and dragged her with him.

"It was you," he whispered in her ear. "You fucking bitch traitor, you talked."

"N-no," she cried.

"We'll see who's lying."

He held the gun to her neck and walked

her out into the open. She squinted against the intense brightness of the industrial lights. How could Cameron see? From the corner of her eye, she saw he'd put on glasses, then remembered how he always wore sunglasses backward, around his neck. Even tonight. As if he'd anticipated what would happen.

"We're leaving!" Cameron called out to the unseen federal agents. "You won't stop us. We have more grenades; we will use them!"

The hand grenades were homemade, and Nora had always been terrified of them. Lorraine didn't seem to think there was anything wrong with having her daughters measuring sulfur, charcoal, and potassium nitrate to create black powder for home-made bombs. The bombs, Lorraine said, were never to hurt anyone. They were to save people from themselves.

Nora realized Cameron had brainwashed her mother. Murder was okay, as far as they were concerned, if it advanced their cause.

Cameron started moving away from the building, across the open yard toward where they had come in.

The FBI would never let them leave.

"Cameron Lovitz!" the voice shouted. "Put down your weapon."

"I'm leaving!"

Cameron continued walking backward, dragging a stumbling Nora with him.

"You're dead, Nora," he growled. "You're a traitor to the cause."

The barrel of the gun dug into her neck and she cried out.

Cameron called out, "Lorraine! Now!"

Another mini-bomb flew over their heads, landing at the edge of the lights.

The explosion knocked them both to the ground. As they fell on hard pavement, Nora realized that Cameron hadn't expected such a powerful blast.

Nora thought she was dead, that Cameron's gun would discharge right into her neck. Clean through, in and out, and her only thought was whether anyone would find Quin and the Jeep.

Cameron fell on top of her, but his hands instinctively reached out to brace himself.

The gun dropped from his grip.

Another explosion, then shouts from everywhere at once, and she thought she heard her mother scream. Cameron reached for the gun. Nora's hand shot out, trying to bat it out of the way, hitting his wrist.

"Freeze! Don't move or I'll shoot."

Cameron slammed her head into the concrete and everything spun out of control.

Nora's mouth filled with blood.

"Fuck you, pig!" Cameron screamed, his hand on the gun, and his arm jerked up and fired without hesitation. Once. Twice?

The report was deafening. Nora's ears rang. So much noise, in her ears, in her head, around her, everywhere. And blood, everywhere blood, she must be dying. The pain was all-encompassing, her head spun, she was suffocating. Someone was on top of her. *Cameron.*

She opened her eyes, barely able to draw a breath as a heavy weight pinned her down. She saw only Cameron Lovitz's dead eyes. Lifeless. He had her trapped.

Four hands pulled her out.

Her head was too heavy to hold up. Her eyelids closed.

"Was she hit? Nora? Can you hear me?"

"Andy." She thought she spoke, but she wasn't sure.

"It's ASAC Rick Stockton. Nora, where were you hit? Nora? Can you hear me?"

Hands all over her. Shouts and orders, but nothing she understood. Someone was crying. A scream. An ambulance in the distance. No, it was close. Flashing lights everywhere, but her eyes were closed.

"She wasn't hit," someone said.

"She's not okay!" Stockton snapped. He

shined a light in her eyes. Stockton. Stockton. Andy's boss. Partner? She didn't know. She didn't remember.

Someone touched her chest and she cried out. Her shirt was ripped open. "Ribs. Cracked?"

"Are they in custody? God fucking dammit, what's going on? Status report!"

Stockton sounded worried. Where was Andy? Why wasn't he here? He promised. He promised everything would be all right . . .

"Andy," she whispered. It was hard to speak.

"I'm getting you to a hospital, Nora. You're going to be okay."

"Critical," someone called from far, far away. Everything began to fade. Voices running away from her.

Maybe they were leaving her here.

Lorraine's shrill voice was like an icepick in her aching head. "I'll sue you fucking pigs! All of you!" An anguished cry. "You killed him!"

"Get her the fuck out of here!" Stockton ordered.

"Lovitz is dead," another voice said. "Wright and Potter are in custody."

"Quin —" Nora said. She tried to get up.

"Don't move, Nora."

"Quin — sh-she's . . ." She couldn't make her throat talk.

"We have Quin," he said. "Quin's safe. We followed the Jeep."

People ran past her. She tried to reach out, to touch someone, but the noises dimmed. Someone grabbed her hand. "I'm not leaving you," Stockton said. "You're going to be okay, Nora. I promise."

Her mind snapped shut and she didn't wake up for three days. When she did, Agent Stockton told her Andy was dead.

CHAPTER ONE

The arson had been hot, fast, and lethal.

The cloying, acrid scent of the extinguished arson fire had FBI agent Nora English breathing through her mouth as she walked carefully through the remains of what had been the research wing of Butcher-Payne Biotech. The bright white light from emergency spotlights cast an eerie starkness throughout the burned building. Her boots sloshing through the water left behind by the firefighters. Tens of thousands of gallons had flowed into this building to put out the blaze, and the fire crew was surveying the structure to insure there were no remaining hot spots.

They'd been damn lucky. Last winter had been dry, creating a summer combustible with dry brush and trees. The hill of dead, brown foliage behind Butcher-Payne, and the arid canyon across the two-lane highway, could easily have caught fire, spreading through the crisp timber and underbrush faster than they could respond. Fortunately, there'd been no wind to push the fire, and the first responders had done a magnificent job saturating the rooftops and surrounding grounds. In addition, the solid exterior and internal firewalls of the five-year-old building had contained the fire within the research wing.

"The fire sprinklers didn't go on as they were supposed to," the Placer County fire chief, Ansel Nobel, said while he escorted Nora to where the body had been found. "The most recent inspection was three months ago; then, they were functioning properly. I don't understand."

"Have you checked the water-pump station? Is this area on city or well water?"

"There's a water storage tank uphill for — damn, that's it."

"Excuse me?"

"The water storage tank is for the hydrants. The sprinklers are on a pump system maintained by the county. We hooked up the hydrants without any problems, so when my crew chief told me the sprinklers hadn't come on, I assumed they were faulty."

He gestured at the ceiling with his flashlight. The sprinkler heads had distended, but had no water.

"I'll ask my partner to check it out." She called Pete Antonovich using the walkie-talkie feature of her BlackBerry. Technically he was no longer her partner, now that she'd been temporarily promoted to squad leader while their SSA was teaching for four months at Quantico. But old habits; she and Pete had been partners since she transferred to Sacramento FBI headquarters nine years ago.

"Pete, it's Nora. Chief Nobel said the sprinklers didn't activate. The pump may have been sabotaged — can you talk to the sheriff's department and get a team over there to check it out?"

"Will do. What's it like inside?"

"Wet."

His voice had a modicum of restrained humor. "I meant damages."

"Same apparent burn pattern as the previous arson fires. Started in the lab and was contained ninety percent there and adjoining offices. The lobby walls have some damage. Hot enough to melt electronic equipment. Arson investigation will know more."

"When's Quin going to get here?"

Nora hesitated a moment. Her sister had a reputation, and she hated to fuel it. But this *was* Pete, so she simply said, "She had a date."

"It's five-thirty in the morning."

"In San Francisco. She promised she'd leave immediately. She wasn't on call tonight," Nora defended.

"I'm not being critical, but we need her. I don't need to tell you they're escalating."

The arson gang they'd been investigating for twenty months had never killed before. The three previous arsons had targeted the same industry — biotechnology — but the first two were set in warehouses, and the third fire in a small genetic research building at Sacramento State University. Nora wasn't certain yet exactly what Butcher-Payne did, but they had "Biotech" in their name and that, coupled with the "message" that had been spray-painted on the exterior — STOP MURDER, signed with the moniker the previous arsonists used, BLF — was enough to make Nora and Pete feel comfortable adding Butcher-Payne to the list.

The only difference in the arson at Butcher-Payne was the victim. Why kill now? Accident or premeditated? Was Jonah Payne targeted because he was Jonah Payne, or simply because he headed the research lab?

"Something else is going on. This just doesn't feel right to me." Nora caught herself twisting her shortish, dark blond hair

36

between her thumb and forefinger. She tucked the loose curls behind her ear and dropped her hand.

"Have you seen the vic?"

"I'm heading that way now."

"I did a field test on the graffiti. The paint is identical to the other arson fires. Chances that this is a copycat drop dramatically."

"Dammit, Pete, they haven't killed anyone before."

"It was just a matter of time, you know that. I'll go check the pumps and get back to you."

Nora pocketed her BlackBerry as Chief Nobel said, "It's happened before."

That seemed obvious to Nora, and should to Chief Nobel, who was well aware of the previous three arsons. "Excuse me?"

"Arsonists setting a fire not knowing someone is inside."

"It still makes them murderers, whether they intended to kill someone or not."

Nobel stood at the entrance to Jonah Payne's office. "Brace yourself, it's not pretty."

Nora buried her emotions deep. It didn't matter how many times she saw a dead body, or in what condition, the anger and deep sadness at a life taken too soon could overwhelm her if she didn't close off her feelings. She couldn't afford to impair her critical judgment. Cops learned to compartmentalize to do the job or they ended up dead or drunk. There was a reason cops had nearly twice the suicide rate as the population at large.

Her ability to fully detach herself had earned her a reputation as levelheaded with those who liked her, and a cold bitch with those who didn't.

Chief Nobel stepped aside. Bright crime-scene tape crisscrossed the charred opening leading into Dr. Jonah Payne's office off the main research laboratory. The metal door was open, the paint burned off on one side. Had it been open or closed when the fire crew came in? The office itself wasn't large, approximately fourteen feet square. Paper fueled the flames in here, soggy remnants of pulp everywhere, higher piles of wet ash and partially burned paper on the credenza behind the large desk. No windows, no natural light — Nora didn't know how anyone could work in such conditions. She'd put skylights in every room of her small country home because she needed sunlight.

The only thing her mother had ever done for her was give her an appreciation of nature.

Good job keeping your emotions in check, thinking of that woman.

Nora focused on the victim, presumed to be Jonah Payne, who lay flat on his back in front of his desk. His position seemed odd to Nora. She'd investigated only one domestic terrorism case that had resulted in fire deaths: in that case, the fourteen victims had been trapped in a burning building and all had died of smoke inhalation. The bodies had been either in fetal positions or prone.

Payne had second- and third-degree burns over all exposed areas of his body. His hair was gone, and the metal from his glasses had melted into his charred skin. His shirt was completely gone, but he'd been wearing jeans, she noted, and while they were black they appeared intact. Denim could withstand fire longer than many other natural-fiber materials. They'd need to put together all these details to figure out exactly what happened to Payne and whether his death was intentional or accidental.

Fire fatalities were among the most difficult crimes to investigate. Much of the damage to the body came from necessary fire-suppression activities, but when firefighters discovered a victim, they did everything they could to preserve evidence while also putting out the flames. Unless there was a bullet in the body, severe blunt-force trauma, or another obvious external force, determining cause of death was extremely difficult.

The man inspecting the body glanced up. "Chief."

"Keith, this is Special Agent Nora English with the FBI's domestic terrorism unit."

"Don't come in," he ordered.

"Nora, have you met our M.E., Keith Coffey?"

"No," she said. "Dr. Coffey, does it seem odd to you that the victim is on his back?"

He stopped his inspection and looked at her. "Yes, it is very odd. But I don't want to jump to conclusions before the fire inspector gets here."

"She's on her way," Nora said. "She was out of town and —"

A raspy voice behind her bellowed, "She? Last I checked I'm still a man, sugar."

Nora bristled and turned. The smoker's voice belonged to a man who looked old enough to be her grandfather. He wore black pants and a red plaid shirt on which was clipped a fire marshal's badge.

The man grinned at her and winked. "Yep, still a man."

"Ulysses, this is Special Agent Nora English with the FBI. I told you about the task force —"

Ulysses waved away the chief's introduction. "Task force," he said with derision. "All talk, no action."

"We should discuss this, Mr. —" Nora began.

"Ulysses."

"I've brought in a consultant from the state fire inspector's office, who's been on the task force since the first fire twenty months ago —"

"This is my jurisdiction, or are you going to flex your federal muscles and screw everything up?"

Nora didn't want friction with the locals, but she would "flex her federal muscles" if she had to. Domestic terrorism fell squarely on the FBI's shoulders. She was about to say that when her sister Quin bounced into the room, the polar opposite of the craggy fire marshal.

"Ulysses!" Quin exclaimed, all petite blond ball of energy fawning over the graying man. She gave him a hug that was longer than it needed to be and Nora watched, bemused, as Ulysses turned to putty.

"If I'd known *you* were coming, sweetheart, I'd have put out the red carpet."

Quin laughed. "Nora is my sister. Cut her cute federal ass some slack, okay?"

"Anything for you, sugar."

Quin caught Nora's eye with a happy smugness that had Nora twisting her mouth to avoid smirking back. At least the victim was in good hands. Her sister didn't take anything but her job seriously, which had been a bone of contention between them for years, and there was no one Nora trusted more than Quin with this case. Quin would catch Ulysses up on the previous arsons, freeing Nora to focus on interviewing Payne's partner and staff. While there was little doubt that this arson was connected to the others, she needed all documentation of threats either in person or writing, a list of any known trespassers over the last few weeks, and information on current Butcher-Payne projects.

Dr. Coffey turned to Nora. "To answer your question, Agent English, I've never seen a case where the victim was on his back except if he was dead or unconscious when the fire started."

Quin crossed over to where Nora stood by the entry and said under her breath, "Sheriff Sanger is here, and he's on a rampage about Professor Cole, yada yada.

That slimy reporter Buttface is here —"

"Belham —"

"Right, Buttface. He's hanging around Sanger, who's giving this hot, tall, and sexy hunk an earful. Don't know if he's Payne's partner, but —" She gave Nora the *I think he's stirring up shit* sideways glance.

"Thanks for the heads-up."

"I'll take care of Ulysses — he's ornery, but he's one of the smartest in the business."

Nora excused herself after one final look at Jonah Payne's remains.

Unconscious or dead before the fire. That would mean his death wasn't an accident — he'd been intentionally murdered. Had he caught the arsonists red-handed? Why not hit the panic button? She assumed he would have a method to alert security quickly, but she'd need to double-check with the security company. What happened to the alarm system? Why hadn't he called the police? Was he unable to? Maybe he had confronted the arsonists and been killed. Or he might have known the perps. Payne's murder could have been premeditated, and the arson merely a way to cover up the crime and destroy evidence. That would make this crime far more personal, and the culprit more likely to be someone who'd benefit from his death: a partner, wife, or relative. But the M.O. matched the other BLF arsons, which made the personal scenario unlikely.

Quin took command of the crime scene the way she commanded everything in her life — fast and completely, with a sugar coating so no one knew what hit them.

Now Nora had to control whatever damage Sheriff Sanger had done by his public vendetta against Professor Leif Cole. This investigation was already sliding down the slippery slope of legal posturing and games, the press circling like vultures because the biotech industry was controversial, and high-ranking politicians were calling Washington wanting to know what was being done in Sacramento and why they didn't have an arrest. Shit runs downhill fast.

Sanger was going to jeopardize the entire case if he didn't keep his big mouth shut.

CHAPTER TWO

Duke Rogan had watched friends die during his tour in the Marines; he had seen and touched the dying, moved and buried the dead. But he'd never felt so damn *helpless*. At least, not since his parents were killed in a plane crash more than a decade ago. Worse, guilt nipped at the edges of his mind, gaining traction. His security system had failed, and a good man had paid the ultimate price.

"Are you certain the victim is Jonah Payne?" he asked Sheriff Lance Sanger. They stood near the front entrance of the burned-out research lab in the unnatural illumination of spotlights attached to the fire trucks. Fire trucks and police cars littered the small parking lot like a child's forgotten game; the fire was out and aftermath activities were methodical, without the controlled urgency necessary while the fire raged.

"Near one-hundred-percent positive,"

Sanger said. "His car is in the lot —"

"Where?" Duke hadn't seen Jonah's red four-wheel-drive Jeep when he'd driven up a few minutes before.

"Behind the building."

"Is that usual?"

"I wouldn't know. I called Jim Butcher, his partner, then you. Jim's in L.A. He's flying back on the first available flight."

Duke wished Jim hadn't heard about Jonah's death over the phone. Jim and Jonah had been friends since college, starting Butcher-Payne Biotech right after graduate school. They'd been deemed by some as young upstarts not putting in their time or paying their dues, but they nevertheless managed to grow their business into a successful enterprise, moving into these larger facilities five years ago after selling a popular patent. Duke had known Jim even longer, since they had lived on the same street growing up, gone to the same high school, even played football together, though Jim was a couple years older.

"Did you check his house?" Duke asked.

"As soon as we discovered the body and his vehicle, we called Jonah's house. No answer. I did a well-being check. No obvious disturbance."

Jonah often worked late at Butcher-Payne,

especially after Trevor, his son, had enlisted in the military when he turned eighteen last year.

Trevor. He was going to be devastated. "Have you contacted Jonah's son in Iraq?"

"Not yet. I needed to confirm the victim's identity before notifying any next of kin."

Duke jerked his head toward the reporter standing only a few feet away not so discreetly eavesdropping. "Trevor may hear about it sooner in the news. I'll call him."

When Sanger glanced at the reporter, the journalist took it as a sign to approach.

"Hello, Rich," Sanger said.

"I saw the M.E.'s car here. Is there a body?"

"I'll be issuing a formal statement after I notify the next of kin."

"I heard it's Jonah Payne."

Duke took a step toward the tall, skinny reporter, straightening his spine to reach his full six feet two inches. Through a tight jaw, he said, "I wouldn't repeat that until it's publicly announced."

Rich took a step back, his hands up, a digital minirecorder in one hand. "Hey, I'm not an asshole."

Sanger coughed into his hand. Duke grabbed the minirecorder, verified it was off, and took out the batteries before handing them back to the reporter. "I don't give you permission to record me or quote me. Understand?"

"It's cool, dude." Rich put the recorder in one pocket and took a small spiral notepad from the other. "Lance, come on, give me something. I already saw the graffiti, I know it's the same group that hit Langlier and Sac State. Is this ELF? ALF? Someone else? What's going on?"

"When I know, you'll know."

"I spotted the arson investigator and a couple government cars. Is the FBI here? Have the feds taken over the case?"

Sanger bristled. A sore spot? Duke had contacts in the local FBI, he'd make inquiries about the other arsons, find out who was running the case. He could help since he had security and background information on all Butcher-Payne employees and vendors.

"The fire was extinguished less than two hours ago," Sanger said. "We have a lot of work to do, and until I get answers, I'm not going on record with anything."

Rich sighed, shoving his notebook into his jacket pocket. "Okay, okay, off-record. Is it Jonah Payne? Did he die in the fire?"

Sanger relented. "We have every reason to believe the victim is Jonah Payne, but we do not have confirmation and until we do, if I hear this in public I will make sure you are banned from every crime scene in Placer County as long as I'm sheriff."

"I'm not going to say anything. I swear, Lance, trust me."

Sanger simply shook his head.

Rich looked at Duke and tilted his chin up. "I know you."

"I don't know you."

"Rich Belham, from the *Bee.*"

He was waiting for an introduction, but Duke didn't respond.

"Rogan!" Rich snapped his fingers when the name came to him. "Rogan-Caruso! Private security, right? You take care of the rich and famous."

Duke tensed. Rogan-Caruso Protective Services handled a wide range of personal and corporate security issues, but inevitably the few high-profile clients they managed became the news. But he wasn't about to get in a discussion about his company with a nosy reporter.

"Are you in charge of security here? How did the arsonists get in? Did they hack into your system?"

The silence was palpable. The reporter had hit the target dead center, and he knew it. Duke said, "I will be investigating the

49

matter thoroughly and reporting my findings to law enforcement. What they do with the information is up to them."

Rich turned to Sanger. "I heard the FBI was talking to Professor Cole at the college."

Sanger's hands twitched, his jaw tightening so hard Duke heard the joints click. "No comment."

"Come on, you've been talking about Cole since the first arson. That he was instigating a riot. You arrested him for breaking into the courthouse three years ago and stealing the confidential settlement between the county and EnviroTech Supply."

Duke remembered that controversy. The county was going after EnviroTech for illegal dumping, but before the trial there was a confidential agreement between the parties. It had been alleged that EnviroTech bribed high-ranking county officials to dump the lawsuit, and that the lawsuit was the county's way of leveraging money from private business. It had been nasty, then seemed to disappear overnight.

"Leif Cole and I go way back," Sanger said. "But you know that, Belham. Don't go fishing in that lake."

Sanger jerked his head toward Duke and said, "I want to show you something." He held up the crime-scene tape for Duke to

50

walk under. They walked just out of Rich Belham's earshot.

"Damn, I hate that reporter," said the sheriff.

"Who's Professor Cole?" Duke asked quietly.

"Leif Cole, head of the social sciences department at Rose College."

"You know him?"

"We went to school together. We used to be friends, but I don't condone civil disobedience, and he's gone too far too many times. Our dads worked for the lumber company and the four of us used to go hunting and camping together every summer. We were responsible out there, my dad wouldn't have it any other way. When Leif went off to college, he changed. His big cause is genetic engineering. Thinks the entire world is going to crash and burn because of it, it's practically a religion to him. His classes at the university are just brewing with trouble. I've talked to him about inciting these kids, and he thinks it's a good thing if they can change the world." He gestured toward Butcher-Payne. "I fear his rants have gone too far. This shouldn't have happened."

No shit. "What's with the initials?" Duke gestured toward the main entrance, where

51

"BLF" was spray-painted in large, bold block letters. "Who's BLF? Is that Professor Cole's group?" He had a million questions, but Sanger interrupted.

"The feds think BLF stands for Biotech Liberation Front, an anarchist group formed specifically against biotechnology, like the Animal Liberation Front, who release research animals and often destroy equipment. Most anarchist groups are loosely formed and there's no obvious connection between the BLF and the ALF. As far as I'm concerned, they're all culpable. A few years ago, a group of teens burned down several houses that were under construction in Rocklin — a firefighter was seriously injured in the last one and is still on disability."

"You think the ALF may have been involved with this fire? How many arsons are we talking about?" Duke was trying to be reasonable, he understood police investigations, but his friend Jonah was dead. How long was it going to take the FBI and police to get their act together? If they knew who was responsible, why hadn't there been an arrest?

"The idiots in the ALF have all been arrested and are in prison. The soonest any of them will be released is late next year. Their ringleader has another decade."

That would have been too easy, Duke thought. "And BLF?"

"This is the fourth arson that they have taken credit for."

Duke didn't miss that Sanger raised his voice a fraction as he continued. "The feds have talked to Cole several times, since he's publicly advocated for the end of the bio-tech industry, but they don't have anything solid."

It was clear Sanger wanted the information out there. Belham, who stood just on the other side of the crime-scene tape, was writing as fast as Sanger spoke.

Sanger continued, "The feds are really mucking this up. The lead agent is this mightier-than-thou bitch. I'm on the regional domestic terrorism task force with her, and she's so focused on the fucking procedures and rules that she makes bureaucrats look like party animals."

Domestic terrorism? Duke almost smiled. If this was domestic terrorism there was only one agent who could elicit such passionate anger.

Sanger glanced left, looking beyond Duke, a tight sneer on his face. "Oh, hello, Agent English." Sarcasm dripped from his voice.

Nora. If there was even a faint silver lining

on this tragedy, it was that Duke would be seeing a lot more of Nora English.

He turned around, watched as Nora realized it was him standing with the sheriff. It was instantaneous. Her confident stride slowed a fraction, her dark eyes widened in surprise. Then Nora plastered on that impassive expression she'd perfected.

But Duke knew better.

No matter how rigid Nora English tried to pretend she was, under that icy shield was a woman rippling with energy and passion. Besides, a woman who looked like Nora, with perfect curves and athletic prowess, couldn't be all hardened cop. That she could deny for the four years Duke had known her that she was as attracted to him as he was to her showed a stubborn streak that Duke had been slowly wearing down the half-dozen times they'd worked together. The last case he'd consulted with her on, only a year ago, he'd been *this close* in getting her to agree to a date, but she'd clammed up and avoided his calls. He'd left the ball in her court, but now all bets were off. He liked puzzles, and Agent English was an extremely complex and sexy puzzle he couldn't wait to put together.

"Duke Rogan," Nora said, unable to keep the surprise out of her voice. "Security?"

She was playing the professional cop, but Duke smiled. "Good to see you, Nora. You're looking terrific, as usual." And other than her tired eyes, she looked even better than the last time he'd seen her.

Her eyes narrowed and she bit her lower lip. "Do you know the principals?"

He nodded somberly. "Jim Butcher and I went to school together, I've known Jonah almost since they started the business, when Jim hired me to run background checks on employees."

"Did you design the security here?"

"Yes." He glanced at the building, knowing that he'd screwed up somewhere. He just couldn't see where. He'd have to go through the logs line by line.

"I didn't know you knew each other," Sanger said.

Nora's chin jutted forward and she said, "Mr. Rogan has consulted for the FBI before."

Mr. Rogan? Duke was bemused. "I've worked with *Agent English* a few times."

She glanced slyly at him, her eyes narrowed as if wondering what he was up to, then turned to the sheriff. "As sheriff, you know that criminals will walk if law enforcement doesn't play by the rules."

"But sometimes you need to push the

envelope. I'm not talking about breaking the law, I'm talking about putting pressure on the bastards we *know* are involved even if we can't prove it."

Duke realized he was in the middle of a long-running debate between Nora and the sheriff. He'd put his money on Nora.

"Agent English!" Rich Belham called, waving his arms to get her attention.

Her voice was as cold as her expression. "Let's take it inside."

Lance Sanger agreed, though he wasn't giving up the argument. Duke followed them. Nora glanced at him, then looked skyward as if asking God: Why her?

Because we are good together.

Duke met Nora when a local congressman, a friend of Duke's partner J. T. Caruso, had received death threats. Duke was attracted immediately upon laying eyes on the woman. But as soon as they had actually started working the case, he'd also known there was something more than physical lust between them. Nora knew it, too. She just denied it. Too vehemently.

"With all due respect, Nora," Sanger said, "I knew Jonah Payne. He was a local-boy-done-good story, born right here in Auburn, left for college and came back to build his business. Brought jobs, good jobs, to town."

The undercurrent of accusation in Sanger's tone was clear: *If you'd put them in prison already, Jonah would be alive.*

Her words were laced with ice. "We've followed every lead, Lance. This case isn't being ignored. And you damn well know that."

Sanger grunted. "People are talking, Nora. They want to know why we — why *I* — haven't arrested Leif Cole."

Nora softened a fraction. "I understand your position, and I'm doing everything I can. I know something about the rules — and which ones I can bend, and which ones are only suggestions. I don't want this group out any more than you do. But you know very well that Professor Cole isn't setting these fires."

"But he may know who is."

They stepped into the lobby, the stone floor slick with an inch of water. Two firemen, coats off, took an ax to the wall between the research offices and the lobby.

Nora tilted her head to the side. "I've interviewed Cole half a dozen times. You know him personally. Would he keep quiet if he knew who had set these fires?"

"I don't know." Sanger ran a hand over his buzz cut.

"And neither do I."

"Do we have confirmation that the victim

is Jonah Payne?"

"Not yet, but we're almost positive. Visually, even with the second- and third-degree burns, the victim resembles Dr. Payne. Same height and build, discovered in his office, his vehicle is parked in the rear of the building, registered to him. He wore glasses like Dr. Payne. We will identify personal artifacts, and when we move the body we'll check for a wallet and any identification, and if possible, the coroner will print him."

"I'd like to see him," Duke said.

Nora looked at him, unable to hide her compassion and empathy. "You don't need to —"

"I do."

Her chin quivered, just for a second, and she took his hand. She understood; he didn't have to explain. "I'm really sorry."

Duke squeezed her fingers. He'd take her sympathy, but what he really wanted was justice.

"You were about to say something else," he said, watching her dark gray eyes. Duke had always been drawn to Nora's eyes — she was the only woman he knew who had truly gray eyes, and they were gorgeous, especially with her long lashes and red lips.

She waited a beat.

"You know I have clearance," he said.

58

"I know." She pulled her hand from his. He didn't let it go without a tug. "My instincts tell me that Cole is not directly involved, but he either knows or suspects who is. He supports legitimate civil disobedience, but he's never advocated murder, nor is he a dyed-in-the-wool anarchist. I've read all his writings, even went to his big speech two months ago. He wants a stop to all biotech research. There is no middle ground with him. But you can't arrest someone for expressing an opinion."

"You can arrest someone for inciting a riot," the sheriff interupted.

"He didn't."

"He's pushing those kids to burn down private property!"

"He's not telling them to."

"Not in so many words —"

"I don't have to tell you how the First Amendment works, Lance. We've had this conversation too many times before. I'll be talking to Professor Cole again. You have to stay out of this."

Nora sounded extremely confident, but Duke also knew that it was extremely difficult to build a case for domestic terrorism. It usually took years before the FBI had enough evidence to get a warrant, and Duke was not that patient.

Sanger fumed. "This fire is in my jurisdiction!"

"And my unit is in charge of all cases of domestic terrorism. I don't want to pull rank. I need your help —"

"Doesn't sound like you want any help."

"You know that's not true."

Sanger grunted. "You don't know these people like I do."

Nora's expression darkened, and her hands clenched so tight that her knuckles turned white, though she tried to hide them behind her back. Nora always tried to conceal her tells. It worked with other people, but not Duke.

"On the contrary, Sheriff, I know these people a hell of a lot better than you or anyone." She turned to Duke. "If you want to view the body, Rogan, come with me. Then I'd like you to walk me through the security system."

Duke watched Nora stride purposefully down the wide hall toward Jonah's office, not looking back. She was upset and angry, out of character for her about something so small as Sheriff Sanger's tit-for-tat argument. Duke had intentionally avoided using his resources to look into her background, though he'd been tempted more than once because few women had intrigued him like

Nora English. He'd always suspected Nora had depth of character and experience that outweighed her thirtysome years.

He'd dated so many women in law enforcement and the military that they'd begun to blend together, the many chips on their shoulders weighing down any chance of true joy. But the society women who'd filled his dance card these last few years also held no lasting attraction — Duke had grown bored with fancy dinners, charity balls, and falseness. It was only Nora he thought about time and time again, and the need to find out everything he could about her . . . from *her* lips.

"Icy bitch," Sanger mumbled. "I'm getting some coffee. Good luck with her."

Good luck with her.

He needed good luck with Nora in more ways than Sheriff Sanger even suspected.

Nora didn't care whether either of the men followed her. She was so angry right now they'd better just stand down for two minutes. Why had she let Sanger get to her? She knew him, knew his type, had been able to manage the sticky relationship for years. The sheriff was more than willing to do anything she asked related to the case, and his two decades' experience in the sheriff's department was immensely valuable to the task force. But his personal connection to Professor Leif Cole, and the animosity he felt toward his old friend, was clouding his judgment. They'd been friendly up until Cole's name had been mentioned during the course of the investigation into the first arson. Now she and Sanger barely tolerated each other.

Of course he didn't know her or her past. In fact, aside from a few people she worked with and Quin, no one knew she'd put her mother in prison. They could find out without looking too hard — the records weren't sealed — but it wasn't something she talked about.

And then Duke Rogan — of all people! — showed up. He drove her absolutely crazy with his arrogant conviction that eventually she'd go out with him. Just because he was attractive, with that black Irish charm, that dark wavy hair, those blue eyes, and that dimple. And he was smart. And confident. And yes, dammit, she was attracted to him, but she didn't have time for too-smart, too-sexy men who distracted her from her job. She didn't want to make the time for Duke Rogan or anyone else. She'd avoided any personal involvement for four years of on-again, off-again working projects. The problem was that it was harder each time to withstand his appeal. And he knew it, which irritated her immensely.

Focus on the case.

The work always grounded her.

She hadn't noticed Duke following her until he said, "I know Leif Cole is a professor at Rose College, but what's his story? Why is the sheriff so gung-ho certain he's involved?"

Nora stopped inside the threshold of the research wing and turned to face him.

"Cole is a social science professor and has been involved in several high-profile demonstrations and speeches against biogenetic research specifically, and biotechnology as a whole. He has several arrests for civil disobedience and trespassing, spent a few months in jail, but has never been arrested for violence or arson."

"But Sanger thinks he's involved."

"Look, Cole's a prick, but he's hardly the raving lunatic Lance Sanger makes him out to be. The First Amendment protects his speech, and we have no proof that his vitriol intentionally incited violence."

It would help if Cole had been more forthcoming with their investigation, but in the absence of proof, Nora couldn't do a damn thing except keep digging. If they overreacted and brought Cole in — or, worse, arrested him — he would be a martyr. She was not letting Cole — if he was involved — or anyone else get off on a technicality. Cases like this were painstakingly built to insure that a conviction held up. Without proof, she'd never get a warrant past her superiors. Without evidence, she couldn't build a case. If she tossed aside the rules, a killer could walk free.

She'd seen it happen more than once. It would not happen to her.

"Do you have someone undercover? Someone in his classes? Talking to his students?"

Nora didn't like the direction the conversation was taking, especially when it involved Duke Rogan.

"Don't even think about it, Duke."

He looked at her wide-eyed, but hardly innocent. "I was just asking."

"Right."

"It's always good to see you, Nora. I'm sorry it's here."

She shook her head. "Just stop."

"Stop what?"

"Save it."

"For later?" he asked, hopeful.

He was playing her. She wasn't going to bite.

"You can consult, but that's it."

"You're the boss."

He glanced over her shoulder at the doorway to Payne's office and sobered immediately. Her heart went out to him, against her better judgment. The victim was Duke's friend, after all, and even after everything she'd seen and done in her life, Nora still retained compassion. It was human empathy that separated the cops from criminals. "Are you sure —"

"Yes," he interrupted, all humor gone. "Let's do it."

She touched his arm and squeezed. "It's pretty bad, Duke."

Duke braced himself for the worst. He pulled together his reserves, but was barely prepared for the sight of Jonah Payne's burned body when Nora moved away from the door.

Jonah was laid out on a white sheet, in the process of being transported. The last time Duke had seen his friend was a month ago, at an end-of-summer party at Jim's house. Once the security system went online five years ago, Duke wasn't needed any longer, just came by a couple times for diagnostic testing, ran background checks, hired I.T. staff as necessary. Most of the system's maintenance was done by the I.T. team, not Rogan-Caruso. Why was it that life, careers, commitments interfered with friendship? With the advances that Rogan-Caruso had been making over the years, the last full day off he had was a friend's wedding more than two months ago. Even Sundays, when he tried to ignore business and take the boat on the river during the summer or go skiing in the winter, inevitably ended as working days.

A blonder, shorter, younger, and spunkier woman than Nora trekked over from the far corner. She gave him a full-body graze before turning to the FBI agent and saying, "It's the same accelerant. I'll take the samples back to the lab, but I know. But get this — the victim had no shirt on."

"Wasn't it burned off?" Nora asked.

"Nope, no shirt. His back has no burns. There'd be remnants of a shirt beneath him had he been wearing one, but the fire didn't burn long enough to incinerate clothing. There's nothing."

Nora frowned. She was about to ask a question, then glanced at Duke. "Quin Teagan, Duke Rogan. Quin is a state arson investigator on the DOMFOR task force. Duke Rogan is with Rogan-Caruso, Butcher-Payne's security company."

Quin smiled in surprise. "*You're* Duke Rogan?" She glanced at Nora. Duke had the distinct impression that Nora had discussed him with this woman. Somehow, that made him both hopeful and apprehensive.

Nora asked Quin, "Is it okay for Duke to get a closer look at the body for a positive ID?"

"Sure. Look, don't touch." She smiled again at Duke, and he didn't miss the double entendre. "Sis, can I talk to you a sec?"

Sis? Quin Teagan was Nora's sister? Curious. He wanted to know what they were saying when the women walked to the far corner of the room — it obviously had something to do with the arson — but he was drawn to the doorway.

"You can come under the tape," the M.E. said, "if you need a closer look. But walk only on that path." He pointed to a white sheet that had been spread from the doorway to the body. "We're trying to minimize contamination of evidence."

Duke lifted the tape to stoop under. He took three steps toward the body and stopped.

The corpse was red and black, much of the skin completely gone. Little hair, no shirt, barely looking human. Duke didn't want to contemplate the smells that mingled with smoke and smoldering metals.

"He didn't suffer," the M.E. said with compassion.

"How do you know?"

"He was found on his back. He was at least unconscious when the fire started."

"You can tell how he died from the autopsy, right?"

"It depends; fire fatalities are among the trickiest to pin down a cause of death."

Duke focused on identifying the body, but one look and he was certain it was Jonah. Even with the burns, it was him. If there were any doubt, seeing his wedding band, covered in soot, on the left ring finger, even though his childhood sweetheart was twelve years in the grave, would have convinced him. But he didn't need the ring, or the glasses, or the other evidence. It was Jonah.

"Rest in peace, my friend," he whispered.

He walked back to the doorway, a deep sadness battling with a driving need to know the truth. He glanced at Nora and her sister the arson investigator, who were huddled in the corner. Nora looked at him. He nodded, glanced back at Jonah, then left the building. As soon as he stepped out into the fresh dawn air, he breathed easier.

He pulled out his iPhone and called his little brother. Sean had been wanting to be more involved with Rogan-Caruso business, and this was the perfect time to give him an assignment.

Sean answered with a groan. "It's six-fifteen in the morning, Duke."

"You're going back to school."

"Hell no."

"Hell yes. Shower and dress, I'm picking you up in one hour."

CHAPTER THREE

Nora listened to Quin's theory. It made some sense, but Nora had more questions. "How can you tell they took the animals instead of releasing them? And how do you know that any animals were here in the first place?"

"On my way back from San Francisco I had Devon working on my laptop doing some research on Butcher-Payne —"

"Devon? Who the heck is Devon?"

"I told you I was in San Francisco on a date."

Nora blinked. "I — I guess I assumed you'd gotten back together with Josh." They'd broken up two weeks ago.

Quin rolled her eyes. The habit had irritated Nora when she was a teenager, and it irritated her more now. "When have I *ever* gotten back together with *any* of my old boyfriends?"

She had a point. "And who's this Devon?

Why are you bringing him into a federal investigation?"

"Ouch, a little passive-aggressive there, Nora?"

"Quin, I had two hours of sleep before the phone rang. Can you just answer the question?"

"Devon is a doctor. He's all over the bio-tech stuff. He's a good guy, not an arsonist or rabble-rouser. I'm not an idiot, Nora."

She silently counted to ten. "I'm sorry. I'm testy."

"Really," she said sarcastically. "I think you need to take Duke Rogan to bed. My God, Nora, I can't believe you didn't go out with him when he asked! Are you insane?"

Nora glanced over at Payne's office. Duke Rogan wasn't there.

Quin laughed. "Made you look. He walked out two minutes ago."

"Let's not talk about my sex life."

"What sex life?"

"Quin —"

"Damn, Nora, you had *that* hot guy interested in you and you put him off?" She shook her head.

"The animals, Quin."

"Right, the bunnies."

"Bunnies?"

"Well, I don't know *what* critters Payne had around, but Devon looked up their projects online — at least what they have publicized. Though they have patents for developing nanotechnology —"

"Nano? Like biocomputer cells?"

"Beats me, I haven't a clue, though I bet Duke Rogan does." She winked. "He could give Apollo a run for his money."

"Apollo?"

"He looks like an Apollo to me. Zeus is too old —"

"Quin!"

"Right. All business, all the time."

Nora reluctantly realized that Duke probably did know a lot about nanotechnology, but she didn't want to ask him if she could get the answers from Quin or someone else. She really didn't want to bring Duke in as a civilian consultant, but he did have clearance and expert knowledge in security, as well as being familiar with Butcher-Payne.

"Forget I told you about Duke, Quin, or I'll never talk to you again about men. What did —"

Quin interrupted. "Do I hear a bit too much protesting?"

"Tell me what your boyfriend said, Quin."

Quin knew when to get serious. "Okay, so their big thing used to be nanotech, but they shifted gears a couple years ago and are now heavily involved in gene therapy. Looking for a cure, or an inoculation, for the avian flu. It's a particularly strong virus that can be spread from birds to people. Other strands can be transferred from pigs to —"

"I'm familiar with avian flu," Nora said.

"Great. So Butcher-Payne has apparently developed a way to prevent avian flu using gene therapy. At least, that's their goal and they've had some minor success, Devon said."

"I don't quite see the implications."

"Well, if no birds are carriers, then they can't pass on the virus to humans, right? Over time the virus will disappear."

"I read an article somewhere that gene therapy was illegal."

"On humans, not animals. There have been several successes with animal testing. We're a lot more complex, I guess. Anyway, it's a truly cutting-edge technology."

"This isn't a copycat, right? Arson to cover up corporate espionage?"

Quin wrinkled her nose and dismissed the idea, as Nora had earlier. "I don't think so," she said slowly. "Unless one of the arsonists is in it for something completely different. It's not a copycat — that I'm almost one hundred percent certain. Same graffiti, same accelerant, same burn pattern, and when I get through this mess I'll bet I'll find pieces of their sneaky little bomb."

"Bomb?"

"Molotov cocktail. Boom. Just like the others, they doused the place in grain alcohol — most likely because it's one of the least toxic when burned and any residual fuel will evaporate. I certainly don't have to tell you about bombs. They burn extremely hot and fast. Light a cloth fuse, attach it to a bottle of grain alcohol, leave it in the middle of the room. When the fire hits the vapors in the bottle, there she blows! Cheap, easy, and gets the job done."

Quin paused and raised an eyebrow. "Sounds familiar, doesn't it?"

Nora knew exactly what she was talking about, because she'd thought the same thing as Quin was talking. "Just like the bombs Lorraine used to make."

"Not that she put them to much use."

"She graduated pretty quick from the modified Molotov cocktail to pipe bombs," Nora said, irritated that Quin was bringing up their mother in conversation. Quin seemed to enjoy digging into the past. "All the information is readily available on the Internet, in the library, and in the *Anarchist's Handbook*."

"Testy, aren't we?"

"Quin, is there anything that differentiates the BLF device from others?"

"No. The bottles they picked can be bought pretty much anywhere in California and most other states. I have enough pieces from the previous arsons to link them, and I suspect this will be no different when I'm done. Find a suspect and bomb-making supplies, and I can match them. There's no unusual signature if that's what you're asking. These aren't people who get off on the fire."

"There's drawbacks in the method they chose," Nora said. It wasn't her FBI training that told her this; it was her childhood. "The biggest being the cloth wick fizzles out and never ignites the alcohol inside, or the air is too cold."

"Bingo! You win!"

"Quin —"

"Right, stay serious. Grain alcohol has a higher flash point, and naturally retains cold. If the alcohol is cooler than fifty-five degrees, it won't ignite." She fanned herself. "Obviously, no problem here. Another major miscalculation is how long it takes for the explosion. I had an idiot standing over a similar device to 'make sure' it ignited. He's dead." Quin shook her head.

75

"The fire spread from this room into Dr. Payne's office because there was plenty of fuel. The door was ajar —"

"How can you tell?"

Quin walked over to the opening. Keith Coffey said, "I'm ready to move him when you are."

"Great, five minutes." Quin gestured at the door. "The door wasn't axed or rammed down. It was ajar or open when the fire started. Now, I need to do some more tests, but I don't think there were any accelerants in Payne's office. They saturated the lab, but the fire in Payne's office was simply papers and wood catching sparks and burning. The fire didn't burn as hot, which is why his body is in such good shape."

Nora didn't think Payne's body was in good shape, but from an arson investigator's standpoint she could see that the body being intact was a huge plus.

"You're incredible, as usual, but you still haven't explained why you think the arsonists took the research animals."

"A cage is missing. Maybe more than one. And I could find no animal remains in the lab."

Nora looked at the wall — what was left of it — and all she saw was a mess of melted steel and ash. Some of the metal could have been cages, but she didn't see — wait. "There's a gap."

"Bingo! You win!"

"We need to get the staff in here and find out if the animals were, indeed, birds and what kind. And if there had been cages here prior to the fire." Nora almost jumped out of her boots. "Wait, don't researchers mark their test animals? With tattoos or bands around their leg or something?"

"Makes sense to me."

If the animals were marked — and the arsonists had kept one or more in their possession — that was hard physical evidence. Enough to get a warrant at the very least. "Quin, you're incredible."

"That's what Devon said after the show last night."

It was Nora's turn to roll her eyes. "I'm calling on Payne's staff. We may have our biggest break yet. I just wish we'd had it before someone died." She glanced around. "By the way, where's your friend, the county arson investigator — Ulysses, right?"

Quin grinned. "I tasked him with an assignment outside the building. I couldn't stand him hovering, and one thing I've learned is that if you give someone something productive to do, they leave you alone."

"So is that why you sent me out to defuse Sanger with the reporter?"

"Of course not. I wanted you to see the hunk Sanger was talking to." She paused a beat. "Though I get more done when no one is asking questions."

"I get the hint. Be available, Quin. No out-of-town dates for the next few days."

"Never in the middle of a job."

Professor Leif Cole had just sat down at his desk with a stack of papers and his morning coffee when his phone rang. It was early, the department secretary hadn't come in, and all calls rolled over to his direct line. All he had wanted was a few moments of peace, but technology thwarted him again.

He considered letting the call go to voice mail, then he noticed that it was his direct line flashing. He picked up the receiver.

"Professor Cole."

"Hi, Professor, Rich Belham from the *Bee*. I'm in Auburn right now, outside —"

Leif didn't care for Rich, but the reporter had given the college and Leif's demonstrations fair coverage, so he didn't simply hang up. "Rich, I don't have time for this now. I have a class to prepare for. Call me —"

"— outside Butcher-Payne along with the fire department and the FBI."

Every muscle in his body tightened as if they were being squeezed by a thousand small vises.

In a voice far calmer than he felt, he said, "I told you the arson fires are off-limits. I'm not involved, I don't know who is, and the FBI is wasting taxpayer resources by hounding me. But what else is new, right?"

"Right," Rich laughed, his voice dripping with falseness. "Except this is much bigger." All fake humor was gone.

Against his better judgment he asked, "How?"

"Murder."

His stomach dropped as if he were on a roller coaster, and he leaned back into his chair.

"Someone was hurt?" he finally asked.

"Someone is dead. Caught inside. I don't have the details, but I have confirmed with the sheriff — Lance Sanger, a friend of yours, right? — that there is definitely one dead body in all that destruction."

"Who?" Leif was whispering. He cleared his throat. "Do the police know who?"

"Not officially."

Rich was quiet. Damn that man, he wanted to play. He didn't know how good Leif was at these games.

"What do you want from me?"

"A quote."

"On what? Shit, Rich, I'm not involved. The fact that the FBI keeps dragging my name and the college through the mud because they don't have enough evidence or intelligence to do their job is inexcusable. They're looking at a lawsuit, and you know it."

"Hey, don't shoot the messenger. I got squat from the feds. It's your friend the sheriff who has it out for your neck."

Lance. He should have known. Lance never understood how Leif had grown up, educated himself, become a better person than he'd been before. Lance was a thug, a cop; he played by society's corrupt rules. Harboring a fantasy that Leif was still the same Boy Scout who raped the earth and killed innocent creatures for sport.

"What do you want?" Leif asked slowly.

"Two years ago, you led a protest against Butcher-Payne for their research into gene therapy, which spurred Butcher-Payne into funding a media campaign to discredit you and your claims —"

"Hold it. You've already gotten it wrong. I didn't lead the protest, I participated in it. And Butcher-Payne has not even begun to discredit my facts relating to Frankenstein's monster — namely, genetic engineering."

"I'm sure they'd disagree. They certainly aren't at a loss for funding, picking up huge private and public grants."

Rich knew how to stick in the knife.

The reporter continued. "So there's no love lost between you and Butcher-Payne. Their research lab was destroyed. Do you have a comment?"

Leif crafted his response. "Human life is as precious as animal life. It is tragic that someone died at Butcher-Payne, but I hope that the other people behind the company realize that their research is just as criminal as the actions of whoever set the fire in the first place." He paused, then asked, "Who died in the fire?"

"It hasn't been released, pending notification of next of kin —"

"I understand."

"Jonah Payne."

"They're certain?"

"Oh yeah, they just want to tell his son first, then it'll be all over the news."

There was no love lost between Leif and Jonah Payne. They'd battled for years about biotechnology in academic journals, mainstream newspapers, and even on national cable news. But Leif didn't want him dead. He didn't want anyone to die.

"An accident?"

"They're not saying."

"Of course not. Look, I have to go."

"Don't —"

Leif hung up on the reporter and sat at his desk, staring out the floor-to-ceiling windows, but not seeing the trees or morning sky.

Jonah Payne had died in the fire. That Leif was innocent didn't matter, for his innocence wasn't pure. He knew too much. He'd known for a long time. And he'd thought he'd stopped it.

He left his office, computer on, email open, coffee cooling on his desk. He had to find out if the group had gotten back together and if so, what the hell for?

At dawn, Maggie unbolted the door of her small, one-room cabin and carefully carried the cage inside, placing it on the round table that took up most of the kitchen space.

The duck wasn't making noise; his spirit had been defeated by the cruelty of those so-called scientists.

She locked and bolted the door out of habit — no one lived anywhere near her here in the middle of nature. People called it "the middle of nowhere" when in fact the few places like her mountainside were the only *somewhere* she wanted to be. It calmed her, and especially now she needed to be calm.

"It's okay, Donnie," she cooed, opening the cage and sitting across from the mallard. He looked at her, waddled forward, and stood there, his wing crooked.

She swallowed her anger, knowing that animals had much better instincts than people, and she didn't want to scare Donnie. First those people did untold things to him, poking him and injecting him with who knows what, keeping him locked in a room for his entire life. What kind of life was that? A prison for innocent animals, yet they were incapable of doing wrong.

And then that jerk, dropping the cage with the ducks still inside! He was lucky she didn't slit his throat then and there. If one of the birds had died, she would have. Then she'd have to kill the others, too, and that would be messy. Her impulsive nature could get her in trouble — she'd had some close calls in the past — so she worked hard to control her reactions.

Maggie had a better way to take care of them. She'd been thinking about it for several weeks. It had been far too difficult to convince them to reunite and continue their plan. Not Scott, but she had him by his cock.

It was Anya she was worried about. Anya, who had an ill-formed conscience. She was feeling *guilty* about the fires. How could she feel any remorse for the corrupt businesses profiting from the torture and abuse of animals? It would only stop when *they* stopped it. People were mostly too stupid to care or understand what was for their own good. Her mother had explained it all to her.

"The masses don't understand what's at stake," her mother said often. "They are content working in a broken system that is spiraling out of control. Until those of us who care about the future take action and protect the earth and plants and animals who were here long before we were, our world is doomed."

Maggie gave Donnie water and bread crumbs. He ate from her hand, tame for a duck. He sensed that she'd never hurt him. She hadn't wanted to keep him in the cage, but with his damaged wing he wouldn't be able to fend for himself. When he was healthy, she'd take him to a lake and free him.

She went to her bathroom and showered in icy water, washing away the dirt and grime from the fire and the lake. Remembered the power she felt when she held the

84

knife to the man who had betrayed her family.

Her mother had told her everything. How Jonah Payne tried to get her father fired only weeks before he died. How he belittled him, embarrassed him in front of his peers. The man was so arrogant in his success, so confident that he was right, Payne never listened to her dad, never even tried to understand his point of view. Just because Payne was the shining star, the kid who could do no wrong, everyone believed him.

While Jonah Payne hadn't killed her father, he had contributed to his death. And for that, he'd had to die. Because the time had come to destroy everyone who'd turned against her and her family.

Cutting him had been better than sex. Watching the blood flow from his arms and legs and chest . . . never-ending rivers of blood. She'd avenged her family and it freed her.

Skin burning with cold, Maggie stepped from the shower and dried her thin body, then cleaned the bathtub. While it filled with cold water, she dressed in jeans, a white T-shirt, and her favorite sweater, one she'd knitted from yarn she'd made herself.

When the tub was full, she turned off the faucet and brought Donnie to the room.

"No more cages for you, Donnie," she told him. He waddled around the bathroom and Maggie left him to explore.

She made tea from plants she'd picked and dried and blended herself, and sat at her laptop. It was eight in the morning, time to take credit for a job well done.

To say his brother Sean looked unhappy with his assignment was an understatement, but he reluctantly agreed that Duke's plan could work.

"Isn't there anyone else?" Sean asked. "I hated college."

Duke pulled into a parking slot outside the administration building at Rose College. "And you were so awful at it," Duke said sarcastically. Sean had an exceptionally high I.Q., started college a year early, and had graduated with two bachelor's degrees and two minors. He became bored easily, which had been a problem from the time he was little, resulting in his being labeled difficult.

"Duke —"

"A few days. Week maybe." He turned off the ignition.

"Investigations like this take *years*."

"It's already been nearly two years. They just need a little inside information to give them direction. The feds have rules and regulations they have to follow. We don't."

"That's not what you said when I wanted to get the goods on that embezzler last year."

"You wanted to break into his office and hack his computer. I'll stretch the rules, Sean, but I'm not sending you to prison."

"I'm good."

Duke shot him a glance. It was true, he probably would have gotten away with it, but Sean was already playing close to the edge and it was Duke's responsibility to keep him on the legal side of the gray line.

"Arrogance will be your downfall, little brother."

Sean grumbled. "Yeah, yeah. Okay, I get the plan — get close to the people in Cole's group and find out if any of them are talking about arson or murder or Butcher-Payne. Or, anyone who seems to be acting weird, guilty, or unusually nonchalant about arson."

"You're here to observe, not act — understand?"

"I got it." He made a move to get out of the car, and Duke grabbed his arm.

"This is serious, Sean. You have good instincts with the brains to match, but you're reckless."

Sean brushed off his hand with a frown.

"I'm not a kid who needs to be bailed out of trouble, Duke. I know what I'm doing. I thought you trusted me."

"I do."

"You say you do."

"Sean —"

"Look, I'm not going to do something stupid. You agreed that I'd be a partner by the time I was twenty-five, and I only have eighteen months to go. Or was that just talk to keep me in line?"

"You know it wasn't —"

"Then let me do this my way. I know what you need. If any of Cole's people are involved, I'll find out who and give you the information."

Duke had to let go. It was hard. He didn't know if it would be any harder if Sean was his son instead of his brother. But Duke, fifteen years older, had always been protective of Sean. And after their parents died, Duke had raised him while their older brother Kane continued to fight other people's wars. Duke hadn't always done a great job — he pushed Sean hard and was often critical — but he was proud of his younger brother.

Duke said, "I already called the admissions director, he's expecting you."

Sean raised an eyebrow. "Someone you know?"

"An old friend."

"Why am I not surprised you know just the right person to get me inside?"

"He might suspect I have another reason wanting you here, but I told him there was a glitch with your diploma from MIT and you need a social science requirement you'd missed as an undergrad. It happens that Professor Cole's class fits the bill. He didn't asked questions. By the time he gets your files from MIT, you'll be out of here."

Sean shook his head with a half grin. "And you think I break the rules."

"I'm bending them." He added, "The only thing, you might want to tone down your background."

"In what?"

"Having two bachelor of science degrees and graduating from MIT might be a tip-off that you aren't a liberal-arts major."

"Got it." He glanced toward the building, but Duke saw his mind working.

"What do you have up your sleeve?"

"Nothing. Trust me, I can blend in, no problem."

"One of them could be a killer. Don't get cocky."

He grinned and winked. "No cockier than the average Rogan."

CHAPTER FOUR

While Quin continued to work her magic at the crime scene, and the M.E. moved the body to the morgue, Nora drove with her partner Pete Antonovich to the town house of Melanie Duncan, Jonah Payne's head research assistant.

"You were right," Pete said as he parallel-parked down the street from Duncan's residence. "The water pump was sabotaged, and whoever did it knew *exactly* what they were doing. Either an inside job or a smart guy with an engineering background. Popped the locks like a burglar, and inside the substation the water was shut off at the source. No computer knowledge necessary, just knowing which screws to turn, so to speak."

"And I'm guessing no fingerprints or tools left around to identify the culprit," she said.

"The sheriff's forensic unit is printing and documenting the scene, but I don't think they'll find anything. The arsonists also blocked the camera."

"How?"

"Simple. Put on a mask and tape a piece of cardboard to the camera lens."

"You'd think," Nora said, "that in the twenty-first century we'd find a better way of surveilling remote locations."

"There is," Pete said as he knocked on Duncan's door. "But city government is behind the curve."

Melanie Duncan came to the door in a robe, her wet, dark red hair dripping down her back. Other than the simple black-framed glasses over bright blue eyes, Duncan was completely antithetical to Nora's image of what a female researcher should look like. She was tall, voluptuous, and attractive.

"It says no solicitors," Duncan snapped when she opened the door.

Nora showed her badge. "Special Agent Nora English. My partner, Pete Antonovich, FBI. Melanie Duncan, correct?"

She frowned, a typical expression when confronted by government agents.

"What do you want?"

"May we come in?"

"What do you want?" she repeated, not opening the door any wider.

"There was a fire at Butcher-Payne," Nora said. She watched Duncan carefully. First reactions were the most difficult to fake, except for the most accomplished pathological liars.

"A fire?" She sounded skeptical, her brows drawing together. "Why are you here? The —" She glanced at Pete, then back at Nora. "The FBI?"

"Ms. Duncan —"

"Dr. Duncan," she replied automatically. She stepped away from the door, and Nora and Pete entered. "I need to call Dr. Payne," Duncan said. "I don't see why you didn't call him, or why the FBI is involved with a fire. Our lab isn't a government facility. We have a grant, but —"

"Dr. Duncan, why don't you have a seat?"

She remained standing, door open. Nora pushed it closed. "Jonah Payne died in the fire."

She blinked. "Died." Her voice was flat. "A fire at Butcher-Payne? No, that's not possible — he's in Tahoe."

Nora raised her brow and glanced at Pete. Pete said, "I spoke with Jim Butcher this morning. He didn't tell us Dr. Payne was supposed to be in Lake Tahoe."

"Jim? Jim's in L.A." She rubbed her forehead and walked over to the adjoining kitchen, where she poured herself a cup of coffee. Her hands shook, Nora noted, and she was clearly dazed. Possibly a very good actress, though Nora didn't think Dr. Duncan was acting.

"Dr. Payne's body was found in his office. The fire started at approximately one-thirty this morning."

"Jonah is in Lake Tahoe," she repeated emphatically. "He went up there Saturday afternoon. He's driving back right now." She picked up her cell phone, which was charging on a small secretary desk in the makeshift dining area.

"Dr. —" Pete began, but Nora put her hand on his arm and shook her head once.

It was clear after a few seconds that voice mail had picked up. With a catch in her throat, Duncan said into the phone, "Jonah, it's Mel. Can you call me, please? It's important." She slowly closed her phone. "He's coming back this morning. We have a ten a.m. staff meeting."

"Why did he go to Tahoe?" Nora asked.

"He goes the last weekend of every month," she said.

"Every month?"

"As long as I've been working for him. He has a cabin. It helps him think. He works seven days a week . . ." Her voice trailed off. "Are you certain? I mean, if there was a fire, maybe it's not Jonah." Her voice cracked.

"Duke Rogan, security consultant, identified the body, which was discovered in Dr. Payne's office."

The scientist sat heavily in a chair. Her bottom lip quivered and she bit it. Tears welled in her eyes but didn't spill over.

Nora glanced at her watch. It was just after eight in the morning. Gently, she asked, "When did you last talk to Dr. Payne?"

"Friday when I left work. It was after seven. Told him to enjoy his weekend . . ." Her voice cracked again, and she looked at the wall beyond Nora.

"Do you have the address for his cabin?"

Duncan slowly rose and went to her desk. She flipped through a notebook, scribbled on a piece of paper, and handed it to Nora, then sat back down as if on auto-pilot.

"And he always goes to the same place?" Nora glanced at the address, then put the paper in the back of her notepad.

"It's his second home. Why would he go anywhere else?"

A regular schedule. Criminals loved habits. They were easy to monitor, giving stalkers and others valuable information about their prey.

She quickly sent an email to the Lake Tahoe satellite office asking them to check out the address as a possible crime scene, giving them basic info on the case.

"Do you know if he arrived in Tahoe?" Nora asked.

She shook her head. "W-what happened?"

There was no use sugarcoating the truth. "The fire was arson."

"Arson? You mean on purpose?" Suddenly her eyes flashed, anger layered over grief. "Is it the same people who burned down Langlier? And the lab at Sac State?"

"On the surface, it appears to be a similar M.O.," Nora admitted, "but we're still in the early stages of our investigation. We have the best people gathering evidence —"

"That didn't do you any good with the other fires!" She jumped up and paced. "Langlier was nearly two years ago. What are you people doing? How could this happen? How could Jonah be dead?"

Nora would forgive her outburst — this time. She herself was intensely frustrated with the slow pace of the biotech arson investigation. That Nora believed someone affiliated with Professor Leif Cole's group was involved meant nothing. Until she could tie him to the crimes, she couldn't compel him to turn over anything, or even force him to talk to her.

But she would continue to push him. Homicide gave her a fraction more weight behind her. And if Cole was true to the anarchist's creed, then he would be repulsed that someone died. Maybe — finally — he would talk to her.

A small consolation to Jonah Payne.

"What about security?" Dr. Duncan continued. "Duke was there? What happened to his fabulous, fool-proof security system? Someone get in? The bastard. Jonah felt *safe*."

Nora resisted the urge to defend Duke Rogan. She had no idea if his system had failed or was hacked or simply never turned on, but she'd seen the pain in his face after he'd recognized Jonah Payne. He blamed himself, and there was no doubt in her mind that right now Duke was working on finding out exactly how the security failed.

Nora doubted it had been Duke's fault if there was a security failure. She'd worked with him too often to believe he wouldn't have triple-checked any system he put his name on.

But Nora needed to figure out how the arsonists got into the lab to start the fire. Plus, where they'd released the animals —

if there'd been any on the premises. Every anarchist or radical environmental group Nora had investigated avoided killing people or animals. At the heart of the movement were politics, and they knew that murder would turn public sentiment against them. Any deaths were unintentional, which made the Butcher-Payne arson doubly interesting, based on the M.E.'s assertion that Payne had been incapacitated prior to the fire.

Nora avoided Duncan's rhetorical question about security and asked, "How long have you worked for Dr. Payne?"

"I've been there for five years, since they opened the new lab. I have a Ph.D. from USC in biochemistry and master's degrees in both human biology and wildlife biology."

Nora made notes as Duncan spoke. "How many people work at Butcher-Payne?"

"All of Butcher-Payne? We have two divisions. Jim's group is all about media and fund-raising. They have ten, twelve people on staff. The lab has six full-time people, plus a vet who comes in twice a week."

It seemed from her tone that Dr. Duncan didn't like Jim Butcher very much, or at least didn't like the public focus of his division. "How was Dr. Payne's relationship with his partner?"

"They were best friends," Duncan said flatly.

"But you don't like him?" she pushed.

"He's a spinner. He doesn't care about what we're trying to do. He has a degree in human biology, but his master's was in business. All he cares about is bringing in the money. And that's important, I know it is, but it feels icky."

Icky? "How so?"

She shrugged. "Jim isn't a bad guy, but he's not Jonah. He'd bring in money that required us to work on specific projects, and so we had to put aside our primary work because the special projects funded our operations. And Jonah did it. He wasn't always happy, but he did whatever Jim wanted."

"What was your primary focus?"

She took a deep breath. "Jonah was on the verge of curing the bird flu — not by inoculating humans, but by genetically engineering birds predisposed to be carriers. By manipulating their genes, we inhibit their ability to contract the virus, which in turn prevents them from passing on the virus to other birds or humans. Influenza kills approximately half a million people worldwide every year. If we can't find a way to stop the eventual pandemic from avian flu, that number will grow exponentially. Six months and we would have been ready for broad testing and trials. We've already started our internal tests. Now it's all gone. It'll take years to re-create. And without Jonah . . . I don't know." She squeezed her eyes closed.

Something Duncan said tickled the back of Nora's brain, but before she could formulate her question, Pete asked, "Have Butcher-Payne or Dr. Payne received any threatening letters? Visits?"

"What day don't we get them? Ask Jim, he'll have them. No one even knew or cared what we did in the lab until last year when Cole's idiot group protested outside the building."

"Professor Leif Cole?" Nora asked.

Duncan scowled. "Yes. They should have all been arrested. They blocked traffic and harassed our employees, not to mention putting up disgusting pictures of dead and bloody animals they claimed were from animal testing. That's not how we operate. But just because we are using gene therapy on birds, they attack us!"

Nora said, "This group has indicated through their graffiti and subsequent letters sent to the media that they're anti-biotechnology, not an animal-rights group like ALF."

Duncan waved her hand and sniffed. "They're all the same nuts."

Perhaps, but the arsonists were specifically targeting biotechnology companies or, in the case of Sac State, bioresearch. Not all of the targets used animals in their research. Nora knew ALF wouldn't have gone after the Sac State lab because it didn't engage in animal testing. The lab was solely involved in agriculture bioengineering, genetically manipulating plants to grow in areas with limited water.

The only commonality between all four entities was their involvement in biotech research. Langlier, Nexum, and Butcher-Payne used animals; Sac State didn't. Unless there was another reason the arsonists targeted the college.

"From my experience," Pete said, "extreme environmentalists tend to come together over multiple issues. There's a lot of overlapping."

Nora concurred. She turned back to Duncan. "You said Jim Butcher has the threatening letters?"

"Bobbie — Roberta Powers — would keep the correspondence. She's Jim's personal assistant. If it was overtly threatening, we'd have sent it to the sheriff."

"Has Dr. Payne fired or let go any staff in the last year?" Pete asked.

"You can't possibly think that anyone from Butcher-Payne had anything to do with arson and murder." It was a statement.

"You're a scientist," Nora said. "You may have a hypothesis, and in your gut know that you are right, but you need to prove or disprove your theory, and that requires extensive research. For us, it requires a lot of investigation. Including asking questions we don't necessarily think are going to give us the right answers. But if we don't ask all the questions, our investigation won't be complete."

Duncan relented, but mumbled that it was a waste of time.

Nora said, "The biohazard team went through the scene and determined it safe enough, but the arson investigator noticed that one or more cages may have been removed."

"Cages? Our birds are kept in a secure room."

"There were no animals in the main area of the lab?"

"No." She looked down, frowning. "South wall? There was a long worktable, several file cabinets, a mini-refrigerator. Empty cages and carriers because we didn't have any more room in storage, but we don't keep animals in the main lab unless we need them. They always go back in their room. How can you tell that a cage is missing? You said there was a fire."

"The fire investigator is analyzing the entire scene and she knows how fire spreads, how it's extinguished, and whether something is out of place. It's not an exact science —"

"Don't tell Quin that," Pete interjected with quiet humor.

"It's based on educated guesses," Nora continued. "In her opinion, something seemed missing. But it could be nothing — it could be a large file box that was moved to storage. It would help, though, for you to walk through the scene and see if something is missing, or something is there that shouldn't be."

"I can do that. Yes, of course, anything." Duncan sat back down, her head in her hands. "I know this is going to sound callous, but Jonah would want us to continue. This was everything to him." She looked up. This time the tears had escaped. "I need to recover any remains. They might be worthless, but if I can get the bodies of the birds, our vet and I can analyze their genes on a cellular level. There should be something — and it could help. All our hard-copy documents are gone — I assume they are — but we have copies of everything in the computer. Not the logs — oh, God, those are going to be impossible to re-create. But at least we don't have to go back to square one. For Jonah, I need to complete this. Jim will agree."

Whether she added that last thought to make it true, or because she believed it, Nora didn't know.

"I don't think there's anything left," she said, but she pictured Jonah Payne's body. Second- and third-degree burns . . . birds were smaller, they'd disintegrate much faster. But Quin would have said something. In fact, she thought Quin was certain they'd been released — or taken in the missing cage. She pulled out her BlackBerry. "I'll ask the investigator to specifically pull aside the birds. How many were there? What kind?"

"Twelve mallard ducks, six male and six female. They were in the room to the left of my office. It's a double room, with an entry and decontamination area, then the chamber where the birds lived, with a small built-in pool."

"How many birds can one of your standard cages hold?"

She looked at Nora as if it was an odd question. "They're mallard ducks. We put one in per cage, sometimes two if they're a mating pair. More than two would be inhumane, but I suppose you could fit four."

Nora was fairly certain they weren't in the lab and in fact had been taken or released. She sent Quin a text message:

Payne's assistant said there were twelve mallard ducks in a room to the left of Payne's office. Are there any remains? If so, can you preserve them? And ask Chief Nobel to debrief his crew and ask if they recall which doors off the main lab were open and which were closed when they went in. Thanks, N.

"When do you want me to go down?"

Nora glanced at Pete. "When did Jim Butcher say he would arrive?"

"He took a seven-fifteen flight out of LAX, but I didn't get confirmation he was on it."

She looked at her watch. About seventy minutes, then another thirty from the airport. He'd be arriving within the next half hour.

"I'll call him," Pete said.

Nora wanted to talk to Butcher without Payne's loyal research assistant around. She also needed to follow up with the Lake Tahoe office about Jonah Payne's house, have her team pull his credit card records and bank information to determine if he ever arrived and if so, when he left.

And she had to ask Duke Rogan to explain the security system. There could even be hidden data that would identify the culprits. Nora dreaded the thought of spending time with Duke, knowing it could weaken her resolve to stay far away from him.

"How about ten-thirty?" Nora asked Duncan. "Does that give you enough time to pull yourself together?"

"I can do it now."

"Ten-thirty is better. The arson investigator isn't going to let anyone walk the scene until she's done with her preliminary walk-through, which takes several hours."

"Was there anything left?"

"It's hard to say. There's of course fire and smoke damage, as well as water damage."

"When can I get in and see what we have left?"

"You mean go through everything? It'll be at least two days, maybe longer. It's a crime scene, we need to keep it intact until the investigators are done with evidence collection."

Pete touched her arm and Nora looked over. He held up his BlackBerry. It was a message from their ASAC, Dean Hooper.

BLF posted a letter online about the Butcher-Payne arson. When can you be at HQ?

She shook her head. She didn't want to talk in front of Duncan, so said cryptically, "There're a half-dozen things we need to check on before memories fade."

"If you want to drop me off at headquarters," Pete said, "I can take care of that situation."

"Thanks. I need some background work done, so I'll go with you for a few minutes."

They stood and thanked Melanie Duncan for her time. Nora's phone vibrated and she glanced down at the message. It was from Quin.

No birds, no ducks, no furry, finned, or feathered creatures at all. The room was empty. The fire did not reach that area of the lab, only smoke and water damage, so if they were there, they'd be slow-roasted, not extra crispy.

Only Quin could make Nora smile at the macabre. She squeezed her lips closed, because this wasn't the time or place. She said to Duncan, "There were no animals at all in the lab."

Melanie shook her head. "All our work. Years. Years. Turned to ash. I don't know enough about DNA to see if we can get something from the ash, I really wanted blood, but maybe —"

"I should have clarified. There are no remains. The room you described wasn't damaged by fire. There were no birds, dead or alive."

Melanie paled.

Nora knew exactly what happened to them. "Animal-rights groups usually release captive animals into the wild or take them to sympathetic rescue facilities."

"Oh no. No. Oh, God, we have to find them."

Nora froze. "Why?"

"The avian flu! Half the birds were infected. We were using gene therapy on them to find a genetic cure to prevent virus carriers. But we're still in the testing phase. They'll infect any bird they come in contact with.

"Worse," she continued, "there's no vaccine, no cure. The virus they have has been genetically altered to be particularly virulent. We were so successful with the weaker viruses, we needed to find a therapy that could attack any mutation of the virus."

"What are the chances the virus will spread to human populations?"

"I don't know. Whenever you're dealing with viruses there is always the risk of mutation. There would need to be prolonged physical contact with the ducks, but the far greater risk is spreading the disease to other waterfowl. It's the end of September. They'll begin to migrate. We have to find them now."

CHAPTER FIVE

At his desk, Duke Rogan stared at the computer logs. What the hell was this? He examined the logs every which way he could, including evidence of earlier hacking attempts, but again and again he came to the same conclusion: Jonah had disabled the security system.

It didn't make sense. There were strict protocols set up in the security plan. The system was set 24/7 to record the exterior of the building, the lobby, the elevators, and inside every entrance, except when in test mode. But Jonah had put the security on test mode, which would have converted automatically to the armed mode in two hours even if he didn't manually reset the codes . . . if there hadn't been a fire.

"You're making assumptions, Duke," he muttered to himself. Just because Jonah's codes were used didn't mean that Jonah himself had disabled the system. But why would Jonah give the codes to anyone? There was a fail-safe; if Jonah was threatened, he could put in false codes that would appear to disable the system, but alert both Duke and the sheriff's department. Duke had successfully used such protocols with high-risk businesses where having a "panic" code worked exceptionally well. Several smaller banks used it as the last resort for their secure areas. There was also a panic button in the lab, in the lobby, in Jonah's office, and in Jim's office.

But the system had been put in test mode at 12:48 a.m.

Sheriff Sanger had told him the 911 call came in from a passing driver at 1:57 a.m., more than an hour later.

There were no video files. They just weren't there. All cameras fed into the main database, and it was replicated every hour to an external server. If the replication failed, the system administrator would be alerted.

The digital files had to be here! Somewhere . . . he would re-create them if he had to.

"Dammit." He'd already left two messages for Russ Larkin, the I.T. director for Butcher-Payne.

Duke scanned the log, making notes on

the pad beside him.

Jonah — or someone with his personal codes — had entered the building at 12:15 a.m. He had turned off internal security, but the doors were still locked, cameras on, and to enter someone would need an employee card *and* a key to the building — and the entry code. It was a backup system — if the card, or the key, were lost or stolen, neither could be used alone to enter the building. It was Jonah all the way. Jonah's pass, Jonah's code.

"Jonah, what were you doing last night?"

He buzzed Jayne Morgan, the in-house computer database manager for Rogan-Caruso, and asked her to come to his office. Duke had worked closely with the young, socially inept genius to code computer security systems for many of their clients. Duke's job was on-site, Jayne handled most of the programming.

Though Duke had a corner office with a view on two sides — one looking down the K Street Mall, the other overlooking Cesar Chavez Park — he grew antsy when he had to spend more than an hour at his desk. His strength was field security, not sitting around analyzing computer data. His favorite assignments were when he was hired to physically break in to facilities and analyze their security systems. Jayne's strength was cyberhacking.

"Is this for Dr. Payne?" Jayne asked.

"Yes. The video backups are missing. They seem to be completely gone."

"Not possible," she said with confidence.

He slid over a notepad listing the details he knew. "Why would he put the system in test mode in the middle of the night?"

"Because you can't turn off the system without alerting us."

"Shit, I knew that." He rubbed his eyes and took a deep breath. "Okay, someone threatened him. Someone manipulated him. But why would he do it? How would they even know about the test mode? That the system can't be turned off?" Any interruption would send an alert to the Rogan-Caruso on-call security supervisor. The logs said no such interruption happened until 1:45 a.m. Which would have been about the time the fire had damaged the electrical system. The disruption prevented the Rogan-Caruso servers from talking to the Butcher-Payne system, which triggered the automatic alert.

"An inside job?"

"Maybe." He frowned. He'd already printed out background reports on all Butcher-Payne employees, past and present.

"Maybe he was meeting someone at the lab, but why so late?" And that still didn't explain putting the system in test mode.

His cell phone rang. He would have ignored it, except it was Jim Butcher.

"Jim," he answered.

"Is Jonah dead?"

"I'm sorry."

"God fucking dammit." Jim sounded tough, but his voice was strained. "What happened?"

"We don't know everything, but I'm consulting with the FBI on this one." Nora had seemed amicable to the suggestion earlier, but he had to play the situation carefully or she might pull him off. Duke didn't want to go over her head, but he would if it meant staying on the case. "I'm not going to stop until I find out who did this."

"Trevor —"

"I called him." Talking to Jonah's nineteen-year-old son had been just about the hardest thing Duke had ever done, even more difficult than seeing Jonah's body. "The press was all over the place. I didn't want him to hear about it thirdhand."

"Thank you. I need to talk to him. This is — shit, it's not right, Duke."

It wasn't, but there was nothing Duke could say to alleviate Jim's pain. All he could do was act. Action he was good at.

"I'm going through the security records now, but someone definitely tampered with the digital camera files. And someone — maybe Jonah — used his personal codes to put the system in test mode."

"Jonah is — was — a brilliant scientist," Jim said, "and a genius on many levels. But he set off the alarms more than anyone. I don't think he even understood what the test mode was."

Jim was right. "Nevertheless, his codes were used."

"What did Russ say?"

"I haven't been able to reach him."

"I swear, if he's off fucking around I'll —" Jim stopped. "You don't think he's in danger? Or involved —"

Duke knew what Jim was thinking. Had their I.T. manager been involved with the arson? Had Russ Larkin killed Jonah?

It didn't make sense. Duke didn't know Russ well, but he had interviewed him, hired him, trained him. Russ didn't seem the type to care about any political cause. His background check had come up squeaky clean. He performed well. And he'd been there for five years, ever since Rogan-Caruso was first hired to develop a security plan for Butcher-Payne. Five years was a long time to wait to

115

kill someone.

But Duke couldn't rule it out until he talked to Russ himself.

"I'll swing by his apartment," he said.

"I just landed. My flight was delayed nearly an hour. I'm driving now to Butcher-Payne to meet with the FBI and God knows who else. I don't know what to expect —"

"I'll meet you there." Duke hung up, gathered his laptop, and packed everything into his satchel. To Jayne he said, "Do everything you can to find those video files. Anything you need to make that happen, it's yours. If you need my office, use it."

"I'm on it, Duke. I won't let you down."

"You never have."

Jayne left and Duke started to follow, then stopped. Slowly, he walked back around his desk and opened the bottom right-hand drawer. Only one thing was stored in that drawer.

The Colt .45 mocked him, lying there with only a box of fifty rounds for company.

He didn't want the Colt.

He didn't need the gun.

He didn't want to touch it.

He'd been a marksman in the Marines, a sharpshooter with any long or short gun the military handed him. He'd killed with a gun, and while it had greatly disturbed him, it had been necessary in battle. Emotions he could put into a box and seal. Something he couldn't forget, but could understand. War wasn't pretty, even undeclared wars the politicians liked to call "conflicts" because that sounded less scary on the six o'clock news.

After his three-year tour of duty was over, he followed in his brother Kane's footsteps — Marines turned mercenary.

Duke closed his eyes and was transported thirteen years into the past, to when he and Kane had worked together. Before their parents were killed, before the twins ran away to Europe, before Duke became the de facto father of his youngest brother.

Duke was pumped. His makeshift tracking system had worked, and he'd earned the rare praise of his big brother in one word: "Good."

Kane called for his team, who were spread across the cocaine field, lying low.

They worked for no one, it seemed. Duke didn't know how Kane got his money, or how he paid his team, but the men were dedicated, and Duke had money deposited in his bank account on the first of every month for the eight months he'd been part of Kane's mercenary squad. When Duke left the Marines, at the age of twenty-four, after his tour in Afghanistan fighting the Taliban before they were publicly declared the enemy, Kane had called him. "I have a position for you."

Of course Duke took it. He'd joined the Marines to follow in both his father's and Kane's giant footsteps, thinking he knew where those footsteps led.

Kane was only two years older than him, but he seemed far more worldly, more scarred . . . decades wiser.

"Kodiak." Kane's command meant something to his team, but Duke didn't know what the hell he meant.

Kane motioned for Duke to follow him. "Stick with me."

"You didn't tell me the plan."

"You aren't ready."

That irritated Duke. After three years in the Marines, he had the stamina and readiness of anyone on Kane's team. He was as good a shot, as strong as any of them, and he was committed. They were actively battling the drug dealers, the smugglers, the bastards growing deadly and addictive crops that were distributed throughout America, killing the innocent and the stupid. Tearing apart families, destroying minds and bodies and futures.

Like Molly, their sister.

"Kane —"

"Follow me. Be alert."

Duke had no choice, but this wasn't the first

time Kane had treated him like a child since he'd relocated to Central America to be part of this team. This wasn't what he'd signed on for, and he'd just as soon reenlist or go home to Sacramento and become a cop. He followed Kane through the field. It was full dark, hours before the sunrise; humidity had fallen but the ground retained the warmth of the previous summer day.

All he knew was that they were going to burn the fields. The coca plants would go up in flames, costing the drug lords millions of dollars in raw material. The tracking device Duke had made with their limited supplies was to better monitor the perimeter guards.

The plan — even without Duke's firsthand knowledge — seemed to go off without a hitch. Kane and Duke set charges, and when they reached the opposite end of the field, the six other team members met them within seconds. Perfectly executed.

Duke had never seen his brother looking so intense. Kane was wholly focused on the job, as if his body had become his mind, every movement with specific purpose, every command with power.

"Ignite," Kane ordered.

Webs lit the four fuses. Each burned virtually smokeless down the rows at regular intervals. Overkill, based on the explosives they'd tamped into each charge, but when Duke questioned the plan, Kane had simply said, "Insurance."

The men dispersed in pairs without comment, and Duke followed Kane. The only thing he'd been told was if they separated to meet at a specific longitude and latitude outside Lancetilla. And not to move north.

Within two minutes, the first charge exploded. Duke was knocked to the ground — he knew they'd put too much black powder in the charge. "Move," Kane said, pulling him up.

Shouts. Voices. Pitch black. How Kane knew where they were going, Duke didn't know. He couldn't see the others, couldn't hear them, but he sensed them . . . they weren't far. Just beyond sight, and trained enough not to make a sound.

Gunfire rang out.

Bang! Bang! Bang!

"Webs," Kane whispered, and crossed himself.

Duke never had figured out how Kane knew Webs was dead, but he'd never rendezvoused with them six hours later, and Kane never spoke of it.

The explosions continued, and Duke's ears rang. Kane kept a hard pace, and Duke followed without breaking stride. This he could

120

do. This was being a Marine.

The click of a rifle had Duke falling flat to the ground, a second before Kane. Somehow, that pleased him, that his instincts were just as good as his brother's.

They lay there. Duke focused on the sounds. The fire in the field. The distant shouts — barely audible. The beating of his heart. Slower. Slower. Slower.

The call of a bird.

The scratching of a cricket.

The footfall of a man.

The glint of a rifle aimed at Kane's position only feet away caught Duke's eye. He fired at the threat. One shot, hitting between the eyes exactly as Duke pictured, though he couldn't see more than a hint of shadow and light. The flash of his muzzle lit the enemy before him.

A child.

A child with a gun.

Duke stared at the young body as it collapsed into the dirt. Kane jumped up, grabbed the gun from the dead boy's hands without glancing at the face, and said, "Move."

The boy wasn't any older than their little brother Sean. A boy. A child sent into the woods to pursue the best soldiers America had trained. Who would send a child to war? Who would send a boy out alone to die?

Duke didn't move; he couldn't. Intellectually,

he knew he'd killed an enemy, an enemy who would have shot Kane in the back without thought. But the enemy was a child, and Duke had killed him without hesitation.

Kane pulled Duke up from the earth. Duke was a full inch taller than his brother, but he felt a foot smaller.

"Soldier!"

Duke closed his eyes.

Kane slapped him.

Duke responded with violence, but Kane caught Duke's fist with his palm, twisted, and brought Duke to his knees.

Without comment, Kane popped the cartridge from the boy's weapon and pressed the end into Duke's hand. It was warm. The pungent scent of gunpowder whiffed into his nostrils.

"Three rounds missing. Three rounds hit Webs."

Kane let Duke's hand go, turned, and disappeared into the darkness.

He expected Duke to follow.

A second later, Duke did.

He paused next to the body of the boy, but just for a moment. A child sent to be a killer, given no choice in growing to be a man.

Duke followed Kane, neither speaking. Five minutes after the team rendezvoused they were airborne.

When they landed outside Mexico City three hours later, Duke told Kane he was going home.

"I understand," Kane said.

Duke turned, certain Kane didn't understand. Maybe couldn't.

"It's war, Duke," Kane said.

Maybe it was Duke who didn't understand.

"You could be one of my best."

Duke closed his eyes. Men like Kane were necessary to battle evil in the world. He finally realized what his brother had been doing, who he was. Kane was too smart, too focused, too disciplined to not understand the stakes, and casualties like the boy were unavoidable. Kane's men were too intelligent to blindly follow a leader. They were all in it together.

But Duke wasn't part of the team. He didn't feel it in his core, where he still dreamed of a normal life. Perhaps he was flawed, not a true Rogan like his father and his brother. All he knew is he couldn't do this, couldn't be part of Kane's unit.

He looked his brother in the eye. "I'm going back to the States. If you need me, call."

Kane stared at him. Something crossed his face, but Duke was too emotionally drained to register what Kane silently told him.

A curt nod. "Call J.T. He could use you."

Duke didn't know if he would. He started to

walk away.

Kane said, "I love you, brother."

It had taken a few years before Duke realized that Kane respected him, understood his decision, and didn't think he was weak, no matter what Duke thought of himself. Duke had made peace with what happened, as much as he could — though the face of the dead boy haunted him at times. Times like now.

Duke stared at the Colt in the drawer. His hand shook. He hadn't fired a gun since that dark morning.

He slammed the drawer shut, the Colt untouched, and left his office.

CHAPTER SIX

Nora and Pete arrived at the medical examiner's office just before noon. She said to Dr. Keith Coffey as he escorted them into the main autopsy room of the small satellite facility, "I appreciate you expediting the autopsy so we could be here."

In a little over an hour, the Department of Fish and Game would arrive at Butcher-Payne to start searching for the ducks, and Nora wanted to be there. She'd spoken to the director and he was putting together a team and gathering the necessary equipment. She'd also talked to Dr. Thomsen, the veterinarian who spent one morning a week at Butcher-Payne, and he was bringing a prototype microchip reader to hopefully aid in identifying the ducks.

"I started as soon as we prepped the body," Coffey said. A basic autopsy took about an hour, not including screenings and bloodwork, but a case as volatile and sensitive as this one — with a physically delicate corpse — needed to be handled exceptionally carefully and thoroughly.

She and Pete pulled paper booties over their shoes and masks over their mouths. She pulled on gloves; Pete stood back. She didn't comment, knowing her partner hated autopsies. She'd told him he could go to headquarters, but he insisted. "You'll need me at Butcher-Payne when Fish and Game starts searching," he'd said, and was right. They were going to need every free body to track the ducks.

The smell in the small autopsy room was clinical and unpleasant, but not intolerable. The forced air circulation kept everything cooler than a typical room, aiding the dispersal of any particularly foul odors. Dr. Coffey's assistant — a young, petite Asian woman — was working on a tray of tissue samples with her back to them.

Coffey had already incised the body. He said to Nora, "Check out the box."

She walked over to the forensic evidence dryer — essentially a big box with HEPA filters to preserve and protect evidence. It was used primarily to dry clothing prior to storage. The only three things in the box were jeans, male underwear, and a pair of athletic socks. The jeans were stained with something that could be blood, and the underwear and socks definitely looked stained with blood.

"From the vic?"

"Yep," Coffey said. "I didn't notice at the crime scene because his body was wet from the fire suppression, but as soon as I pulled off the jeans I realized we were dealing with murder. They tested positive for blood."

"This looks like a lot of blood." Only an unusual amount of blood loss could account for this much blood. "Are you sure this is only blood? Not —" She didn't know what else it could be. "Maybe something from the fire?"

"The jeans are burned, but not substantially, and as you can see I turned them inside out."

Nora actually hadn't noticed that until the M.E. mentioned it. The stains had seeped through, and nearly every inch of the jeans above the knees was saturated.

"I tested several samples. Only type A-positive, which matches the vic's blood type. It's common, but I suspect most, if not all, the blood is from his body."

"But no shooting? Stabbing?"

"Nothing that tells me what caused that much blood. Except —"

He hesitated.

"What?"

Coffey spoke carefully. "The injuries are inconsistent with a stabbing — no plunging knife. No internal organ damage. And on the surface, I can't tell whether the injuries were life-threatening — the fire damage is too extensive to get a good gauge on the depth. However, I can tell you that he was restrained."

He picked up a rubber-tipped pointer and lightly touched Jonah Payne's wrists. "You can't see the damage easily on the surface because his hands were burned, but see here? I peeled away the charred skin and there is damage to the muscles."

He motioned for Nora to walk around to the other side of the table. "We have to be gentle, but I want you to see his back. I've already taken pictures."

They carefully turned the body onto its side. "There's some sort of indention," Nora said. "From the beginning stages of rigor."

"Exactly."

"Then why isn't it purple or black? If he was supine for a few hours, then there should be pooling on his back." There was a faint purple hue, but it wasn't the right color.

They eased the body back on the table.

"You're right, there should be. I looked everywhere on this body, there is very little pooling, and what there is, is only on the back — but it's not visible to the naked eye."

"Did it evaporate or something? Because of the heat?"

"The fire didn't last long enough to cause such extensive blood loss, and even if it had, I would have seen a discoloration on the muscles where the body had been during the early to middle stages of rigor. I examined the cuts. They're shallow — they only look deeper because of skin splitting."

Pete paled and stepped back. "Skin splitting?"

Coffey nodded. "In the heat of the fire. But I've looked at every external inch of this body and I don't believe any of them are more than an eighth of an inch deep. And that's stretching it."

"What are they caused from?" Nora asked.

"That's almost impossible to tell because of the fire damage. Some sort of knife, thicker than a razor blade, but beyond that I can't give a more accurate example."

Nora stared at the body. "There're at least thirty marks on him."

"Thirty-eight that I can positively identify. No apparent pattern, except that the majority of them are on the arms. Only six are on

129

the torso."

Nora asked, "Were you able to determine whether he died in the fire or before?"

"I haven't looked at the lungs yet."

Nora let the M.E. do his job, watching him, focusing on the process so she didn't have to think about the victim and who he had been.

"Hmm," Coffey said.

"What?"

He didn't say anything for a long moment, and Nora stepped forward, though she didn't know what she was looking for. The insides of the recently dead were messy and the organs almost indistinguishable to a novice. But when Coffey pulled out a large organ, Nora recognized it as the lungs.

"See the lungs? No internal smoke damage. The throat isn't burned, at least to the degree that it would be if he were breathing when the room filled with smoke."

"That makes me feel marginally better," Nora said. "Then how did he die? These?" She gestured to the knifelike incisions on the torso and arms.

"I honestly don't know."

Coffey continued with the autopsy, and Nora refrained from asking too many questions.

"Look at his heart," Coffey said.

Nora didn't know what she was looking at, but looked anyway.

"Did you see that?" he asked.

"What?"

"Exactly! There was little to no blood pressure when he died. Usually I get a spurt when I cut out the heart, but only a little trickled out."

"You mean there was low blood pressure when he died?"

"Yes. Considering the amount of blood on the jeans, he very well could have bled to death."

"From what evidence? Can you state with certainty he died of exsanguination?"

He looked irritated. "You have all the evidence I have. Right now I can only tell you how he *didn't* die. He didn't die in the fire, from burns or smoke inhalation. He was dead when the fire started."

"But how can someone die from shallow wounds like these?"

Coffey said, "I don't know. I've ordered his medical records, and I talked to his doctor just before you arrived. He wasn't a hemophiliac, he wasn't on any medication — prescription at least — that would hinder his blood's ability to clot, such as warfarin. I've taken blood samples and hope to get tox reports back by tomorrow morning. I

131

rushed them."

Nora was stumped. "So you can't confirm he died of exsanguination?"

"I'm not putting it in writing — if he did die of a Class Four hemorrhage, then there would be a secondary determination, but I have to run some more tests, check the bloodwork, maybe run some more tissue and blood tests. I'm not closing it yet."

"I didn't see blood evidence at the scene. Would it have been destroyed by the fire?" Nora asked.

"No — there was no blood at the scene. Your crime-scene folks cut out the carpet after I bagged the body. I didn't see even a noticeable bloodstain — if any. But you'll have to ask them."

Pete asked, "What about the marks on his back? What does that mean?"

"Right, that's the other thing. So his body didn't leave the usual discoloration, though there was some pooling. But the weight of his body did press into a hard, uneven surface. I also found trace fibers on his back, which I've bagged as evidence."

Nora said, "I'd like samples for the FBI lab. We can expedite the tests."

"Great, because otherwise I'd send it to the state. We have a great lab for most things, but for trace evidence we have a very small department. I'll have a sample of everything couriered over to your office."

"Thank you," Nora said.

"Do you think the marks mean Payne wasn't killed at Butcher-Payne?" Pete asked.

"They might. Because the fire messed with the rate of decomposition, I can't give you a time of death — in fact, I can't even give you a tight window. I can say that rigor mortis had already begun before the fire. He had been dead a minimum of six hours. Possibly longer, up to twenty-four hours. But your investigation may yield a better window. He died approximately eight hours after eating. We're running those tests now because I couldn't tell by sight what he'd last eaten."

Pete excused himself and left the room.

Nora said, "The fire started around one-thirty in the morning. So he'd already been dead for six hours." That put the latest time of death at approximately seven-thirty Sunday evening, the earliest Saturday afternoon.

Nora emailed Duke and asked him if he'd yet accessed the security logs for the weekend. What if Payne was dead in the office long before the arsonists arrived? That seemed an unlikely coincidence, but something she needed to rule out.

"So what do you think caused those marks, Dr. Coffey?" Nora asked.

"I think the body was transported shortly after death. Rigor mortis set in while lying on a hard, smoothly ridged surface."

"Smoothly ridged? That seems an oxymoron."

"I won't put this in writing until I get a mold done and compare with the books, but I think he was in the back of a pickup truck for several hours after he was killed. The truck was likely enclosed or I would have seen evidence of greater insect activity."

"And because it would be obvious to passersby that a partially naked dead man was in the back."

He cracked a grin. "Right."

"So we're looking for a pickup truck with a camper shell or another similar secure top."

"And probably a long-bed. The vic is six feet two inches tall. He was at a diagonal in the truck — you can tell by the ridges. And he was flat — they didn't break rigor to move him."

Pete stepped back into the room. "Fish and Game just arrived at Butcher-Payne. The guy in charge is looking for you."

134

Sean Rogan slid into a plastic chair in the cafeteria of Rose College, stabbed the salad in front of him with his fork, pretending he was punching Duke in the face.

Play the part, Duke said. Be one of them, Duke said. You'll be fine, Duke said.

Duke could go pound sand for all Sean cared. He hated college, had hated MIT while he was there, straight A's notwithstanding.

Straight A's except for one damn *B minus* in English from that stodgy female professor who didn't like him.

Sean slumped in his seat and ate the leaves in front of him. How could people survive on this rabbit food? His nose twitched, the warm, tantalizing scent of grilled hamburgers making his stomach growl.

Duke owed him big time.

Jonah is dead.

Sean sighed away his anger and devoured the salad. Then he downed two of the four pints of milk in front of him. At least the milk satisfied the hollow feeling in his stomach.

"You drink *milk?*"

Sean looked up as he wiped his lips with

his napkin. A cute brunette who didn't wear makeup — and didn't need it — stood in front of him with her tray in one hand and her other hand on her hip.

"I have problems with my bones," he lied automatically. "My doctor insisted that I drink milk for the calcium." He prayed she didn't ask any details, because he'd have to make them up.

"You can take pills for that."

"He said it wasn't the same." Sean didn't know *what* he was saying, but it sounded good. If he had to pretend to be a vegetarian for the next week or two, he could live — but he was *not* giving up milk. Not even for Duke.

She put her tray down on the table and her pretty ass in the chair across from him. The raw veggies on her plate wouldn't be able to keep Sean thinking coherently for five minutes, let alone sustain him for an hour.

"Doctors are all quacks," she said. "I have a great nutritionist. I can hook you up with him if you want."

"Sounds good," he said. Nutritionist? What would he tell Sean that he didn't already know? *Eat a well-balanced meal, stay away from sugar, exercise.* "I didn't catch your name?"

"Anya."

"Anya. That's nice. Russian?"

She shrugged. "I don't know. I never asked."

"Asked?"

"My parents."

"Why?"

She shrugged again. "I was never able to talk to them. They don't understand, you know?"

Sean remembered why he hated college. He couldn't stand his peers. *I wish I had my parents alive to not understand me.*

"And you're . . . Sean, right? From Social Justice."

"Good memory."

She smiled. She really was pretty, Sean thought. Though he was only twenty-three, he felt a decade older than most of the students here, had felt that way even back when he'd been in college. But he still admired pretty coeds. "I really liked how you stood up for the innocent."

Innocent? Sean searched his memory . . . right, during a discussion during the two-hour class, he'd made a point of taking an extreme position on protecting the rights of animals, living creatures who couldn't protect themselves or their own rights. It had sounded good at the time, but Sean didn't remember exactly what he'd said. Something about how people couldn't be saved on the dead bodies of animals because we're just animals, too.

"Thank you," he mumbled. "I didn't mean to overstep my bounds."

He couldn't believe his plan had worked so well. He'd hoped to draw out the activists, but after one day?

"You're new. Where'd you transfer from?"

He rolled his eyes. "I didn't. It's a long story, but I had this jerk professor who flunked me. I graduated in June — or, I would have, except for him. So I have to take this class to get my degree."

"Who was it? Brigger? He's an asshole."

"Not here. I went to school on the East Coast, as far from my family as I could get." That was true, but not because he wanted to leave Sacramento. Duke said the MIT opportunity couldn't be missed. Maybe he was right, but Sean hadn't fit in there any more than he'd fit in at high school or at Stanford. True, unlike high school, at MIT he had intellectual peers, but few people he connected with. He'd been restless and bored. He tended to get into trouble when he was bored, and Duke always bailed him out. Like when Sean had hacked into the dean of students' computer and pulled out the porn the jerk had downloaded, then sent the files to the college board and student council. The dean was fired, but Sean had been expelled. That was Stanford, when he'd been a seventeen-year-old freshman.

Sean thought it was grossly unfair. The asshole *had* been surfing porn and downloading disgusting videos. Sean was all for looking at gorgeous naked women, but not the violent sex acts this idiot had jerked off to. Sure, Sean had illegally hacked into the computer — originally as an April Fools' Day joke — but it wasn't like he'd been changing grades or putting the porn on his computer in the first place.

The dean had even tried to accuse Sean of planting the movie files. Duke stepped in and proved that wasn't the case. But in the end, though the prick was fired, Duke had been disappointed in Sean's conduct, and Sean hated when Duke was disappointed in him.

"Hey, Sean," Anya said.

"Yeah?"

"You look sad."

He grinned widely. "Me? Naw, I'm a party animal."

"I'm in this group — you might be interested. We meet a couple times a week, write articles for the paper, do some demonstrations, help keep the campus green. It's not easy."

"I know," he said, though he had no idea what she was talking about.

"You're a great spokesperson. We could use someone like you."

"I have to catch up in the class — Professor Cole said he wasn't giving me extra time just because I enrolled late."

"Leif is a softie."

"Leif?"

"Leif Cole. No one calls him Professor Cole. I'll bet he loved your speech today, he just tries not to play favorites."

"He seemed preoccupied," Sean said.

Anya said nothing for a minute. "Maybe a bit tired. We all have those days. But he'll be at the meeting tonight, he always comes. Once you sit down and talk to him, you'll realize how brilliant he is."

Did professors have groupies? If so, Anya led the pack. Sean suspected she had a crush on the guy. What did a pretty coed like Anya see in a middle-aged academic with a receding hairline and ponytail?

But Sean nodded. "Great. Where?"

"The lounge in Edward Albee Hall. Seven-thirty tonight." She looked over his shoulder, giving body language signals to someone behind him. He avoided checking out the distraction.

"I'll be there." He smiled. "Thanks. Maybe this semester won't be a total drag after all."

I hope I'm not overdoing it.

"See you there. I have to go."

She picked up her tray and walked away. Sean drained his milk and glanced discreetly over his shoulder. Anya emptied her tray, sorting the trash from the recyclables into separate containers, but he couldn't see who she'd been making eyes with. As soon as she rounded the corner, he cleared his tray and trailed her.

Leif met Anya in the organic garden.

They rarely were alone on campus because it would have been improper, but why Leif worried about the conventions of society in matters of love, he didn't know. Today, however, he didn't have a choice. He'd tried to see her before class, but there were too many people around. After class, he couldn't break free in time to catch her before lunch, and then she was eating with the new kid.

He'd felt a whiff of jealousy seeing Anya with the handsome young man, which was unlike him. But what could he expect? She was lovely, a wisp of a girl really. Leif was twice her age. Not only were his feelings inappropriate, but the fact that he'd acted on them, that he'd pursued a relationship and had sex with a student — had fallen in love with a student — would get him in deep trouble. Though Rose College was progressive in academics and philosophy, the board could be rather uptight in matters of sex. Why wasn't he surprised that such a forward-thinking institution would cave in to rigid societal mores, all for money? Because ultimately, they feared losing the tuitions from the wealthy parents who sent their children to the exclusive college.

But Anya's spirit beckoned to his. She was an old soul as well as a fresh idealist. He needed her like he needed water to survive. Leif loved her, an odd feeling for him. He'd never felt so strongly about another human being. His life's work, his mission, had always been far more important than any emotional or physical attachment. But with Anya, he'd give up his tenure if that's what it took to keep her.

They'd agreed to keep their relationship discreet, even though Leif was the only one with something other than his heart at risk.

In May, when she graduated, he'd ask Anya to share his life. Not within the constraints of man-made matrimony, but where it mattered. They'd be together for as long as their spirits complemented each other. For as long as they were satisfied and complete.

When Anya approached him in the organic garden, wearing her customary long, flowing dress that made her look as sweet as her kind disposition, Leif couldn't resist taking her hand and squeezing it just for a moment. He ran his thumb up and down her palms. There were dark circles under her eyes, and her pale skin was even more translucent.

"Are you okay?" he asked quietly. He dropped her hands in case someone approached.

"Yes, of course," she replied. "What's wrong?"

"How was your lunch date?" He hadn't meant to ask, it just came out.

She blinked, unsure of what he meant, then said, "Sean? He seems very aware. Do you remember, he spoke up in class?"

He remembered, though at the time of Sean's impassioned plea for animal rights, Leif had been preoccupied with the news of Jonah Payne's murder.

"Was he with you last night?" Leif asked.

"I — I don't know what you mean. I just met him this morning in class, talked to him at lunch. What's wrong?"

"I know what happened."

He didn't need to elaborate. Her eyes fluttered downward almost demurely.

"Was he *there* last night?" he asked again.

"No. It was the same people."

His stomach tightened and he grabbed her hands again. "You promised me it was over."

"It was important. They were —"

"Shh." He cut her off. They'd never spoken of Anya's arson activities out loud. He *knew*, but they'd talked around it. They never said the words or names out loud. But Leif blamed last night's disastrous outcome on Anya's roommate. He'd thought Maggie had left for good.

"So Maggie is back?"

Anya nodded.

"Why didn't you tell me?"

"It — I — I don't know."

"She told you not to."

Anya nodded, tears in her eyes. "Leif, please forgive me. I didn't mean to break my promise to you, but there's so much at stake."

He had always admired Anya's passion and that she'd acted on her passions — something Leif had always wanted to do, but was too fearful. Freedom was more important to him than action. He talked a good game, but he'd never put his freedom on the line in a substantial way.

And he didn't want Anya to lose it.

"Anya . . ." How could he tell her? If not him, someone else would. She would know what happened.

"Leif — you're scaring me."

"Someone died."

She stared at him, not registering what he'd said. Then she shook her head, her big eyes glistening. "I don't understand."

"A reporter called me. Jonah Payne was found dead in his office." Anya began to tremble and Leif took her in his arms, reputation be damned. "Shh," he murmured.

Her pain was palpable as she sobbed on his shoulder. It had been an accident! Anya could no more intentionally kill anyone than could Mother Teresa — her life would never be the same. Leif couldn't say *I told you so*, though he had in the past. After the security guard was injured during the arson at Sac State, Leif had told Anya that she meant the world to him, and her life was too precious to risk death or imprisonment. And Anya had agreed. She knew the stakes, was willing to risk both, but in the end she said their love mattered more to her. And that together, after she graduated, they would find more powerful, long-lasting ways to change public opinion. Between his words and her face, they could do it, Leif knew. But now . . .

"What happened?" she cried.

"I don't know," he admitted. "Payne could have been asleep in his office, or maybe he tried to put out the fire. They may never know."

She pulled away. "Someone might see us."

"I don't care."

"You're too important for me to jeopardize your career," she said.

That she'd said it made Leif realize how selfish he'd been these past two years. Making Anya keep their relationship a secret.

"I love you, Anya."

Her lip trembled. "I killed someone."

"Not intentionally."

"It doesn't matter."

"Stop thinking that way. It was an accident. I can't lose you, Anya. I can't bear the thought of you being in a cage. Please, honey, you must protect yourself."

"I have to go."

"No —"

"I have class this afternoon."

"Anya, please —"

She tried to pull away, but Leif held her

wrist. "Don't worry," she said. "I'll protect you."

"There's nothing to protect." That was true, to a degree. He hadn't known about the arsons until after the second fire, and he didn't know details. He didn't know for a fact who else was involved — though he had his suspicions. Anya had never told him anything, he couldn't be called to testify. He *knew* but he had no evidence, no confessions.

"I killed someone," she repeated, whispering it this time.

Leif put it out of his mind. As far as he was concerned, Anya had never said it.

"Promise me," he said to her, "that you'll protect yourself. Do not talk to the police without an attorney. Say nothing. They will use your words against you. They'll try and make you feel guilty and I know your heart: it is kind and good. Someone has to protect your rights."

She nodded, eyes wet with tears. *I love you, too,* she mouthed, then ran off.

Leif removed his glasses and squeezed his burning eyes. An overwhelming sense of despair and foreboding enveloped him until he felt suffocated. Life as he knew it, as he loved it, was ending. And there was nothing he could do to stop it.

CHAPTER SEVEN

Duke listened to Jim Butcher as he accepted that his life's work was gone, and his best friend was dead. Jim didn't know what to do. Duke struggled to reassure him by saying, "I'm not walking away from this."

They sat in an office across the two lane highway from Butcher-Payne. A friend of Jim's had let him have a space for the duration of the police investigation. It was both good and bad that the office had a window with a view of the partially destroyed Butcher-Payne office building. Right now there were two sheriff's cars, the arson investigator truck, and three large California Fish and Game vehicles parked in the lot.

Jim stared at him. "The FBI didn't do jack shit on the other arsons, and now my partner is dead."

Duke stiffened. While he understood Jim's frustration, he also knew that the FBI had vigorously worked the case. That's what they did. And Nora English was one of the very best — Duke had seen her work first-hand on half a dozen assignments where their paths had crossed.

"I know the agent in charge of this investigation, and she's not going to let up."

"Fantastic!" Jim said sarcastically. "How many people are going to die because of these lunatics? They're fucking insane."

Duke changed the subject. "I swung by Russ's apartment. He wasn't there. No sign of him. His neighbor hasn't seen him since Saturday, but that's not saying much. She admitted she doesn't know him well. Did Russ mention to you that he might be going out of town?"

"No," Jim frowned. "Is something wrong?"

"I don't know." He sent a quick email on his iPhone to his partner, J. T. Caruso.

Run a full search on all financials, recent travel, etc for Russell Larkin, IT Director, Butcher-Payne. Address 1010 Rocklin Rd #16, Rocklin.

"Russ wouldn't be involved in anything that might hurt Jonah," Jim said. "What do you think is going on?"

"I don't know," Duke repeated, hating not having the answers. "Russ is the only one besides me who knows all the security codes and understands the system well enough to manipulate it."

"You're missing something. That just can't be," Jim said, though without conviction. Jonah was dead, all their research destroyed, anything was possible.

"I'll find him," Duke said.

"Melanie Duncan called me and said the FBI has already been out to talk to her. Is it true the research ducks were released into the wild?"

Duke hadn't spoken to Nora since sending her a copy of the security logs when she asked for them an hour ago.

"I haven't heard any information about that. If the FBI said they were, it's likely true."

"This is fucked." Jim ran a hand through his thin hair, leaving it sticking up in places. "I don't know what to do. I'm a damn media consultant and I don't have any idea what to do!"

Duke said, "Do what you do best, and by that I mean gather the facts. Before you go public with anything though, you should first talk to the FBI."

Jim said, "Agent Pete Antonovich told me to meet him here ten minutes ago, I gave him this address."

"He'll be here."

"Duke, I'll pay anything to find these

150

people."

"I'm not charging."

Duke saw an unmarked sedan pull into the lot. The car had "fed" written all over it. "I think Antonovich and English are here," he said.

He watched Nora slide out of the driver's seat. Pete Antonovich said something to her, then started toward the building where Duke was sitting with Jim. Nora went to talk with Fish and Game.

Duke looked at his long-time friend. "If you want me to stay while you talk to Agent Antonovich, I will. Otherwise, I want to see what I can get out of Agent English."

"Go. I'm fine. I have nothing to hide. I didn't kill Jonah, or want him dead." His voice cracked. "He was practically my brother. Losing him is devastating for Butcher-Payne, but for me, personally, it's . . ." He threw up his hands. "I've lost my best friend. The business means nothing to me without Jonah."

On the short drive from the morgue to Butcher-Payne, Nora spoke with the Centers for Disease Control. They were a bunch of pricks. Necessary, but pricks nonetheless. At least the jerk she'd spoken with was. But she hoped she had them under control.

They were on alert, but weren't about to respond to this potential emergency without more proof that they were needed.

When she drove into the parking lot she was pleased to see that Sheriff Sanger had set one of his men on the entrance to check IDs to keep the media and others away. She didn't want anyone without official clearance — especially the media — to get wind of the fact that there were twelve research animals potentially infected with a deadly virus loose in the area. She noted that Quin's truck was still on-site. Arson investigations took time and painstaking attention to detail. All of which was vital when and if anyone went to trial.

She introduced herself to the team leader from the Department of Fish and Game. Kevin Barry was a tall, skinny, bearded wildlife biologist with long dark hair restrained with a rubber band. He and his people pored over a map of the area, identifying nearby bodies of water, while close by Melanie Duncan paced. When Nora approached, Duncan was on her cell phone talking to the vet who was driving in from UC Davis with a prototype electronic reader that could register the microchips embedded subdermally in each duck.

Nora let them do their job while she

looked at her own map.

"Hello, Nora."

She immediately recognized the low, sexy voice behind her. She braced herself against the presence of Duke Rogan before turning to face him. Even though she was prepared, she was still stunned that he had such a strong impact on her.

To compensate for this reaction, she got right to business.

"Anything from your security disks?" she asked him.

His face went from subtle flirt to serious. She almost regretted it.

"Jonah's codes were used to get into the building. My staff is working on reconstructing the video surveillance."

"What happened to it?"

"I wish I knew. It's just not there."

Nora saw that the lack of answers bothered Duke even more than her. Her job was, in part, *finding* the answers, so the search might disturb her at times, or irritate her often, but it was simply part of the process in an investigation. For a man of action like Duke Rogan, not knowing struck at his core.

"You'll find it," she said.

"I went by Russ Larkin's apartment on my way here. He runs the I.T. department for Butcher-Payne. He's not there."

"He's not here either. The sheriff's department is keeping tabs on employees, neighbors, and potential witnesses, but I'm in the loop." She caught the worry in Duke's expression. "Are you concerned about Larkin's well-being?"

He didn't directly answer her question. "I put someone on his apartment. She'll call me if he shows up there."

"All right," Nora said, "I'll issue a BOLO for him if you think it would help. We do need to talk to all staff."

"Good thinking," he said. Duke gave her Russell Larkin's vital stats and the make and model of his car. Nora sent the information to headquarters.

She began, "You don't —"

He interrupted and gestured toward the Fish and Game trucks. "What's this? Jim said some ducks are missing?"

Duke never made it easy to get rid of him. "We have reason to believe that the arsonists released the research ducks into the wild."

Duke's face darkened and he said in a low voice, "They killed Jonah to let some ducks out? They're fucking nutjobs."

Nora had no answer for him. It seemed wholly incomprehensible to her as well.

Kevin Barry looked up from marking his

maps and said, "Can we identify them from their bands?" He specialized in birds, and Nora had immediately sensed his competence when first talking to him.

Nora said, "Most likely, the arsonists would have cut off the bands. They don't want the ducks recaptured."

"They should have thought about it before they released them," Barry said.

Duncan was within earshot, and the researcher hurried over to where they stood in the staging area on the far side of the parking lot. "Release?" she balked. "How do you know the ducks were released? Why wouldn't they take them home?"

Nora explained. "Animal-rights activists rarely, if ever, keep research animals as pets. Twelve mallard ducks? Where would they keep them? In their swimming pool? When the news gets out about the missing birds, neighbors and relatives could become suspicious and turn them in. In addition, they don't believe that wild animals should be in captivity, by researchers or even themselves."

"But you said they weren't animal-rights nuts. That they were opposed to genetic research." Duncan's tone was accusatory.

"Yes," she said, "but the fact that they took the ducks would suggest that they're involved in more than one political cause."

"Why do they think they can get away with it?"

"By cutting off the bands, the twelve ducks blend in with the thousands in the area. They've given them a chance of freedom."

"You sound like you agree with them!" Duncan said.

Nora didn't need to explain herself to this semi-hysterical woman, though she well understood Duncan's anger. Nora was angry, too, but she didn't have time for social niceties. In a clipped voice, she said, "Part of my job is to think like them, to understand their motivation and their goals. Their goal is to liberate the birds, not keep them as pets."

Barry interjected, "Well, they'll be neither free nor captive after we find them. They'll be dead."

Duncan panicked. "Can't you return them to me?"

Barry shook his head. "Gotta kill 'em. Them and any duck in the area. We can't possibly risk this virus spreading. And after, we'll have to sample birds in a wider area, make sure we got them all and the virus didn't spread."

Duke leaned over to Nora. "Is that true?"

156

She nodded. "I hope we find them all quickly."

Duncan resumed pacing, then glanced up at a van whose driver was showing credentials to the deputy manning the entrance. "Finally!" She strode over to the car that had just been waved through by the deputy.

Nora assumed it was the veterinarian and said to Barry, "Are you ready to go? I think that's the vet with the equipment."

"Almost." Barry pulled a map from his pocket. "These nuts could have taken the birds anywhere. Do you have any idea which direction they'd go? Looking for a dozen ducks in the Gold Country is harder than finding a needle in a haystack."

Nora considered what she knew about how these people operated. "Maybe not as hard as you think," she said slowly as she looked at the map and the areas the Fish and Game staff had already marked. "First, they're not going to keep the ducks for too long. They left here between one-thirty and two in the morning. They wouldn't take the ducks anywhere near their work, school, or residence. That would increase the odds that someone they know would see them releasing them."

"And you know where they live?" Barry asked sarcastically.

She ignored his comment and put herself in their shoes — easy to do, since she'd learned from one of the best animal liberators: her mother. "They won't take them to the closest lake — they'd assume that's where we'd go."

She remembered the times she'd freed research animals with her mother. When she was little she thought she'd been doing the right thing, the humane thing. But she'd learned far too quickly that freedom didn't mean safety, at least not for animals who were raised and cared for by people.

If Nora had taken the ducks, she would have found a place for them where people came to toss bread crumbs. A place with a lot of water, so the ducks could escape little kids who didn't know better when they chased them, and teenagers who did. But people were a must, because anyone worth their salt in the animal-rights movement knew that captive animals would have a difficult time fending for themselves. These birds needed food, water, safety.

"They won't be able to tolerate any quacking, thinking they were hurting the animals by caging them," Nora said. "And the ducks would have been crammed tight in the cages they took — they can't hold more than four ducks each. The arsonists would be nervous as well, having evidence in their possession."

"Well — how many miles?"

"I'm not sure, but not more than thirty minutes away. They wouldn't risk being pulled over if someone called in the arson quickly and the police were looking for a specific vehicle. A body of water off a freeway — preferably a protected area." That reminded Nora to check with Sanger about the canvass his men were doing earlier and if they had tracked down any potential witnesses.

"Hmm." Barry pondered his map.

Nora looked at the map upside down. If she had a dozen semidomesticated waterfowl and wanted to give them the best chance of survival in the wild, what would she do?

Steady supply of food. Lots of water. A park.

Finding such a place would be secondary to getting out of the vicinity, so they would pick a place along their escape route. She speculated that the route would be in the opposite direction of their final destination.

Barry said, "There are several ponds in this area. Some are seasonal and dry now, but —" He pointed to three less than two miles away. There wasn't anything special about them — no parks, no people. They bordered industrial areas. No, the arsonists would be concerned about toxins in those ponds.

She shook her head.

"How about Lake Arthur?" Barry pointed to a larger pond — hardly what Nora would call a lake — east of their location, right off I-80.

That was a possibility, ideal for escape. So was a group of man-made ponds in Newcastle, about ten minutes west. Except there wasn't a nearby park. It was also a new development near a light industrial area. Less pollution from business, convenient to dump the ducks, but it wasn't good enough for the animals. Nora would never have left them there.

"Here." She pointed to Lake of the Pines. "That's it."

"There're at least a dozen locations just as good that are closer."

The more Nora thought about it, the more convinced she was that she was right. The other locations just weren't *as good*. Lorraine would have chosen Lake of the Pines. Nora thought it ironic that she was thanking her imprisoned mother for lessons learned.

Nora said, "From Lake of the Pines they can head up Highway Forty-nine to Highway Twenty and cut across to Maryville, then head north to Chico or south to Sacramento. It's longer than going virtually anywhere via I-Eighty, but it gets them out of the area and they don't have to backtrack past the scene of the crime."

"You're amazing," Duke said.

Surprisingly she'd forgotten Duke was standing next to her. He usually wasn't so quiet. "Thanks." She was trying to be sarcastic, but it came out differently, almost as if she cared what he thought of her. Which she didn't.

All right, she did. But she wasn't about to admit that to him.

"This is a huge recreational area," she continued. "There are people, pets, kids — the ducks will be well fed. They'll be concerned about that. They don't want the ducks to die of starvation, and that's always a risk."

"Well," Barry said, folding up the map, "they'll be dead any way you slice it. And all the other ducks on that lake. We're talking hundreds of ducks. I hope you're wrong."

Nora's heart thudded in her chest and she felt sick. It pained her that innocent animals had to die, but the risk of the virus getting into the duck population was far too great

161

to chance it. Thousands of wild ducks could die, species decimated from Canada to Mexico, and there was the additional risk to humans if they didn't quickly eliminate the threat.

"We'd better go now," she said.

"I hope you're wrong," Barry repeated as he folded his map.

"Me, too." But Nora knew she was right. "I'll meet you there. Take Dr. Duncan and Dr. Thomsen with you. They've agreed to assist."

"It'll take us a bit to set up, and I hope Dr. Thomsen's reader works. I've never heard of one working more than a couple feet away from the source." He walked off to dispatch his team.

To Duke, she said, "Did you see Pete?"

"He's talking to Jim Butcher across the street."

Duke followed her. He'd seen the worry on Nora's face. He was hugely impressed with her analysis, and not a little curious how she came up with it. He'd always admired Nora's intelligence and quick thinking, but this was different. It was as if she could read the minds of the anarchists. But of course that was silly. And Duke knew, from working with Kane, that good soldiers became great warriors when they could put themselves in their enemies' shoes and anticipate their every move.

Good cops weren't much different.

They stopped outside the building where Jim had set up temporary shop.

"We'll find them," Duke said.

"The ducks or the arsonists?"

"Both." He reached out and touched her chin, lightly, but he couldn't help himself. She was so sad. "Chin up, Nora." She was so drained. Not a surprise; she'd been up since before dawn.

"Jonah Payne was murdered."

"I know. We —" He stopped. "You mean he was intentionally murdered? That his death wasn't an accident?"

"Pete and I came here from the autopsy," she said. "Dr. Payne was dead long before the fire started — six hours or more. And based on the evidence, he was killed somewhere else."

Duke tried to wrap his mind around what Nora was saying. He spoke almost as if to himself.

"It's far too coincidental that someone disconnected from the arson killed Jonah and dumped his body in his office the same day that a group of anarchists came to burn down the lab and free research animals."

"That's exactly what I thought. But this

163

behavior is completely out of character from what I know about anarchist terrorist groups. And I know quite a bit. This is more like the work of a psychopath."

Duke frowned. "How was Jonah killed?"

"It's inconclusive, but the M.E. believes he died from massive blood loss. There were multiple shallow cuts on his arms and torso. No major arteries were hit, but when Dr. Coffey dried his jeans there was a substantial amount of blood."

It sounded like torture to Duke. He couldn't figure out why — Jonah was a scientist. A bit absentminded maybe, but brilliant and dedicated.

Nora said softly, "I just don't understand. Everything about this case is textbook perfect for a standard environmental extremist group. The arsons, the spray-painting, the messages they sent. Everything . . . except premeditated murder."

"You said this sounds like a psychopath. Are anarchists exempt from being psychopaths?"

Something changed in Nora's expression. "No. I knew one a long time ago."

Taken aback by this admission, Duke wanted to ask her about it, but Nora abruptly entered the building. Again, he followed her. He'd make certain she'd tell him later.

Chapter Eight

Under other circumstances, the beautiful Lake of the Pines community — predominantly populated with the vacationing and the retired — would have enticed Nora into a long walk along the shore, or renting a paddleboat to soak in the sun, or taking a cold swim. Though it was a popular spot for picnics and outdoor recreation, the area was well maintained, with numerous garbage bins encouraging people to throw their trash where it belonged. For the most part, people complied — probably driven to comply by the signs prominently posted advertising the steep fine for littering.

A light breeze cooled the heat from the day, and Nora remembered why she loved Indian summer best. The remnants of summer during the day, the hint of winter at night, warm colors and vibrant life surrounding her wherever she went. The time for harvest, the cycle of life, the greens and golds, reds and browns. Autumn was a time for reflection, of celebrating the end of one year and anticipating the next.

It was late in the afternoon, nearly five, and early commuters had stopped at the sight of police activity. The media had arrived; there was no stopping them from reporting. Fish and Game and the CDC had come up with a statement that bordered on the truth: Several ducks had turned up with a deadly virus and in order to prevent the spread of the disease, they had to destroy the infected ducks.

Dr. Ian Thomsen showed Kevin Barry how to use the prototype scanner. "It'll read fifty feet away, provided there are no obstacles."

"Fascinating." Barry looked at the model. "The ones we use you have to be practically on top of the animal to get a beep."

"The company making this one is going into mass production next year. Part of the difference is the implanted microchip itself."

Thomsen and Barry started their walk around the lake with the microchip reader to see if it picked up a signal while everyone else waited at the staging area that had been cordoned off. Nora stood rigid, watching the men and not the ducks who swam up to them or waddled along the shore, looking for food. So trusting. If Nora's hunch was right, all these animals would be killed.

Pete and Jim Butcher were talking with the CDC representative, and Duke stood by her side. She was finding it hard to compartmentalize her feelings.

"You don't have to watch," Duke said.

"I'm not going anywhere. You wouldn't understand."

"Try me."

How could Nora tell him anything when she barely understood it herself? It wasn't that she felt responsible for what had happened at Butcher-Payne or what the arsonists had done with the ducks; it was a more ethereal feeling of helplessness and the need to be enraged in order to be more effective. She had to watch the end result of their stupidity to both hone her analysis and, perhaps, to punish herself. All the bad things she'd done in her past . . . not because she'd wanted to, but because she hadn't known any other life.

"Nora?" Duke said softly.

"Not now." Maybe not ever, but she couldn't talk as she watched Thomsen and Barry walk toward her with the microchip reader.

Beep.

"Does that mean —" Duke began, but

Nora put up her hand. She couldn't explain, she needed to focus.

It beeped again. The beeps were faint, but definitely audible. The two men continued walking along the shoreline; the beeping stopped. Barry turned and walked along an inlet filled with reeds. The beeping started again and grew stronger. As they approached, the beeping increased in both tempo and duration.

They stopped and talked. Nora joined them, and Duke followed. She didn't want to admit that she was glad he was with her.

"What are these numbers?" Barry asked Dr. Thomsen.

Nora glanced over. Numbers flashed across the device's small display.

Dr. Thomsen frowned, then nodded. "There're several ducks — I've never used it in broad scan mode, only the individual scan. This may be a glitch, but it looks like the display is flashing all the numerical codes it's finding."

Barry looked at the lake, then at the display. "Agent English, do you have that map I gave you?"

Nora pulled out the map of the immediate area. He handed her the microchip reader and looked at the map, then talked into his radio. "We hit paydirt. Get the nets.

No guns."

"You're going to save them?" Nora asked, hopeful but unbelieving.

Barry shook his head. "We don't have a choice. They'll be killed and sent to our lab. I don't think we can handle this quantity, and I'm sure the CDC will insist we ship every one off to Madison."

"Wisconsin?"

"Right. The lab there has everything. A regular animal CSI unit."

"But you said no guns."

"One shot and we get one duck, the rest will scatter. Then we're screwed. They'll go in all different directions. If all twelve are here, our job is done when we get every duck in this area."

Nora must have looked confused, because Barry added, "We'll snap their neck. It's instantaneous. Painless."

Nora's phone rang. It was Quin. She didn't want to be interrupted now, but Quin might be calling about the case.

"Hi Quin. I'm kind of busy."

"Lance told me you're with Fish and Game at Lake of the Pines. Why? Did you find the ducks?"

"Yes. I have —"

"What are they going to do?"

Quin sounded panicked. Nora wished she

170

had had the time to explain it to her sister earlier. "You know what they have to do, Quin."

"How can you participate in a mass slaughter?"

"It has to be done or thousands of ducks are in jeopardy. You know that."

"I — I can't think."

Lorraine had done a number on Quin. For some reason, Nora had never adapted to Lorraine's way of life. She'd rebelled from an early age, knowing deep down what they were doing was wrong but not knowing how to stop. Quin had wanted their mother's approval and attention so badly; she'd taken everything Lorraine said as gospel. It had taken Nora years to get Quin to think for herself and not spout out slogans and rants on every political subject under the sun.

"Honey, it's going to be okay. Are you done there?"

"What? Yes, yes, for now. I'm coming."

"Go home. Call your boyfriend and have him take you out to a nice dinner."

"I can't even think about eating when I know what's happening."

Barry said to Nora, "We're about to begin."

She nodded, and Barry motioned for his team to fan out.

171

"Quin, please go home. I'll call you later."
Quin hung up and Nora frowned.

"Something wrong with your sister?"
Duke asked.

"She's upset." But Quin's panic surprisingly calmed Nora. She did much better when she had a crisis to resolve; talking to Quin had put her in the proper mind-set.

Barry and his team were working along the western perimeter of the lake. They all wore protective breathing masks. Dr. Thomsen and Dr. Duncan handled the microchip reader.

It was an assembly line with multiple approaches. Fish and Game employees captured the ducks with a net or their hands, brought them to Duncan and Thomsen. After twenty ducks, they still hadn't found a bird from the lab. The ducks they'd captured were put in the back of an enclosed truck. If they couldn't get a positive identification of a lab duck, all the ducks would be freed. But if they found even one from Butcher-Payne, the captured ducks would be killed.

The work was painstaking and methodical. The wait was agonizing. The sun dipped lower in the southwest; the air grew cooler.

Duke stood as close to her as he could without touching. She closed her eyes and wondered if she was crazy for wanting to

172

give in to her attraction, but right now the idea of having someone come home with her, someone to hold her close, someone who understood her job and what she did and still cared . . . she wanted it.

How Nora could want something she'd never had, she didn't know.

You wanted a home before you ever had a real one.

A loud beep cut through the silence and her eyes opened.

Thomsen inspected the duck, nodded. Melanie Duncan started crying silently as Thomsen handed the duck back to Fish and Game. "That's one."

Barry ordered the ducks already captured destroyed, and he took the Butcher-Payne bird from his staffer. Without hesitation, he snapped its neck and placed the bird in an individual bright orange plastic biohazard bag and sealed it. The other ducks were killed and then put in large clear plastic bags, ten to twelve per bag.

Nora stood and watched as duck after duck was scanned, killed, and sorted into an orange bag or clear bag. Even the wild ducks would be tested — blood drawn and dissected — in case the virus had spread in the day they'd swam with the contaminated birds.

It wasn't the sight that bothered Nora the most.

It was the sound.

Like a thin, dry tree branch, each slender neck was snapped, the carcass disposed of in the correct manner.

Nora watched with wide eyes, fearing that if she only heard the sound she'd fall apart.

She remembered the day, years ago, when Lorraine had freed the wild horses. The horses Nora's mother told her had been born free, and should be let free. Nora had helped. She desperately wanted to please Lorraine, who just told Nora the day before that she was pregnant.

Nora would never forget the stampede. Hiding in the brush. The shouts and curses of men and women trying to recapture the animals. The horse falling in front of her, the snap of his leg loud enough that Nora knew he was lame.

When a man found the distressed horse, Nora saw pain in his expression. Pain and shock and anger. He talked to the horse quietly, whispering so softly, so soothingly that Nora was almost lulled into believing what he said, that the horse was going to be okay, that he was safe. Nora didn't hear the words, but she felt the rhythm, the tone.

It's okay, boy . . . You're safe . . . Shhh, relax.

The man, who looked like he might have been a cowboy though Nora had never seen one outside of a book, knelt by the horse's injured leg. He gingerly touched it and the horse tried to stand, stumbled, and fell, his whinny full of agony.

"I'm so sorry."

The cowboy took a gun from his belt and put a bullet in the horse's head.

Nora froze. Stunned. She'd believed . . .

Then the man turned away from the horse, looked at the sky, his face wet from tears. Before then, Nora had never seen a man cry. She'd never seen such real pain.

Later, her mother told everyone who would listen, "That bastard just killed the poor animal in cold blood. Didn't even try to save the horse. Probably enjoyed it. Or didn't even think about it, just a stupid animal," she added sarcastically.

Nora went to her mother later and said, "He was crying, Mama."

"No he wasn't," Lorraine said. "And don't call me Mama."

That had been the day Nora realized that her mother was wrong, and if she would lie about the sad man, she could lie about anything and to anyone. That had been the day Nora started believing in herself and not in her mother, the day Nora had decided

175

she wanted a different life, and she would do everything to get away.

Quin was born six months later, and Nora realized she couldn't let her beautiful baby sister grow up like she had. She would find a way for both of them to be free.

Nora had been nine.

As Duke watched, a pair of mallard ducks, male and female, waddled up to where Nora was standing on the edge of the gruesome scene. Some of the Fish and Game people were enticing the ducks from the water with bread — they were all quite domesticated. Evidently, these ducks thought Nora had food for them.

"Hey, Agent English, can you grab those for me?" one of the men called.

Nora didn't move. Her face was hard, icy, her entire body rigid. Something was wrong, even though he couldn't see her eyes through her sunglasses.

Instead, Duke managed to catch the birds and bring them over to the assembly line. A moment later, Dr. Thomsen, the vet, ran a scanner over them. It beeped.

"That's ten and eleven," Melanie Duncan said, her voice thick with emotion as she sealed their dead bodies in the biohazard bags. Her face and eyes were swollen from tears, though her red eyes were now dry.

"Team B is done as well," Barry said. "That's it."

"We're missing one," Melanie said.

"It's not here," Barry said. "But I'll send the team out to canvass the area one more time." He walked away, wiping his brow.

Duke went back to Nora. "Hey."

She didn't acknowledge him.

He reached out and touched her shoulder. She jumped, her body so tense he expected her to snap. Her face was pale, as if all the color from her tan had been leached out of her skin. "Please don't touch me," she whispered.

"It's okay. Hey, Nora, it's okay."

"Go away."

Was she angry with him for handing over the ducks? "They're done for now," he said. "Why don't you sit down?" He looked around, saw a private place about twenty yards away, shaded by trees.

"Leave. Now." She swallowed. "Please, Duke, leave me alone."

Her voice cracked and Duke realized how precarious her emotional balance was right now.

Barry from Fish and Game approached. "That's it, one's missing. I sent everyone out to scan the area one more time, but we've already been around it three times. The vet said he'd drive around with me along the entire perimeter. Dr. Duncan said it's a male, and he couldn't have gone far, since their wings are clipped. I'm sending these other birds to the lab now. The CDC guy is getting a bee up his ass with the media here, and wants me to clear out ASAP. Is that okay with you?"

Nora nodded.

Duke had a half-dozen questions he wanted to ask. Then another voice from behind them called, "Sheriff, I found these in the Dumpster behind the bathrooms."

Duke turned and saw a deputy carrying two cages.

Duncan exclaimed, "Those are from the lab!"

The sheriff of Nevada County, Donaldson, approached. "Tag them as evidence, Boyle."

"Will do."

"Agent English," Donaldson said, "I think we should sweep the public restrooms. Don't know that we'll find anything — they're not the cleanest of facilities — but we might get lucky. Is your lab handling the evidence? This is getting to be a jurisdictional problem, but we don't have a big lab here. We send most of our big cases to

Sacramento or the state lab."

"I'll take care of it," Nora said, her voice restrained.

"Great. I'll get it packaged up and off to your people. Wish this wasn't so damn depressing. When my kids see the news footage, I'm not going to hear the end of it."

Nora jerked her head toward the sheriff and snapped in a surprisingly harsh tone that sounded nothing like the Nora English Duke knew. "When criminals break into high-security labs and steal what doesn't belong to them, bad shit happens."

Her stance shifted, she tightened her jaw, making her cheekbones appear sharper.

"It's a tragedy," Duncan said. "Didn't they think through what they were doing? A man died last night because they wanted to free a dozen research animals — and one hundred fifty-seven ducks are dead because of their reckless act."

"Who's talking to the press?" the sheriff asked the assembled group.

"The CDC," Nora said.

"I'll give him the stats," Barry said. "He's going to need some spin on it."

"They'll keep the lake closed for a few days, until we find that last duck," Dr. Thomsen said. "We need to look — every minute we waste . . ."

He didn't have to finish his thought. The group dispersed and Duke stood alone with Nora.

"Nora?" he said, gently but firmly putting his hands on her shoulders. He pulled off her sunglasses. Her eyes were dry, so dry they were red. She grabbed her glasses and put them back on, though the sun was setting and she no longer needed them.

"Why don't I take you home?" he said. "Your partner can take the car back, right?"

"I'm fine," she said.

She was anything but fine.

She stepped forward and a loud snap had her jumping as if she'd seen a ghost. She looked down and saw she'd stepped on a tree branch.

"Dammit," she whispered. "It's just a damn branch."

Duke said, "I am taking you home, Nora."

She didn't object. She turned back to face him, her chin quivering, and said, "Thank you."

Nora was grateful she didn't have to drive back with Pete and listen to details about the case. It was after seven, and she'd been moving nonstop for sixteen hours. The sun was sinking, and so was she.

"Agent English!" a news reporter called out.

She jerked her head up. Everything was dark, but she didn't take off her glasses. Not until she had her emotions completely under control.

"No comment," she called, but no one heard her as a group of bystanders started shouting at her.

"Murderer!"

"The ducks didn't do anything to you!"

"Killer!"

"Bitch!"

She noticed the flying object a second too late to avoid being hit in the chest by an open, partially filled soda can. The dark, fizzy liquid splattered across her chest like dark, watery blood.

She faced the crowd. They had no idea what was going on and why those poor animals had to die.

She saw Duke make a beeline toward the twenty-something girl who had thrown the can, a defiant look on her face. She wasn't scared — or if she was, she hid it well.

"Rogan!" Nora called. He hesitated. The anger in his face was palpable. It gave her the strength she needed to shake out her memories, to put her mother behind her for the rest of the night. "It's okay."

She walked back to the reporter and said, "I have a brief statement."

181

She was going to get reamed by her boss for this, but she wasn't going to let the truth be shoved under the rug by the CDC, who would give no real information, other than that the public was safe. Everyone would believe that the government had overreacted and killed animals without good cause.

The news reporter rushed over, followed by the cameraman. Nora said, "I'm only saying this once."

"Can I ask —"

"No," she said emphatically.

"Okay. Okay, fine. I need your name —"

Nora reached into her pocket and handed him a card. She cleared her throat, saw that the camera was rolling, and began.

"The tragic killing of one hundred fifty-seven ducks today — specifically, five different species of ducks and two species of geese — is solely the result of a small group of criminals who broke into a private laboratory and released twelve quarantined ducks. The thieves believed that they were helping the birds by releasing them into the wild. On the contrary, they are responsible for all the dead animals you saw today." She paused a moment, and when the reporter looked like he was opening his mouth, she added, "But even worse, they set the labora-

182

tory on fire and a human being died as a result."

She wasn't going into details regarding Jonah Payne's death. She had some ideas about how to draw out one or more of the arsonists, and she didn't want to give information that they might decide to keep in-house for the time being.

"Rest assured," she continued, "the FBI, the domestic terrorism joint task force, the Nevada County Sheriff's Office, and the Placer County Sheriff's Office will do everything we legally can to find and arrest those responsible for this tragedy."

She paused a second, then said, "Cut."

"Can I —"

"No."

She turned and briskly walked away. Amazingly she felt better. She'd been so scared earlier that she was going to completely fall apart — her compartmentalization technique hadn't been working. Every snap, every duck, reminded her . . .

Don't think about it, Nora. Don't think about it.

She shook her head, needing to put it aside, and stumbled.

A strong arm wrapped around her waist. She hadn't realized she was on the verge of falling until Duke pulled her up and held her against his side for a moment of time that was several beats too long for the chivalry of the act. And she liked it. A lot. His broad chest a perfect resting place for her heavy head; his warm, muscular arm holding her close. Just for a moment, just for a glimpse of what it would be like to have someone to call her own, someone who cared . . . but she'd given all that up long ago.

"You did good," Duke Rogan whispered in her ear.

"I'm sorry for — earlier."

"No apologies."

Nora took off her glasses and put them in her pocket, then reluctantly took a step away from Duke. "Thank you for being here."

Duke touched her cheek lightly. "I think I have a shirt in my trunk."

She'd almost forgotten about the girl who'd pelted her with the open soda can. She glanced over her shoulder, but Duke said, "She's gone."

"Just an unhappy bystander," she said. "I'll live."

CHAPTER NINE

Sean was sorely out of place at Rose College, especially at the meeting of Leif Cole's Action Now! group.

Twenty or so students gathered in the student union and talked well into the first hour. Cole was late, and Sean hadn't seen Anya since he'd followed her to the garden, where he saw her meet up with Cole and behave rather intimately. Though they didn't kiss, it was the familiar way they had touched, the way they had spoken to each other, that told Sean they were romantically involved. It bothered him, not just because she was Cole's student but because Cole was twice her age — or more.

What he wouldn't have given to have bugged the bench and listened in to their conversation. *Something* had happened, and Anya had gotten very upset. Cole hadn't looked too happy himself. Had their conversation been related to the arson and Jonah

Payne's death? Duke had told Sean that the FBI felt someone in Cole's group was responsible. Sean wanted it to be Cole, not Anya, but it had looked to him like both of them had been worried and upset.

A girl ran into the student union and interrupted the "meeting" that hadn't really started. "Turn on the TV!" she exclaimed. "The news. Channel Ten."

One of the kids flipped on the television set nearby.

The station was in the middle of a report. The film showed plastic bags full of dead ducks.

One of the students cried out, "What happened?"

"The police," gasped the girl who'd told them to turn it on. "They killed them all!"

Murmurs. Sean was surprised to glimpse Duke in the background, just for a second or two.

The newscaster was saying, ". . . related to Butcher-Payne Biotech —"

Several boos came from the students.

". . . in a fire early this morning. Sources close to the investigation told News Ten that the arsonists released ducks infected with a genetically altered virus into the lake here, at Lake of the Pines."

"Genetically altered!" a student exclaimed. "Serves them right."

"Someone died in that fire," Cole said, but Sean suspected he was the only one who heard the man.

The newscaster said, "Residents were shocked and upset by the activities."

Cut to an elderly woman. "I've never seen anything like it. They just broke their bodies in two and tossed them into garbage bags."

A teen boy said, "They were sick."

An older man said, "My wife had to lie down, she was so upset by this tragedy. We bring our grandchildren to the lake, but neither of us will forget all those little bodies."

A professional-looking woman commented, "I can't believe this happened, but I think it's more shocking that the people who brought them here burned down a business in Auburn."

The scene cut to the on-site reporter, who said, "Twenty minutes ago, I had the opportunity to talk with Special Agent Nora English of the FBI's domestic terrorism squad."

The lighting was different, certainly twenty minutes or more earlier, Sean thought. He couldn't hear what she was saying at first because of the boos and complaints from the students gathered in the room. Cole said, "Shh, listen."

". . . broke into a private laboratory and released twelve quarantined ducks. The thieves believed that they were helping the birds by releasing them into the wild. On the contrary, they are responsible for all the dead animals you saw today. But even worse, they killed a human being."

"I don't fucking believe that fascist fed!" a tall, older student exclaimed.

"Shh!" Cole admonished. The kid continued to grumble and Sean strained to hear the television from his position on the far side of the room.

Agent English was saying, ". . . Sheriff's Office will do everything we legally can to find and arrest those responsible for this tragedy."

The on-scene reporter was back, and it was now dark and he wore an overcoat in the breeze. "The California Department of Fish and Game are still out here, but refused to say why. Speculation is that there are more infected ducks, or they're looking for additional evidence. The Placer County Sheriff's Department recently confirmed that the victim in this morning's arson fire was in fact Dr. Jonah Payne, a genetic scientist from Auburn. Unconfirmed sources claim that the same group that attacked three other facilities, including a laboratory at Sacramento State University, is responsible for the Butcher-Payne arson."

The broadcast returned to the studio, where a newscaster said, "The Placer County sheriff, Lance Sanger, issued a statement that his office was cooperating fully with the FBI. When asked whether officials were looking into Action Now!, the environmental activist group founded by conservationist and Rose College Social Science Chairman Leif Cole, Sanger confirmed that Action Now! and other groups were all being looked at closely, but he wouldn't comment on whether any one group is under investigation."

Cole turned off the television.

His students ranted on his behalf.

"Okay, everyone!" Cole tried to get their attention. It took him several minutes before he could speak without raising his voice.

"I know that you're all upset by what happened," Cole said. "But we need to put this in perspective. What the FBI and Fish and Game did was wrong —"

"Absolutely! Fascist pigs," a voice called.

"But," Cole continued, "we also have to think about the loss of human life. That goes against everything we believe, and I know that all of you agree with me."

There were still rumblings. One girl said, "But Leif, why did they kill the ducks? I don't understand how they could be so cruel."

"Neither can I," Cole said.

Sean waited thirty minutes after the meeting had broken up. He finally got Leif Cole alone.

"Hi, Professor Cole? I'm Sean, I'm new here."

"I remember you from my class this morning."

"Anya Ballard invited me to this meeting, but she's not here. Do you know where I can find her?"

Professor Cole was suspicious, Sean saw it immediately. Suspicious or jealous. "I saw her earlier," he said. "She wasn't feeling well."

"Oh. Too bad. I'll see you Wednesday morning."

Sean felt the man's eyes watching him leave.

In the campus parking lot, he got into his car. He had planned to head home, but a niggling worry about Anya had him getting out and heading over to the dorms. Earlier, he'd looked up Anya's dorm room number, and now he knocked on the door.

She answered, her eyes tired and red.

"Sean," she said, surprised.

"I missed you at the meeting tonight."

He looked over her shoulder, trying to maintain discretion. There were others in the room. Two boys sitting on the floor that he could see. One of them had been at the meeting.

"I'm tired. We were studying and time got away from us."

"Sorry to bother you," he said. Had he been wrong? He glanced at the kid who'd been at the meeting. Sean remembered his name had been Chris, and he'd left early. Maybe he'd come here to study . . . but Sean didn't see any books or papers nearby.

"I'll see you tomorrow, okay?" Anya said.

"Wednesday," he said. "I don't have class tomorrow."

"Wednesday. Maybe we can have lunch again." There was no romantic interest from her tone, just friendship, but Sean was emboldened.

"I'd like that," he said.

She closed the door, and he could have sworn he heard a female voice asking, "Who was that?"

"Who was that?" Maggie asked Anya. The guy hadn't looked familiar. Though she didn't know why, he'd given Maggie bad vibes. Maybe because he was so clean-cut, but she hadn't seen him very well through the crack in the door.

"Sean — he's a new student," she said.

"Oh." No one interesting. "I forgot Leif's meetings were on Mondays. Sorry I kept you."

Anya shook her head. "I wasn't planning on going." She sat back down on the edge of her bed. "It's over," she said.

"We're not talking about it," Chris snapped. That had been one of their strictest rules: Never discuss past actions.

"I'm not. I'm stating a fact. I can't live with myself if there's another accident, if someone else —"

"Anya!" Chris shouted. "That's enough."

Tears welled in her eyes. She didn't like being yelled at.

Maggie played the part of her defender. "Cut it out, Chris. We're all upset. This wasn't supposed to happen."

Scott stared at her, but he didn't say anything. He wouldn't. He was as guilty as she was. Well, he hadn't actually *cut* Jonah Payne, but he'd helped Maggie bring the body back from Tahoe, and he hadn't said boo about it. Of course not. He was always too stoned to care much about anything but when he was getting his high. He was stoned now. Not too heavily, but enough to mellow him out.

"I'm sorry, Maggie," Anya said. "I can't do it anymore. It's wrong."

Wrong? Anya had said the *wrong* word. There was nothing *wrong* in burning to the ground corrupt businesses. There was nothing *wrong* about killing bastards like Jonah Payne who destroyed lives without a thought. Lives like Maggie's father, who had just wanted a platform like everyone else . . .

"We're done," Scott agreed. "I'm out. Chris?"

"Yeah." Chris acted like a tough guy, but he'd gotten sick earlier. He didn't have the stomach for action, and Maggie was glad they were quitting.

"It's unanimous," Maggie said. "I'm relieved." Relieved that she had a plan to take care of these fools.

Anya hugged her. "I'm glad you're back, Maggie." She tried not to feel guilty, but she squirmed.

"Me, too." Maggie pulled back, blinking away tears.

"What's wrong?"

She shook her head. "I'm just — the ducks. I'm so angry and upset. They didn't need to do it." That was the truth. Agent Nora English, the things she'd said. The things she'd allowed to happen. Maggie couldn't think about that now. Later, later when she was alone and didn't have to worry about what she said or did or thought.

"I'm thirsty," Maggie said. "Anyone for iced tea?"

"Water?" Anya asked.

"Sorry, none here." She'd gotten rid of it, knowing Anya preferred water to anything else.

"Iced tea, then," Anya said.

Maggie poured the tea into cups and handed them around. She reached into her pocket, looked at her cell phone. "Damn, it's my mother." She rolled her eyes. "I gotta talk to her. I'm going in the hall so she doesn't think I'm having a big party or anything." As she opened the door she said, "Hi, Mom."

She closed the door, pocketed her cell phone, and walked quickly away.

"Something's up with her," Chris said to Anya and Scott.

"Maggie?" Anya shook her head. "She tried to get back into college, but Rose said they needed the money from last semester before they would readmit her. She doesn't have enough. I gave her three hundred dollars, all the extra money I have." She drank her tea. It was icy cold and tasted like oranges.

"Too much sugar," Scott said after sipping, but he gulped it down anyway.

"I think this whole thing is fucked," Chris said. "The accident, then the feds killing all those birds. I just want to get out of here. Do you think they might, you know, put it together?"

Anya put a hand on her stomach. She had gas, pretty bad, but she didn't want to ask Chris and Scott to leave just yet.

"I think I ate too many cookies," Scott said.

Chris didn't say anything, but his face was turning purple.

"Chris?" Anya stood, stepped toward him and fell to the floor, her stomach clenching. Suddenly she vomited uncontrollably.

Chris started convulsing, and Anya panicked when she couldn't catch her breath. Intense pain radiated through her limbs and she couldn't get up.

She crawled — slithered — to the door. Behind her, Scott started vomiting, the sound so deep, so violent, that Anya feared for him.

She couldn't see, her head was floating, her body so tight. Her throat burned as if on fire.

It seemed like hours, but it couldn't have

taken her more than a couple minutes to reach the door. She pulled herself up against the wall, could barely touch the knob. Her vision blurred and she couldn't turn the handle.

"Help!" she called, but couldn't hear her voice. "Help." Her throat wasn't working. All she heard was her own breath coming in raspy moans.

Her hand wasn't cooperating. Her vision faded, the pain so intense she just wanted to die.

She was dying.

Leif.

Help.

She retched again, down her front, and saw blood. *Help.*

Her hand fell from the knob and she slumped against the door.

CHAPTER TEN

While Nora changed her clothes, Duke walked around her house, curious. He'd never been here before, and he was pleased to see that it was both what he expected — private, tasteful, neat — and what he didn't expect: open rooms, lots of windows, large garden, and an extensive collection of knick-knacks.

The house itself wasn't large, but it rested at the end of a short, private street in a hidden community in the middle of Fair Oaks. Each room was oversized, with high, vaulted ceilings and large windows. The windows in the rear looked out into a yard that distinguished itself by being simple: A deck overlooked a wide expanse of mowed grass, with established oak trees along the back hillside, a small, elegant pool to the right, and a rose garden to the left. The lighting was well placed, and the yard was one that would be comfortable year-round — there was even a gazebo in the corner for rainy days.

Duke had expected Nora to be more of a minimalist, but her home had built-in bookshelves in nearly every room, bursting with books and knickknacks and pictures, mostly of her and her sister Quin. Nora seemed to collect . . . things. One shelf of small clear glass animals, another shelf of seashells, another of ceramic elephants, and yet another of coffee mugs from twenty-one of the fifty states. He counted them.

In the den there were stuffed animals of all shapes and sizes and vintage crowding a loveseat in the corner. It made him wonder why she couldn't part with any of them, why she clung to mementos. Above the couch was a framed photograph of Nora accepting an award, rifle in hand. He looked closer and was impressed, but not surprised, that she'd made FBI Sharpshooter.

There were two bedrooms on either side of the great room, each with its own bathroom, but Duke avoided those, not wanting to walk in on Nora dressing. Not true. He absolutely wanted to watch her dress — or undress. But not tonight. They were exhausted, and he just wanted to make sure she was okay after the afternoon at the lake. The experience bothered her on many levels, and Duke had finally gotten her to start opening up.

He found her in the kitchen. She'd changed into sweatpants and a faded FBI Academy T-shirt. She still looked gorgeous. She'd washed her face, and though she wore little makeup during the day, now she was fresh-faced and looked younger than her years.

"I boiled some water — I'm having chamomile tea, no caffeine — nothing to interrupt my sleep tonight. I also have caffeinated bags —"

"Chamomile sounds great." It sounded like drinking weeds, but Duke wanted any excuse to stay.

"Do you live far from here?"

"Rancho Cordova."

She shot him a look. "You don't seem the type."

"Because it's a working-class city?"

"Maybe."

He shrugged. "It's my parents' house."

"You live with your parents?"

"They died. A plane crash."

"I'm sorry. Recently?"

"Thirteen years ago. Now it's just me and Sean."

She put the tea in front of him, slid over

the honey. He sipped it, then added some honey.

"What happened?" she asked.

He realized she thought his entire family was gone. "I should say, it's just Sean and me in the house. My older brother Kane is a soldier for hire in Central America. The twins, Liam and Eden, are younger than me and live in Europe."

"Europe?"

"They run their own personal security company there. For the rich and famous." He laughed, but it didn't sound funny. Maybe because he'd never thought it was a good idea.

He changed the subject. He didn't mind talking about his family, but he wanted to find out more about Nora. "I like your house."

Even in her exhaustion, she brightened. "Thank you. I've been here seven years. Bought it just after I turned thirty. It's always been my dream . . ." Her voice trailed off and she grew melancholy.

"To own a house?"

"To have a home."

There was a distinction, and Duke was curious. "Did you move a lot growing up?"

She didn't say anything for a long minute. "Yeah, you could say that."

"What would you say?"

"You don't really want to know."

"I do, or I wouldn't have asked. I'm not making small talk."

"Then what are you doing?" She looked him in the eye. She was suspicious, wary, and sensitive. But there was something about her tone, something *hopeful.*

Duke leaned back. "I'm getting to know you. It's what people do when they work together. When they like each other. When they've been interested for, oh, four years. It's called conversation."

"I must have missed that lesson." She glanced down at the mug, but there was a half smile on her lips, a smile she didn't want him to see. She sighed and said, "I didn't have a conventional upbringing. I didn't go to school, for one. Lorraine claimed she was homeschooling me."

"Lorraine is your mother?"

"Unfortunately. Her idea of education was teaching me about her favorite social causes. I learned how to pick a lock, paint a protest sign, and make bombs."

That wasn't the answer Duke had been expecting. He didn't know what to say. How could he have worked with her on half a dozen cases over the years and not known?

Nora waved her hand as if it didn't matter, but Duke saw it mattered greatly to her. "Some of Lorraine's friends were saner than she was. I learned how to read because of Gigi, a wonderful but eccentric woman who followed the Grateful Dead around for fifteen years, earning her way by knitting and selling sweaters. I used to have some. My mother left me with Gigi for a few months when she went off on one of her crusades. The first time was when I was five, but I stayed with Gigi quite a bit. She had a pickup truck with a camper shell. Almost like a home."

The wistful angst in her voice twisted his heart. No one should grow up like that.

"I assume your father wasn't in the picture."

She shook her head. "Not mine, not Quin's. Different fathers. So we think. Lorraine knew who my father was — at least his name. I tracked him down much later. He died at the age of thirty-two, drunk. He fell off the cliffs near Soquel. Lorraine doesn't know who Quin's father is — never cared, either. She named her Quin Teagan because Teagan was the name of some guy she liked — but admitted to me that she'd never slept with him. I don't know where she got Quin from. I think she took it from a Bob Dylan song, but spelled the name wrong. Probably on purpose. Lorraine never liked conventions."

She looked out the window into the dark.

"I didn't mean to bring up bad memories —"

"You didn't. Today — it was just a hard day."

"The lake."

"That, and the arson, and the killer — you said something earlier."

"About the psychopath."

He remembered it well, because it had affected her.

"I knew a psychopath once. Cameron Lovitz. My mother met up with him when I was nearly sixteen. She'd always been a criminal, a petty criminal. Nothing more violent than graffiti, trespassing, and petty theft. A few bombs — but they rarely worked. She didn't know I'd been sabotaging her plans for years." Nora sighed. Duke didn't interrupt. She needed the time to tell her story the way she wanted.

"I was just waiting until I was eighteen," she said a few moments later, "but honestly, I didn't know if I would leave — I couldn't leave Quin. I was the one who made sure she went to school, and I taught myself with her schoolbooks. I used to live in libraries . . ." She cleared her throat, sipped her tea. "But Cameron Lovitz was a terrorist. He boasted of sinking a boat off Santa Barbara that was carrying a high-ranking oil executive and his family. I didn't know if I could believe him, but at the public library I researched his claim and learned a board member of an offshore oil drilling company had died in what was apparently an accident. Did Lovitz do it? Maybe.

"But I became less skeptical of his claims when he pulled my mother into crazy plans. Setting bombs in new housing developments, planning to derail a train carrying toxic waste to show the dangers of toxic chemicals. Lorraine bought into it. And I was in the middle of it."

She got up and poured her half-gone tea down the drain, rinsed the cup, and left it in the sink. "Lorraine was so stupid. And blind. And she said she loved Cameron and would do anything he asked her. Including breaking into Diablo Canyon nuclear power plant. Knowing what I know now, there was no way their plan would have worked, but that wasn't the purpose. I think the purpose was to scare people. And maybe they should have been scared."

"What happened?"

"I turned FBI informant when I was seventeen. Worked with the Los Angeles office, gave them everything, and they were there to catch them."

"But they didn't?"

"Cameron Lovitz is dead. The others are in prison, including my mother."

"And then you joined the FBI?" It seemed incredible and unexpected, but it fit Nora.

"I didn't know what I wanted to do after my world fell apart." She walked over to the counter, leaned against it. "My handler lied to me. About a lot of things, but I didn't know that until he died during the operation. I hated him, but I didn't. I understand why, now, but at the time . . ." Her voice trailed off. "I met another agent out of Los Angeles, Rick Stockton. He's now a director at the FBI lab. He was everything that Andy Keene was not. And he taught me a lot, helped me gain custody of Quin, helped me get my GED and go to college. Urged me to take psychology because of my aptitude tests."

"Psychology? Are you a profiler?" It made sense, the way she analyzed where the arsonists took the ducks.

"I have the certification. The BSU offered me a position, but it meant a lot of travel."

"You don't like to travel?"

"One week here or there for vacation? Sure. For my job? No. I wanted a home. A place of my own. A place for my stuff." She laughed at herself, but it was a sad sound, and Duke rose from his chair and crossed over to Nora. He took her hands into his, and squeezed.

"Home is everything," Duke said. "I didn't realize how important it was until my parents died, and it was gone. So, yeah, I understand exactly what you're feeling."

She swallowed, trying to extract her hands from his, but Duke didn't let go.

"I also finally figured out what makes you tick."

"You don't know me —" she began.

"On the contrary. Do you realize that every decision you make is always about someone else? From turning FBI informant to raising your sister to joining the FBI."

"That's not true —"

"Would you have stayed with Lorraine as long as you did if Quin wasn't in the picture?" he interrupted.

"Probably not, but —"

"And why are you here in Sacramento? Because of your sister?"

"Family. You said it yourself, home is everything. Quin's my only family, why are you picking on me?" That came out wrong. She sounded immature and stupid, and it wasn't what she meant, but she didn't like how Duke Rogan had a way of looking at her as if he knew her better than she knew herself.

"You have a beautiful house, but you're never here to enjoy it. You work fourteen hour days, seven days a week. I don't think you've ever put yourself first, or factored in your dreams ahead of Quin or your partner or your boss or the damn FBI. It's never, 'What does Nora want?' It's always, 'What does someone else need?' What do you do for fun? Do you like to swim in that incredible pool out back? Do you like skiing? Camping? Going to amusement parks?"

Tears sprang to her eyes, and she blinked them back, averting her gaze.

"Oh, sweetheart, I'm sorry. I didn't mean anything by it. Just that I want you so much, Nora, but even more than that, I want you to be happy."

"I've never been to Disneyland," she said softly. "I can't believe I'm upset about it."

Nora should have anticipated Duke's kiss, but it surprised her nonetheless when his lips touched hers.

It was light, airy, for only a moment. Then he pressed his solid body against hers, his hands wrapped around her waist to hold her against him, and he took the kiss from warm to scorching in seconds.

The heat radiated from his body, his mouth claimed hers, hard and intense, sending a lightning bolt through her nerves. Her hand went up to his face, touched it, and he shivered against her.

The kiss was all she could think of, her mouth drawing in his tongue, his taste and scent wrapping around her senses so she couldn't think. She was on fire, a good fire, a yearning and need for Duke that she'd kept simmering on the back burner for far too long. The fear was still there, but she pushed it aside as her hands reached into his hair and a moan escaped her throat.

He pulled his mouth from hers, kissed her jawline, her ear, and whispered, "I've wanted to kiss you for years." He feathered kisses on her face. "I should go."

She nodded her agreement. It was a lie. And he knew it.

He kissed her, held her chin in his palm. "Next time I'm going to stay."

Her knees buckled as a hot wave of anticipation jolted her. He smiled, as if he knew what he'd done to her.

"I'm going to go before I find it too hard to leave. Set your alarm, and I'll see you bright and early tomorrow morning at FBI headquarters."

Nora was speechless. She followed Duke

to the front door. Her voice seemed to have disappeared. She cleared her throat.

"Tomorrow," she whispered.

He turned and stared at her, a deadly serious half smile on his face. "Sweet dreams, Nora." But his tone was anything but sweet. It was spicy and held the promise of his words, *"Next time I'm going to stay."*

Then he left.

She locked the door behind him, set her alarm, and stood there, calming her racing heart, still feeling his lips on hers, his mouth hot and seeking, his hand on her chin.

There was no going back. She'd tasted the forbidden fruit, and she wanted more.

It wasn't Duke Rogan who was forbidden; it was anyone who tried to get too close. He was dangerous to her carefully arranged life, her quiet home, her peace. She'd built everything around her with care: her friendships, her relationship with Quin, her career. Someone like Duke could throw it all off balance. Though with someone like Duke, she almost didn't care if he turned her life upside down.

Still, she was terrified of losing herself, losing everything she'd worked hard to achieve. But mostly she was scared that the wall that kept her from getting too close to anyone or anything would melt under the laser blue gaze of Duke Rogan.

While her sister Quin had made a point to date many men as often as possible — all smart, professional, attractive, eligible bachelors — Nora's sister's relationships were fleeting. Quin never put her heart on the line, therefore she couldn't be hurt. But neither was she happy — though she'd never admit that.

Nora was the opposite. She'd been involved with very few men since Andy Keene. She had always put everything on the line — and each time, the relationship had ended badly. Nora liked her present life. She longed to come home at the end of a busy day. She loved sitting on her deck and reading until the last sunlight disappeared. If she wanted to have cereal for dinner or cold pizza for breakfast, she could, without commentary or criticism.

She was content.

But contentment was lonely.

CHAPTER ELEVEN

Nora walked into FBI headquarters before eight in the morning while talking to Agent Nathan Dunn of the Lake Tahoe satellite office on her cell.

"It was dark when we finally made it last night," he told her. "We had a warrant to deliver, and it ended up being a testy situation. Payne's place was locked up tight and we had no indication that anyone was in immediate danger."

"The man is dead," Nora said bluntly. "We confirmed that he left his Auburn residence at oh seven hundred on Saturday, and his intended destination was his house in Lake Tahoe. The medical examiner confirmed that he wasn't killed at the research lab, so yeah, I think we have probable cause to enter his house. Do it and call me right back." She hung up, not giving him a chance to argue. Technically, she wasn't his supervisor. He and his partner worked

211

independently, running the Lake Tahoe office. But she'd worked with them many times over the years, and she was the acting SSA of the domestic terrorism squad while Nolan Cassidy was at Quantico. She had no problem using the little authority she had if it got the information faster.

The tight rules and regulations that Nora worked under day in and day out were beginning to annoy her. For once she wished she had the freedom to act when she knew damn well something was up. If Payne hadn't been killed at his vacation house, they needed to know that ASAP. If he had been, they needed their evidence response team on-site immediately. And while Dunn was a competent agent, too many times he and others had their heads knocked around by the U.S. attorney's office for overstepping procedural boundaries. And with the recent electoral changes, nearly every U.S. attorney had been replaced. No one quite knew what to expect from the new people, and thus were doubly sensitive.

But a man was dead and an anarchist group apparently had a psycho in charge, which made almost everything Nora had learned since becoming an agent fifteen years ago irrelevant. She had to go way back for lessons in this kind of aberrant psychology, to the two years she had lived under the same roof with Cameron Lovitz. His powerful personality had convinced her mother that breaking into a nuclear power plant was a good idea.

Who had that kind of charisma? Leif Cole for one. However, after reading his published works and talking to him half a dozen times over the twenty months since the first arson at Langlier, Nora had thought the academic a highly unlikely suspect. Just because he was the most vocal opponent of genetic research didn't make him an arsonist, or a killer.

But maybe she was wrong. She needed to talk to him again. Pressure him to help.

If a traditional anarchist cell had killed someone, it would have been an accident, and most likely they would then disband. There was still one cold case from five years ago where that had happened. After a homeless man died in an arson fire at a new apartment development, a string of seventeen related arsons stopped cold.

But Jonah Payne's death was premeditated murder. A psychopath, even one with a political agenda, operated under a different set of guidelines. Would the public outrage slow him down or encourage him?

She sent a message to her team to meet in the main conference room at 0830 for a debriefing and assignments, then stopped by SSA Megan Elliott's small office. Megan handled violent crimes.

Kincaid, Nora reminded herself. She rarely worked with Megan, and it would take time getting used to the fact that she'd gotten married over the summer. Nora had never thought about how she might manage her workaholic life within a marriage. It was all so much easier when no one else depended on you and you could make your own schedule.

Megan was at her desk, and motioned for Nora to come in while she wrapped up her call. "What's going on?" Megan asked.

"I'm dealing with a psychopath in the Butcher-Payne arson, and that's your area of expertise."

"Lucky me," Megan said.

"I've called my team together for a debriefing in twenty minutes. Would you mind sitting in and sharing your thoughts and wisdom?"

"Count me in. Any word on Nolan?"

Nora shook her head. "Nothing new. He loves it at Quantico."

"You ready to take over for him?"

"I'll cross that bridge when I come to it,"

Nora said. She'd thought about it, and while being in charge of her squad didn't intimidate her, she wasn't entirely confident that she was the best person for the job. As Pete always told her, she got too emotionally involved with her cases.

"Nolan wouldn't have put you in charge of your squad if he didn't have one hundred percent confidence in you," Megan said.

"Thanks. I appreciate that." She glanced at her watch. "Fifteen minutes?"

"I'll be there."

Back in her cubicle, Nora checked her messages and wrote a quick update for her ASAC, Dean Hooper. He'd just been transferred from Washington the week Nolan went to Quantico, and Nora was still a little nervous around him. Hooper had been an assistant director at headquarters, specializing in white-collar crimes, and took the lower position when he'd married a local immigration agent.

Quin walked into her cubicle, startling Nora. "Hey, sis."

Nora frowned. "You said you couldn't make it."

"I only have a few minutes, but I went to the lab first thing this morning to grab the test results on the accelerant." She slid over a thin folder. "There's your copy. Exact same brand of vodka. And that's something the press never knew."

Nora read the printout. She said, "And you were right, no trace of accelerant in the office."

"Nothing we didn't know."

"You didn't have to come down."

Quin shrugged. "You asked me to. I don't mind. But I have to get downtown by ten for a staff meeting, then Ulysses and I are meeting at Butcher-Payne to catalog everything, then turn it over to your ERT by tomorrow morning."

As they walked together to the conference room, Nora's phone vibrated. She glanced at the number. Dunn.

"English," she answered. "Did you get in?"

Dunn's voice was strained. "You were right. We have what appears to be a major crime scene."

"Where in the house?"

"In the bedroom. The bed is saturated with blood. There's also other biological matter — the place stinks to high heaven."

"Don't touch anything. I'm sending the ERT there. Secure the scene and start the canvass. Any neighbors who saw him arrive, when, if anyone spoke to him, saw him with anyone, whatever you can find out. Then send me a report."

"This place is in the middle of nowhere. It doesn't get much more private than this."

"I'll have research shoot you off his recent credit card transactions and phone records. See if you can follow up on any of them. I'm going into a briefing, but call me if you find anything."

She hung up.

"Payne was killed in Tahoe," she told Quin as she shot off an email to the ERT leader and ASAC Hooper about the crime scene and asking for a group to go to Tahoe to process the scene.

They entered the conference room. Within minutes, her entire team had gathered, as well as Megan Kincaid. Nora wondered where Duke was, but she didn't have time to call him.

"I'm going fast because we have a lot to do. First, to bring everyone up to speed, Nathan Dunn called from our Tahoe office. There is substantial evidence of violence in Dr. Payne's vacation home. We've secured the house and are sending the ERT. We'll need to confirm that Dr. Payne was killed there, but all evidence points in that direction."

She sipped water and continued. "Everyone should have gotten my notes from the coroner's office and the crime scene. Dr.

Coffey hasn't made his report official, but we're going off the preliminary until we hear something different. The victim was dead at least six hours before the fire started. He was killed off-site and transported in an enclosed pickup truck bed. Dr. Coffey is working on matching up the marks on his back with a make and model. It may give us our first real lead."

From the minute Dr. Duncan said Jonah Payne was a creature of habit and went to his vacation house the last weekend of every month, Nora had known that he'd been killed there. Organized murderers plan their kills down to the last detail. They follow their prey, plan the best method of attack, and pounce.

Before she could share the additional information, ASAC Hooper opened the door and said, "Nora, when you have a minute I need to see you in my office. Go ahead and finish up here."

He left, but Nora was distracted. She glanced at Megan, who just shook her head, not knowing what was going on.

Finish up here. Right.

She looked at the team. "I asked Megan to be part of this because she understands psychopaths. And whoever killed Jonah Payne is not a typical anarchist."

Megan said, "I've been thinking about it, and I'd like to go through like crimes, see if there are any unsolved cases similar to Dr. Payne's, but not connected to genetic research or arson. I'm looking at the manner of death. If you don't mind, I'd like to talk to the M.E. myself."

"Please do," Nora said. "Pete, can you follow up with both Sheriff Sanger and Sheriff Donaldson on the canvasses at Butcher-Payne and Lake of the Pines yesterday? See if they've found anything new, have them walk you through it. They might need a fresh pair of eyes."

"Will do. What about Cole?"

Nora was trying to avoid going there until she had a chance to reassess her previous analysis. "We need to talk to him again."

Pete cleared his throat. "Without meaning to offend, Nora, but are you the best person to do it?"

Nora knew where he was going with this. Pete had always felt that she was too close to the investigation, that Nora tried too hard to think like the arsonists. He worried she was overly sympathetic, but nothing could be further from the truth.

"Yes," she simply said, "I am."

Nora turned to Ted. "Duke Rogan with Rogan-Caruso sent over the background reports on Butcher-Payne staff. Go through it with a fine-toothed comb. Anything odd, you know what to look for — flag it and follow up." To Rachel she said, "Learn everything you can about Jonah Payne and Jim Butcher. We can't rule out that Butcher — who has the most to lose because he isn't a scientist — may be peripherally involved. Maybe someone wants to punish *him* by killing his meal ticket."

"That doesn't sound like anarchists," Pete said.

"No, and anarchists don't generally kill. But someone died yesterday."

"Unless it isn't connected."

"A bit too coincidental to me," Nora said. "There's a reason why Dr. Payne's body was brought back to the research lab. Maybe it was just to watch us run around trying to figure out the unexplainable, but that would have been thought out by the killer. I doubt it's so immature a reason, but there's got to be a reason. When we find it, we may just discover the killer."

She glanced at her watch. Ten minutes had passed.

"Go," Pete said. "Let me know what's happening when you're done."

She thanked her team, said good-bye to Quin, and went directly to Dean Hooper's office.

Duke Rogan shook Dean Hooper's hand when he entered his office. "Good to see you again, Hooper."

"Likewise. How's Sean?"

"Good." He refrained from saying anything about Sean at Rose College this week. Better that Hooper didn't know. Plausible deniability, should Sean learn something important to the investigation.

"I appreciate you coming in," Hooper said.

"I was coming in anyway. What's going on?"

"I had a disturbing call from Quantico. Our key profiler went over the case and wanted to discuss it immediately."

There was a knock on the door, and a moment later Nora entered. Duke wanted to talk to her alone — hell, he just wanted her alone — but she was all business as usual.

"You wanted to see me?" She caught Duke's eye and for a second, Duke knew she was thinking about last night. Good. That would keep her on her toes. He winked at her and she diverted her eyes, a faint blush rising.

Damn, but that was sexy.

"Yes. Everything taken care of? I read your

report," Hooper said.

"ERT already left for Payne's cabin."

"I'm planning to talk to Leif Cole again today." She put up her hand before Hooper could object. "I know he's threatened us with lawsuits every time we say boo, but I honestly believe that he knows something. I don't think he's involved —" Her voice trailed off and Duke wondered what, exactly, she *did* think. "But he has to suspect someone. Though they operate independently, it's not a huge group of people."

"You're not going to get someone like Cole to turn state's evidence."

"No, but I might be able to feel my way around the situation and see if I can prod him hard enough to give up something without realizing it. It's worth a shot, because right now we have next to nothing — unless ERT picks up a fingerprint in Lake Tahoe that we can match," she added with a hint of sarcasm, enough to make Duke think she didn't believe it would happen.

"Good plan," Hooper said. He hit the speakerphone button, then dialed. "Hans Vigo called this morning and wanted to talk to us about the last letter sent by the BLF arsonists. Since Rogan here has been consulting, I hope you don't mind I asked him to join us."

"No," she said, clearing her throat. She glanced at Duke, and he smiled at her.

Hans Vigo picked up the phone himself.

"Hans, it's Dean Hooper. I have Nora English and Duke Rogan here with me."

"Thanks for getting back to me so quickly," Vigo said.

"What's going on?" Hooper asked.

"I've been analyzing the four letters BLF sent after each arson, and I think we need to revisit the references to Agent English's past cases."

Duke straightened. "I hadn't heard about that." He glanced at Nora, who looked ill.

Hooper passed over a photocopy of the set of letters to both Nora and Duke. "The last one is on top. The places it references are all cases that Nora worked as an undercover agent."

Duke watched Nora read. The way Hooper spoke . . . "Are you suggesting that the killer knows Nora?"

"No," Nora said automatically. Somehow Duke didn't even think that she'd heard what he'd said.

Hooper said, "When Hans called I pulled the cases that Nora worked. Only two were on file in the system."

Nora tapped the letter. "The first two

listed here I was an informant, not an agent."

Hans spoke through the phone. "Which makes me think that the person who wrote this letter knows a lot about you. Killers who reach out to the media want attention," Hans said. "And I think that this killer wants *your* attention."

Duke's chest tightened and he shifted in his seat. He didn't want Nora under the gun from *any* nutjob.

"My attention?" Nora said. "What the hell for? Anarchists like the group we're dealing with want attention for their political cause. Not from the FBI or anyone in it."

"Correct," Hans said. "It's why they spray-paint their message on buildings, publish their 'manifesto' of action, and escalate. The letters posted on the newspaper message board are their way of making sure that they put their spin on their crimes — before the public is even aware of the arson from the regular news media, the arsonists post their reasons for the crime. Corrupt companies, animal testing, gene manipulation, whatever their specific cause is."

Duke didn't like the direction this was going. He skimmed the first three letters while Dr. Vigo spoke, then read the fourth letter carefully. It had a different tone and focus.

Vigo continued. "The first three letters focus on the individual entity and their so-called crime. For Langlier, it was that they engaged in animal and genetic testing to develop their pharmaceutical products. For Sac State, it was genetic engineering in agriculture. For Nexum, it was using animal by-products for profit. But for Butcher-Payne? That letter mentions in passing the use of animals in genetic research, but the *primary* focus of the letter is the actions of law enforcement in *resolved investigations*. None of these listed cases are open."

Hooper said, "The earlier cases where Agent English was an informant aren't cases where there was any doubt. All parties were convicted on solid evidence. I reviewed them thoroughly."

"All it tells us is that another person in the group wrote the letter." Nora put the letter aside, but the way she kept looking at it had Duke concerned. Because Nora was worried, no matter what she said.

"Yes, you're right," Vigo said. "But why?"

"Maybe there's a new person in the group," Nora suggested.

"Possible," Vigo responded skeptically.

Nora said, "Based on past cases, we know that there are usually three or four people

225

involved in these types of groups. Maybe one of them dropped out. Maybe someone else wanted to take a stab at public relations." She sounded sarcastic, a way to distance herself from the intensity of the situation.

"Nora, you can't ignore this," Duke said.

"Let's assume — just for a minute — that the killer fixated on me as the person trying to stop him. He does a little research and — *voilà!* — learns of my high-profile cases and is trying to distract me."

"Possible," Vigo said once again.

The idea of a killer targeting Nora terrified Duke. He had no problem with Nora being an FBI agent working dangerous cases; he had a huge problem with her being the focus of a psychopath. His specialty was personal security, and he wasn't letting Nora English out of his sight.

"This last letter is personal," said Vigo. "It focuses on the 'corrupt' government — a phrase often used by these people when talking about both politicians and federal law enforcement. I went through the files on all those cases, and there are no other common factors except Agent English."

"And the types of investigations," Hooper said, "were all domestic terrorism cases."

"I'm hardly the only agent who works

domestic terrorism," Nora said.

Duke watched her closely. She was thinking about what Vigo and Hooper were saying, but she didn't want to believe that somehow this case was becoming about *her.* Nora didn't want to be the focal point. She didn't want to think of herself as a victim.

Hooper said, "I'm having an analyst pull all Nora's cases and see if anyone she's arrested is out of prison."

"Have them look into relatives of prisoners as well," said Vigo. "Someone who lives on the West Coast. Originally, I thought the killer was older, but this letter seems to be singsong, taunting — a younger, immature voice. Under thirty, with no college degree, though, who likely spent some time in college and is comfortable around students."

"Leif Cole," Nora mumbled. "He doesn't seem the type. And he's older. Also, I don't think he's a killer."

"He didn't write this letter," Vigo agreed, "but he may be familiar with the unique writing style. Remember that it was Ted Kaczynski's brother who recognized his distinctive phrases in the published manifesto."

"Cole hasn't been willing to help on any level," Nora said, "and he wouldn't even look at the other letters, but I'll try again.

Now that the group has escalated to murder, maybe he will help." She didn't sound optimistic, but Duke had complete confidence that she would push Cole hard.

"What's our next step?" Hooper asked.

Nora rose from her seat, agitated. "To keep the investigation moving forward," she said. "I have a great team working on this case, covering all the bases. The answers are out there, and we'll find them."

"Yes," Vigo agreed, "but I think the fastest way to find the answers is to find out who is so angry with you, Agent English, that they created an elaborate and drawn-out plan to draw you into their game."

"Maybe I should put Pete in charge and have Nora take some time off," Hooper said. "I've only been here six weeks, Nora, but I've looked at your personnel records and you haven't taken a vacation in years."

"That's not true," Nora said, but Duke could see her thinking about it. Of course it was true, he thought. He knew her better than she knew herself. "I'm not giving up this case. Call Nolan, my SSA. Dr. Vigo, find him and he'll tell you that I am the best suited to getting to the bottom of this. I *know* these people. I *know* how they think."

"Your safety is more important," Hooper began, "and there are other trained agents who may work this case without a personal connection."

Dr. Vigo said, "I don't know that pulling Nora is the right thing."

"Of course it's not!" Nora said. "If it was Pete, would you pull him?"

Duke heard the tremble in Nora's voice, the fear. Not of the killer, but of losing her identity. She *was* her job. And Duke wondered if he could ever claim enough of her to where he was as important to her as her work. And was it even fair of him to ask?

He didn't care about being fair, not about this.

"I'll take responsibility for Agent English's personal safety," Duke said.

She faced him with shock and something like distrust. He didn't want to read too much into it, she was on an emotional roller coaster, and one he realized she'd never ridden before. But he was irritated that she didn't try to understand.

He needed her to trust him. Without trust, there could be no relationship.

"I can accept that," Hooper said. "Hans?"

"Great. We need to go over the cases, and it wouldn't hurt if you reviewed them as well, Nora, when you have a chance."

She quickly calmed herself, and said in a measured tone, "I understand your point,

Dr. Vigo, but I can't imagine anyone who would have a personal vendetta against me, to such an extent that they would kill to . . . to do what?"

"Nora, you understand terrorism. I understand psychopaths. This is a case where the two have collided, and I think we have a wholly new, and dangerous, monster on our hands. Be careful."

Duke's phone vibrated and he looked at the message. It was his partner, J. T. Caruso.

He stared at the message with a heavy heart, but not surprise. Maybe he'd already sensed the truth, because he couldn't imagine that Russ Larkin had any part in killing Jonah. But it didn't make the news any easier to swallow.

He told the three FBI agents, "Russ Larkin's car was found in Reno. He's dead."

CHAPTER TWELVE

By the time Duke and Nora arrived in Reno, nearly two hours later, Russ Larkin's corpse had been taken to the morgue. Nora contacted the Reno FBI office after Duke had been notified by Reno PD about the latest murder, and Agent Sara Ralston met them at the crime scene: a squalid parking lot behind an abandoned warehouse.

Duke felt damn guilty that he'd harbored ill thoughts about Russ being a villain in this mess. When both Russ and his computer had gone missing, Duke's first thought was that he was guilty. Only later did it occur to Duke that Russ might be in trouble.

"Did you see the victim?" Nora asked Agent Ralston.

"Just. When I got here, they had already removed him from the vehicle, had him bagged and tagged. The deputy coroner on scene is an acquaintance, gave me the basic. Dead more than twenty-four, how much more he won't know until the M.E. does his job. Dressed in jeans and T-shirt, sneakers, no visible damage aside from the slit throat. Cut deep, likely from behind."

"Passenger seat or driver's seat?" Duke asked.

"Driver's," she said. "Seat belt still on, and there was a clean strip of shirt where it hit him, so I'd say the belt was on when his throat was slit."

Why the hell did Russ drive all the way to Reno and park behind an abandoned building? Twenty-four hours would have put him there at two p.m. on Monday, well after the arson fire. "Could he have been dead longer?" Nora asked.

"Could be, I really don't know my decomp well. I'm white-collar crimes, but we have a small satellite office here, and my violent-crimes squad is out in the middle of nowhere handling a murder-suicide on federal land. Nasty stuff. Don't know how you do this every day."

"I'm domestic terrorism, not VCMO," Nora said. "But I get my fair share of the dead."

"The M.E. is fairly friendly. We might be able to get an answer before the official report."

"I heard there was a note with the body,"

Duke said. "Do you have it?"

"Saw it, don't have it. Reno PD has it."

"We'd like a copy," Nora said.

"Go ahead and ask. They're territorial here."

"Whatever it takes," said Nora. "We need that note — it'll help with the profile."

Duke crossed over to where the CSI team was processing Russ's car and getting it ready to transport to their garage for further evidence collection. He picked out who was in charge easily enough, and crossed over to the twenty-something kid. They were all young, which surprised him.

"Duke Rogan, I spoke with Lieutenant Rob Prentiss two hours ago about the victim."

"Prentiss? He's at the station."

"He asked me to come because the victim was in my employment and has classified information in his possession."

The kid said, "Take it up with Prentiss. This is my crime scene, and you're in it."

Duke pushed. "He said I could get a copy of the note that was attached to the body."

"I don't know anything about that. He didn't talk to me."

"Call him."

"I'm busy. You're not from our jurisdiction, are you?"

"Sacramento."

"Sacramento what? You're not a cop, so I don't know what you think you're going to get from me."

Nora was suddenly at Duke's side, and the kid gave her the once over. "Hello," he said.

She said, "Officer Dressler, correct?"

"Yes, ma'am."

"Special Agent Nora English, FBI attachment to the Department of Homeland Security," she said rapidly. "Mr. Larkin, the victim, works for a contractor of DHS, Rogan-Caruso Protective Services, and in such capacity, has sensitive and classified information pertaining to national security. Mr. Rogan, the principal of the company, is a security-cleared consultant to the JTDP for both DHS and FBI and as such, I'd expect you to give him whatever information he needs to insure that the health and safety of all Americans is not jeopardized, which any delay could risk."

Dressler blinked. "What is —"

Nora glanced at her watch, and said, "We're on our way to another crime scene, and the killer in question is crossing state lines, which actually puts this case squarely in my jurisdiction. I've been told that Reno's CSI unit is extremely competent.

I'd rather not call in my team, but I don't have time to dick around. Either we get what we need — now — or I'll secure this scene personally until my ERT arrives."

Duke was impressed. He'd never heard anyone bullshit so completely and have it sound so legitimate. He kept the grin off his face, but he wanted to kiss Nora for her quick thinking. He didn't think she would appreciate it here, especially with her *if you defy me I'll win* arrogance.

Dressler mumbled, "A minute," and walked away.

Nora turned to Duke, her lips turning up just a fraction, and she winked.

"I need Russ's laptop and flash drive," Duke said.

"He'll give you everything you need. I'll sign an evidence receipt and give Dressler the car to process, which will make him happy. Ralston told me he's a stickler for details, which makes him a bastard to deal with in jurisdictional issues, but a godsend in the evidence room."

Dressler returned a moment later. "Prentiss said to give you what you need." He was obviously unhappy with the order.

Nora softened and gave Dressler the benefit of her smile. "Thank you, Officer Dressler. I appreciate your cooperation. All we need is the letter and any computer equipment in the vehicle, which is the property of Rogan-Caruso. There may be highly classified information and we need to know what the killer may know, in order to protect the well-being of American citizens. However, I would greatly appreciate it if you could process the car and trace evidence from the victim. I'll trade you information. This is a highly charged case, and I promise your expertise will be much appreciated."

He wanted to argue, but didn't. "I'll prepare an evidence receipt."

"Thank you," Nora said. "And as soon as you have any information off the vehicle, please contact me directly." She handed him her card.

While Dressler went to gather the sealed evidence, Nora asked Duke, "Why would Larkin be out here? Do you have clients here?"

"Russ didn't work for me, I hired him for Butcher-Payne. He was employed by Jim and Jonah. I did the background check on him, I don't know what I missed —"

"Maybe nothing."

"When I get into his laptop, maybe I can figure it out. But this just doesn't make sense. He drove all the way to Reno . . . why?"

"Jonah Payne's vacation house is only thirty or so miles from here, in Dollar Point. Were Dr. Payne and Larkin friends outside of work?"

"Not that I know of. Jonah's weekends away were always private after his wife died. He didn't date much, if at all. He was all about his work. Russ was young, smart but only about computers. He didn't care about the science end of Butcher-Payne, only the computer end. I've been going over his files, and nothing jumps out at me."

"Where did Larkin go to college?"

"Fresno State. Graduated in 2003, worked for the state for two years, then I hired him for an insurance company we consulted for in 2005. It was in Fresno, and he wanted to move up here, so I was looking for something for him, and Butcher-Payne needed an I.T. guy when they expanded in 2006. He's been there since."

"Why did Larkin want to move to Sacramento?"

"I don't know. Probably job opportunity. He was from a small town in the central valley, and Sacramento is a lot more appealing than Fresno."

"Could he have been seduced?"

"Into what — giving away security codes? I don't think so. He didn't seem the type to be so naive."

"But if he was involved with a woman, maybe she had access and he didn't know."

"Possible, but that doesn't explain how the killer knew about the test code. When I trained Russ, we did it on-site. There's nothing written down."

"He didn't write anything down?"

Duke considered that. It was possible, sure, but after all this time . . . "I don't know."

Dressler came back with a box. "Sign this." He used his chin to gesture to the slip of paper on top.

• One (1) HP Laptop Model 8730 recovered from passenger seat, in leather case.

• Two (2) Flash drives, 2 MB. Blue: in center console. Green: in pocket of leather case of laptop.

• One (1) Wallet, black, leather, initials RAL embossed on front. Contents: California Driver's License D-0009874 Russell Anton Larkin, Roseville. $67 cash. VISA check card from Golden 1 Credit Union. VISA Credit Card from Chase. Shell Gas Card. Three wallet photos. Membership card, fitness center. Starbucks card. Medical card. Electronic security card, unmarked, blue. One blank check number 988 in victim's name and address. Three receipts: Shell Gas, Roseville CA dated 9/26/09 for 14.5 gallons; Starbucks #NV731 time-stamped 10:05 a.m. 9/27/09 for $9.55; Shell Gas, Reno NV dated 9/27/09 for 7.6 gallons, time-stamped 11:58 a.m.

• One (1) backpack, dark green. Contents: T-shirt, jeans, socks, underwear, toothbrush, toothpaste, floss, prescription Motrin filled 7/17/09 at Raley's Pharmacy, Roseville, Dr. Booth; disposable razor.

• One (1) Key ring with five (5) keys. One key for Honda Civic, registered to vic; four keys unknown.

• One (1) day planner, rubber-banded.

"Thank you for your diligence," Nora said as she signed the receipt. They each kept a copy.

Duke barely heard her. He was reading the list carefully and was itching to open the planner, head over to the Starbucks to see if anyone remembered Russ, and crack open his laptop. Something was here, he had to find it.

"Don't break the chain of evidence," Dressler admonished.

"I'll be careful," Nora said, taking the box. They walked back to Sara Ralston. Nora

239

said, "Can you ride him and see what you get from the car? Prints, fibers, anything. If you think we need to take anything to Sacramento, let me know and I'll get my ASAC on it. We have an escalating serial killer on our hands, and time is critical."

"I love getting to play the big, bad fed," Sara said. "And getting out of the damn smoky casinos for the next few days? I owe you one."

"You can pay it back now —" Nora opened the box, pulled out the individually bagged receipts. "Where's this Starbucks and this Shell station?"

"Easy. The Shell station is five or six blocks down East Forty-third, right at the exit." She pointed to the intersection. "The Starbucks — that's the one closest to the state university. Hop on the freeway, head east, take the next exit, and I think this street runs right into the main drag. Before you hit the entrance, it's a one-way street on your right."

CHAPTER THIRTEEN

Nora and Duke swung by the gas station first; the owner, likely from India, based on his thick accent and appearance, had been working on Sunday, but either didn't understand Nora's questions or didn't remember the man in the blue Ford Explorer who came in Sunday morning. He did, however, understand her badge. When she pointed to the security cameras, he brought them around to his side of the counter to show them four black-and-white televisions, which showed static angles of the two gas pumps, the bathroom entrance, and a wide shot of the inside of the small convenience store.

Duke inspected the equipment and shook his head. "It's live feed. Not recorded."

"Meaning there are no tapes?" Nora asked.

"Exactly."

"What's the point of having security if you

don't have recordings?"

"It's supposed to be a deterrent, and to give the clerk an advance sign if there's going to be trouble."

"Seems shortsighted to me," Nora mumbled.

They left the gas station and drove to the Starbucks where Russ had been only hours before his death. This neighborhood fit the image of a college town with several cheap restaurants, a few clothing stores, bookstores, and a large corner Starbucks with tables inside and out. It was noon and the sun beat down on the desert city. They stepped into the cool, air-conditioned Starbucks. It was busy, half full with mostly college students, some chatting, some working on laptops, some doing homework alone or in groups. The scent of coffee had Nora's stomach growling.

"What do you want?" Duke asked.

"I'm fine," she said.

"Your stomach says you're lying. My treat."

"She should shut up." She was mildly embarrassed that her hunger was audible. "Iced mocha, with whipped cream."

"Nora has a sweet tooth."

"Nora needs the sugar," she replied with a half smile. When they reached the cashier,

Duke ordered and Nora asked to speak to the manager.

Shortly after their drinks were served, a cute blonde, not more than twenty-five years old, approached. "Can I help you?" Her long hair was pulled back and she wore no makeup. The green apron was tied three times around her impossibly skinny waist. Her nameplate read *Sandy, Assistant Manager.*

Nora introduced herself and Duke and asked if they could speak with her in private.

"We don't really have the space in back," Sandy said. She motioned to a vacant table in the corner.

It would have to do. They sat and Nora asked quietly, "We're interested in this man." She pushed over a photograph of Russell Larkin that Duke had brought. It was his DMV photo, enlarged, and printed on quality photo stock.

She looked. "I don't know. Should I know him? I see a lot of people, and he might look familiar, but he has a familiar face, you know?"

Larkin was average, clean-cut and pleasant-looking without being a standout. "He's just over six feet tall and thin. He was here Sunday morning."

"I don't work weekends — let me grab

the schedule and see who was on then."

The girl jumped up and Nora sipped her iced mocha. Duke had gotten her the largest size. It hit her empty stomach and felt like heaven. She really needed to eat regularly. She told herself that all the time, but still rarely managed to eat two meals a day.

"Thank you."

"Watching your face is thanks enough," he said.

She didn't quite know how to take the comment. Duke just grinned at her.

Sandy returned with a petite Asian girl named Summer. "Summer worked Sunday from opening until two," Sandy said.

The girl looked at the picture with interest. "I remember him. He used his Starbucks card. It was one I hadn't seen for a long time, two people in a car with a dog."

Nora showed the card through the clear plastic evidence bag. "Like this?"

She frowned. "Yes. Is something wrong?"

Sandy was also concerned. "Do I need to call the regional manager?"

"No, this isn't related to your business, but the owner of this card was murdered the day he came in here, and we're retracing his steps."

Summer put her hand to her mouth. "Oh no, that's horrible."

"The receipt shows that he ordered two drinks and pastries. Do you recall who he was with?"

"He came in alone, ordered the drinks, and went outside to the patio. We had our Sunday morning special, buy one, get one half off. He went out on the patio and I was at the register, so I couldn't see him from my position, but about twenty minutes later we had a lull and I went out to wipe down tables. He was sitting with a girl."

"A girl? What did she look like?"

She shrugged. "Brown hair, round face, very pretty."

"Would you recognize her if you saw her?"

"Maybe, I don't know. I think she's been in here a couple times, but not recently, and maybe I'm wrong? I'm good with faces, but I tend to remember those who come in regularly."

"Anything that stood out about her? Height, weight, a mole or anything else?"

"Not really. She was on the skinny side, but kind of turn-your-head gorgeous. She had big round eyes, I remember now. I think one of the guys was talking about her eyes. I wish I could help, but really, it's just a vague memory."

"You've done great," Nora said. "How long were they here?"

"They were still there when I came back inside, and then gone next time I went out to straighten up, but that was at least thirty minutes later."

Nora looked at the receipt. Russ Larkin bought the coffee just after ten in the morning. Approximately 10:30 a.m., Summer went out and saw him talking to an attractive brunette. By 11 a.m., they were gone.

"How did they act together?" Nora asked. "Friendly? Romantic? Upset?"

"I guess friendly. They weren't laughing or fighting or anything, just having a conversation. Low-key."

"Thank you for your time." Nora handed her a card. "If you see the girl, or remember anything else, please call me as soon as you can."

"I will."

As Nora and Duke left, she said, "I'm going to have Sara Ralston follow up with the male staff, see if anyone has something more to add to Summer's statement."

In the car, Duke climbed in the passenger seat and held up two sandwiches. "Turkey or cheese and avocado?"

"You don't look like a cheese and avocado guy," Nora said, taking that sandwich. They'd parked under a shade tree and Nora rolled down the windows. A warm breeze tamed the sun.

"I wasn't sure if you were a vegetarian or not."

"No, but I love cheese and avocado." She unwrapped her sandwich. "That was thoughtful of you."

"You haven't eaten all day. It has to be messing with your thought process. When I'm hungry, I can't concentrate."

"Does the pretty brunette ring any bells?" she asked Duke.

"No. I don't know Russ that well."

"He had an overnight bag."

"Possibly — but he could have that with him all the time. I have an emergency kit in my car."

"You do?"

"Don't you?"

"Yes, but I'm a first responder. A requirement of my position." She paused. "And sort of habit. We often moved when I was growing up, usually on the spur of the moment. Sometimes because my mother just felt like it, other times because we had to. I was used to traveling light and keeping what was important to me in my pack at all times." *And my bag with me at all times, too.*

"That's hard."

"I was a verifiable bag lady." She laughed humorlessly. "I grew up more or less homeless, not because my mom couldn't work, but because she refused to. She did odd jobs here and there, but there were times when we lived in a place, usually with a group of people. She also had a scam going from county to county claiming to be a victim of domestic violence, so we could get a place for a couple weeks, she'd get a temporary job, and when she had enough money to split, we were off again on the next 'adventure' as she called it. Mostly she stole what she wanted and never felt a moment of guilt. I hated it."

She put down the second half of her sandwich, her face flushed. "I can't believe I told you all that."

"I'm glad you did."

Nora was angry with herself. She had sounded bitter, but she wasn't. She'd come to terms with her past, and maybe that's why she could speak of it to a virtual stranger. No, she was deceiving herself. While she'd accepted her past, it wasn't something she discussed with anyone . . . just Duke. She felt comfortable with him, and she wanted him to know, to understand who she was. But here? Now? It wasn't the place or the time.

"That was highly inappropriate." She started the car. "I'll attribute it to hunger."

Duke took her hand and squeezed until she looked at him.

"Thank you for telling me."

She smiled.

Yeah, she was glad she'd told him.

Duke watched Nora as they headed back toward Sacramento. Even as she expertly maneuvered the vehicle, he saw that she was lost in thought. Thinking about the past? About her cases? About this case? Maybe everything.

Up until their parents were killed, the Rogans had led a charmed life. They hadn't been wealthy their entire life, but right before the twins were born, Duke's parents, Paul and Sheila, ended up with a patent for law enforcement and military gear that went big.

Still, even before that change of fate, the Rogans always had a home. Duke was born and raised in the same house he still lived in. When they had the money, they remodeled the hundred-year-old farm-style house in Rancho Cordova. The area was known for tract homes and lower-income families, but the Rogans had a five-acre parcel that butted against the American River. He hadn't wanted to move after the plane crash to avoid uprooting Sean when he desperately needed stability. And now? It was comfortable. It wouldn't occur to him to move anywhere else.

The house had long been a gathering spot. J.T. and Jax Caruso had practically lived there, since their parents were divorced and neither cared much about what their kids did. The kids from the neighborhood had always come by after school; Sheila had always said it was better to come to her house than to get in trouble on the streets. She had fed the neighborhood, monitored potential problems, and always listened.

That was what Duke missed the most about his mom. She'd always had time for him and his brothers and sister. Even when she was working, even when she had outside commitments, she listened. She rarely offered advice unless directly asked, but she'd always ask one or two questions that guided you to the right answer. His dad was more cut-and-dried, right-and-wrong, but he, too, believed that family was everything, and as long as the Rogans were together, they could handle anything.

Their deaths left such a gaping void that the family split apart. Duke never understood how it had happened. Duke had been back from his months fighting Kane's wars in Central America for less than a year when their parents died. Kane returned and tried to be the patriarch, but it was not in his blood. He handled grief differently from most people, Duke supposed. So the responsibilities fell to Duke, and too soon the twins left the country to run their own security business and Kane turned over the business he started with J.T. Caruso to Duke, and returned to Central America. And Duke and Sean kept the house up, though it was far too big for the two of them.

But through it all, if Duke needed anything, Kane was there. Home base was always . . . home. And having the foundation that his parents gave him was irreplaceable.

He stared at Nora. She was now aware he was looking at her; he could tell by the way she drove, keeping her eyes on the road, her focus on the other drivers. Everywhere but on him. He made her nervous, and he didn't know why. He was the one in awe of what she'd accomplished in her life. To have grown up in that situation and to turn out not only smart and sharp, but to be a cop. A fed. It couldn't have been easy, but at the same time she was well-suited for the job. She believed in what she was doing, understood the people she fought against, and had incredible compassion for all concerned. A rare, rare trait, and perhaps that, more than her own conflicts about her childhood, was what made her so tense. To be able to see all sides of an issue, to understand the predators as well as the victims, was not easy. Duke had known a lot of cops, local and federal, who burned out far too fast because they couldn't tame their emotions. Nora's grim steadfastness was an act, and Duke saw right through it. She had a shield that kept her sane, but that's all it was — a shield to protect her.

He wanted to get under that shield and see Nora English for the woman she was. The Nora English that kissed him last night, the Nora English who was inside.

And he would. Duke got everything he set his mind on.

When the car started down the mountain on the California side of the Sierra Nevadas, Duke's phone vibrated. He had a voice mail.

He listened, his face falling.

"That was Sean," he said. "He left a message."

"Your brother?"

Confession time. "I've had him snooping around Rose College the last couple days."

She didn't say anything, but he could tell she wasn't happy about being kept in the dark.

"Three students were found this morning, dead, apparent suicides. And they left a note claiming they killed Jonah Payne."

CHAPTER FOURTEEN

Rose College was in mourning.

Nora walked through the campus amid a sea of shocked faces. The media had been held at bay by the sheriff's department, and Sheriff Sanger was speaking to the dean of students in the lobby of the dormitory where three students had apparently killed themselves.

Nora herself was stunned. For the forty minutes it took from when Duke got his brother's call until they arrived she tried to reconcile political activism with serial murder. It didn't make sense.

"Sheriff," she said as she approached.

"Agent English," Sanger said formally. "That was fast."

She raised her eyebrow. "Excuse me?"

"I just talked to your office ten minutes ago."

"Funny. I heard about the suicides forty-five minutes ago, and even then the informa-

254

tion was old. I should have been contacted as soon as the suicide note was found."

Sanger's jaw tightened. He introduced the dean. "Greg Holbrook, Special Agent Nora English. And Duke Rogan."

"We're all in shock," Holbrook said. "All three of them exemplary students. All seniors with promising futures. Suicide —"

"I need to see the letter," Nora said.

"Excuse us, Dean Holbrook," Sanger said, moving away. Nora and Duke followed.

Once they were out of earshot, Nora said, "Why did you wait so long to contact me?"

"First, the letter isn't a full-out confession, and it took responding officers time to put it together. By the time they did and I came on scene, I called your office."

Nora released her pent-up anger. "I'm sorry. I didn't mean to jump down your throat, Lance, but we just came from the scene of another homicide; Russell Larkin, the head of Butcher-Payne's I.T. department, had his throat slit."

"I didn't hear about that," Sanger said.

"It happened in Reno, and he's been dead a couple days. Probably since late Sunday morning."

"Sorry to hear it," Sanger said to Duke.

Duke acknowledged his condolences and asked, "What happened here?"

255

"Three seniors dead. The dorm room is a mess — they all vomited violently. The medics came in and tried to resuscitate the female, who still had a pulse, but she was declared DOA at the hospital. She never regained consciousness. We found the letter on the desk. The M.E. took the bodies about twenty minutes ago, and my deputies are upstairs collecting evidence." In Placer County, the sheriff's deputies doubled as crime-scene investigators, which was common in many of California's smaller counties.

"Pills?" she asked.

"Seems so, but until the autopsy we don't know what they took."

"How were they discovered?"

"The girl across the hall smelled something foul and knocked on the door early this morning. She didn't get an answer, went to class, and then when she came back she tried again, and found the door unlocked. It was a pretty ugly scene. The poor girl is a wreck."

"And the three just stayed in the room vomiting and didn't try to get help? Did the female have a roommate?"

"No, she didn't. And apparently, they wanted to die," Sanger said.

Or maybe the ingested drugs had a paralyzing effect, Nora thought. Still, it didn't seem right to Nora. She'd seen pill-related suicides. They weren't pretty, but she wouldn't call them violent. Generally if vomiting began, the individual would purge enough from their system to survive or regret their decision and seek help. "Such a violent reaction seems unnecessary," Nora said.

"Excuse me?"

"If they planned it, they would know how many pills to take to do the job, and what type of pills would minimize pain and suffering. Most suicides try for the most painless, easiest out they can find. They also talk about it to someone — even if that person doesn't know the suicidal person is talking about killing themselves. They show signs of despair and depression —"

"But they faced prosecution for arson and murder," Sanger pointed out.

"Did they? I don't have a suspect right now, do you?"

Sanger hesitated. "I see what you mean."

"Do you have an ID on the three?"

Sanger checked his notes. "Anya Ballard, twenty-two, originally from Portland, Oregon. She's been here for four years. Chris Pierson, twenty-three, from Richmond, California, also here for four years. Scott

Edwards, twenty-two, from Los Angeles, California. He transferred two years ago from UCLA. He was a computer engineering major until he came here, then switched to environmental studies, like the other two."

Sanger looked at her. "I pulled their schedules. I wasn't surprised that all three of them are in Leif Cole's Social Justice class."

Nora raised her eyebrows. "Did the letter incriminate him or anyone else?"

"No. It's bagged and in the van, but I'll have someone fetch it." He spoke into his walkie-talkie.

Duke asked, "Do we know about what time this happened?"

"Just sometime last night. They weren't at a meeting people expected them at, but no one thought twice about it. My deputies are interviewing everyone in the dorm, their political groups, and their classes. Holbrook has given us the student union for the duration of the interviews and investigation. As soon as we clear the dorm room, we'll release the third floor."

"Duke!"

Nora turned and saw a kid who could have been Duke's younger twin on the opposite side of the crime-scene tape.

"It's my brother," Duke said.

Nora said to Sanger, "Can you let him through?"

Sanger frowned, but motioned for the deputy at the door to let the younger Rogan in.

Nora glanced at Duke. "I'm still not happy about this," she said quietly.

"Noted," Duke said. He introduced his brother. "Sean, this is Special Agent Nora English and Sheriff Lance Sanger with Placer County."

Sanger asked, "Are you a student here?"

Sean hesitated, and Duke explained. "I got him in so he could keep an eye on Cole and his activist group. Nora didn't know, it was my call."

Sanger looked impressed. "Well Nora, I guess you don't mind bending the rules."

He didn't believe she hadn't known, and Nora didn't correct him. What would be the point? Instead, she asked Sean, "Were you at the meeting last night?"

He nodded. "They really didn't have a meeting. Mostly, they ranted about the ducks being killed at Lake of the Pines. It broke up early, a little after eight. I went to Anya's room to see if she was okay."

Duke said, "So you knew her?"

"I met her Monday morning in class. We

had lunch together."

"What was her behavior like then?" Nora asked.

"Cheerful, I guess. Normal. She invited me to the meeting and I said she would see me there. She was distracted near the end of lunch, though, and so I followed her when she left. She met Professor Cole in the organic garden. I couldn't hear what they were saying, but it seemed obvious that he told her something that upset her. And I had the impression they were involved."

"Involved?" Nora asked. "Romantically? Did they kiss?"

"Sort of."

"Sort of?"

"It wasn't like a passionate kiss, but it was more how they touched and stuff. They stood really close, not like us here, but like this." He stepped close to Nora and took her hands. They were about a foot apart. "Yeah, like that. And they held hands."

He stepped back, embarrassed.

"Why did you go up to her room?" Nora asked.

"Because she didn't show up at the meeting and she'd invited me."

"Did you talk to her in her room?"

"Just briefly at the door. She said she was studying and time got away from them. But

Chris, who I saw through the door, had been at the meeting. He left early, before it started."

"Did you see anyone else?"

"No, but I heard someone. A girl."

Nora straightened. "A girl?"

Sean paused. "I can't swear by it. I only saw Anya and Chris, and part of another guy — he had big feet in white sneakers. But I heard another person. Maybe it was a guy."

Nora went with Sean's first impression, which was probably accurate. But it wouldn't hold up in court because he was already backtracking — if in fact there had been another female in the room who knew what the three were doing and didn't do anything to stop them, she could be in serious trouble. Suicide was still a crime in California.

"What else did Anya say?" Nora prompted Sean.

"I told her I'd see her Wednesday in class and she said maybe we could have lunch again."

"She was making plans?"

"Well, it wasn't set in stone," Sean said. "More like if we saw each other at the cafeteria we'd eat together."

People who were contemplating imminent

suicide did not generally make future plans, even lunch in two days.

Sean added, "When I was leaving the meeting, I asked Professor Cole about Anya. He said she wasn't feeling well."

"So he already knew she wasn't coming to the meeting? Why would he say she wasn't feeling well if she was studying?"

It was a rhetorical question, but Sean answered anyway. "Professor Cole seemed very protective of her. But I already knew they had something going on."

"Thank you, Sean. Oh, one thing, you heard a third person, thought it was female. Was there another reason you felt the third person was female?"

He shrugged. "The door was closed — almost. Closing, I should say. But it wasn't Chris."

It wasn't definitive. There were three dead, and three known people in the room, and perhaps Scott's voice had been effeminate. But three college students who were environmental activists slitting the throat of an I.T. director to steal security plans? Or torturing Dr. Payne and letting him bleed to death? None of it made any sense to her. But she had to go with the evidence, and the evidence right now had the three confessing to arson and murder.

Three deputies came down the stairs carrying an evidence box. They wore booties, gloves, and face masks.

"Sheriff," one of them said after removing his mask, "we found four bottles of one-fifty-one proof vodka and green spray paint. We also found Ballard's computer. And a journal. It doesn't appear to claim credit for the arsons, but it documents the so-called crimes of the businesses that were attacked, plus others that weren't attacked. We're still bagging up evidence, it'll take the rest of the day."

Nora said, "Did you dust for prints?"

The deputy glanced at her, but the sheriff answered. "I know how to process a suicide. It's always treated as a crime scene."

"Can you send me a copy of the pictures?"

"I'll get you copies of everything. You may get a chunk of the evidence as well, because I'm sure the U.S. attorney is going to want undeniable proof that the arsonists are dead."

A deputy walked into the lobby with an evidence bag, and Sanger motioned for the two other deputies to take the other boxes to the crime-scene van. Sanger handed the letter, wrapped in plastic, to Nora.

The short letter was written on college-ruled notebook paper, one side only, in blue ballpoint pen. The paper had never been folded, though half was crinkled. There was some biological matter dried on the letter. It read:

To our parents and friends:
  We're so sorry for the pain we've caused you and we're sorry that we have to do this. We never wanted to kill anyone. Things just got out of hand and then we couldn't stop.
  We only hope that maybe a tiny good can come from our actions. People need to wake up and look at how we're destroying our planet. Stop screwing with nature. Stop polluting the water and the plants and the air. Stop eating genetically altered food. Stop before it's too late.
  We all agreed that this is the best way.
                    Anya, Chris & Scott

Nora read the letter three times and didn't quite know what to make of it. They didn't come right out and say they were responsible for the four arsons and murdering Jonah Payne or Russ Larkin. It was short — common with suicide notes — but suicide notes themselves were rare. Only one in four suicides left a note. Most were impulsive acts.

Many suicides did occur to avoid imprisonment or other punishment, but these kids weren't yet on Nora's radar. She'd been to the college several times to talk to Professor Cole, but she hadn't brought any students in for questioning because no evidence had pointed to any individual student. Why would they kill themselves before there was an active investigation into their actions? Out of guilt? Nora would have to pull out her old psychology books, but suicide for guilt alone was somewhere at the bottom of the list.

"What?" Duke asked. "You're frowning."

"I'm thinking," she said.

"What's the problem?" Sanger said. "It's pretty cut-and-dried."

"They don't admit to the arsons or murder."

"They say right there that they didn't want to kill anyone but it got out of hand."

"They could be referring to the suicides themselves. That they planned it and didn't know how not to go through with it. We don't know, but —"

"The evidence is coming out of the room right now," Duke said. "The vodka and the paint —"

She nodded. "I know. It seems convenient."

"You can't possibly think that they were framed," Sanger said. "You're really stretching this."

Nora wasn't going to get into an argument with Sanger in front of his deputies with college students coming and going. They'd sealed off the third floor of the dorm, but the other floors were accessible to residents; soon, they'd release the third floor as well.

Something bothered Nora about the letter, but she couldn't put her finger on it. Had they left evidence of their crimes, but the police just hadn't yet found it? Or had one of them felt guilty? Perhaps it was a murder-suicide. The letter was written in feminine script, difficult but not impossible for a man to forge. Pills and other poisons were commonly chosen by female suicide victims, while men preferred firearms. Ironically, perhaps, the choice of weapons for female killers was poison as well. Could Anya have killed her partners, then herself?

"Did you find any empty pill bottles, a knife? We have two victims, Jonah Payne and Russell Larkin. Neither fit with the M.O. of this group."

"What M.O.?" Sanger said. "We know the same people were involved with the four arson fires — your sister proved it, right? Same accelerant, same bomb, same type of target. We've matched the spray paint. They escalated — they often do. Serial arsonists want bigger, more violent fires."

"But serial arsonists set fires to watch the fire and achieve sexual satisfaction. Anarchists set fires to make a political statement and damage the offending businesses economically."

"Why are you so antagonistic?" Sanger asked. "You should be happy that the case is solved."

"Solved? It's far from solved."

"What the hell do you mean? We have three dead college students who have claimed responsibility, or at least have provided good solid evidence of responsibility. It'll take a few days to match up, but I'll bet it matches the evidence we found at the crime scenes. They fit the profile that you yourself gave me: early-to-mid-twenties, college-educated, Caucasian, known environmental activists."

What he said was true, but, "That was before someone was killed. If Dr. Payne had died in an accident, then yes, I could buy this. But he was tortured and murdered, his body moved from his vacation house to his business. His colleague Larkin had his throat slit while he sat in his car behind a deserted building. These are not the acts of traditional anarchists."

"Maybe they're just plumb crazy."

Nora remembered her conversations with Megan Kincaid and then Hans Vigo earlier this morning. That the manner in which Jonah Payne was killed was the work of a psychopath. "Maybe you're right," she said quietly.

But she wasn't done, not by a long shot. She needed to be one hundred percent sure that the three suicides were solely responsible for the murders and the arsons. She wasn't closing the case anytime soon.

"Sheriff, I'm going to talk to Professor Cole. He knew all three students, he may have some insight or information. Would you like to join me?"

"I was getting ready to talk to him as well. I'll give you a ride."

She frowned. "A ride? His office is just on the other side of campus."

"As he's been so reluctant to comply with this investigation, I had him taken into custody. He's at the county jail."

Duke and Sean followed Nora back outside to the car. "You did good, Sean," Duke said.

Sean seemed surprised by the praise, and Nora wondered if Duke was that rare with compliments.

"Thanks," the young man answered.

Nora grabbed her briefcase from the backseat of Duke's car. "I just emailed Pete and asked him to stick with the evidence, I want everything to come through my office, but I didn't want to say that to Sheriff Sanger. I'm hoping Pete can convince him that we have more resources to quickly process it." She pulled out a notepad and copied the names and stats of the three suicide victims, then handed it to Duke. "Would you mind running backgrounds on these three? I sent the information to my office, but it's getting late and I don't think I'll get answers tonight. And" — She glanced from Sean to Duke. — "your backgrounders on Butcher-Payne staff were extensive."

"The Butcher-Payne employees agreed when they applied to provide us with Social Security numbers and other vital statistics. With those, I was able to go deeper."

"What I want is basic, but I'm looking for any further connection between these three and Leif Cole, and anyone at Butcher-Payne. Specifically look at Payne himself and his son, Trevor."

Duke was stunned. "Why Trevor? You don't think he's —"

She shook her head and interrupted, "Of course not, but he's twenty and college age, even though he's in the military. Maybe one of these kids went to high school with him. Maybe they played on the same Little League team. I don't know, but it's just bugging the hell out of me that these kids killed themselves when they didn't have a good reason. We weren't investigating them!"

"But you *were* investigating Cole," Duke pointed out. "Maybe Anya Ballard was trying to protect him."

"I wasn't officially investigating Cole," Nora corrected. "I just suspected that he knew more than he was saying."

"Sounds like splitting hairs to me."

"I pushed him, Duke. I didn't let him off. But I didn't have one teeny shred of evidence to tie him to any of the arsons. And the only thing that's tying him to Butcher-Payne is his academic tit-for-tat exchanges with Dr. Payne."

"People have killed for less," Duke said. "And you have one more connection. His relationship with Anya Ballard."

Nora rubbed her eyes. Duke tapped her chin up. "Hey, don't fall asleep during the interrogation."

"I'm not tired. I'm frustrated. This seems too convenient."

Sean said bluntly, "I don't think Anya killed herself."

Nora turned to the younger Rogan. "Why?"

"Sean," Duke said, "the evidence seems clear. It should be relatively easy to match the materials found in her room with the evidence at the crime scenes."

"I didn't say Anya wasn't an arsonist. I don't know about that." He frowned and glanced back toward the dormitory still rife with police activity. "I just don't think Anya could slit anyone's throat. She didn't seem violent."

"Sometimes," Duke said, "people are not who they appear to be."

"Don't talk to me like I'm a child," Sean said. "I'm giving you my opinion based on spending an hour with her yesterday. Did you meet her?"

Duke was surprised at Sean's retort. "I didn't mean to talk down to you. I was stating a fact." Maybe he stated the obvious too often with Sean. He didn't realize it bothered his brother.

Nora said, "I don't think we can make a determination one way or the other regarding who killed Larkin or whether those three kids killed themselves or —" She cut herself off.

"Or what?"

"Or they were murdered."

She turned to Sean again. "I want your honest opinion, Sean. When you saw Anya last night and heard the third voice, how certain are you that it was a girl?"

He didn't say anything for a moment, he was clearly reviewing the exchange. "Eighty percent," he said finally.

"That's good enough for me," Nora said. She punched numbers on her cell phone. "Ted, it's Nora. I need you to grab the DMV photo and the Rose College student photo of Anya Ballard, the female deceased, and send it to Sara Ralston in the Reno office. Ask her to show the pics to all Starbucks employees at the address that's in my report — it's near the university. She needs to find Summer, who was working this morning, and make sure she sees Anya's photo. I want to know if Anya Ballard was the girl seen with Russ Larkin Sunday morning, or if anyone else there recognizes her. And can you ask Rachel to get a copy of the suicide letter and fax it immediately to Quantico for handwriting analysis and assessment? Specifically, I want to know whether the person who wrote the suicide note also wrote the letters that have been sent to the media. . . . Great, thanks." She hung up. "He's on it."

"Did I miss something?" Sean asked.

Nora said, "We know that Larkin met with a college-aged girl the day he was murdered. If we can rule out Anya Ballard, that gives us more reason to trust your memory about what you may have heard."

She spotted Sheriff Sanger driving up to take her to the county jail. "Sanger's here," she said, glancing at her watch. "Can we meet later at FBI headquarters? Say around seven?"

"I'll be there. I'm going to work with Jason on Russ's laptop, see if we can find anything after your ERT prints it."

"How do you know —" She stopped herself. "You've worked with him before."

"I recommended him for the job," Duke said. "He used to work for Rogan-Caruso part-time while in college."

"I should have known." But she smiled. "Thanks, both of you, for your help."

Help? That was kind of formal. But before Duke could banter with her about their kiss yesterday, she walked off and slid into the front seat of Sheriff Sanger's truck. They drove off.

His help. He might be a consultant on this case, but he was going to be far more than mere *help* to Special Agent Nora English.

"I'm going to stay on campus," Sean said, "keep my ears open and my mouth closed.

I might be able to pick up on something, like who the fourth person was."

"If there is a fourth person," Duke said, "and he or she had any part in the suicide, then that person is dangerous. Especially if she killed them and tried to make it look like suicide."

Sean bristled at the suggestion he couldn't take care of himself. "Duke, when are you ever going to treat me like a grown-up? I'm nearly twenty-five. I have two college degrees, a master's, and an I.Q. that exceeds yours."

"Smart people do dumb things." Duke realized he said the wrong thing — his "stating the obvious" problem with Sean. He was about to apologize when Sean hit the roof of his car.

"I'm going to work for Kane."

"Like hell you are."

"You're not my guardian anymore, Duke. I don't even know if you're my brother."

"I say the wrong thing and you jump down my throat? I'm concerned about your safety. You think maybe you're overreacting here —"

"I'm not overreacting," Sean said. "You treat me as if I'm incapable of making tough decisions. You don't like my friends, you won't let me work for Rogan-Caruso, and when I *can* do something that helps, you balk because it's dangerous. You can't protect me for the rest of my life. Dammit, Duke. You were the only person I had after Mom and Dad died. Kane had his causes, Liam and Eden had each other, and I had no one — but you never walked away. I love you for that. But I can't be coddled, protected, and managed. I don't want to be. I want to contribute to Rogan-Caruso in a meaningful way, not under the watchful eye of my big brother."

Duke had never heard Sean articulate his feelings like this before. Sean usually mumbled his discontentment and walked away. Duke had always chosen to ignore Sean's complaints rather than get to the heart of the matter. It was easier for Duke to pretend that he was still in control than to accept that Sean was a man who could make his own decisions, and was smart enough to make the right ones.

Still, if anything happened to Sean because of a case or job that Duke had assigned him, Duke would be lost.

"I'm proud of you, Sean."

Sean shuffled his feet. "You've never told me that before."

"Of course I have —" Duke stopped. Hadn't he? Sean stared at him, dead serious. "I'm sorry," he continued. "I've always been proud of you."

"Even when I was expelled from Stanford?"

"Furious as anything and I wanted to beat sense into you, but secretly proud that you'd devised and executed such an ingenious plan."

"Even when you were called to bail me out of jail in Massachusetts because I'd hacked into the Boston Police Department's database and erased all my parking tickets?"

"You could have saved me a lot of money if you'd been able to do that five years earlier with Eden and her hundred and sixty-some tickets."

Sean raised his eyebrow, his dimples showing his good humor. "You're not serious."

Duke shook his head, then grinned. "But Sean, every time you've broken the rules — except for maybe the parking tickets — it was to help someone else, to defend the underdog. You weren't doing it for personal gain, and I admire that greatly. It's why I have tremendous respect for Kane. Our brother can be a real jerk, but he's never done anything in his life for personal glory or wealth. Everything he's done he's done for others, and it's hard not to admire his selflessness."

"You're the most selfless person I know," Sean said.

Duke shook his head. "Okay, go. But I swear, Sean, you watch your ass or I'll be kicking it hard."

"Thanks." Sean started walking back toward the dorm, then turned back. "I'm serious, Duke. Maybe I never said it before. But you were my age when you took the responsibility of raising me. You sacrificed a lot for me. That's pretty damn selfless."

"You're my brother," Duke said. He'd never thought about anything he did or didn't do because he had Sean in his life. "It wasn't a sacrifice."

"But I'm not your son. And for a while it was okay for you to act like my father. But now? My father is dead. My brother isn't. I need a brother."

Duke understood. Damn, he loved his brother. "Okay."

He walked two steps and turned around again. "By the way, I like that FBI agent. She's hot."

Duke coughed. "She's too old for you."

"I'm cool with older women."

Duke frowned. Sean couldn't be serious. Not only was Nora more than ten years his senior, but she wasn't available as far as Duke was concerned. Especially to his little brother. Until she told Duke to take a hike, he was going to keep coming back until she gave in to him. Because Duke knew she wanted to. He saw it in her eyes, tasted it on her lips last night.

"Sean, I don't think —"

"Gotcha!" Sean pretended to lick his finger and made a mark in the air. "She's not too old for you, bro. Don't think I couldn't see how you looked at her."

"I do not look at Nora any particular way."

Sean laughed.

"I'm serious," Duke protested.

"I can see you're serious," Sean grinned. "I approve."

"I'm so glad I have your sanction, little brother."

He watched Sean saunter off, this time with a wave.

But if he was going to be perfectly honest with himself, he was glad Sean liked Nora. He just hadn't known his attraction was so obvious. Or maybe Sean was just more observant than Duke gave him credit for.

CHAPTER FIFTEEN

Nora followed Sheriff Sanger into the county jail. Since the FBI didn't have detention facilities, she'd been here many times over the years to interview suspects. After arraignment, the accused generally stayed in county jail until trial; then, if convicted, they were transported to a federal penitentiary.

Nora didn't like how Sanger had made a snap judgment on the suicides. The three could certainly have killed themselves out of guilt, but she needed more. And she needed more than Sanger's theory that Cole was the instigator. Evidence and motive for a start.

None of this fit in with her experience. And if she couldn't rely on her experience, what good was she on the squad?

Did she want to be right so badly that she was jeopardizing the case? She didn't think so, but at the same time she'd had the very strong and very instant reaction that these suicides didn't fit the mold. And while human behavior certainly couldn't always be predicted, when someone went way off the reservation, Nora couldn't help but question it.

"Please bring Cole to interview room two," Sanger ordered the desk sergeant.

"He's with his attorney in interview four."

"That was fast," Sanger said.

"It's better this way," Nora said.

"How the hell is it better?" growled Sanger.

She motioned for the sheriff to follow her, and the desk sergeant buzzed them into room two.

Nora faced Sanger and leaned against the table. It was better not to be too aggressive with him, but she couldn't deny she was in a fighting mood. "Cole has never spoken to us without his attorney present. You think he's going to suddenly open up after you arrest him?"

"I've known Leif Cole for years. I can get him to talk."

"Great. Talk about conflict of interest."

"What's your point?"

"You and Cole have a history."

"That has nothing to do with this."

"Maybe not," she said, not believing him,

"but we still need information and evidence. If you honestly believe that Cole is responsible, then we need to find that evidence, because he's sure as hell not going to confess when we have nothing."

"But he doesn't know what we do or don't have."

"If you play him wrong, he'll never talk. He would love to bring the ACLU down on your ass, Lance. And neither you nor I want to spend our limited resources battling that giant."

"You know what I think?" Lance said. "I think that they killed themselves to protect Leif Cole and that maybe he was the one who told them to kill Payne. Payne was a thorn in his side for years."

If Leif Cole was guilty, Nora had been working off the wrong profile from the beginning. That was a poor excuse. Any decent profiler knew that a psychological assessment of a suspect when you didn't have a suspect was nothing more than a guideline; it wasn't rigid. She'd adapted when she learned Payne had been tortured — adding in the psychopathic factor. Was Cole a psychopath? If so, she'd missed it during their previous interviews. If not, which of the three students had killed Payne? Had they been in it together? Who had been the instigator? Groups behaved differently from individuals, and anarchist cells had a small-group mentality, each member goading the others into acts of civil disobedience and felonies.

"Maybe you're right."

Sanger was surprised. "I didn't think you would cave that easily. You were certain he wasn't responsible."

"I said *maybe* and what I've always *said* is that Leif Cole wasn't involved in the arsons, but that he *suspected* who was. Sean Rogan said Professor Cole was involved with the student Anya Ballard."

"We'll have a hard time getting that admitted into court. His defense will argue that it's hearsay."

"Sean Rogan will make a good witness on that point," Nora said. "Let me be the lead on this, okay?"

Lance didn't want to cede control — Nora saw it in his face and posture — but he reluctantly relented. "All right. I wouldn't mind seeing you in action, anyway."

Before she could respond to that surprising statement, Leif Cole walked in with his attorney. The lawyer introduced himself as Gavin Shepherd.

Shepherd got right to the point. "My client may or may not answer your questions, depending on whether he believes it's relevant to determining what happened to the three students in question. You should also know that I am petitioning the court for immediate release for false arrest."

Sanger said, "False arrest? He refused to answer questions at the college, and I offered to interview him at the station. He got in my face, so I arrested him for attempting to intimidate a police officer."

That was interesting, Nora thought. Sanger hadn't told her the charges. And Nora thought Shepherd had a point, especially if Sanger told the judge that Cole "got in his face." Intimidation wasn't the same as assault, and Sanger had forty pounds and two inches on the professor.

Leif Cole slammed his palm on the table. "I asked you one simple question and you refused to answer."

"It doesn't work that way," Sanger said. "I ask the questions, you answer — or refuse to answer."

Nora cleared her throat while Gavin admonished his client. "Professor, what was your question?"

"Is Anya okay? She was taken away in an ambulance. I just want to know if she's going to be okay."

Sanger shifted uncomfortably in his seat.

Nora realized the importance Sean Rogan's observations yesterday had on why that information was important to Cole.

She said, "I'm sorry, Professor. She died en route to the hospital."

Cole's body shook, his hands fisted, and his jaw moved, trying to prevent a sob from escaping. He lost that battle and the gut-wrenching cry that was pulled from his heart brought goose bumps to Nora's skin.

She waited a long moment to give Cole time for initial grief. Her opinion about the propriety of a professor's relationship with a student was put on the back burner; there was no doubt in her mind that Leif Cole cared deeply about Anya. This was no act.

"Why?" Cole asked, his voice rough. "Why would she kill herself?"

"Professor," Nora said gently. "I'd like to ask you some questions about Anya and the others."

He didn't respond.

She plunged in. "I have a witness who said that you and Anya had an intimate relationship. Is that true?"

"That has nothing to do with this," Shepherd said. "It is irrelevant whether my client had a sexual relationship or not with Ms. Ballard."

"I'm trying to establish the relationship

284

between Professor Cole and a student who died under suspicious circumstances. Let me ask it this way: Did you know Anya, Chris, and Scott outside of the classroom?"

"Yes," Cole said.

"Did you ever think for a minute that one of them was contemplating suicide?"

"Never. Especially not Anya."

"Why do you say that?"

"I did have a relationship with her. I loved her. She was going to move in after graduation. I know what you're thinking, I'm forty-two and she's twenty-two, but it worked."

Sanger shifted in his seat and Nora shot him a look. He'd better not blow this.

"When was the last time you spoke with Anya?" Nora asked.

"Monday afternoon. In the organic garden. I tried calling her later that night, about ten or ten-thirty, after I got home from the meeting, and she didn't answer. I knew — I didn't think anything of it."

"How was her disposition in the garden?" Nora asked.

"She was upset about something."

"Do you know what?"

He didn't answer.

Shepherd said, "My client doesn't have to answer that."

"If Professor Cole has information on why

Anya Ballard killed herself, then yes, I think he should answer it."

"Should is not a compelling reason," Shepherd said.

"Did you know that Anya and the two boys were arsonists?"

"We're not going to answer that," the lawyer jumped in.

"Did you know that there was a fatality in the Butcher-Payne fire? That Dr. Jonah Payne died?"

Cole said, "A reporter called me Monday morning and told me about that."

"Why would a reporter call you?" asked Nora.

"Because of you," Cole snapped. "Your investigation keeps sniffing around me, and I've told you time and time again that I had nothing to do with the arsons, and I certainly had nothing to do with the Butcher-Payne arson or the death of Dr. Payne."

"When did you find out he was murdered?"

"We're not going to answer —" Shepherd began, but Cole cut him off.

"You would be hard-pressed to get first-degree murder from an accidental death," Cole said.

"In acts of domestic terrorism, yes I damn well can get first-degree murder," Nora stated evenly. "But Jonah Payne's death wasn't an accident."

"What the hell are you talking about? The reporter said that Dr. Payne died in his office. I assumed he'd been working or fallen asleep there when the fire started."

Professor Cole's frustration seemed genuine. Nora assessed Professor Cole's posture and eyes and she believed *he* believed Payne's death had been an accident. It seemed that the first Cole had heard of Payne's death was indeed when the reporter phoned. Things began to click into place for Nora.

"Dr. Payne's horrible death was no accident. It was cold-blooded, premeditated murder. Payne was tortured prior to bleeding slowly to death."

"You're lying through your teeth, and you know it," Cole objected. "I'm not playing these games with you, Agent English." He began to stand, but Nora waved him down as she pulled files from her briefcase. Without comment, she laid several of the crime-scene and autopsy photos in front of him. Again, the shock on his face wasn't faked. Leif Cole looked ill.

"You're a smart man," she said when she'd finished laying out the gruesome pictures. She tapped the photo of Dr. Payne in his office, lying on his back. "He wasn't killed here in his office. He was killed —" She turned her cell phone around and displayed a photo that the evidence response team had emailed her of the blood evidence in Payne's Lake Tahoe bedroom. "— here."

The digital image of dark red on the white sheets was stark. It had the desired effect on Cole.

"The M.E.'s preliminary report," she said, gesturing toward several autopsy photos, "indicates that Dr. Payne bled to death" — she held up her phone again — "and was transported in a covered pickup truck eighty miles to his office. The research lab was doused with accelerant and set on fire. The sprinkler system was disabled in order to cause maximum damage, very likely to destroy evidence on the body. Or to make Dr. Payne's death appear to be something that it wasn't."

Though that didn't explain why the killers didn't pour fuel onto his body, it did explain why they had disabled the sprinklers. Had Dr. Payne's body been burned for a longer period of time, the authorities wouldn't have discovered that he'd bled to death. Perhaps the arsonists had run out of 151 vodka. Or maybe they were running short on time. Or maybe the killer didn't want the others to know about the cut-up corpse.

Ever since the autopsy, Nora had felt that Payne's murder was personal, but still in some way related to his professional position. But maybe it had nothing to do with the fact that he was a biotech scientist. Maybe he'd been killed for other reasons and the arson had been merely a convenient distraction.

It explained the time gap between fires. Anarchists generally escalated, the time between attacks coming closer as the players relished the idea of getting away with it. But in this case, the hits had grown farther apart.

According to Sean Rogan, who was truly the only impartial observer, Anya Ballard was cheerful and generally happy when they had lunch together. Yet Sean saw that she had been upset in the garden . . .

Nora looked Cole straight in the eye. "Professor, when you were in the garden with Anya, did you tell her about Jonah Payne's death?"

Cole considered his response before answering. "Yes. I told her that a reporter called with the news."

"And what was her reaction?"

No comment.

Nora was getting irritated with his selective answers.

"Professor, let me explain something. Accelerant that is a likely match to the arsons was found in Anya Ballard's dorm room, as well as the exact same spray paint used on the exterior of the target business. We have a thumbprint from the Nexum arson that I'd bet my pension belongs to one of the three suicides. And I have a suicide note that takes credit for the fires and expresses remorse for Dr. Payne's death." She was exaggerating the last point, but there was no law saying she couldn't lie to suspects while in questioning.

Cole's face remained impassive, his eyes never leaving her face.

Nora continued, "This is what *I* think: Anya, Chris, and Scott took what you preached and put it to action —"

As if on cue, the attorney objected, "Professor Cole has *never* advocated arson or murder."

Nora frowned and glared. "I'm not out to get your client, and I never was. I don't think he's a killer. I don't think that he burned down Butcher-Payne. What I *think* is that he knows damn well who did and out of a misguided sense of loyalty or guilt, he has kept quiet. Why? Because, up until two days ago, no one had been killed.

290

Things, not people, were destroyed." She turned to Cole. "I've read everything you've written, Professor," she said, staring Leif in the eye. He was clearly surprised by her statement, and she continued. "And in your writings, you have an incredibly strong theme of preserving human life. You wouldn't condone murder, and you wouldn't be able to live with yourself if you didn't do something to stop it."

Nora continued. "Maybe at first you didn't know about Anya and the boys. But you've admitted to a relationship with Anya, and you probably figured it out. If I had to guess . . ." She mentally ran through the three previous arsons. ". . . I'd say it was after the security guard was injured at Sac State. Anya would have been distraught at hurting a human being. She probably confessed everything, or hinted enough so you knew — and you told her to say no more. So she kept quiet about her other activities."

Nora raised an eyebrow. "I have doubts as to whether those three kids killed themselves. Maybe it was a murder-suicide." Nora wasn't about to let on that the suicide note had been written by a woman.

She watched the professor's mind working, as he tried to figure out how to talk to her without incriminating himself.

"I would say —"

Shepherd cleared his throat. "Leif, I need to advise you to —"

Cole shook his head and continued. "There are many truths in your story."

She'd nailed it. He didn't incriminate himself, but gave her what she needed — information.

"If Anya learned that she had accidentally killed someone," Cole said cautiously, "she would have been extremely upset. But never have I imagined that she could be suicidal. She loved —" His voice cracked and he cleared his throat. "She loved everything. The outdoors, flowers, animals. She valued life, all life, human and animal and plant."

"What about Chris and Scott?"

"Chris is a hothead and his academic work is hit-or-miss, and Scott's quiet, restrained, a solid student. Chris is the one who speaks up in class, Scott never raises his hand. But I don't see either of them killing Anya. They loved her."

Lance Sanger spoke up for the first time since the beginning of the interrogation. "Maybe," Sanger said, "they disliked your relationship with her. Maybe we're dealing with a love triangle."

Nora refrained from shaking her head.

292

That didn't fit, though she couldn't articulate exactly why.

It ticked off Cole. "That's bullshit and you know it, Lance. Chris and Scott were Anya's best friends, and they knew about us. Have for a long time. And Scott had a girlfriend. He wasn't thinking about Anya like that."

Nora's ears practically twitched like a cat. "Who's Scott's girlfriend?"

"Maggie O'Dell, Anya's former roommate."

Cole's eyes widened at the same time Nora had the sense that she'd just heard something crucial to her case.

"Who's Maggie O'Dell?" Nora asked. "Anya doesn't have a roommate this year."

"Maggie left last Christmas."

"Why?"

"I don't know. Anya didn't know, Maggie simply told her she was dropping out of college."

"Was Maggie one of the gang?"

"Don't answer that, Leif," his attorney said.

Cole said, "Where Anya went, Maggie went. They were inseparable. I heard she was back."

"I want my client released immediately," Shepherd said.

He glanced at his attorney, then said, "Where's Anya now?"

"I don't know," Nora said. "Possibly the hospital or maybe she's been transported to the morgue. You don't want to go in there."

"I want to see her. Please."

Nora glanced at Sanger. They really had no reason to hold Cole. Yes, he knew about the arsons and was an accessory after the fact, but he hadn't said anything that could be used against him. He had been forthcoming without being self-incriminating, a great trick if you were a criminal with information cops needed.

"I'll take you," Sanger said.

"I'll take him," Shepherd insisted.

Sanger glared at him. "I'll do it." He said to Cole, "I'll let you out if you promise to stay in town. No major trips for the next couple weeks."

Cole wanted to argue. Then he flipped like a switch. "I understand. Thank you, Lance."

Chapter Sixteen

By the time Nora pulled back into Sacramento FBI headquarters, it was after seven in the evening and she was both exhausted and exhilarated. Two long days notwithstanding, she had her first, solid lead.

And no one was in the office.

That wasn't completely true. Duke was with computer analyst Jason Camp in the small computer room. She poked her head in. "How's it going?"

"The hard drive was wiped," Jason said, frustrated. "We're trying to capture some of the data. If we can get enough, we may be able to rebuild the drive. But we're not going to have answers tonight."

"Thanks," she said. To Duke, "Anything on the backgrounders?"

"On your desk, sweetheart," he said.

She frowned as she walked away. "Sweetheart"? Did he think that because he'd kissed her she was now his sweetheart?

Her heart raced. She was panicked and excited at once. But now was not the time to think about relationships, especially a relationship with Duke Rogan. She'd turned him down a dozen times in the last four years, couldn't he take a hint? She did not want to go out with him.

She closed her eyes as she sank into her chair. She was interested in Duke Rogan, had been from the beginning, but she had no time for a serious relationship. And though Duke flirted and joked, when he looked at her she saw that he wasn't going to be content with a few dinners, hot sex, and sayonara, baby. He wanted a long-term commitment. She didn't want a relationship. Any involvements were few and far between, and Nora didn't want to risk her heart again.

She opened her eyes and looked through her inbox, finding on top Dr. Coffey's autopsy report on Jonah Payne. Attached was a note.

Nora:
I just received two of the three apparent suicide deaths. I'm waiting for the third before doing the autopsy, so if you want to attend it'll be early tomorrow — seven-thirty a.m.

The tox screens came back on Payne.

Payne ingested a modified version of Rohypnol that included speed and some other things that aren't identified yet. Since the tests were inconclusive, I sent a blood sample to Quantico to see if they've seen anything like it. It almost appears home-made. But if it behaves anything like Ro-hypnol at the dosage he received he could have been experiencing memory loss, fatigue, insomnia, and dizziness. His reflexes would have been slow, and his hearing and sight impaired. This wasn't a pill, it was liquid, and could have been ingested with anything, food or liquid. I got this from his stomach contents, which sug-gests that he consumed it four hours or less from the time he died.

In addition, his blood tested positive for heparin, a blood thinner. It acts fast, gener-ally within thirty minutes, and is always administered as an injection. Other similar drugs take four to twenty-four hours to work. Heparin is not a known street drug, but a pharmaceutical drug. Hope that helps a bit, and I'll get you the results of the suicides as soon as possible.

— K. Coffey, M.E., Placer County

How the hell did the killer get ahold of

heparin? Unless the killer required it for some reason. Nora logged into the FBI database and looked through drug theft reports in the area. Hospitals kept track of their medicine, and certain drugs were flagged if inventory was off. But either heparin wasn't flagged, or no one had stolen it recently.

Nora also knew some hospitals weren't so good at record-keeping; if a small amount went missing they might not have noticed, or didn't want to file the paperwork. But this suggested to Nora that the killer had access to medical supplies . . .

She picked up the phone while pulling the Langlier file from her desk. She was reading the notes when Quin finally picked up.

"Quin Teagan, at your service."

"Quin, it's Nora."

"You're back."

"Yes, and I need information about Langlier. They stored cancer-fighting drugs at their warehouse, correct?"

"That's their bread and butter," Quin said.

"What other drugs?"

"I don't know — it's in my report. They gave me a list — I attached it."

"I can't find it —"

"I'm not home right now. If it's important, I can be home in thirty."

Nora heard a male voice in the background. "No, no — here! Found it."

Quin read the list of losses. The drugs were listed in alphabetical order, and there were only five.

Heparin was third on the list.

"Thanks, Quin."

"Oh, sure, I solved the whole case," she said sarcastically.

"You might have, with your detailed reporting. I know now where the killer got the blood thinners used on Payne. Keith Coffey alerted me that the drug used wouldn't be easy to get, and so I thought of Langlier —"

"But Langlier was nearly two years ago!"

"Speaking of Langlier, there was a triple possible suicide at Rose College today."

"Suicide?"

"Possible. Or murder. The students who died were definitely involved with the arsons, but I think there's one more student or former student involved, and I have a line on her. It's one of the victim's former roommates."

"Good luck. This is fantastic."

"Enjoy your date."

Nora hung up and pulled all the background reports Duke had run for her. She yawned and her stomach grumbled. She packed everything into her briefcase and walked to Jason's office. She glanced in. Jason was alone. "Where'd Duke go?" she asked.

"He had a call."

"Tell him I said good-bye and I'll see him tomorrow."

Maggie opened the door to Donnie's cage and let him walk around. She hated keeping him locked up like a prisoner, but she couldn't risk him getting away. She didn't know exactly how the police had tracked down the other ducks, but it had something to do with an implant, according to the news. She didn't know where it was, had inspected Donnie carefully, and she didn't want to hurt him. He was the innocent victim in all this. It wasn't his fault those people had experimented on him. He'd done nothing wrong.

Tears welled in her eyes and she dry-heaved as she remembered what the cruel cops had done to all those ducks. They'd gotten off on it, the sadistic bastards. Snapping their delicate necks like tree branches. One after another after another . . .

But it was all done on the orders of that bitch, Nora English.

Maggie had gone a bit too far when she

threw the soda can at Nora at Lake of the Pines, but Maggie had never been so close to her before. She'd wanted to cut her so bad it hurt, make the federal agent suffer for the pain she'd caused the movement. The pain Nora English had caused *her* personally. But Nora didn't know her, couldn't know her, though Maggie wished she did. Nora had ruined her life and didn't even know it. She'd acted callously, without regard for anyone she damaged in the process. Without a care of who went to prison, whether they were guilty or innocent.

The cause was more important than any one person. Maggie had killed fighting for what was right, and she would die for it. Some ideals were bigger than individuals. Bigger than her life. What was guilt but a judgment by a corrupt judicial system? Had any of Maggie's comrades been *guilty* under the natural order? No! They were guilty only because of man-made rules and laws, not because they had actually done anything wrong.

Donnie waddled over to the sink she'd filled with water. He drank, then jumped in. Maggie smiled. She wished she'd taken two ducks. She would have taken them all, but she hadn't known the feds were going to torture and murder them. She'd kept Donnie because he was injured, that brute Scott had just stuffed the ducks into the cages as if they were children's toys, not nature's creatures. His wing was broken, and Maggie couldn't free him without chance of survival.

And yet, he was the only one who had survived.

Maggie picked up her favorite knife and stared at the blade. Under the light, the blade looked angelic, sparkling, blinding. She turned it and it was dull again.

She took out her special stone and sharpened the knife slowly, with sure, firm purpose. Sharpening her blade calmed her like nothing else. The *scrape, scrape* of the stone on the hand-forged metal. She remembered making this exact knife with her stepdad. She remembered each knife they'd made together, the patience he taught her, the respect for the fire, for the steel, for the cutting edge.

She'd used this knife on Jonah Payne. He didn't understand, but she didn't expect him to. He'd died because she needed practice. She had to have it perfect.

Nora English would pay for her actions. For putting innocent people in prison, for slaughtering Donnie's winged brothers and sisters, for working for the corrupt system and against nature. Nora English was very much part of the bigger problem.

When Maggie was done with her, Nora would beg to die. And Maggie would let her do just that . . . eventually.

Jonah Payne had not been her first kill, and Nora English wouldn't be the next.

Someone else had to come first. Someone who had hurt her. Someone who'd turned people against her.

Maggie didn't like it when people didn't do what they were supposed to. When they didn't do what she wanted them to do.

She'd learned a lot since the first time she'd killed. That time . . . that was messy. She missed Clay sometimes, but he'd deserved it. He was going to leave her.

They lay on the blanket under the big oak tree, Maggie and Clay. It was the last weekend in April, and spring was supposed to be the time of rebirth and beauty, everything green and flowers blossoming. But today, though the sun shone hot over the treetops in the small Central Coast town of Paso Robles, her blood turned cold and she shivered.

She knew before he spoke that Clay was going to make a huge mistake. She couldn't let him, instead postponing his confession with a kiss.

"Shh," she said, tucking his pretty hair behind his ears. His parents didn't like that his hair touched his collar, but she did. She liked everything about Clay Baker: his hair, his smell, his smile, his commitment to the cause, and most of all his commitment to her. He *was* hers, now and forever. They'd been together all of high school, she'd had sex with only Clay, and she loved him. He owned her heart, and she his.

He kissed her back, but it wasn't like before. It wasn't the same as last month, before he got that damn letter.

He was already three thousand miles away.

"Maggie, we need to talk about this."

"I don't want to," she pouted.

"Graduation is only four weeks away. I don't want this hanging over us for all that time."

"No."

"Maggie, just listen. It's the opportunity of a lifetime. A full scholarship to SUNY! It's what I've always wanted. You need to be happy for me."

"I'm sad for us. You can't go."

He touched her hair and sighed. "I'll miss you, too."

"I'll come with you."

"And not go to college?"

"I'm only going to community college." Her grades had been borderline. Maggie was lucky to even graduate. Her entire life her teachers had told her and her parents that she was an underachiever, that her test scores showed she was very intelligent, too intelligent to be getting C's and D's.

"You just need to find yourself and your place," Clay said.

"My place is with you. I'm going to Syracuse."

She didn't like the look on Clay's face. It was as if he'd already known what she was going to say and had prepared a response.

"Maggie, you can't come with me. You would be a distraction from my studies. This is important to me. Try to understand that. Everything I've wanted to do in environmental science, I can with a degree from SUNY. I'll be back in four years, and if we still feel the same way —"

Her stomach turned sour. "If?"

"Four years — Maggie, people change in four years."

"You're dumping me."

"We have email and I'll call every week."

He was telling her what he thought she wanted to hear. The only thing she wanted to hear was that Clay Baker was not dumping her.

He took her hand, kissed her neck. "We

have all summer. Let's not worry about later, okay?"

He hadn't told her he loved her in weeks. He hadn't made love to her in weeks.

He didn't know that she knew Cindy Tomlinson was going to SUNY, too. Or that she'd been watching how he looked at Cindy since those college letters arrived last month. They had bonded over a damn college! It wasn't fair. Maggie was as smart — no, smarter! — than both of them. And Clay was going three thousand miles away with Cindy Tomlinson.

Maggie let Clay kiss her, touch her breasts, push up her skirt. They had made love under this tree the first time.

And now, the last time.

He held her for a minute, then went to dispose of the condom. She told him she'd be right back, and walked naked down to the creek where they'd stored the cooler after their picnic.

Clay's mother had made the lemonade. Mrs. Baker didn't like Maggie, but she'd been nice today. Nice in one of those "I know something you don't" ways, so mightier-than-thou. The bitch had sabotaged Maggie's relationship with Clay. She had convinced Clay to dump her. His future, his life, his dreams. What about *her?* Margaret Love O'Dell, with hopes and dreams of her own. And they centered around Clay Baker.

At least for one more day.

She'd seen the water hemlock growing when she first put the cooler in the water. She'd seen it before, as this was their spot. Clay didn't know what it was, or if he did he never commented on it.

She took a cloth napkin from their lunch basket and used it as a glove of sorts, wrapping her hand in it while she crushed the water hemlock leaves, breaking the membranes and releasing the poison. She didn't want any to be absorbed through her skin. It would take a lot of leaves because the poison didn't mix well with cold water. She stuffed the leaves into an empty water bottle, then poured lemonade into it and shook it well. She let it sit for a minute, watching the leaves. She pretended she could actually see the poison leaching from the leaves into the pale yellow liquid. It was turning a darker color. That she wasn't imagining. It was working.

"Maggie! We only got thirty minutes before curfew," Clay called from beyond the grove of trees.

His *mother's* curfew. Six p.m. on Sundays. So they could have a *family* dinner. One they never invited Maggie to. She'd bet they'd invite Cindy Tomlinson.

She strained the lemonade into another

water bottle. It didn't quite look right. Would he notice? Maybe. She put everything back in the cooler, then re-packed the basket and cooler and brought everything over to the oak tree. The wet hemlock leaves were stuck in the bottle — she'd have to dispose of it later.

Clay lay on his back, watching her.

She put everything down and pretended to drink the lemonade. "Still cold, but a little tart. Want some?"

"My mother never puts in enough sugar."

He took the water bottle and chugged half the poisoned lemonade, then grimaced. "Yeah, I think it was in the sun too long."

He screwed on the cap and tossed it on the blanket. He patted the spot next to him, and she sat down.

"Don't worry about tomorrow," he told her. "Just here and now. Today, everything's fine, right?"

Maggie smiled. "Everything's perfect."

CHAPTER SEVENTEEN

With the background reports spread out on Nora's dining room table, a glass of buttery chardonnay in front of her — her one and only for the evening — she finally hung up her phone.

In the two hours she'd been home, she'd been productive. She'd heard back from Sara Ralston that Anya Ballard was *not* the woman with Russ Larkin on Sunday in Starbucks, even if she had dark hair, according to Summer, the coffeehouse employee who had seen her. Then she'd talked to Rachel about running a background check on Maggie O'Dell, including all variations of the name "Maggie."

"Make sure you get a photo from the DMV and Rose College. Get her transcripts as well — if they squawk, let me know. We'll get a warrant. We have more than enough cause."

She was satisfied that Rachel would hop

on the assignment first thing in the morning, and they'd debrief at nine with the rest of the team, after Nora observed the autopsies of the three students. Coffey would send her the information, but she'd rather stop by and get it faster. It wasn't too far out of her way to head up to Placer County before going to headquarters.

She made notes on Anya, Scott, and Chris. While they shared their major and college, they were born in different towns, went to different high schools, and didn't seem to have had any contact prior to attendance at Rose College.

She went through the Butcher-Payne employees yet again, to see if she missed something. When Nora's doorbell rang, she jumped.

Embarrassed even though no one saw her reaction, she walked cautiously to the door and glanced through the peephole.

Duke.

Nora opened the door. Before she could say anything, Duke said, "You disappeared."

She tilted her head. "Hardly."

He stepped across her threshold without an invitation. She stepped back. She'd had to, to avoid touching him.

"You didn't tell me you were leaving headquarters," he said.

"I didn't know I was supposed to." It took all her willpower to look him straight in the eye and not remember the kiss. "I told Jason," she said.

The kiss. Hardly something she could forget. Anticipation fluttered in her stomach and she told herself it was hunger.

Right, hunger. Go ahead and try to convince yourself you want a can of soup more than you want Duke Rogan.

She stepped back again, though he hadn't moved. He smiled, a Cheshire cat grin, as if he knew something she didn't.

He stepped all the way in and shut the door.

She turned away from him and walked down the hall toward the dining room where she had her work spread out in front of her. "I'm working," she said over her shoulder, hoping distance might extinguish the growing heat between them.

"You're always working." He was right behind her, and his long legs cut the space between them quickly.

She hardly thought he was one to judge, and she spun around to tell him just that.

Duke was mere inches behind her. His right hand wrapped around her neck and pulled her mouth to his without hesitation, without asking permission, without a doubt

311

in his mind that she would resist.

She didn't.

Her mouth opened, her body pressed against his and Duke pulled her closer, his left hand around her back, under her shirt, molding her back, holding her tight against him.

Everything fell away, the pressure of her job, the memories of the past, worry for her team and her sister and the victims. Everything disappeared, and it was only the two of them, her and Duke, as if nothing else mattered, nothing else was important but for the first time in her life giving in to what she wanted.

Duke had been right when he said she'd never factored in her dreams in any decision she made.

She made a decision for herself right now. She wanted Duke Rogan, and she was going to take exactly what she wanted.

Nora pulled his T-shirt from his jeans, ran her hands up his hard, broad chest. Her thumbs circled his nipples and Duke's hand fisted in her hair as he tightened his grip, his tongue shooting into her mouth, mimicking sex. She shivered, a moan trapped between their lips, and wrapped her arms around him to keep from falling to her knees.

His free hand grabbed her ass and held her up, his fingers massaging her, squeezing, teasing. Between them, the temperature rose and Nora burned. She grabbed the ends of Duke's T-shirt and pulled it up; he grabbed it with one hand and pulled it over his head. She stared at his sculpted body, wasted when hidden by clothes. She swallowed, but her mouth was dry, and then he was kissing her again, a kiss that promised her everything she'd wanted but denied herself. A kiss that told her he wasn't going away, a kiss that told her he knew her better than she knew herself, and that from the beginning she'd wanted him.

He was right.

His hands came between them, flicking her blouse open with confident fingers, exposing her flesh and lacy white bra. Her head dipped back as his firm lips moved from her mouth to her jaw, his tongue tracing a line that sent hot chills racing along her nerves, down to her neck where he lightly bit her, then drew her skin into his mouth, leaving her breathless.

He fell to his knees, his face against her chest. He unhooked her bra with one hand, tossed it away without thought, his mouth drawing in her breast without hesitating, then switching sides, back and forth, his hands moving as if they knew exactly where she wanted to be touched. Nora's breath caught in her throat when his hands pulled down her slacks with an impatient jerk, and then squeezed her ass, his mouth moving down her stomach, past her waist, until his tongue flicked out and tasted her through her panties. She gasped, a high-pitched yelp that sounded nothing like her, caught between foreplay and sex. Her knees buckled, her legs spread, and she began to sink to the floor, but Duke held her up, one hand supporting her back, the other pushing her most intimate place closer to him, where his mouth suckled as if he were dying of thirst.

She couldn't see, she couldn't think, the edge of the cliff was there, in front of her. She grabbed Duke's shoulders, holding on as if she would drown; a rainbow of light burst, and she exploded with a cry that sounded far, far away.

She tried to catch her breath while trying to find his mouth with hers. But instead of kissing her, he hauled her up off the floor, and over his shoulder as if she weighed nothing. Duke carried her down the hall to her bedroom. He tossed her on the bed and she finally opened her eyes and saw him, looking as hot and needy as she felt. His skin glistened with perspiration, and between her dining room and her bedroom, he'd lost his jeans. He towered over her naked, his cock long and hard in front of him.

"God, you're gorgeous." His voice growled, rough and gravelly, as he bent over her, his hands on either side of her head, slowly, until he kissed her again.

Duke had wanted Nora English since the first time he'd seen her four years ago. Every time he'd consulted with her squad, before the arsons, he'd wanted her even more. One look at her, and he'd known she wanted to explore him just as much, but she wouldn't let herself. Nora never gave herself a minute to indulge in what she wanted. He needed her to open up to him, to talk to him, so he could find out everything about her, why she was so driven, so serious, so dedicated. He needed her to open her body to him, just like this, though her wanton response was far more thrilling than he'd imagined. He thought he'd have to work harder, but as soon as he called her out for her feelings, she caved, and he loved it. She was an open book, and everything he thought he knew about her was both very right and wrong at the same time. Nora was everything she appeared to be, but *more.* She had more depth, more passion, more *everything* than what appeared on the surface.

And here, now, the way she looked at him, giving herself fully and completely to him and their mutual pleasure was turning him nearly desperate with lust.

He wanted slow and easy, he wanted to show her how strongly he felt about her, but the depths of his desire were greater than he could control. He gave, she took and returned everything back, her hands firm and unwavering in their exploration of his chest, his back, and then she reached down and grabbed his cock and squeezed. A guttural growl escaped his chest.

He swallowed her mouth, grunting with restraint as she moaned out his name.

"Nora," he whispered into her ear, sucking the lobe, kissing the soft, delicate skin behind her ear. "Nora," he said again, "You had me from the beginning." He kissed her neck, her body moving beneath him, her hands moving back up his body, her short nails scraping neither too light nor too hard up his back, but with confidence.

She grasped his hands, squeezed, and pulled them above her head, trapping herself beneath his body, holding tight, her body moving to a tempo they both heard in their collective heart.

He didn't need a road map, his body

moved into position, his cock twitching between her legs as it sought ground zero. When he touched her, she gasped, her eyes fluttered closed, and her heart raced against his chest.

Duke sank slowly into her, a nearly primal groan vibrating his chest. Nora gasped beneath him and held her breath, her mouth open, her eyes closed, her face an open book of pleasure tinged with discomfort. He realized then that she was sharing something precious with him, that she didn't jump in bed with just anyone, that she was opening up far more of herself than he'd hoped for. And he would take it all, and pray he could return every ounce of trust she'd placed in him.

Nora couldn't remember the last time she'd had sex, but she knew it had never been like this.

She released Duke's hands and wrapped her arms around his back, her fingers pressing into his hard muscles as she stretched herself for him. There was nothing in the world like this, being here, with Duke. Her mind didn't wander, her body didn't betray her nervousness. In fact, she wasn't nervous. She had a confidence that emboldened her, that pushed her to seek more from Duke, more from herself, than she'd thought she'd wanted.

She arched her back and without having to say anything, he pushed himself fully into her. She bit back a cry as she lost her breath. The needful sounds, the rich, earthy scents, the texture of his body on top of her, inside of her, wrapped around her, heightened her perceptions. It was as if she were fully and completely absorbed into this man. She didn't know where she ended and Duke began. She didn't want to know. Never had she felt so at one with another human being, never had she felt so desired or hungry. He filled her, melting her, becoming part of her.

He pushed up off her chest, giving her air she didn't want but sorely needed, his hands on either side of her head.

"Nora," he whispered, his voice throaty and deep, sending shivers that vibrated through her body and made him grunt.

She opened her eyes, his deep blue eyes only inches from hers, his square jaw set. She couldn't tear her eyes away as his hips moved, slowly up, then down until she gasped, a tornado building again inside her, bigger, stronger, more powerful than the twister that overtook her in the dining room.

He knew it, too, his face darkening, as he

forced himself to go slow. She felt his biceps; they were hard, his veins pronounced as he controlled his movements. His sweat dripped onto her skin, their scents mingling. Her entire body responded to Duke, her hips meeting his as they quickly developed a perfect rhythm, a tempo that with every beat increased the pace.

In another flash of light and heat, Nora cried out, her body arching as if pulled up by an invisible string, and she wrapped one leg around Duke's waist to hold him there, right there, as waves of her orgasm crashed into each other, one after the other. Duke wrapped his arms around her back and pulled her tight to him as his own orgasm exploded into her. The intensity, the incredible high of their shared pleasure, left Nora dizzy and completely satiated.

Duke eased down on her, his heart pounding so hard she was lulled by the rhythmic power. He kissed her on her cheek, her neck, her lips, soft whispers of affection, of satisfaction, of comfort.

"That was . . ." she began, but her mind was mush and she smiled and sighed, squirming beneath him.

"Incredible," he finished. He rolled over, pulling her with him, and managed to find the sheet that had fallen she didn't know where. He wrapped the sheet around them, and held her.

"I'm not going anywhere," he said emphatically.

"Good," she whispered and snuggled into him. Her eyes closed and she sighed with contentment. She couldn't imagine being anywhere else.

Duke watched Nora as she drifted off to sleep. Her hair was damp from their activities, and he tucked it behind one of her ears so he could see her profile. So soft, so beautiful, so peaceful in rest. She looked vulnerable, something that she hid very well most of the time.

The urge to protect was common to him; it was part of his job. But the need to keep Nora safe overwhelmed him. This wasn't Duke's job, this was more. He couldn't bear for Nora to be hurt, he had to keep her safe and protect her not only from predators, but from her own relentless drive, her strong empathy, and sense of guilt for things she had no control over. Nora never had anyone looking out for her: not her mother, not her boss, not even her sister. And certainly not Nora.

But now she had Duke. This was far more important than a job. It involved his heart,

and he was losing it to Nora faster than he
could tell her he loved her.

CHAPTER EIGHTEEN

Overwhelming despair washed over Leif Cole as the sheriff drove him home from the morgue. Anya was dead and Leif felt more than partly responsible.

She'd been so upset when she found out someone had died in the fire at Butcher-Payne, Leif should have stayed with her. He'd never imagined she'd kill herself.

He also knew that if Jonah Payne had been murdered in cold blood, Anya had played no part in it. She wouldn't kill any living creature intentionally. Nothing Sheriff Lance Sanger or FBI agent English said would ever convince him otherwise. The arson? Yes. Murder? Never.

Lance turned down the long driveway that led to Leif's small but private ranch house in pricey Granite Bay. His former friend had been surprisingly kind during the morgue visit and subsequent drive. Leif had been in no shape to pick up his own car that he'd left at Rose College when Lance arrested him, but he could call a friend for a ride or get a taxi tomorrow. If he went to classes tomorrow. He had a lot of thinking to do. Thinking and mourning.

Anya had been too young to die.

"Thank you," Leif said, his hand on the door handle.

"I'm sorry for your loss," Lance said, distinctly uncomfortable.

"She's gone," Leif whispered. He cleared his throat. "She didn't kill Jonah Payne, not in the way Agent English said."

"I'm not going to discuss the investigation with you."

"Fine, just listen then. Anya made mistakes, but her motivations were good. Murder — it's not in her blood. I can't believe she killed herself. I don't know if I believe it."

"We're investigating all three deaths thoroughly," Lance said. "I assure you we'll find out what happened."

"It won't bring her back." His voice caught in his throat.

Lance shifted in his seat, and Leif knew it would be expecting too much to ask him to come in for a drink. Lance was a cop, but more than his career, Lance didn't understand why Leif believed so passionately in his ideas. Time had divided them, and ideas kept them apart. When your core values differed, there was no seeing eye-to-eye.

"I know, don't leave town," Leif said, opening the door.

"Leif —" Lance began.

Leif glanced at him.

Lance said, "I'm sorry I was a jerk when you came back from college. I missed our friendship, and you weren't the same."

"We all grow up. You changed too," Leif said. "We aren't the same kids we were. But I'll never forget when we put the dead skunk in Ms. Knudson's office after she accused us of cheating."

Lance grinned. "She knew it was us, but could never prove it. She couldn't get the stink out for weeks."

"Thanks for driving me home," Leif said, leaving the rest unspoken.

"Do you want company for a while?" Lance offered.

Leif almost took him up on it. Almost. Instead he shook his head. "I need time alone."

"Don't drink too much."

"I won't. I'm okay, I just need to think." Leif got out and walked to his front door. He rarely came in this entrance, usually pulling into the garage and coming through the kitchen door. He fumbled for his keys, found the right one, and waved as the sheriff drove away.

Leif stood on his porch for a minute and looked up at the stars. It was a beautiful night, a night that Anya would have appreciated. She loved the stars, the vast space, the entire earth. She cared about everyone and everything, with a sincere compassion that few people possessed. The world was worse off with Anya gone.

He squeezed his burning eyes closed and rubbed the back of his neck. He'd loved her. Damn, he loved her. There was no bringing her back.

He pushed the door open and slammed it closed. He'd promised Lance he wouldn't drink much, but he needed something to dull the pain in his heart. Something to help him sleep. A triple shot of whiskey might help. A hot shower.

Leif grabbed his sole bottle of whiskey, Chivas Regal that the dean had given him last year when he'd had an article published in a prestigious academic journal. He took it and a water glass to his bathroom, poured a near-full glass, and took a large sip. The liquid burned his throat the way his eyes burned from the pain of losing Anya. Spread the pain, he thought, and coughed out a sob.

He turned on the shower, stripped, leaving his clothes in the middle of the bathroom floor. He took another long drink of whiskey, this one sliding down much easier.

The water was still cold when he stepped into the shower, but he didn't care. Physical discomfort was nothing compared with the pain inside.

The water warmed and he sobbed, bawling like a little kid, and sank to the tile floor of his shower. He'd failed Anya in so many ways.

It was a long time later before he emerged. Leif wrapped a towel around his waist and reached for his glass of Chivas. He drained the remainder and considered pouring another, but his stomach churned. He should never have drunk whiskey on an empty stomach. He couldn't remember the last time he'd eaten . . . breakfast? Coffee and a scone. Hardly a meal.

He rummaged through the kitchen cabinets looking for crackers or chips, lightheaded and dizzy. He grabbed a box and stumbled into his bedroom, collapsing uneasily into his reading chair. He closed his eyes, head spinning. He knew better than to drink. He was such a lightweight.

He drifted to sleep. *Anya* . . .

A sharp pain in his arm startled him. Leif didn't feel awake. His head was thick, as if he had a hangover. A bad hangover. From a couple shots of whiskey? Maybe. Had he drunk more and not remembered?

He tried to stretch, to shake the cobwebs from his mind, but his limbs were heavy, he couldn't move. He tried to open his eyes, but they felt plastered shut.

A light, flowery scent consumed him.

A woman. Perfume. Not a scent he was familiar with. Not Anya's. Anya was dead.

Someone was in his house.

"What?" His tongue was thick.

"Good fucking morning," a female voice said, her breath on his face.

He forced his eyes open, squinting, the lights too bright. He didn't remember turning on any lights.

"Who are you?" he asked. It sounded like he was hearing himself in a tunnel, complete with an echo. He tried to stand, but stumbled and sank heavily back into his seat. He couldn't move his hands.

"Don't worry," she said.

The realization that someone had broken into his house while he was sleeping — or passed out — and tied him to his chair cleared his head a fraction. And there was something familiar about her voice.

"What? What are you d-doing?" he said, trying to get the words out clearly. He opened his eyes again, slowly, adjusting to the too-bright light.

"It's your fault. You made me do it."

Maggie.

Maggie O'Dell? He struggled against his restraints. Duct tape, long pieces over his wrists and taped down the sides of his upholstered chair. He pulled, but couldn't break free. He looked down the side and saw that the tape had been crisscrossed to better restrain him.

"Maggie?"

He saw her then, her brown hair and big brown eyes. She had always been a beautiful girl, but Leif had never liked her. He didn't know why.

She slapped him.

"You made me kill her."

His head spun. "What?"

She slapped him again, then started pacing. The violence cleared his head some and he stared at her. She looked both angry and panicked. When she reached his desk in the corner of his bedroom, she picked up the monitor and threw it against the wall with surprising strength from such a slender girl.

Leif pulled at his restraints, but couldn't

loosen the tape. His fingers were numb.

"Twenty minutes," Maggie mumbled.

"What?" Leif said, not knowing whether she was talking to him or not.

She walked back to him, straddled him on the chair and that's when he realized the towel around his waist had slipped off and he was completely naked. But there was nothing sexual in her expression.

"It's all your fault. Your fucking fault!" Her hand reached out and grabbed his neck and squeezed. "I hate you, hate you, you fucking prick. You messed up everything. *Everything.* I didn't want to kill her. I loved her more than a sister. More than anything, but *you made me do it!*"

She squeezed until his body tightened, fighting for air.

Then she jumped off and started pacing again. "Fifteen minutes," she said.

She was crazy. Certifiable.

I didn't want to kill her.

The truth of that statement hit Leif like a bullet. "You killed Anya."

"*You!* You killed Anya. You turned her against me. We had a good thing going, and you screwed with my plans. It was a major setback, you selfish prick, but you don't care about anyone but yourself. You used her."

"I loved Anya."

She barked out a laugh. "You loved having a young girl to fuck, old man."

She walked back to him and straddled him again, this time grinding herself against his limp dick. "Just a pervert," she said.

"What do you want, Maggie?"

"I want you dead. I want you to suffer like Anya. I didn't want her to suffer, but I didn't have much time." She jumped up, then kicked him in the balls and he screeched. She didn't seem to notice.

"She called me and said that someone had died in the fire and we had to confess. Confess! Right, like I was going to admit that I'd killed a man. A man who deserved to die for all the pain and heartache he caused."

"You killed Jonah Payne." Leif's voice was a whisper. He shuddered in pain.

"He thought he was so brilliant, and he wanted everyone to know how brilliant. He didn't care who he hurt just to prove he was right."

"There are . . . other ways." Leif took a deep breath.

She continued as if he hadn't spoken. "Payne was only one problem. Anya would have been with me for all of it, but you got to her. You corrupted her. You turned her against me. I hate you. I hate you!"

She kicked him again and Leif's vision darkened. He closed his eyes and held his breath. Everything hurt. His hands were numb, his groin throbbed, his head spun.

"It was your idea," he whispered.

"Most of it was my idea. Scott came up with the arson. He got off on setting fires. Anya and I picked the locations. Well, I picked the first place because I needed something from Langlier."

"What?"

She continued without answering his question. "We were good. We were a great team. Then you started fucking Anya, and she was so goo-goo about you, what a sucker. I told her you just wanted to screw around, but she didn't believe me. I even told that wuss Holbrook and he didn't care. Said he would look into it, but he didn't."

Leif remembered last year when the dean came to him and asked if he was involved with a student. Leif had denied it, called Anya to warn her, and she'd also denied it when Holbrook called her in. Chris backed her up on it. It had never occured to Leif that it had been Maggie who'd turned on them.

"I had to leave before I did something stupid. I wanted to kill you so bad, but I didn't have a good plan. It's all about the plan. I needed to think, to get my head clear. I knew . . ." Her voice trailed off.

Leif couldn't hear her, he couldn't see her. Where had she gone? He fought the restraints. His vision sharpened and took on odd hues of color. Almost like when he'd dropped acid in college. He blinked rapidly and they disappeared, but his head again felt thick and he became nauseated. He had difficulty focusing, but when he closed his eyes the dizziness returned. He looked for Maggie, turned his head each way, but couldn't see her. Where was she? What was she doing?

Dead silence for a full minute. Longer. Had she left? He was sweating. Another minute slowly passed. He closed his eyes and tried to slow his racing heart.

"It's time."

He opened his eyes. She stood in front of him. Had he passed out for a minute? A second ago she wasn't there.

His eyes fell to the knife in Maggie's hand. It wasn't one of his. She'd brought it with her. She'd come to his house to kill him. His body shook and the more he tried to control it, the harder he vibrated.

"Please," he begged, his voice high and terrified. "Don't."

She looked at the knife without emotion,

then pressed it against his forearm. He felt only a mild sting, like a paper cut. He stared at his arm and saw blood seeping through the slit skin, dripping down his arm, sliding down the side of his chair. Little pain, but so much blood . . .

The blade touched his skin again, an inch farther up his arm. More blood. Again, again, again. His arm was drenched in blood. Blood that dripped. It seemed to be pouring from his arm. He couldn't stop watching, knowing that he was going to die.

Calm down. Leif, calm down.

Anya had stopped cooperating with Maggie's plans, so Maggie killed her. Now she would kill him.

"Why?" he asked, failing to keep rising terror out of his voice.

"I told you why, you prick."

She cut him again, smiling. She enjoyed hurting him.

"Maggie — Anya never hurt you. She was upset when you left last year. She missed you." His vision began to fade. He saw little except his blood flowing out of shallow wounds.

Maggie took the knife and made a stabbing motion, stopping as the tip of the knife pierced his chest. Though the blade went in not even a quarter of an inch, pain pulsated through his body, and more blood flowed from his wounds. She pulled out the knife and blood ran down his chest. A panicked cry escaped his throat.

"You hurt me, Anya hurt me. She would have talked, and I couldn't have that when *my plan is not finished!*" She started pacing again.

Leif was dying and Maggie continued to rant.

"You're no better than any of them! You sound like you care, but it's an act and you would have betrayed the cause just like she did!"

Maggie came back and walked around to his other arm. Her face was feverish, her eyes wide, her mouth pursed as she cut his arm without comment, one, two, three times, the blood dripping down, sliding, Leif's vision blackened from the outside in. He swallowed, but that simple act was laborious.

Maggie had been Anya's best friend, but she'd killed Anya. She was killing him. And she wasn't going to stop.

My plan is not finished!

Play possum. Let her think he was dead. She'd leave him alone, right? Leave him for dead and someone would find him when he didn't show up at the college in the morning. He could survive. Mind over matter. He would survive.

Calm down. Close your eyes.

So tired.

Maggie stared at Professor Cole's bloody body, her breathing rapid, her skin flushed. She dropped the knife, stepped backward, and tripped over a stack of papers, falling on her ass. She sat there, her head in her bloody hands, and breathed deeply.

It's over it's over it's over.

She waited until she was calm, waiting until she could think again.

Then she looked at the professor.

He was dead, his entire body slick with blood. She didn't remember cutting him so many times. His arms, his legs, his chest.

"It's your fault," she accused the dead man.

She rose from the floor, picked up the knife with her gloved hands, and walked into his bathroom. She stripped naked, the clothes she had bought at a secondhand store earlier that day falling on top of Leif Cole's earlier discarded clothing.

She turned the tap and stood under the icy cold water, watched as blood ran off her body in rivulets that soon came clear. She scrubbed her body with his soap, washed her hair with his shampoo.

Maggie didn't go back to the bedroom. She didn't need to see him again, and she definitely didn't want to get any more of his blood on her. Leif Cole was done. She wouldn't think about him anymore.

Anya missed you.

Maggie knew that no one missed her. No one wanted her. Anya and the professor had been so wrapped up in each other, now they were gone. Jonah Payne had his work and now he and his research were gone, destroyed.

But Maggie wasn't done.

She pulled on a thin dress that she had stowed in a bathroom cabinet before Cole had come home. Slipping on her sneakers, she was about to leave the way she came through the side door and across the open field in the back to where she'd parked when she saw the cat door.

Why hadn't see noticed it before?

She rummaged through the kitchen until she found cat food, then shook the box until a small, black cat slipped through the kitty door. She scooped him up and he purred loudly. "Aren't you sweet?"

She smiled and rubbed her face against his furry neck. Then she left with the cat and his food, with no thought of the dead man.

CHAPTER NINETEEN

"Jimsonweed," Nora said when she walked into the FBI conference room five minutes late for the briefing she'd called.

She dropped her briefcase and slid a stack of stapled papers to Rachel and motioned for her to take one set and pass the rest along.

"Jimsonweed?" Pete asked from the back of the room.

"Specifically, *Datura stramonium.* Commonly known as jimsonweed. It grows in warm, dry climates, particularly areas that are wet during the winter but completely dry in the summer. There are several areas in the valley where it can be found. It's easily recognizable, and too often teenagers use it to get high since, in small doses, it causes hallucinogenic effects."

"So it was an accident?" Rachel asked. "They were trying to get high?" She frowned.

"They left a suicide note," Pete pointed out.

Nora said, "Even in a fraction of the amount they consumed, they wouldn't have survived. The boys had twice the level as Anya, which is why she held on a bit longer. But even if she'd been found immediately, chances of survival were next to none. The poison is deadly and paralyzing, which was why they couldn't leave the room for help."

Pete said, "Why would they kill themselves with a drug that was going to cause such a violent reaction?"

"Good question," Nora said.

Rachel was reading from the coroner's notes. "The iced tea they drank was brewed with jimsonweed leaves? That's insane. What's this about orange peels?"

"The iced tea was essentially liquid poison," Nora explained. "It was heavily sweetened with liquid sugar and orange peels to disguise the bitter taste."

"Disguise? Because they didn't want to taste it or because they didn't know?"

"That's the million-dollar question," Nora said.

"You're thinking this might be murder?" Pete asked.

"Murder or murder-suicide," Nora said. "I spoke with two witnesses yesterday relating to Anya Ballard's demeanor in the hours leading up to her death."

The conference room door opened. Entering was Agent Steve Donovan from Violent Crimes, who doubled as the ERT team leader. Donovan nodded to Nora and sat down next to Pete.

"Both witnesses who saw Anya within hours of her death," she continued, "said that Anya was upset, but had made plans with them for that week. Highly unusual for someone contemplating suicide. We also learned that Anya had a roommate last year who may have been involved with the arsons. Maggie O'Dell. Rachel? What did you find on her?"

"No California driver's license. I called the college and they won't release her records without a warrant. I called the U.S. attorney's office with the information and they're supposed to get back to me."

"Follow up in an hour if you don't hear from them. Our probable cause is that she's wanted as a person of interest in the ongoing domestic terrorism arson investigation. We need that information today." Nora had another thought. "Hey, go down to Rose College and look through the yearbooks in the library, see if we can get a picture. Check the school newspapers as well. If that fails, ask around the dorm and see if anyone has a picture of her. Picture, address, any information about where she might be."

"I can go now, unless you need me here." Rachel gathered her papers.

"Great, go now. Finding O'Dell is a priority. And when you get a picture, send it to Sara Ralston in the Reno office. She'll know what to do with it. Oh, and on your way out ask Jason to surf the Internet and look for any Rose College websites with captioned photos, if the three dead students had blogs or websites, anything that might yield information about Maggie O'Dell."

Rachel left and Pete said, "Is she a suspect?"

"I'd say a person of interest," Nora said. "At present, we have no physical evidence that Maggie O'Dell was involved with the arsons, or that she was involved with the poisoning, or that she is even in town. One witness implied Maggie was involved, but had no personal knowledge of her involvement. So I want to talk to her."

She turned to Steve Donovan. "Steve? You have an evidence report?"

"I sent you an email with the findings for your records. The blood at Payne's Lake Tahoe house is Payne's. We confirmed that he was in Lake Tahoe Saturday afternoon.

A neighbor saw him walking outside about four o'clock. Payne waved to him, they chatted for a few minutes. The neighbor is a full-time resident, knew Payne casually. He said Payne seemed like he always did, happy but preoccupied. The neighbor invited him for dinner, which Payne declined. Apparently there's nothing unusual about that, either. He usually declines."

"You checked with other neighbors?"

"It's very secluded in his little area. Can't see any other houses from Payne's house, there're lots of trees. It's not one of the places with a grand lake view. You can only see the lake if you crane your neck on the far corner of the deck. But it's nice and private."

Private enough that you can be murdered and no one will hear, Nora thought. She was about to ask another question when Steve added, "The neighbor gave me the contact information for the house closest to Payne, which is owned by a San Francisco couple. They were up for the weekend and left Sunday night. I spoke to the husband who said he saw a dark-colored truck he didn't recognize parked in Payne's carport, next to his Jeep. He didn't think much of it, except that he hadn't noticed it on Saturday when he walked past the property."

"He didn't by chance get a license plate?"

Donovan shook his head. "But Scott Edwards has a 2003 dark blue Ford F-150 registered in his name. It has a camper shell."

"Bingo," Nora said. "You could have woken me with that information."

"I talked to the witness ten minutes before I walked in here."

"Where's the truck?"

"I contacted the sheriff's department and they don't have it. I sent a tow truck and an agent to the college to impound it. Anya Ballard has a Volkswagen Beetle, one of those new trendy ones, and that's next up on the tow list. The other dead student didn't have a car registered to him. We're looking into two vehicles that are registered to his parents to see if he regularly used one."

"Great job. Let me know what you find and put out a BOLO on all vehicles. We don't know whether Maggie O'Dell had access to them, and since she has no car registered in her name she may have taken one of theirs. Keep in mind that they transported ducks late Sunday night, that could tie them to the crime scene."

"She doesn't have a driver's license," Steve pointed out.

"She doesn't have a *California* driver's license," Nora said, "but she could be from anywhere. And even if she has no license, that wouldn't stop her from driving." Nora's mother never had a driver's license, but they'd borrowed plenty of cars. Lorraine had never been pulled over.

Steve made a note. "Pete and I spent half the night going through the evidence from the dorm rooms," he said. "We sent Anya Ballard's journals to Quantico for comparative analysis against the letters that were sent to the media claiming credit for the arsons. The one thing we noticed right off is that so far we have found nothing in her room, or the boys' room, that has evidence of brewing the iced tea that killed them. No utensils, no containers, no jimsonweed leaves. But this morning when I was going over the logs, I saw that the sheriff's department had documented four glasses with the tainted tea."

"Four?"

"I triple-checked, and there were definitely four. I reviewed the crime-scene photos and there was one glass on the dresser, full."

"Where is it now?"

"Bagged, the tea sealed, but there were some problems."

"What problems?"

"The glasses were bagged properly, but they were labeled wrong. They were numbered, but no one put the numbers in the logs so we don't know who had which glass. Trace is currently printing the glasses, but we can't definitively state which glass was on the dresser."

Pete said, "Whichever glass doesn't have one of the three kids' prints."

"What if one of the dead kids handed out the drinks? What if the glass was meant for someone who didn't show?"

Nora straightened. "What if someone pretended to drink, then left?"

"You mean chickened out at the last minute?" Ted asked.

"I mean never intended to drink the tea in the first place. It could be first-degree murder if the three dead students didn't know their tea was poisoned." She said to Steve, "Make printing those a number-one priority. Maybe we'll get lucky. Do you have Ballard's computer? An address book or cell phone?"

"Yes, but we haven't gotten to her computer yet."

"When you go through her things, specifically look for anything about Maggie O'Dell."

"Will do."

"Anything else?" she asked.

He grinned. "That's not enough?"

She smiled. "It's great."

"I have one more thing," said Steve. "We processed Payne's Jeep yesterday afternoon. Someone much shorter than he drove it last."

"That's terrific."

"And she —"

"She?"

"The strands of hair we found on the driver's seat were fifteen inches long. Possibly a male, but more likely female."

"DNA?"

"It's on its way to Quantico. But I can tell you definitively, it doesn't match Anya Ballard."

Pete said, "Leif Cole has longish hair."

Nora asked, "What color?"

"Brown."

Anya was blond, and Leif Cole was light brown and gray. "Light brown? Dark brown?"

"Medium. Unprocessed. But that's all I know until Quantico gets back to us. I rushed it, but the response time really depends on what's on the schedule before it."

"Thanks, Steve."

Ted asked, "Any word on the missing duck?"

"No," Nora said. "Fish and Game is supposed to let me know if they find it."

Jason Camp, resident computer expert, stepped into the room. "Nora, sorry for interrupting, but I got something off Larkin's computer."

"Good news?"

"Depends on how you look at it. Butcher-Payne's security logs are wiped, but I can tell that someone accessed password-protected files on Sunday afternoon, only a few minutes before the data was corrupted. But I think I figured out why they wiped the drive. Emails."

"Something in the emails the killer didn't want us to know? Why not just take the laptop?"

Jason beamed. "That I know. LoJack."

"The computer was LoJack-protected?"

"Yep."

Nora frowned. "Why didn't Duke trace it on Monday when he was looking for Larkin?"

"He didn't know. I just got off the phone with him, and he said the laptop wasn't Rogan-Caruso property."

Nora got the facts straight in her head. "So the killer realized the computer had

346

tracking equipment and took the information right there. Maybe threatened Larkin, or maybe hacked into it after he was killed."

"That I don't know, but I can tell you that I can't get the emails back."

"So why do I need to know this? You still have nothing."

"I have the ISP."

"How does that help us?"

"The ISP for Russ Larkin is Rogan-Caruso. They have their own server. It's how their security system replicates itself."

"But wouldn't that compromise security if it was used for Internet access?"

"No — the replication is just information, not actual monitoring. It's like syncing your iPod, but only one way. I talked to Jayne Morgan, the computer chick over there, and she's going to pull all emails to and from Larkin for the past two weeks. It's going to take a bit because they're compressed and archived, but she said she'd have them for me today."

"If you learn anything —"

"You'll be the first to know." Jason left.

Nora finally felt that she was making forward progress in this investigation.

"Pete, can you dig deeper into Russ Larkin? Rachel was working on it, but she's sidetracked with Maggie O'Dell. Specifically, any connections with the three students who died or O'Dell. Maybe we're missing something. A relative, a friend, something that connects Larkin to one of them."

She glanced at her notes.

"Ted, can you check and see if the autopsy report is in from Reno? If not, call Sara and ask her to follow up with the coroner. Also trace evidence in Larkin's car."

Ted wrote everything down. "Got it."

Pete asked, "What about the three college students? We need backgrounds on them."

She'd asked Duke to run the background checks, as well as an FBI staff analyst. "Already being done," she said. She wondered where Duke was. When they'd parted this morning, he'd said he would meet her here. It was already after ten.

As if on cue, the door opened and Dean Hooper walked in, Duke right behind him. Duke winked at her, just out of Hooper's line of vision. Nora glanced at her squad. Had Pete and the others seen that? She tried to control the blush rising up her neck to her cheeks. She glanced down at the table and shuffled her papers.

"Thanks, guys," she said, dismissing the team. "Let me know if you're having any problems."

Hooper said a few words to each agent as they left, and when it was just him, Duke, and Nora, he said, "I just got off the phone with Dr. Vigo. He reviewed a sample of Anya's journals and concluded that she wrote the first three BLF letters, but definitely not the last one. Style, word choices, tone — everything was different." That confirmed their assessment from yesterday regarding the fourth letter, but also gave them more physical evidence tying the dead students to the fires.

"I need a sample of Maggie O'Dell's writing," Nora said. "Maybe she has an article published in the newspaper or we can talk to her professors and get an essay she wrote. Rachel is on her way to the college now, I'll —"

Hooper interrupted, "We already have it. It was in the evidence Steve sent yesterday."

"He didn't tell me —"

"He didn't know. It was a handwritten letter folded into Ms. Ballard's journal that began 'Dear Anya' and signed 'M.' Whoever wrote that letter, Dr. Vigo says wrote the fourth BLF letter. And moreover, whoever wrote that letter also wrote the suicide note. And it definitely wasn't Anya Ballard."

"Is the letter 'M' wrote important?"

"Possibly." He handed her a copy of the

letter. "We dusted the original for prints. We have a few partials from two different individuals, but they're pretty degraded. Quantico is working on enhancing them, but it'll take time."

Nora read the letter. It was undated, but based on the content it was given to Anya around the time Maggie left Rose College last December.

Dear Anya,

How could you choose him over our cause? I'm <u>very</u> disappointed in you. Don't you <u>care</u> anymore? Don't you want to be part of the solution? Your boyfriend yaks it up like he cares about the cause, but he's part of the problem. He's Establishment. He's never done <u>anything</u> to help. You know it. He talks and talks and likes everyone to think he's this big, noble Progressive Environmentalist who cares about the earth and animals that the Industrial Complex is killing so the masses have soap and makeup to disguise their ugly hearts.

~~Fuck you both!~~

"M" had crossed out that last line, but Nora noticed that while the text started out small and tight, it grew bigger and tilted more to the right — retaining the same tightness but with sharper points and more pressure on the pen. The letter continued with smaller script, but still with the heavy-pressured rightward slant.

I'm sorry. Anya, I love you. I wish you were my sister. You know about mine. I can't even talk to her. I wish we could be friends again, friends like before. I'm going to miss you, but I have to go. I hope someday we can do everything we planned. Don't listen to that jerk. He'll be screwing around with another student soon enough, then you'll see him like I do. A walking penis. He was in his office for a long time with that whore Ashley Corman on Monday. I'll bet they weren't talking about midterms. Ask him. I <u>dare</u> you. Or would you rather be ignorant and used?

We can do so much to <u>really</u> change the world and make a <u>real</u> difference. <u>We can do it</u>, Anya. Believe. I'm the only one who understands how you feel. Remember when you cried in my arms when that mama bear was killed by an SUV? She was just protecting her bear cubs. You cried and I told you we'd fix it. We'd make it right. And we did, didn't we?

<u>He</u> wouldn't do that for you.

I'll be thinking about you. We have more to do. You promised. Call me.

M

"She's certifiable," Duke said.

"Maybe," Nora muttered.

"What's wrong?" Hooper said. "Does something stand out in the letter?"

"First," she said, "her sister. We need to find her sister. Maybe that's where Maggie's hiding out. Rachel's at Rose College, we need that warrant ASAP."

"I'll call the U.S. attorney myself," Hooper said. Nora smiled. Hooper had connections that most FBI agents didn't have.

"What else?" Duke said. "You look worried."

"I'm very concerned. Look at the writing. She's like a tightly wound clock ready to break. She's impulsive and angry. She's young, which is why she's been able to get away with it. Parents and teachers tend to let young people get away with erratic behavior thinking they'll grow out of it. I don't think she'd be able to hold down a job for long. I doubt she has much control over her outbursts, though she is able to rein herself back in. Like a three-year-old who pushes down a kid and takes their toy. They'll give it right back when they're told to, but they were unable to control the impulse to take it in the first place. That's learned behavior, to resist taking what we want when we want it. I don't think our Maggie has control over that."

Hooper said, "I'll put out some feelers about that bear story. She mentions they 'fixed' it. Sounds like something that might be an unsolved crime."

What would people like her mother do under those circumstances? She said, "If the identity of the driver who hit the bear was made public, that's who they targeted."

"You don't think they killed him?" Hooper asked.

"Not Anya, if we're to believe what Leif Cole said about her. If she was truly that upset when she thought that Jonah Payne had been killed by accident, then she couldn't have participated in cold-blooded murder. But that doesn't mean she wouldn't destroy property he cares about. Like the offending SUV."

"I'm on it."

"Can I keep this?" She held up the letter.

"Sure, it's a copy."

She stared at it again and frowned. "There's something familiar here. I'm wondering if we've seen similar letters come through our squad. The use of the word

'Establishment' stands out. That's a clear anarchist statement. But 'Industrial Complex' sounds out of place, almost like she felt like she had to put it there to sound like she knew what she was talking about."

"You don't think she's a true anarchist?"

"She is. She believes in her cause, but her cause is not solely extreme environmental activism. It's more focused."

"You can tell that by this letter?" Duke asked.

"Some," she said. "And thirty-seven years of experience, on both sides of the law."

"I'm going to have Jason work on finding out about that case and seeing if there was any retaliation," Hooper said. "Duke."

There was a silent exchange between them, and Hooper left.

"What was that about?" she asked.

"You aren't blind to the fact that something's going on here. You heard the profiler yesterday state that the last letter was focused on *you*. Then his opinion today about the suicide note. I was in that conversation. Three handwriting experts confirmed that whoever wrote this" — he tapped the letter from 'M' in her hand — "wrote the fourth letter, which specifically mentioned cases *you worked.*"

"You and Hooper spoke to Dr. Vigo about

my case? Without me?"

"You were at the morgue. Why is it so hard for you to accept help?"

Duke was challenging her. She was completely out of her element, psychopaths and revenge. "I don't have any problem accepting help. I have my entire squad hunting down pieces of this puzzle, and I let you come on board as a consultant. So don't tell me I don't accept help."

"Let me rephrase it. You don't want anyone singling you out for special consideration. You don't want personal protection. But you've got it. Hooper and I agree that this woman has some reason in her head for not liking you. Until we find her, we need to be cautious."

Nora didn't like the direction this conversation was going. "Let's be logical about this. If someone had a vendetta against me, they'd come after me, right? Personally. I don't know Maggie O'Dell, I've never met her. Why would she come after me?"

"Why would they go after the driver of an SUV because he accidentally hit a bear? He certainly didn't do it on purpose, his car was probably totaled and he's lucky to be alive if he hit the poor animal with any speed. And why would this woman kill Jonah Payne? There's no logical reason. And her friends — she probably killed those three college students, kids she knew, a girl she said she loved like a sister. So don't think for a minute that you're not at risk!"

Nora was taken aback by Duke's passionate anger in getting his point across. She pulled at her hair, never feeling so out of sorts. "It doesn't make sense. It has to make sense!"

Duke firmly rubbed her arm. "I'm not a shrink, but I know people pretty well. Some of them just aren't very nice. Maybe this game she's playing is as much psychological as it is physical."

"I don't have any personal connection with the people she's suspected of killing."

"Maybe they're not connected to one another, but connected to the killer," Duke mused.

She looked at him. "I was thinking that earlier, but Jonah Payne is the odd man out. The only possible angle is to Leif Cole because of their public disagreements over biotechnology, but that's really stretching it, don't you think?"

"Let's put Anya Ballard and her friends aside for a minute. And Russ —" Duke swallowed uneasily.

She said, "He had information that the killer needed. But why not leave Dr. Payne's body in Lake Tahoe? Why transport it to his lab?"

"I don't know. The theatrics?"

Nora considered. "But it draws attention to BLF."

"And they're dead."

"Maybe the killer worried about them saying something."

"This Maggie O'Dell, we don't know where she is. Maybe Dr. Vigo's wrong about there being only four cell members," Duke said. "Maybe Maggie and her partner are the two we need to be looking for. Maybe it's Maggie and her sister."

"She says she doesn't talk to her," Nora pointed out.

"Maybe a boyfriend? A mentor?"

Nora considered. "Scott Edwards was her boyfriend, according to Professor Cole. He probably knew more about her than anyone. If Scott Edwards's truck was really in Tahoe, then that confirms there had to be two people — one to drive the truck with Payne's body and one to drive Dr. Payne's Jeep back to Butcher-Payne."

"Why would they bring the Jeep back?"

"I don't know. Theatrics, as you said. I don't see how they could possibly think that we wouldn't have been able to figure out that his death wasn't an accident."

"Our overcrowded prisons are a testament to the fact that criminals aren't always smart."

"This one killed five people that we know of," Nora pointed out. She didn't know what to think. Her head spun as she processed all the information she'd received in a short period of time. She called upon her classes in criminal psychology. "Females rarely use knives to kill."

"But I haven't heard of any other cases where the killer lets their victims bleed to death. Maybe you have. I remember a girlfriend of Sean's in high school who used to cut herself. She had scars all up and down her arms. She never left the house wearing anything but long sleeves."

Maybe . . . maybe Duke was on to something. Nora was well-versed in the psychology of "cutting" behavior. "O'Dell left around Christmas and there were no more BLF attacks. What was she doing during the nine months before she allegedly came back?"

"Good question. When we find out exactly who she is, maybe we'll know."

"So O'Dell leaves, everything is back to normal. She returns . . . why?"

"To finish her revenge."

"Why leave at all? Just because her roommate was having an affair with her professor?"

"Maybe there was another reason we don't know yet."

"She was angry with Anya. Very angry. But it would be easy to manipulate her old anarchist cell into arson, especially when there were animals in jeopardy. So she's mad, throws a tantrum, leaves, returns, everyone is friends again as they plan to 'rescue' the ducks. But Maggie has murder in mind, and gets her boyfriend Scott to help her."

"And genetic testing is Professor Cole's big voodoo doll," Duke said. "It makes the entire situation high-profile."

"But it still doesn't explain why she felt the need for the big show, other than for the platform."

"Maybe we won't know until we find her. Or maybe it was to get you on the case."

Duke stared at her, worry wrinkling his forehead. She understood why he and Dr. Vigo thought that Maggie O'Dell had some personal issue with her, but Nora wasn't quite ready to buy into that idea. It could be, but the woman was on the edge. She could have fixated on Nora simply because she'd put domestic terrorists in prison.

"I want to follow up with Leif Cole, show

him this letter, and see if he has any idea of who Maggie O'Dell is or where she lives. Maybe something came to him overnight." She turned, but Duke didn't follow. "I thought you were my personal bodyguard." She didn't mean for it to sound so snide. She tried to smile, but it wasn't natural.

He tensed. Maybe this was better, she thought. After last night . . . she didn't know what to think. This situation was foreign to her. When she did have a relationship, it was always on her terms, at her pace, and someone not connected to law enforcement. Someone not connected to *her.* She didn't like the intermingling of her personal and professional life.

Maybe that's why it had never worked out with anyone. Nora only *had* a professional life.

"I know what you're doing, Nora."

He stepped toward her. The way he looked at her, with such intensity, made her nervous and jittery. Butterflies fluttered and she remembered how amazing she felt making love to Duke. She didn't want these feelings. She didn't want to care about anyone this much.

Her voice cracked as she said, "I'm not doing anything, Duke. I'm tired, I have a lot of work to do, and I don't like being watched."

"Get used to it."

She bristled. He sounded so confident, as if he had a right to her. Maybe after last night she'd given him that impression. Maybe last night she'd *wanted* him to have that impression. But today, she didn't know anymore. She was confused, upset about Dr. Vigo's analysis, worried about her job, her team, and now a pending relationship. Something had to give.

"Duke, about last night —"

"Don't. I'm not going to believe you."

"You don't know what I'm going to say."

"I do. You're trying to backpedal. You're trying to ignore your feelings so that you can do your job and not think about yourself. I'm here, I'm staying, and you are going to have to address your feelings and think about yourself for a change."

That Duke understood her so well unnerved her, so she steeled herself and snapped, "I can't believe how arrogant you are!"

He smiled, as if he found her anger amusing. "It runs in the Rogan blood."

It was really hard to stay mad at Duke when he revealed that solitary dimple.

"I need space," she pleaded.

"I don't give space."

"But I need it." She was panicking. She'd never been the sole and complete focus of anyone in her life, but the way Duke Rogan's blue eyes pinned her, she seemed to be the *only* thing in his sight.

"I'm sorry," he said without sounding one bit sorry. He caressed her cheek with the back of his hand. She wanted to turn away, this was inappropriate, especially here. But she couldn't. He was a powerful magnet, and she was helplessly drawn to him.

He kissed her lightly, then stepped back. "You do all the thinking you need to do, but in the end, I'm not walking away, no matter how hard you push. Not only are Rogans arrogant, but we're stubborn."

CHAPTER TWENTY

Nora had never seen so much blood at a single-victim crime scene.

Blood coated Leif Cole as if he'd bathed in it. The beige carpet under the chair where he was strapped down was soaked, as blood from multiple shallow wounds from his wrists to his shoulders had dribbled down his arms and onto the floor. The chair was slick with it, where he sat soaked, the brown denim material nearly black where the blood had seeped for more than eight hours, according to the coroner.

Cole was naked. Evidence showed he might have been getting out of the shower when confronted by his attacker. What small areas of skin weren't coated in blood were extremely pale. His wrists had been crudely but efficiently duct-taped to the chair. His feet were unrestrained. How anyone could have incapacitated him without a struggle, Nora didn't know — unless he'd been drugged.

"Any sign of him being drugged?" she asked.

"He had whiskey last night — there's an empty glass in the bathroom that smells of it," Sanger said. "It's bagged into evidence. He told me he wouldn't drink."

"Excuse me?"

Sanger turned his red-rimmed eyes from Cole to her. "I should have stayed."

"You couldn't have known he was a target. Leif Cole doesn't fit —" Then she realized she had no idea why or how the killer was selecting his — or her — victims.

All the evidence pointed to the mysterious Maggie O'Dell. No driver's license, no records, no photo.

Nora and Duke had found Cole's body after Nora couldn't reach him on any phone — house, cell, or the college. She called Sheriff Sanger and confirmed that Cole had gone home the night before, leaving his car at Rose College. At first she wasn't concerned — he could be sleeping late, a common sign of grief. But when he didn't respond to knocking or the doorbell, she'd searched the property and discovered the garage door unlocked.

Cole had given them Maggie's name, but Nora didn't see how Maggie could have found out. Did she fear he would lead them to her? Did Cole know more about Maggie O'Dell than he said last night?

She looked back at Cole, and the wall that separated her cop mind from her emotions faded. She'd known Cole. She'd talked to him just last night. Seeing him like this . . . it was more than a tragedy. Nora wasn't going to forget.

Duke put a hand on the small of her back. Subtly and discreetly, but the simple gesture supported her and helped keep her focus on the crime scene.

There was very little blood spatter on Cole's body, the chair, or the wall, as far as she could tell. Each cut seemed to have been made slowly, carefully — at least four dozen incisions. There was some cast off from the knife on the carpet and the side table, suggesting the killer was right-handed.

Keith Coffey was grim. "I think he bled to death. There's little or no clotting. Someone check his medicine cabinet for warfarin or another anticoagulant. In fact, grab all medicines."

"These cuts look the same as Payne's. Can you run tests on heparin?"

Keith looked at Nora. "I was thinking the same thing, but Payne's body was clean."

"Clean?"

"There wasn't blood like this."

"Would the fire have taken care of that?"

"Not necessarily. And his back would have been stained. There would have been smearing and his unexposed skin — under his arms and back — would have had dried blood. Since he'd been dead for several hours, even brief exposure to water from the fire hose wouldn't have cleaned him so effectively."

"On the surface, it looks too similar to discount a connection to Jonah Payne's death," said Nora. "We're going to assume it is until proven otherwise. I just don't know why."

"A college professor seems an unlikely target for this killer."

Nora said, "Not to Maggie O'Dell."

Duke raised his eyebrow and Sanger was about to speak, but Nora put her hand up. "Bear with me a minute. I might be making a stretch, but if we believe what Cole said yesterday, Anya was calling it quits with BLF. She was highly distraught when she heard about Dr. Payne, and at the time she thought it was an accident. Maggie didn't want them to quit, but she couldn't trust that they'd keep quiet."

"So she poisons them?"

"Convenient. Take out all three witnesses.

Maybe she thought Cole would expose her."

"He did," Sanger pointed out. "Last night."

"He was the only other witness to her involvement in the arsons," Nora said. "A good attorney could block his statements without the ability to cross-examine."

"What if she was angry?" Duke motioned toward the corner of the bedroom where Cole's computer monitor was shattered, a deep gouge in the wall.

"Angry at Cole?" Nora said.

"For talking to us last night?" Sanger asked. "How would she know?"

"Could she have followed him?"

"I would have noticed someone following me," Sanger said defensively.

One of the deputies walked in with a clear bag of evidence. A wet gob of multicolored hairs. "This came from the shower drain and tested positive for blood. Bloody female clothes were found in the bathroom."

"She came prepared," Nora said.

"Why didn't she take the clothes with her?" Sanger asked.

"I think she's deranged," Coffey mumbled.

He might be right. Nora couldn't reconcile the methodical, vicious way Maggie O'Dell had killed her friends and a man Nora doubted she even knew, Jonah Payne. "She's young," Nora said. "Early twenties. Impulsive."

"She's going to be caught."

"Either she doesn't care or she doesn't think we'll find her. She's an anarchist — we know that from BLF activities. She's learned to be sly, sneaky, live off the grid. She was probably raised that way." The similarity to Nora's upbringing was unsettling.

"Why these people? Why now?" Sanger asked.

Nora had been wondering the same thing. "Maggie left for nearly a year, dropped out of college and disappeared, then came back. What was she doing during that time?"

She glanced at Pete. He said, "I know what you want. I'm on it."

"You need her college transcripts. We have to know who she is. Maggie O'Dell isn't popping up anywhere we've looked. If we had an address or financial aid information, *anything* to point us at least to her parents."

Pete was already on the phone with Rachel as he left the crime scene.

Another deputy came in. "We have footprints coming to and from the house, leading across the field. We lost them in the grass meadow, but there's a street only a quarter mile from here. I sent two men to check it out and canvass the neighbors."

There was something else they weren't seeing. Nora glanced at the broken monitor, then at the chair. "She was enraged about something. Look — she stabbed the chair. Not Cole — she has some control — but the chair has three . . . five, six holes."

One of Steve Donovan's ERT, Agent Chow, stepped in. "The killer got in through the garage door. The kitchen door was unlocked, but the garage door leading to the back has a flimsy lock. Someone jimmied it. A novice might take five minutes, an expert five seconds."

"She needed help with Payne because she moved the body, but not with Professor Cole," Nora said. "If he was drugged he might have passed out. Or maybe he wasn't drugged, and just drunk."

Coffey said, "I'll rush the tox screens and alcohol test."

"You're on the right path," Duke said. "Only, there has to be something else in common between Payne and Cole. Another reason they were targeted."

"They did something to Maggie."

"What?" Sanger said, irritated. "You think they did something to her? Like what?"

"Something personal. They probably

didn't even know what. She was slighted, and she made them pay in the only way she knew how."

"But she's so young," Duke said in disbelief.

"They start younger and younger," Nora said. "Duke, do you have the background check on the three kids?"

"It should be done by now," he said.

"Let's go back to headquarters and take a look. There is a common factor between all these victims. We just have to find it."

As they walked out, Duke whispered, "I could find out about Maggie O'Dell faster."

Nora was very tempted. "Let's give Rachel one more hour to get the warrant. I don't want this case thrown out because of a technicality."

Duke stood in front of the driver's door of Nora's car with a concerned expression. "You want to drive?" she asked.

"You said something inside — that maybe Maggie O'Dell grew up off the grid."

"It explains why we're having a hard time getting any information on her. No license, no —"

He interrupted. "You grew up the same way."

Nora shifted uneasily on her feet. "Your point?"

"What if she's targeting you because she sees you as a traitor?"

"Our analysts are going through all my cases, looking for a possible connection. Maybe a relative or friend —"

"She doesn't seem to need much of a reason to kill," Duke said hotly. "It could be as simple as you being raised the 'right' way in her mind — fighting the 'Establishment' — and then doing a complete one-eighty and becoming a cop."

"That was my mother's fight, not mine," Nora snapped. She didn't want to talk about her upbringing here.

"Maggie doesn't know that. She could think that you'd infiltrated the anarchy movement because you had personal knowledge of them and could pass for one, then you had them all arrested. Maybe she's targeting you because of your job, and she doesn't even know you from Adam."

"I'm a hypocrite," Nora said.

"No!" Duke said emphatically. He reached for her, glanced at the cops all over the place, and barely grazed her arm before running his hand over his head. "I didn't mean that, I don't think —"

"Not you, but Maggie. Hypocrite or traitor, they're one and the same to people like her. But you're right about one thing. She

371

is deranged, and if she can set her sites on Dr. Payne, Professor Cole, her best friend, and an FBI agent because of perceived slights against her personally, or a political cause, she can justify killing anyone. We have to find her damn quick or anyone who gets on her bad side is at risk."

They didn't have to wait an hour. Thirty minutes later, Duke and Nora were back at FBI headquarters, and Rachel followed five minutes later, breathless.

"I got Maggie O'Dell's file!"

They brought the surprisingly thin college transcript file to the conference room. Nora opened it.

There was no photograph; there were just admissions records, grades, and a disciplinary report. There was an emergency card.

Margaret Love O'Dell. Nora had to look twice at her middle name, but it was clearly "Love." Her birthplace was Paso Robles, a little town near San Luis Obispo on the central coast.

Nora had lived in SLO during the year before she turned FBI informant against her mother. It was where Lorraine had met Cameron Lovitz. A chill ran through her, as if her life was coming full circle. She hadn't spoken to her mother in nearly twenty years, since the trial. She was in prison, and because a federal agent died during Lorraine's terrorist act, she would be in prison the rest of her life.

Nora rarely thought about it, but these last few days she couldn't avoid it.

Establishment.

It was a word her mother used regularly. Along with *Industrial Complex,* which had sounded so out of place in Maggie's letter. And the questions. *Don't you care?*

"Paso Robles," Duke muttered.

Nora swallowed uneasily. "That mean something to you?"

"Russ lived there for most of his childhood."

One more connection to the area. "Which would give him a good reason to meet with her and not think that something was unusual," Nora said.

She looked back at the forms. "Father, David O'Dell, sixty-four. Mother, April Plummer, fifty-nine."

April Plummer. It had to be a coincidence.

But even as Nora thought that there was *no way in hell* that Maggie O'Dell's mother was the *same* April Plummer that Nora had known most of her childhood, Nora knew that it was.

Paso Robles, so close to where April had

lived for years in SLO. Same age as April would be.

She remembered April at her mother's trial. She wasn't pregnant. She'd always been rail-thin. Nora would have noticed if she were pregnant, the hearings and trial went on for months and months . . . maybe April got pregnant after the trial. Though that would make Maggie a little young for college.

But there had been one pregnant woman at the trial.

"When was she born?" Nora cried out, a bit too loudly. "Dammit, where do they put the birthdays on these stupid forms?" She sounded panicked.

Duke pointed to a box near the top of the form.

December 12. Maggie would be twenty in December.

The timing was right.

Nora dropped the file, a hand to her stomach. She swallowed bile as she realized the unthinkable. This couldn't be, but there wasn't any other explanation.

She shoved the file toward Rachel. "Call the SLO field office and have them send a pair of agents to talk to David O'Dell and April Plummer about Maggie. And find out where her sister is — the one she mentioned in the letter she wrote to Anya Ballard."

Rachel took it, looking at Nora as if her head was about to spin around. "Anything else?'

"Just that. For now."

With Rachel gone, she breathed marginally easier.

What if she was wrong? They could be going down the wrong path. They could be wasting time. Only, she didn't think she was wrong. She *knew* she wasn't wrong.

Her mother had lied. Lying sounded exactly like something her mother would do.

Nora hated Lorraine. She squeezed her eyes shut, willing away the waves of pain and anger that washed over her like the ocean hitting rocks during a storm.

For seventeen years Nora had lived without a home, without a place to belong. For seventeen years Nora had tried to understand her mother, had wanted to please her, had done things she knew were wrong but didn't know how to say no to the woman who'd raised her.

Until Quin was in trouble; then Nora turned. When it was Quin in danger, Nora put herself on the line. And Lorraine went to prison. But that didn't make the pain go away. It took years before Nora was able to truly make her own path. Quin never understood why Nora refused to let her visit Lorraine in prison, why Nora didn't visit her. They'd often argued about it, but Nora had always won.

Nora was determined that Quin would not be corrupted by their pathological liar mother.

Duke put his hands on her shoulders and made her look at him. "Nora, what's going on?"

She took a deep breath and the truth spilled out. "When my mother went to trial, she asked for leniency because she was pregnant. I didn't even know until the pretrial motions, but it was confirmed — she was five months pregnant by that time. She had the baby right before the trial, in December, and the judge told me that the baby was put up for adoption.

"I didn't want anything to do with it. I didn't want to see it, I didn't want to feel any connection to the baby. I asked for no details, because as long as my mother didn't raise the baby, he'd have a decent life."

"He?"

She shrugged. "I didn't know if the baby was a boy or girl. I didn't ask. I never told Quin because there was no reason to. She didn't have to testify at the trial, why should she be dragged into everything? She was a little kid. I didn't want that for her. I didn't want her to live with the pain and guilt I did for so many years."

Nora didn't realize tears were running down her face. She was so angry — furious! — and emotionally wrung-out. Remembering the trial, what she said on the stand, the way her mother had looked at her. As if she'd cut her heart out. Betrayed her.

"April Plummer was a friend of my mom's. Single then, as far as I knew. April was truly a flower child. She took way too many drugs in her youth and ended up kind of simple, but very sweet. We lived with her for a while — a few weeks here, a month or two there. I always thought my mother used her, manipulated her. April would do anything you wanted her to, especially for my mom."

"And you think that this April adopted your mother's child?"

Nora nodded, wiping away the tears. She took a deep breath. She had to do this. She had to face the truth. "Fifty-nine — I don't know how old she was, but my mother is fifty-seven. When Dr. Vigo said that the killer was pulling out only my old cases, those were cases my mother might have known about. At least the first two. I was an informant at Diablo Canyon. That's where her boyfriend was killed, where she was arrested." Her boyfriend, Cameron Lovitz. The father of Lorraine's child, the father of Nora's half sister.

The father of Maggie O'Dell. And he was a psychopath, just like her.

"The second case she mentioned in the letter I worked as an informant against Lorraine's friends. They were planning to set oil wells in Kern County on fire."

Nora looked at Duke. "That was twenty years ago. Maggie O'Dell is nearly twenty now. April came to my mother's hearings, I saw her several times, and I never saw her pregnant."

"It should be easy enough to find out," Duke said.

"I know I'm right."

"We need confirmation."

Duke was right, they had to confirm the facts, but Nora knew in her heart and soul that Maggie was the daughter of Lorraine and Cameron. Her life was being ripped apart and trampled. She'd have to tell Quin, and that hurt just as much. But the truth would get out as soon as Maggie O'Dell was caught, and Nora didn't want Quin hearing about it from anyone but her.

Nora would find Maggie O'Dell and stop her.

"My past — it's coming back. I thought it was over, but now —" She didn't finish. What could she say? "I'm sorry."

Duke grabbed her by the arms and gave her a firm shake. "You had nothing to do with this. Nothing! Don't even think for a minute that just because you share blood with someone that it means you're guilty."

He pulled her into a tight hug. She accepted his embrace, needed it. Needed him.

"You call your contacts, I'll call mine," Duke said, talking over her head. "We're going to get to the bottom of this, Nora. I promise."

CHAPTER
TWENTY-ONE

Once again, having Dean Hooper as her ASAC ratcheted up everyone's response time to Nora's requests. Warden Jeff Greene called her less than ten minutes after she had explained the situation to her boss.

"How can I help, Agent English?" the Warden asked.

"You have a female prisoner, a lifer, Lorraine Wright. She was convicted of domestic terrorism which resulted in the death of a federal agent."

"Assistant Director Hooper filled me in on the basics."

Assistant Director? She didn't correct the warden. "I need to know if Maggie or Margaret O'Dell has visited Wright in the last two years, or perhaps even before that. Do you have that information?"

"All prisoner visits are logged into the computer. We go back fifteen years electronically. Anything older than that is on hard copy."

"Going back fifteen years should be fine."

"I can fax you the list of Wright's visitors, if you'd like."

"Thank you." She gave him her fax number. "Is it possible you could tell me right now if O'Dell was a visitor?"

"Yes, she's been visiting monthly as far back as we have. She's listed as next of kin. You know that O'Dell is Ms. Wright's daughter?"

Though Nora had thought as much, the confirmation still took the wind out of her. "Yes," she said, her voice low. "When was O'Dell's last visit?"

"September ninth."

Less than three weeks ago.

"Thank you. I'll wait for the fax."

"Agent Hooper said that this may involve a federal crime?"

"O'Dell is wanted for questioning in an act of domestic terrorism that resulted in a death." Nora didn't feel a need to share all the details.

"I'll flag her name," he said. "If she shows up to visit her mother, I'll detain her."

"I appreciate it. Thanks, Warden."

She hung up. Duke asked, "And?"

"She's a regular visitor. Her daughter."

Before she could say anything else, Hooper

walked in with a fax. At first, she was amazed at Warden Greene's speedy response; then she saw the fax wasn't from Victorville.

"What's this?"

"A copy of Margaret O'Dell's adoption records. It was an open adoption; the files aren't sealed. Under the terms, the adoptees, David O'Dell and April Plummer, agreed to bring the child to visit Lorraine Wright at least one day each month until her eighteenth birthday."

Nora skimmed through the documents. They confirmed Hooper's summary. She saw who'd signed the documents. "This isn't the judge for her trial. He told me she gave the baby up for adoption."

Duke leaned over and looked at the name. He typed it into his laptop computer. A moment later he said, "Newman is a family court judge."

"But don't they talk to each other?"

Hooper said, "Family court would be county. Wright was tried in federal court. They're not in the same building, and rarely have cause to interact."

"Why didn't they tell me? I assumed they wouldn't let that woman anywhere near a child, after —" Nora cut herself off. The system always tried to keep children with their parents, even criminals. She just didn't know that twenty years ago.

Duke asked gently, "Nora, what would you have done about it had you known? Tried to get custody? A seventeen-year-old without a high school diploma or job?"

Nora looked at Duke, stunned that he would throw that out at her. It didn't matter that it was true — she'd never have gotten custody in those circumstances — but it hurt that he'd publicly brought out something she'd told him in private.

"I would have petitioned the court to deny the open adoption," she said. "Obviously, Lorraine isn't fit to be an influence on a child. Look at how Maggie turned out."

"You don't know that Lorraine —"

"You don't know her, you didn't grow up with her." She jumped up and paced. She was humiliated in front of her boss, embarrassed at her outburst, distraught over what she'd just learned.

Hooper changed the subject. "There's more. Donovan's team can't locate Scott Edwards's truck. We're operating under the assumption that O'Dell has possession of it and have put out an APB on both the vehicle and O'Dell."

He stood and walked to the door. "I'd tell you to take the rest of the day off, but you won't, so I'll just admonish you to be alert and let me know if you need additional assistance."

"I appreciate it," she said, and meant it.

Hooper walked out, and Duke said, "I didn't mean to hurt your feelings, Nora."

"You used my past against me."

"I didn't."

"That's not how it sounded."

He stood and walked across the room to her. "You would have seen the truth if you weren't so upset. You were lied to, and that hurts. But you couldn't have changed it then, and you can't change the past now. All you can do is focus on finding the girl."

"She's my sister." Nora could barely get out the words.

"You want Hooper to assign someone else?"

She shook her head. "He probably should. I'm too close to this."

"That's your greatest asset as well as your greatest weakness. You understand how Lorraine thinks, and therefore you understand how Maggie O'Dell thinks. No one else has those instincts. But you can't think of Maggie O'Dell as your sister. She's nothing like you."

"She doesn't think like Lorraine," Nora said. "She thinks like her father. Cameron

Lovitz. He was a psychopath — methodical and organized."

Emboldened, getting a sense of Maggie O'Dell, the killer, Nora continued. "She's different. She likely has his charisma in order to convince people to help her, but she has less control of her temper. She's both organized and disorganized. She's ruthless. And it's all personal."

Nora paced, putting herself in Maggie's shoes. What would it be like growing up knowing your mother was in prison for trying to blow up a nuclear reactor? Visiting her every month. Hearing the stories about saving these animals and those trees and stopping a developer from building on a pristine meadow practically single-handed. And the exaggerations . . .

The stories.

"Lorraine romanticized everything, exaggerated the good and the bad," Nora said. "We'd be involved in some demonstration and she'd be pushed by a cop. That night the story turned into she was beaten with a billy club and she was lucky to be alive. Or if she freed research animals, it was fifty and she found homes for all of them, rather than twenty animals she'd released into the wild. All bait for larger predators."

And Cameron. Nora remembered exactly

what Lorraine said on the stand.

"Cameron didn't have a gun. He despised guns, just like I did. Nora brought it with her, and Cameron took it."

A flat-out lie, but Lorraine likely believed it because she wanted to. She was a pathological liar, which had been proven during her trial. What had Lorraine told Maggie about her father? About what they'd done and how they'd lived? What had their mother said about Nora?

"You think that Lorraine convinced Maggie that before the arrest, your family had an idyllic life?"

Nora nodded. "And I stole that life from her. That's why Maggie wrote that letter highlighting the cases where I was undercover. I had 'betrayed' the cause and the good people who'd trusted me. That's also why Maggie killed her cohorts. Because they betrayed her. They wanted out, and she wouldn't let them go. Couldn't. If they didn't do what she wanted, they deserved to die."

"And what about Professor Cole?"

"He had turned Anya against her. Anya turned the others. Or at least Chris. Scott Edwards, I'm not so sure. Maybe Maggie felt if she killed the other two she had to kill him as well. Or he did something that irritated her." She squeezed her temples.

"Headache?" He crossed the room and massaged the sides of her head.

His fingers felt incredible and she relaxed. "I'm out of my area of expertise here. I don't understand psychopathic killers any more than I understand —" She searched her brain. "— how to launder money. Hooper gave us all a crash course when he got here, but I was completely lost."

"You understand more than you think."

Duke kissed her temple as if his lips could cure her pain. Maybe, with a little time and privacy, they could. Nora leaned into him, giving in to his affection just for a moment.

A rap on the conference room door had Nora jumping a foot away from Duke, blushing to the roots of her hair. The receptionist walked in without waiting for an invite and handed Nora a thick stack of paper. She mumbled a thanks and looked at the information to hide her embarrassment as the woman left. But Nora pushed her personal thoughts aside: The fax was from Victorville Federal Penitentiary.

Each page had one line entry per visit. The name, date, relationship, time entering and time ending. The print was small and there were fifty or so entries per page.

April Plummer and Margaret O'Dell.

Over and over. Occasionally another name Nora recognized, a few she didn't. Theresa Lovitz visited five or six times in the first two years. Nora didn't know who she was, but she was likely related to Cameron. A few other people visited Lorraine in the early years: Glenda Chastain. Mina Ro. Roger Nelson. As time passed, the visits from revolutionaries diminished. April still came by, sometimes with David O'Dell. And always Maggie. By the time Maggie was ten, she was visiting on her own, sometimes more than once a month. Maggie, Maggie, Maggie . . .

Quin Teagan. Daughter.

Nora had to go back and look again. She couldn't be reading the logs right.

Quin Teagan. Daughter.

Nora flipped rapidly through the pages in disbelief. She went back, counted. Counted again. Twenty-three visits in the last eleven years. Twice a year Quin visited Lorraine. The first time the month she turned eighteen.

Nora wanted to believe it was a mistake. But of course it wasn't. It was here in black and white. Quin had lied to Nora. She'd been seeing their mother all these years and had never said anything.

"Hey, what's wrong?" Duke asked, looking over her shoulder.

"Quin," she mumbled. She shoved the papers at him, hitting the stack with her fist as he took them. Nora was shaking, her knuckles white. "My sister. All these years. Going down there to see *her*."

"You mean Lorraine?" He put the papers down. "You didn't know?"

"Damn straight I didn't know! I told her never to talk to her."

Duke didn't say anything, and Nora whirled around, willing herself to stop shaking. She didn't know if she was more angry or scared. Duke looked closely at her, uncertainty in his eyes. He still didn't say anything. "What?" she snapped. "Why are you looking at me like that?"

"You told Quin not to have contact with her mother."

"*Mother?* That's rich. What *mother* has her nine-year-old daughter making bombs? What *mother* has her daughters playing decoy on the docks of San Francisco at midnight while she and her *friends* spray-paint graffiti on the storefront of a furrier? What *mother* tells her daughters to throw red paint on women wearing fur coats?"

"Nora — Quin was nine when Lorraine went to prison."

"What difference does that make?"

389

"She wasn't old enough to understand."

"Cameron left her alone in the middle of nowhere at night and my mother went along with it. Quin was always terrified of the dark." Duke didn't understand. Maybe he never could. Suddenly, Nora was alone again. Deeply, irrevocably, alone. She'd been lonely most of her life, and she knew better than to think that would ever change.

She turned away from Duke. She had to protect her sister. Quin was all she had. "I need to talk to her."

"Nora, you're not in this alone. I told you earlier — I'm not walking away."

Duke tried to pull Nora to him, to hold her, just for a minute, to prove to her that he meant what he said. She pulled away, took several steps back. From the look on her face, she didn't believe him. Righteous anger began to creep up within him, but dissipated when Duke realized that Nora was scared. She'd taken so very long to let him inside, even just a little, because she was terrified. She'd been alone for thirty-seven years, practically since she was born, raising herself and then Quin and never having anyone to count on.

She'd even said that the FBI agent who'd been her handler had lied to her. That must have hurt her almost as much as her mother's selfish behavior. Maybe more, because she must have deeply trusted him in order to be his informant.

Duke watched Nora storm out of the room. His heart twisted with her pain. But there was no way he was letting her leave alone. He followed.

She needed him, whether she acknowledged it or not.

Maggie sat at the bus stop and ate an apple as she watched Quin leave her downtown Sacramento office building and walk down the street with three people from the state fire inspector's office. Even if Quin happened to glance her way, she wouldn't recognize Maggie. She'd put her long hair up in a baseball cap and wore sunglasses. Hardly incognito, but the disguise didn't stand out. The sun was bright and a lot of people wore sunglasses and caps.

She tossed the apple core into the trash can chained to the bench and followed her sister with her eyes until Quin turned the corner and disappeared from sight.

If it wasn't for Nora English, Quin would have been her sister. Her full sister. They would have grown up together, been best friends, done everything together. Inseparable.

Eleven years ago, April brought Maggie to visit her mother. At the prison, Maggie told April to leave them alone. She didn't like her listening in on her private conversations with her real mother. April was dumb as a doornail and always said such stupid things.

April was happy to leave. Said she'd be back when the hour was up.

Mother and daughter met in the recreation room. It was where the female prisoners with good behavior could meet with their children. Sometimes, when Lorraine was in trouble, Maggie had to go to a small room with a table and hard chairs and a mean guard glaring at her through the window. Maggie hated that. She hated being in a box with no windows and no sun. At least in the rec room there were windows that opened — even though there were bars on them — and lots of light.

They sat on a stiff couch with rough fabric. Her mom was happy today. She said, "Guess who visited me last week?"

Maggie frowned. Why was someone else visiting HER mother? She pouted.

"Don't be sad, Maggie." Lorraine beamed. "You should be happy like me! Quin came to see me! And she's coming back, she promised. I can't wait for you to meet her."

A sliver of jealousy cut through Maggie. Her mother talked about Quin all the time, how she was stolen from her. Did her mom love Quin more? Why did it take so long for Quin to visit? She was a bad daughter. When Maggie didn't want to come one day last year because Lorraine had made her mad, the next visit Lorraine told her she was a bad daughter for missing their scheduled visit.

"Why? She's never been here before."

Lorraine scowled. "Nora kept her from me. All these years, I thought Quin didn't want to see me. But it was Nora all along. She wouldn't let her come. Quin turned eighteen and came right away to visit. And she's coming back."

Maggie knew who Nora was. Nora had killed her father. Maggie hated her. If Nora hadn't betrayed her own mother, Maggie would now have a real family. Not the stupid April and the sickly sweet David. She called them her stepparents. She didn't like them, but she'd figured out how to do pretty much anything she wanted.

"Why so sad?" Lorraine asked.

"Do you still love me? Even though Quin came back?"

"I'll always love you the best. You never left me. You're a good girl."

Maggie smiled. "I want a sister."

"Quin is lovely. She'll like you. Someday you can meet her."

"When?"

"She has to be very careful. Quin said Nora would be furious if she found out, and I don't want her to find a way to stop the visits. She's an FBI agent now. She can probably stop me from having any visitors."

Maggie's stomach felt sick. Lorraine was the only person she could really talk to. Her mom was the only person who talked to Maggie about her father, about all the incredible things he had done to save the earth, to save animals, to change things.

And Nora had killed him. She had sent their mother to prison, and had stolen Quin away.

"I hate Nora." Inside, Maggie felt her emotions raging.

"Don't say that. Hate is a negative emotion. It turns us inside out and we make mistakes. Nora doesn't know better. I don't know what I did wrong, I don't know why she set your father up to be killed by the police. They must have lied to her, brainwashed her. She's even so misguided she's become part of the Establishment. But not Quin. Quin still has me in her heart, and I know we'll be great friends, the three of us."

Maggie wasn't so sure. But her mother was happy, and Maggie liked it when her mother was happy.

Maggie frowned as she stared at Quin's

office building. Quin had gone off with friends to lunch. Laughing, living a normal life with a normal job, Maggie's sister never called her anymore. The last time Maggie had seen her was two years ago, when Maggie had decided to go to Rose College. Maggie had shown up at Quin's town house to surprise her. Quin wasn't happy. She said that Maggie and Lorraine were another part of her life, separate from her job and friends here in Sacramento.

Maggie had hated her then, had very much wanted to hurt her. But then Quin had apologized, said she was sorry, but Nora couldn't know.

Nora stood in Maggie's way.

She'd *always* been in Maggie's way. Basically, from Day One, Nora had ruined her life. After killing her father, imprisoning her mother, and stealing her sister, Nora became one of *them,* the Establishment. Maggie had learned a lot about Nora English, and was determined to find the very best way to make her pay. To make her suffer. To hurt her more than she'd hurt Maggie. She could kill her the way she'd killed Scott and the others; she could kill Nora the same way. Watch her get sick and fall over paralyzed and in pain and lie there for hours suffering until she croaked.

But then she'd be dead and out of pain. There had to be something worse than death, and Maggie had spent months figuring out what that was.

Now she knew.

She rose from the bench and walked down Eleventh Street until she hit O Street, then turned west. She'd been to Quin's town house before. Quin was now at lunch. Maggie would break in and make herself at home while waiting for her sister.

Nora would kill Quin. It would be her fault. And how she would suffer! She'd feel so guilty. So angry. Full of revenge. And then, Maggie could make her suffer even more. Push in the knife and twist, twist, twist it.

Nora would pay with her own life for killing Maggie's father. But not until she was emotionally and physically devastated.

CHAPTER
TWENTY-TWO

"She's at lunch!" Nora got in the passenger seat and slammed the car door shut.

"It *is* twelve-thirty," Duke said.

"I can't tell her in front of her friends and colleagues. But I have to warn her. And try to figure out why she lied to me."

"Email her, ask her to come by Rogan-Caruso right after lunch. We'll wait for her."

"I have to get back to headquarters. I should have called her first, I was just so mad I thought she'd hear it in my voice."

"You can work from my office for an hour. Make your calls, I'll help go through the background information with a fresh set of eyes, see if we missed anything. Any connection between Maggie and Jonah, Maggie and Russ, anything. And Jayne, my computer expert, said she wanted me to look at something in the video files."

"I thought you were the computer expert."

"I'm the security expert," Duke said with

a half smile as he pulled onto the street. "I break into computers and security systems. Jayne works on keeping me, and people like me, from doing that."

By the time they arrived at the sleek office building where Rogan-Caruso occupied the eighteenth floor, Quin had emailed Nora back. "She said she'd be here in forty-five minutes. Wants to know why."

Duke offered an oblique response for her. "It's about the case, isn't it?"

"Gotcha." She typed a vague message to Quin into her BlackBerry.

Duke was worried about Nora and how she was going to handle Quin. He kept thinking about Sean and how close he'd been to chasing him away — away to Kane and far more dangerous situations than he'd face working here at Rogan-Caruso.

They went up to his office, and Nora admired the layout. "Wow. This is really nice."

"Thanks." He glanced at his email. "Jayne's with a client, but she'll buzz me when she's done."

Nora stood looking out the window, but Duke doubted she saw the downtown view, particularly impressive on this sunny day.

"I warned her," she said. "I told her Lorraine was a pathological liar, she couldn't believe her, and she'd make Quin crazy and confused. I thought she understood. I mean, it wasn't always easy with the two of us, but it's better now. Quin has a great job, we don't argue much, we're friends. Maybe — maybe I could understand why she wanted to see her again. But to continue to visit? A couple times a year? I just don't get it."

"She was young when all that happened. She didn't have your experience. Nora, you practically raised yourself. You took responsibility for a young girl, not just after Lorraine went to prison, but before that. You raised Quin more than your mother."

Nora spun around and faced Duke. "Then why didn't she listen to me? Why didn't she do what I said? Why did she have to lie to me?"

Nora didn't have a traditional upbringing. She didn't understand how teenagers rebelled and did what they wanted. Duke said, "I had a great relationship with my parents, but I didn't do everything they told me to. I did what I wanted."

"But this was serious — not sneaking out of the house to go joyriding."

Duke ignored her sarcasm and said, "My father told me not to work for Kane, my brother. Told me I wasn't ready, and he didn't know if I ever would be. I took that to mean I wasn't good enough, or at least as good as Kane. I resented my dad for saying it, and went and joined Kane's mercenary group. I had been a United States Marine, I could do anything. I said that to him, too.

"I knew third day in that I was in over my head. I could do the physical work, no problem. Even emotionally, until I left, I could handle any situation. I became the unit's go-to guy for fixing the unfixable. But it was the seriousness of the day-to-day job. There was no downtime. Downtime was relaxing in the jungle where you never really relaxed because someone could be sneaking up on you. Your senses always on overdrive. I was miserable. I could do it, but I wasn't happy doing it. And Dad knew that. But it was something I had to find out myself."

Nora rubbed her temples and sat down on a chair at the large round table in the corner. "I appreciate that, and I understand where you're coming from, but you got out of the bad situation. You learned your lesson and moved on. Why is Quin *still* seeing her? What lies is Lorraine feeding her?"

"Maybe Quin just wants to see her mother. Maybe she feels sorry for her. Maybe she doesn't want her to be so alone.

Lorraine's locked away for the rest of her life. Quin has a lot of compassion, just like you."

"I have no compassion when it comes to Lorraine."

"That's fine. But Quin's in a different place and she doesn't recall the bad times like you do. I risked alienating my brother Sean. You raised Quin most of your life — I got Sean when I was twenty-seven. He was nearly fourteen. Yet I tried to protect him from my mistakes. It wasn't until he threatened to work for Kane — and I said, 'Fuck no' — that I realized it didn't matter what I said, Sean was over eighteen and he could do whatever he wanted. He could work for Kane and learn what I did, or maybe be able to stomach that life. I only thought he'd be killed. But I shouldn't have said anything, and let him go. Kane would never take him on, Sean has no military background, and while he's smart as hell — his I.Q. higher than even mine — he doesn't have the experience."

He grinned, hoping to get Nora to lighten up a bit. While she did relax a fraction, he couldn't get her to smile.

"Cut her some slack, okay?"

Nora said, "I will."

Duke wasn't sure of that, but he gave

Nora the benefit of the doubt. "Quin will be here in a few minutes. Eat —" He gestured to the sandwich he'd picked up for her downstairs in the lobby. "I'm going to check on Jayne and let Reception know to send Quin back here. I'll give you two some privacy. Just — think about what I said, okay?"

"Thanks, Duke. I'm going to make some calls, follow up with the agents talking to David O'Dell, keep myself busy."

"Good." He leaned over, put his palms on the table behind Nora, and trapped her between his arms. He kissed her lightly on the lips. "You might be noticing that I'm giving you space."

Now she smiled. "I thought Rogans don't give space."

"Maybe just a little now and then."

Maggie walked through Quin's entire town house. Nice, a little boring. Everything in earth tones, subtle. Quin was so funny and talkative, her town house seemed sedate compared to her effusive personality. She didn't believe in keeping stuff around. But there were pictures on the walls, pictures of Quin and Nora, Quin and a variety of boyfriends. At the fair, at the circus, on vacation in Hawaii. Quin, Quin, Quin.

Where was Maggie? Where were the snap-shots of Quin and Maggie?

Maggie took an old picture off of Quin's dresser. Quin was about seven, and Lorraine was in the picture. So was Nora. They were all holding signs. Lorraine's read: "Meat is Murder." Quin's was, "I don't eat anything with a face." Nora's message was partly cut out of the picture, tilted at an angle. "Stop" was the only word Maggie could make out.

Quin and Lorraine were smiling, Lor-raine's arm around her. Nora had space between them, neither smiling nor frown-ing. Just staring blankly at the camera.

Maggie realized that this was Nora's problem — already so sour and depressing. She was clearly jealous of Lorraine and Quin. Is that why Nora betrayed them? Because she didn't fit in? Didn't want another baby around who fit in with the family when Nora didn't?

"You fucking bitch!"

She flung the picture across the room. It shattered on the wall, bits of glass raining onto the carpet.

"I hate you!" She went through the town house and found every picture of Nora she could and destroyed them. She shredded them, stabbed them, and with one she put it in the sink and poured bleach over it until

403

the colors faded, then disappeared.

She'd make Nora disappear.

"I. Hate. You!"

The rage was so great inside that Maggie felt as if she was going to burst. She hadn't felt so out of control in a long time. She'd let her temper get the better of her a couple times when she killed Payne and then Professor Cole, but that was just a little. This was a building rage.

Stop. You'll make a mistake. You must not make a mistake.

Grabbing her backpack, Maggie ran upstairs to Quin's bedroom. She sat on the bed. With trembling hands, she pulled out her knife and placed it on her arm.

Control. Control. Control.

If she couldn't get her rage back, she'd die, and that was okay. Sometimes she wanted so much to be dead.

But then Nora would win.

She breathed deeply. The disturbing thought that she'd lose to that bitch calmed her.

Deep breaths. The sharp pain in her arm put everything in focus. Good. Calm. Breathe.

When she opened her eyes she saw all the blood. One . . . four . . . seven cuts. Quin would be angry. The blood had soaked into her carpet as well as the bed with its pretty white comforter.

A bit light-headed, Maggie stood and went to the bathroom. She put the knife down and cleaned her arm. Each mark was a perfect one inch apart, just deep enough to draw blood. Perfect in every way. She stared at the incisions, pleased with her control.

She was ready now. She could battle her evil sister and win.

Nora hung up with the agents in Paso Robles. David O'Dell had refused to let them in his house, said he didn't know where Maggie was, and that even if he did know he wouldn't tell them. No threats worked, and the federal agents left empty-handed. They were trying the high school next, to talk to Maggie's former teachers and principal and get a fuller picture if possible.

Pete called and Nora was glad for more work so she didn't have time to think about Quin. Who was late.

"Hi, Pete, what's going on?"

"Good news, I think. I'm at Butcher-Payne with Jim Butcher, and I think I may have found a connection with Jonah Payne."

"Dr. Payne and Maggie?"

"Payne and Cameron Lovitz."

405

Nora froze. The man was coming back to haunt her. She'd never forget the look in his eyes when he was pounding her head into the cement. He'd wanted to kill her. She'd thought she would die.

"And?" she managed to get out.

"Payne did a semester at Cal Poly SLO during grad school. His professor in neurobiology was Timothy Guttenburg. Guttenburg's research assistant was Cameron Lovitz."

It was a connection, but it didn't necessarily mean anything. "And?"

"That's all I have."

"Is Guttenburg still around?"

"I haven't called yet, I wanted to tell you —"

"Call, dammit." She squeezed her eyes closed. "Sorry. I'm testy today. Just call, talk to him if you can, or anyone who knew him and Lovitz. Find out why Lovitz's daughter would want to kill Dr. Payne, if you can."

"Will do."

Nora realized she hadn't told Pete about the connection with Lovitz. "Pete, how did you find out about Lovitz? I didn't know about Maggie O'Dell's connections until after you left."

"Hooper called. I know it's sensitive, I'm being discreet. I'm sorry, Nora. I know this

406

is tough for you."

"Thanks," she mumbled, and hung up. She should have called Pete herself and filled him in. She hadn't even thought of it.

The door opened and she hoped it was Duke. She needed — what did she need? She didn't know. She just wanted to see him. To help her prepare for the rest of today.

"You summoned me?" Quin bounced into the room and closed the door. "Nice digs. Subtle and sexy, just like the hunk who works here."

Nora couldn't reconcile the Quin she knew and loved with the Quin who'd been deceiving her for years. She said, "I have something to tell you."

"That's why I'm here!"

Nora didn't know how to tell Quin about Lorraine's baby, but she was angry about her sister's deception so she spilled everything.

"Our mother was pregnant when she was arrested. I never told you because from the beginning, the judge told her if convicted, she would need to put the baby up for adoption if there were no relatives who wanted it. And I didn't. I didn't even know how I was going to take care of you." Nora took a deep breath. She almost wished Quin would say something, but she just stared blankly, watching. Quin hadn't gone to the trial. She'd seen Lorraine once after the arrest, and once after the conviction ten months later. After the baby was born and adopted. Quin had never seen Lorraine pregnant.

"I know this is a shock, and I would never tell you about it except there's a serious situation you do need to know about. The baby, a girl, was adopted by April Plummer, Lorraine's closest friend. It was an open adoption with visitation rights. That girl is Maggie O'Dell."

Quin stared at her and shrugged. "I know."

CHAPTER
TWENTY-THREE

Comprehension slowly hit Nora as she rose from the chair. "You know? You know what?"

Quin stood in the middle of Duke's office, arms crossed over her chest. Defiant. Just like she'd been as a little girl. Stubborn. When Nora put her foot down, Quin would stand just like this and challenge her.

"I know about my sister." Her chin jutted out.

"Did Lorraine tell you?" Nora's voice shook. The anger and frustration and failure she'd felt for the last two hours boiled over. "When you went to visit her?"

Quin squinted, though she couldn't hide her surprise. "Yes."

"I can't *believe* you went to see Lorraine without talking to me first!"

"You never let me visit her! My own mother. I begged you, and you kept saying no."

"You were a child. Lorraine is a pathological liar who's in prison for terrorism and murder. You didn't need her warped influence."

"Nice of you to be my protector. The last time I asked, I was sixteen. You still said no, and that was it. End of story. The Great Almighty has spoken. So, yeah, I waited until I was eighteen so I could see her without your damn permission."

Nora remembered what Duke had said about Quin not having the same experiences with Lorraine as she had. She was trying to understand, but the years of living homeless, living off others, never having a home, never going to school, no friends . . . she wanted none of that for Quin. Didn't Quin remember how hard it had been? Didn't she remember the times they'd been left alone? When she was three and Nora was twelve and Lorraine disappeared for two weeks? They lived in a tent, and Nora hid them from the cops because she feared they'd take Quin away from her, put them in a government institution where they would never see the sun, where they would live like slaves.

That's what Lorraine had always told Nora. And some of it was true. If they had been found, the government would have

410

split them up. They might have lived in a virtual prison. Or foster care. Would that have been better?

There were too many times when Nora had learned the hard way. And damn if Quin was going to live through the same.

"I'm trying to understand," Nora said, biting back her frustration. "Visiting Lorraine once, maybe I can understand. But you went back. Twenty-three times you went back, most recently in *June.* The week you told me you were going to L.A. with your boyfriend of the month."

"I did. We just made a stop first."

"Why? I spent my life protecting you from her!"

"Maybe you didn't need to."

Nora stared at her sister in disbelief. It was like she was seeing Quin for the first time. Had she messed up that badly? Had she missed all the signs? Had Quin been brainwashed by that woman?

Quin said, "Lorraine made mistakes, I know that. I'm not saying she shouldn't be in prison, but she never hurt us."

"She had us making bombs."

"Just the components —"

"How can you talk like that? You were mixing and measuring black powder from the time you were seven! It was your damn math lesson! And when Cameron held you off that freeway overpass so you could hang his stupid fucking banner, I wanted to kill him."

"Well, in a way you did."

Nora's mouth opened, then closed. Quin damn well knew what had happened. She knew the truth about that night. "They were going to plant bombs at a nuclear power plant."

"Don't be so naive. You know as well as I do that the security at those places is so tight no one was going to get in."

"They did get in! They got through the gate. They'd never have succeeded in their plan, but they got in on their own. Someone could have been killed. A security guard, an engineer, an innocent person so Cameron and Lorraine could make a damn political statement!"

Quin shuffled her feet, glanced down. She *knew* Nora was right, why couldn't she just admit it? Where was all this animosity coming from? These last few years they'd gotten along so well. They had the relationship Nora always wanted for them. Quin never talked about what happened then, and Nora sure as hell didn't bring it up. But this defense of Lorraine? Nora was livid.

"I'm not saying they were right," Quin

412

said, "but they didn't intend to hurt anyone. You set them up. You got him killed."

"He was trying to *kill me*. The bombs Lorraine and Kenny threw killed a federal agent. Lovitz was a psycho, just like his daughter!"

Quin stared at her. "What are you talking about?"

"Maggie O'Dell." Nora paused. She breathed deeply and told Quin the rest. "That's why I wanted to see you, so I could —"

Quin threw her hands up in the air, then ran them through her hair, her face tight. "You are a piece of work. You have lied to me my entire life and you think you can just start ranting about Maggie? You don't even know her!"

Nora froze. "I've never lied to you."

"Let me count the ways. You lied to me about Mom having a baby. You wouldn't let me go to the trial so I wouldn't know about the baby."

"I was protecting you. It was awful. I wished I didn't have to be there. I hated it."

"Oh, poor Nora English, long-suffering. Get over yourself. So we didn't have the perfect life. Lying to me was okay?"

"I thought she gave the baby up for adoption. You didn't need to know."

"Why not?"

"You were a little kid. Lorraine is a pathological liar."

"You keep saying that, but you're the one who lied to me about my father!"

Nora blinked rapidly. "What?"

"Yes! His name was Randall Teagan. Sure, it wasn't a big romantic affair, but she told me all about him. How smart he was, how kind, how much he cared about the earth. She didn't know she was pregnant, and when she found out, he had moved out of state for a job. She didn't want to saddle him with a couple kids, so she took care of us herself. It's not easy being a single mom. She did the best she could."

"She lied."

Quin pointed her finger at Nora. "No, you lied! I looked him up. I found him living in Denver. I went to see him." Quin's eyes were glassy. Nora had always known that Quin had a hard time about her father, not knowing who he was or why he wasn't around, but she thought that time and maturity had helped. "I watched. He has a beautiful wife, two beautiful children, a nice house . . . I couldn't tell him the truth. I didn't want to hurt him."

She sounded so forlorn. "Oh, Quin, honey

—" Nora tried to hug her, but Quin pulled away.

"You could have told me. Maybe if I'd gone to him when I was nine, I could have had a father. You took that away from me. My mother, and my father."

Nora felt gut-punched. "I did *not*. Lorraine doesn't know who your father is."

"His name is on my birth certificate!"

"She lied! She met Randall Teagan at a rally two years before you were conceived! She never had sex with him. When you were born, she picked his name because she thought it sounded good with 'Quin.' "

"No. That's *not* what happened!"

Quin was calling *her* the liar? She'd lived through it. She'd lived with the guilt of her mother's deceit. "Let's see, when she was pregnant, she went to a bunch of guys and got abortion money. She didn't have the abortion, but it kept us fed for a long time, whatever she didn't spend on her political causes. Then after you were born, for nearly two years, she went to every guy she remembered having sex with, roughly figured out when, told them you were whatever age fit, and blackmailed them into paying her money so she didn't tell their wife or girlfriend or go after them for child support. We had more money during that time

415

than all the years I remembered combined. Until one of the guys wanted to share custody. He'd become a born-again Christian and wanted to be responsible and take care of you and make sure you went to college. He offered to marry her and adopt me. And you know what? Even though I knew she was lying through her teeth, I wanted him to take us in. He had a house and a good job —"

Tears streamed down Quin's face. "Why are you doing this to me?"

Nora felt like shit. She'd never meant to tell Quin any of this. It had been her cross to bear, something she'd promised she'd protect Quin from. And in anger, she'd now thrown it at her, her words sharp as knives.

"I never wanted you to know. I'm sorry, I'm so, so sorry. Please believe me." Nora put her hands on Quin's shoulders, but her sister shrugged them off and took a step back.

"You made a lot of sacrifices for me, but you didn't have to. Mom made mistakes. She admits it. But you took me away from her, away from my *mother*. I didn't have a father, I didn't have grandparents or aunts and uncles or cousins, I had you and I had her. And you never let me see her. After I saw her in prison, I knew I needed to leave you. I needed to figure out who I was and what I thought *for myself.* Because I didn't know anything anymore. I came to Sacramento for college, and you followed me."

Nora shook her head. "It was two years later —"

"When I told you I was moving back to L.A. after I graduated, you said you could transfer. Why?"

"You're my family."

"I stayed because I got that great job with fire inspection. Found out afterward that you got it for me."

"I didn't. I gave you a recommendation. You knew that."

"Right. FBI Special Agent Nora English," she mimicked sarcastically.

"It was just a letter of recommendation!"

"You didn't mention you were my sister."

"I don't know what that has to do with anything." Nora's head was spinning. The entire conversation had gotten out of control.

"It has to do with you trying to control my life. From the minute you put Mom in prison."

From the minute you put Mom in prison? "Lorraine is the one who broke the law, not me. She committed hundreds of crimes before she got caught."

"Why do you call her Lorraine?"

"Because she told me not to call her 'Mom.' "

"She said it was because you refused to."

That was the last straw. "I'm telling you the truth. I don't care if you believe me, but Lorraine has fed you a crock of shit. Hell, she probably believes it! Maggie O'Dell, the woman you call your sister, is a murderer. She's killed six people. *Six.* Starting with Jonah Payne. She tortured him and killed him because he had slighted her father in some way. She poisoned three college students with jimsonweed. They are dead. She killed Professor Cole by injecting him with heparin and cutting his arms and chest so he slowly bled to death. The woman is seriously disturbed. She's going to be caught. I want to catch her before she claims another victim. Before she comes after me, or you."

Quin stared at her with wide, disbelieving eyes. Her mouth opened and closed. "Wh-why do you think Maggie is involved? It's not like her. I don't believe it."

"I can show you all the evidence and lay it out for you like I would the U.S. attorney before an indictment. Or you can believe me."

Quin turned away.

Nora's heart broke. That Quin doubted

her sliced her to the bone. She said quietly, "Maggie attended Rose College for three semesters. Her roommate was Anya Ballard, who we believe was one of four arsonists in the fires you investigated. We have evidence from her room, and a journal we've proven is her writing. Based on our investigation so far, Maggie recently returned to Roseville and joined Anya and two young men in the arson fire of Butcher-Payne. We have a witness who identified her boyfriend Scott Edwards's truck parked at Jonah Payne's Lake Tahoe residence. Dr. Coffey right now is comparing the truck bed liner with the marks found on Payne's body. Not with Edwards's truck — it's been missing since he was murdered — but against a similar make and model.

"What tripped her up, however, is her thinking she was going to outsmart the police. She planted a suicide note with a poor attempt at copying Anya's handwriting. Ironically, there were no prints on the iced tea jug that the poisoned tea came in. Whoever poured it wore gloves or wiped it clean. She or Scott Edwards slit the neck of her old high school friend Russell Larkin, who was the I.T. guy for Butcher-Payne. We're not sure how, but they retrieved codes off Larkin's computer that enabled them to get into Butcher-Payne without detection. I have agents in Paso Robles where Maggie grew up trying to locate her. I have an agent at the college interviewing students who knew her. I have another agent poring through property records, and Duke Rogan is reviewing all background information one more time in the hopes of finding out where she is hiding."

Nora stopped, her heart racing. Quin still didn't look at her. Nora felt like she'd irrevocably damaged her relationship with Quin. She ached for her sister, wished she could take back the harsh words, wished she could understand. Maybe she'd been wrong keeping Quin from Lorraine. All she'd wanted for her small family was stability.

"Quin — we've been friends now as well as sisters. Please. Look at me."

Quin slowly turned. Her face was splotchy, her eyes red. "Leave me alone," she whispered.

"I can't. I fear for your safety."

She laughed, the pitch high and fake. "Maggie? Even if you're right, she would never hurt me."

Nora didn't believe that for a minute, but knew it would be fruitless trying to convince her now. "Do you know where she is?"

Quin shook her head. "I saw her in June. I didn't know she was in Sacramento. *If* she's still in Sacramento."

Nora tried not to let her words sting. "If you hear from her, you need to let me know immediately. She's dangerous."

"I'll take it under advisement."

Quin walked out the door. Nora sank into the chair behind Duke's desk and put her head in her hands. She had to believe that Quin would see reason when she calmed down. Quin wasn't stupid, she was just hurt, upset, and confused.

Tears never came easily for Nora, but her eyes burned and she squeezed them shut. She knew better than to let the guilt in. If regretted, every decision, including those she made about Quin, would be threatening a flood of remorse. Quin, things she'd done as a child, her resentment of her mother — even turning state's evidence, though the right decision, weighed down her heart. She'd protected Quin because it was all she had to cling to, Quin was all she had that kept her strong when too often she'd wanted to disappear.

She couldn't lose Quin, but could she accept her sister's relationship with Lorraine? How could she constantly battle the lies from Lorraine's mouth? She didn't want to defend herself and her decisions, right or wrong, for the rest of her life. She felt defeated and alone.

Duke entered his office after he saw Quin run out, obviously upset. Nora had her head on his desk, her shoulders slumped and quivering with tension and restrained emotion. He ached for her, wanting to wash away her anguish.

Walking over to her, he put his hands on her shoulders and squeezed. "I'm sorry. That must have been hard."

She sat up, leaning back into his hands as he rubbed her tense shoulders. "She's believed Lorraine's lies about so many things — I don't know where to begin to set her straight. I lost her long ago and I didn't even see it. I was in over my head and didn't know it. I wish to God I could take back some of the things I said." Her voice cracked and she bit her bottom lip.

"Quin's smart. She just needs to think it through."

"She thinks I've been lying to her about important information. Like her father." She rubbed her eyes. "I can't believe I've been so blind. She's resented every decision I've made."

Duke wished he could do something, but this was between Nora and Quin. All he could do was stand with her.

"Did Jayne have anything for you on the security tapes from Butcher-Payne?" she asked him.

"I know how they messed with the video. Actually quite smart. They brought in a computer that directed a completely different feed into the digital recording, essentially recording blanks over the actual images. I think that's how they corrupted Russ Larkin's computer as well. It's impossible to get the true recording, but I'm glad Jayne figured out how they did it. My security system had a fatal flaw, now I can fix it."

"It's not your fault," she said.

He spun her around in the chair, his face inches from hers. Her big round eyes were filled with heartache. "And it's not your fault that Quin is having problems accepting the truth."

He heard a rattle on his table in the corner. "Your cell phone is vibrating." He walked over to the table and brought the phone to her.

"Thanks." It was Lindsey Prince, one of the agents in San Luis Obispo.

"I got news for you," Lindsey said in a rush. "First, a photo of Maggie O'Dell from high school. We're at Kinko's now, scanning it in, and will email it pronto."

"Terrific. Send it to both me and ASAC Hooper. He'll need it for the APB and I'll distribute it to my team."

"There's more. We talked to the local sheriff and he knows Maggie O'Dell very well. She was quite the juvenile delinquent. Mostly vandalism and petty crime, and her parents always paid restitution when she was caught. It's a small town, they didn't do anything more about it. Except, the sheriff has long suspected that she killed her boyfriend. He just can't prove it."

"How?"

"Hemlock."

"Hemlock?"

"Specifically, water hemlock. But she denied even seeing him that day, no one saw them together, and her father vouched that she had been sleeping most of the afternoon because of a flu bug."

"Was he lying?"

"The sheriff thought so, but had no physical evidence to tie her to the death. Some people thought the kid accidentally ate the hemlock. Others thought he was killed. His parents received a substantial amount of money from an insurance policy they had on him. But even so the sheriff always suspected Maggie. From the start, her reaction didn't fit for him. But she didn't rattle."

"How did the boyfriend ingest water hemlock?"

"The autopsy was unclear — there were no undigested leaves or roots in his stomach. But the pond nearby had a considerable amount of water hemlock growing near the shore. There have been documented cases of cattle being poisoned from drinking water that had been saturated with the plants. The sheriff, under pressure from the family, closed the case as an accidental poisoning. Because he couldn't prove murder, there was the possibility of suicide, and the insurance wouldn't pay on self-termination."

It fit Maggie O'Dell's M.O. — there had been no traces of jimsonweed leaves in the Rose College students; the water had leeched the poison from homemade, deadly tea bags.

"And," Lindsey continued, "the victim was supposed to picnic with another girl that day, but her grandfather died the night before and she left the state. The victim's mother said that he'd broken up with Maggie weeks before, and wouldn't have gone to see her."

"That probably didn't sit well with Maggie," Nora said. "Anything on Russell Larkin?"

"He was Maggie's neighbor, though graduated several years before she started high school. His younger sister was in O'Dell's class. I want to talk to her next, but she's on a plane now, flying in from Northwestern for Larkin's memorial service."

"Down there?"

"Yes."

"If you can get to her tonight or tomorrow morning, find out what she knows about Maggie O'Dell."

"Will do. Watch for the photo."

Nora hung up and said, "I'm getting a photo of O'Dell."

Duke watched Nora's phone. A few seconds later, a message came in. She clicked it.

The photo loaded fairly quickly. In ten seconds, they were staring at a stunning girl with long brown waves of hair and huge, round brown eyes. The shape matched Nora's, but nothing else resembled her. Nora didn't know why she was relieved.

Maggie looked a bit familiar. Not just because of the eyes, but . . .

Duke snapped his fingers. "She was the girl who threw the soda at you on Monday."

"Are you sure?"

"Positive."

There was a tap on Duke's door and J.T.'s stellar administrative assistant, Heather, walked in, sharply dressed in a pricey business suit. "We found an apartment," she said, handing Duke a folder.

Duke opened the thin red folder.

5100 College Blvd., #A124, Roseville.
Rented to: Margaret Lovitz.
Landlord: Ted Albany.

"Heather, you're incredible."

"Thank you," she said. "Do you need anything else?"

"Not right now, but thanks."

Nora looked at Duke, weary, her fight with Quin draining her.

Duke tried to offer a reassuring gaze. "I had our staff call every apartment building in Placer County starting with those near Rose College. Bingo — I found one. Rented to Margaret Lovitz."

"How did you find it?"

"I gave Heather a list of likely aliases — O'Dell, Wright, Plummer, Lovitz — and a time frame: rented after June of this year."

"I'll call Hooper to get a search warrant." She stood and smiled. "Thank you. For this

— and everything."

He caressed her cheek. "Anytime," he said slowly. "For you, anything."

Maggie bolted upright in bed, panicked. Where was she?

Quin's house. Quin's bed.

She let out a long, quiet breath and listened. Something had woken her up. Finally, Quin had to be home.

She glanced at Quin's simple, old-fashioned alarm clock, the kind with the bells on top and a traditional clock face. It was only four in the afternoon. Had she left work early? Why?

Someone was moving around downstairs. Into the kitchen, the creak of the linoleum a slightly different, louder sound than the soft carpeted footfalls. Water running. Turning off. Footsteps again.

Maggie swung her body out of bed, picking up the knife. She wished she hadn't cut herself so much. Quin was going to see the blood. But that couldn't be helped.

Now was the time to convince Quin that they should be a team. Just the two of them.

On the stairs, Maggie coughed twice and cleared her throat.

It wasn't Quin she glimpsed downstairs. It was a man.

Maggie scurried to the closet, grabbing the comforter on her way. She practically threw herself inside and closed the door.

And was very, very silent.

CHAPTER TWENTY-FOUR

Maggie O'Dell's apartment would alone convict her.

At first, Nora saw nothing out of the ordinary in the small ground-floor garden apartment. In fact, it was virtually empty: The living room had a secondhand couch; the dining/kitchen area a small table with two chairs; and the bedroom a mattress on the floor with sheets and a blanket pulled tightly around the corners. But as she dug deeper into the dark crevices, Maggie's crimes became clear.

The pristine kitchen concealed death well. A container in the refrigerator matched that one with the fatal iced tea in Anya Ballard's dorm room. This one, too, was full. Nora didn't know if it was poisoned, but they would find out.

In a drawer, jimsonweed was spread on paper towels, drying. In the drawer next to it, a set of knives, handmade, perfectly aligned in a special tray that appeared to have been built for this set of knives.

One knife was missing.

Nora wondered if one or more of them would test positive for blood.

It was the bedroom closet that had Nora most on edge.

The closet was a walk-in, nearly as large as the bathroom. The few articles of clothing hung far to the left side. Every inch of the walls was covered with photos and articles. For a moment, Nora thought she'd walked onto a cheesy movie set when she saw a picture of Jonah Payne taken from a distance at his Lake Tahoe house. Written in black permanent marker across the top:

You're dead.

Pictures of Maggie with Scott, with Anya, with Quin. *Quin.* What was going on? Nora resisted the urge to pull them down, and swallowed, focusing on the unspoken message Maggie was leaving.

The captions were everywhere. *You're dead. I hate you. I want you to beg. I hate you. Slut. Pervert.*

There was a picture of Anya Ballard in a naked embrace with Leif Cole, taken from outside a window. A picture of Quin with . . . Danny? Yeah, Danny. Whoever was the guy before the new one, Devon. They were at a house Nora didn't recognize, probably Danny's. The woman was a voyeur.

The picture of Maggie and Quin bothered Nora the most. Centered on the wall with a big heart around them. She recognized Quin in the picture. It was taken three or four years ago when Quin had gone through a short-hair phase and sported a sleek bob. They both were smiling, Quin's arm slung over Maggie's shoulder. The image unnerved Nora. Quin trusted Maggie, and that trust could get her hurt, or worse.

"Nora," Duke said quietly.

She turned around. He'd closed the door. On the back side was a violent shrine dedicated to Nora.

Traitor. Bitch. Traitor. Murderer. I hate you I hate you I hate you.

Over and over, covering pictures of Nora taken while she worked, while she went to the store, while she was sunbathing in her backyard earlier this summer.

One of the pictures had her head cut off. Another, her throat slit with what looked like dried blood around the edges. And another had her heart cut out.

"Oh God," she gasped.

Steve Donovan called her name from the

bedroom.

She opened the door with a shaking, gloved hand.

"Donovan." She motioned him to go inside while she stepped out.

"Holy shit," he said.

"She doesn't stay here," Nora said, looking around. "It's too dark, too barren. No privacy. This is her stopping-off point. A place to hide, to regroup, to keep her supplies close. Donovan, we need every photo analyzed to see where it might lead us. Every nook and cranny and hiding place. She has another house. It's private, no neighbors. That's where she's living."

She stepped outside, close to being claustrophobic in the sterile apartment. She dialed Quin's cell phone. With each unanswered ring, Nora's fear grew. She should never have let Quin leave Rogan-Caruso without an armed guard. What had she been thinking? About her own pain and guilt, forgetting that she was dealing with a killer who had a connection to her family. Her *only* family, Quin. If anything happened to her sister it would be her fault.

Voice mail picked up, Quin's cheerful voice proclaiming, "Hello, buttercup, this is Quin Teagan, I'm not available — ha ha — but leave a message and I'll call you when

433

I'm free."

Nora said, "Quin, call me as soon as possible. Wherever you are, stay there. Let me know where. You need police protection." She hung up and bit her bottom lip.

"After seeing that you think she's going after Quin?" Duke sounded both angry and scared. "Did you see what she did to your pictures?"

"But —"

"You're the one who needs protection."

"She knows she can't get to me, not easily. Especially now — you've hardly left my side, I've been working, I haven't been alone. Quin is my Achilles' heel. Maggie knows I'd do anything to save her." And Nora would. She'd delivered Quin nearly twenty-nine years ago. She'd been terrified of hurting the baby, certain from her mother's screams that Lorraine was dying. Then she held her, wrapped in a towel, and knew true love.

"How does she know this?"

Nora pushed aside the memories. "Quin told her I was overprotective and controlling. And I'm sure it sounded worse. Maggie is a good judge of people. That's how she was able to manipulate her boyfriend and Anya for so long. How she was able to fool people into thinking she had a conscience. She knows how to behave. But it's an act. She's full of rage and can easily snap. We have to find Quin."

"Let's go."

She glanced at her watch. Seven-thirty. "I doubt she's still at work. I'll have police check her house and if she's not there, her office."

After she talked to Sacramento PD dispatch, Nora called Quin on her house phone on the chance she'd left her cell phone in the car, while Duke sped out of the parking lot. It rang four times; then voice mail picked up.

"Hiya Sexy, it's Quin, leave a message and I *promise* to call ya back."

"Quin, it's Nora. If you're there, pick up the phone. Please. I need to talk to you."

Nothing. Nothing. Nothing.

"Dammit, Quin, now's not the time to be stubborn. I'm worried. Call me back."

Weather permitting, Quin walked to work because she lived only fourteen short blocks from her office building. Today, she wished she had driven. She didn't want to go home. She wanted to drive away. Anywhere. Away from Sacramento. From Nora. From her mother. She'd tried to reach Devon, hoping he'd take her to Lake Tahoe. If not, screw him. She'd go herself and find a hot guy on a roll and fill the emptiness inside with good sex. Nora disapproved of her lifestyle, which had spurred Quin on. Who was Nora to judge, anyway?

But Quin didn't want to find just any guy. She wanted Devon. She really liked him. He was smarter than most of the guys she dated, funnier, cuter. And a doctor. He cared about his work the way she cared about hers. Which is why she'd buried herself in work after walking out on Nora this afternoon.

She turned up the short walk to her town house. She liked the three-hundred-unit complex that took up two square blocks near the river, Old Sac, the movie theater, the K Street Mall. It was convenient, clean, and attractive. Her two-bedroom town house even had a small, private garden area.

She stopped briefly to water her plants before unlocking her front door. She heard the shower running, and her heart skipped a beat until she saw Devon's keys and black bag on her entry table.

He could even sense when she needed him. She might just be falling in love with the man. Hot shower sex was just what she needed to get her mind off Nora and Maggie. Because she felt like shit for what she'd said to Nora. Maybe it was true, well, a lot of it was true — Nora had been micromanaging her life since she took over the role of mother when Quin was nine. But Nora wasn't a liar, and all day Quin feared she'd believed her mother because she was desperate for something indefinable.

She took the stairs two at a time. The upstairs was moist and humid. How long did that man shower? She pulled off her T-shirt with the State Arson Investigator logo on the pocket.

"Devon, it's me!"

Before she opened the shower door, she knew something was wrong. No one was in the shower. There was no steam, the air thick with cool water vapor. The pebbled glass door distorted her view, but she could swear Devon was sitting on the shower floor. Unable to stop herself, her hand already on the handle, she pulled it open.

Devon was slumped on the shower floor, his skin so pale it was translucent, long bloodless gashes down his chest, back, and arms. His eyes were open, and they were no longer bright, vibrant blue. They were glazed, faded, and lifeless.

She screamed, then covered her mouth with both hands. He was dead. No, no, no!

"You weren't supposed to find him."

Quin spun around and Maggie stood there in the doorway between her bedroom and bath. In that split second, Quin realized everything Nora had told her was true. Fear crept up her spine until she could barely think.

"All I did was go to the garage because I thought I heard something, and I wanted to be there when you drove up. But your car was already there."

"I — I walk to work." Quin looked around for a weapon, but the only one she saw was the knife in Maggie's hand.

"I wanted to talk to you." Maggie sounded like a child. "You like her more than me, don't you?"

"Wh-who?"

From her pocket, Maggie pulled out a picture of Nora. It had been mutilated, but Quin knew exactly what it was. Nora at Quin's college graduation.

Nora had always shown up at her soccer games. Or when Quin took first place in the state spelling bee. Every play she was in, whether she had a small role or a leading spot, Nora had been there. At her high school graduation, her college graduation, her promotion party.

Quin had taken Nora for granted. *Resented* her because she *wasn't* her mother.

She was her sister, and Quin alternately loved and despised her.

Quin had broken up with one of her boyfriends, one she'd thought she'd loved, when he'd suggested she talk to someone about her problems with Nora. "She's been nothing but cool to you," he'd said. "I don't see why you are so hot and cold with her."

No way in *hell* was she seeing a shrink, she'd said, and she'd booted him out of her house and out of her life. Quin wasn't crazy, and she could deal with her own emotions just fine, thank you very much. After that, she rarely introduced her boyfriends to her sister, and if she did it was a brief event.

But it niggled at her like a sneeze that wouldn't come, and now — for the first time she recognized that she'd been grossly unfair.

Quin was paralyzed. She wasn't a cop, she was an arson investigator. A nerd. She was smart, not street-savvy.

The television shows always had the good guys trying to keep the bad guys talking until the cavalry showed. "What do you want, Maggie?"

"I wanted my father. I thought that's what you wanted, too."

When she first got to know Maggie, Quin's little sister had been just nine, the same age

Quin was when their mother was sent to prison. But it wasn't until a few years later that they really had meaningful conversations. And one of them had been about their fathers.

It was then that Quin told Maggie that Nora had lied about her father. She'd believed what her mother said — she'd been so lucid, so detailed. And Quin had found him. Randall Teagan was a real person.

Nora hadn't denied that, only that he wasn't her father.

Quin had believed her mother because she'd wanted to. Needed to. And that was really the point when she'd bonded with Maggie. Because Nora had taken away her father, too.

You've been such an immature brat.

She prayed Nora would forgive her.

"Why did you kill him?" Quin couldn't look at Devon again. Guilt fought with fear.

"I thought he was an intruder."

"An intruder in my shower?" Her voice broke into a sob.

Maggie shrugged, then glared at her. "I needed you. But I can see you're just like all the others. A selfish bitch. Now I won't feel guilty."

Quin watched as the picture of Nora floated to the floor. She should have kept her eyes on Maggie, she thought in the split second before two metal darts hit her stomach and she collapsed in terrible pain, her limbs jerking.

I'm sorry, Nora.

Maggie dropped the Taser and her knife in the deep pockets of her peasant skirt. Quin's body danced with the electrical charge flowing through her nerves. Maggie grabbed her under the shoulders and pulled her from the bathroom.

CHAPTER
TWENTY-FIVE

"Where are the police?" Nora asked, jumping from the car as soon as Duke parked it. "I called it in more than ten minutes ago."

Duke said, "It was a well-being check."

"I'm a federal agent, you'd think they'd hop on it." She walked briskly down the path toward Quin's town house.

"Hold it, Nora."

"We don't have time —" But she slowed down. "I know. I just need to know she's okay."

"I understand. Do you have a key?"

She held out her key ring by Quin's key.

"How many entrances?"

"Two. Garage, which is downstairs under the town house. It has stairs going up to the first floor. And the front door. There's a sliding glass door, but it's not keyed."

"I'll go around to the garage and get in that way."

"You need a remote to open that door."

He gave her a half smile. "Garage remotes are not a problem. Give me a count of sixty to get in place, then enter. I'll come up the back stairs. Just in case. Stay alert."

Nora nodded. "Hers is the third garage from the end."

Duke waved and jogged back down the path and around to the garage. Nora began counting.

One. Two. Three.

She bounced on her feet as she mentally counted while standing outside the privacy fencing around Quin's small courtyard. She heard nothing inside and peered through a crack in the fencing. The kitchen light was on in the back, and the upstairs master bedroom light was on. Energy-conscious, Quin never left her lights on. She had to be home.

Fifty-eight. Fifty-nine. Sixty.

She already had the key in the outer lock. She turned and pushed, took four long steps to the front door, inserted the key, and turned. Her hand was on the butt of her gun as she listened for any sound. The shower was running upstairs. Relief flooded through her.

The door from the stairs leading to the garage slowly opened. Nora stood out of the potential line of fire, saw that it was

Duke, and motioned him inside.

"She's upstairs," Nora whispered. "The shower's running."

"Her car isn't in the garage." Duke locked the garage door behind him and did a security check on the first floor. Hall closet, half bath, kitchen pantry, cabinets. There were not many hiding places on the first floor.

Nora frowned. The air had a strange, cool, moist feeling. She drew her gun and cautiously walked up the stairs, Duke two steps behind her, instincts on full alert. Up here the air was almost wet, leaving an odd, chilling coat on her skin.

As soon as she stepped through the open master bedroom door, with the moisture so thick water dripped down the walls, she feared Quin was dead. Duke motioned toward the open bathroom door. Water had pooled on the floor.

Duke mouthed, *Let me,* and motioned toward the bathroom.

He obviously thought Quin was dead, too. He wanted to protect Nora from it, and this time she let him.

He peered around the corner, still anticipating an attack.

"Shit," he said.

A tight moan escaped her lungs as she

said, "Quin."

"No."

She looked inside. The shower door was wide open, and a naked man lay dead on the tile floor.

Duke said, "I'm checking the rest of the second floor. Wait."

She looked around the bathroom. The man's clothes had been loosely folded on the bathroom counter. She walked over and saw there was a nametag on the shirt pocket. *Dr. Devon Blair.* Quin's boyfriend. On the floor, wet from the water splashing out of the shower, was the red T-shirt Quin had been wearing earlier that day.

Nora stared at it. What had happened here? Also on the floor was a photograph. Nora didn't dare touch anything; preserving the evidence was crucial and they'd already walked the entire house and probably contaminated the crime scene. But she bent over to see what it was.

It was a picture of her, defaced with her throat scratched as if it had been slit and her eyes carved out. Quin had snapped it while Nora had been unaware, looking up at the stage after Quin's college graduation ceremony. Quin had asked her what she'd been thinking that had her looking so pensive, and she'd replied that she was so proud of Quin that it had overwhelmed her for a minute. That wasn't the complete truth. She had been proud, but more than that, she felt that she'd done what she'd promised Quin and herself — making sure Quin had a solid foundation on which to build her future. With that personal goal completed, Nora had been both elated and sad.

Duke returned. "No one's here. But you need to see something."

"She has Quin." She gestured to the T-shirt.

"I know." Duke glanced at the photo, at first not recognizing it was Nora, then frowning when he did.

He led her out of the bathroom. He pointed to the dresser. She registered the destruction. All the framed pictures, broken. The photos destroyed. Years of memories that Nora had painstakingly created for Quin because their mother had so few photos of them growing up.

"There is blood on the comforter. Not a lot," Duke added quickly, "but it was stuffed in the closet. I only moved it to make sure no one was hiding under it."

Or dead under it.

"Where would she take her?" Nora's voice cracked. "Not her apartment, so where?"

446

"We'll find her."

Downstairs the bell rang, followed by loud knocking.

The police.

Nora paced the FBI conference room while on hold waiting for Warden Jeff Greene at Victorville to pick up. A dozen agents and analysts were working tonight digging through property records under a variety of names — anyone Maggie might know — phone records, and emails trying to get an idea of where Maggie had taken Quin. Every law enforcement officer in the western U.S. had a memo on Quin's car with her photo and Maggie's photo.

An hour ago, just before midnight, Scott Edwards's truck had been found parked on the street three blocks from Quin's office. It had been towed to the sheriff's impound lot. Steve Donovan's team was going through it now.

They'd already tried to trace Quin's cell phone. It was in her purse, left behind at her town house. Her car, which she rarely drove, didn't have GPS or any trackable security device.

Upon arrival at Quin's town house, the coroner determined that the victim, Dr. Devon Blair, had been dead for several hours, but the exact time would be difficult to determine because the cold water had lowered his body temperature. After talking to hospital staff, they learned he'd left Sutter General at four in the afternoon.

At Maggie's apartment Duke and Nora, along with three specialists, had meticulously searched for any clue — a receipt, note, journal — that might lead them to where Maggie had taken Quin. There was nothing. In fact, other than a familiar alias on the apartment rental agreement, nothing they had come across even suggested that Maggie O'Dell lived there. ERT went through printing the place and pulling trace evidence, and had felt confident that they could prove that she was there through physical evidence, but the lack of personal belongings suggested Maggie was far more shrewd than most young killers.

She had no credit cards or bank accounts, so tracing plastic or a checking account was out. They ran her father's credit card and came up dry; it had only been used by him locally.

The pair of agents who had interviewed him yesterday went back and asked for his help, but he refused. He didn't believe them when he was told that Maggie was under suspicion for murder and kidnapping. He owned no other property in the state, though ownership was certainly not a requirement for Maggie's purposes. She would pick a place that was private and accessible to the highway. An abandoned cabin or empty vacation home would work for her purposes. Thinking of that, Nora had sent the pair of agents in Lake Tahoe to check on Jonah Payne's place. That, too, was empty and the police seal undisturbed.

Hans Vigo at Quantico seemed positive that Maggie would contact Nora directly before harming Quin. But it already had been more than six hours.

Nora had done everything she could that night. Making sure every branch of law enforcement had recent photos of Quin, the high school picture of Maggie, and a copy of the more recent picture found in her closet. A description of Quin's car, Scott Edwards's truck, sending agents to re-interview students at Rose College, pushing Donovan on the evidence. It was one in the morning and she had nowhere to turn, nothing to do except think about the danger Quin faced.

She did have one more option. Her last option. God knew that she'd never attempt to speak with Lorraine unless she had no other choice. Lorraine might know something about where Maggie was living. Maybe she would help. Quin's life was at stake; she *had* to help!

She dialed Warden Greene at the Victor-ville Federal Penitentiary and worked on controlling the desperation that rose in her chest. If Lorraine knew how scared Nora was, she might clam up just to hurt her. Nora had to prove to Lorraine that this was about Quin. That was the only way she'd help.

"Sorry to keep you waiting, Agent English."

"I'm sorry to drag you from bed, Warden, but it's an emergency. I need to talk to a prisoner immediately."

"I know. That's one of the reasons I took so long. I had Lorraine Wright woken and asked her to take your call. She refused."

"She can't!"

"I can't force her to talk to you."

Nora rubbed her eyes. Lorraine would never change. Selfish, angry, distrustful. "Please ask her if she knows where Maggie is staying. If she has any idea where she *might* be living. Tell her that her daughter Quin is in danger."

"I'll ask. Hold the line. This may take a few minutes."

"I'll wait, thank you."

Duke stood at her side and took her hand. She said, "Lorraine won't talk to me."

"Dr. Vigo said Maggie would call you." Hooper had already put a trace on all her phones. If Maggie called, they'd quickly pinpoint her location.

"But he doesn't *know* that she'll call. And that puts her in the driver's seat. We need to find out where she is *first.* Otherwise, she'll jerk us around."

"Everyone is working on it."

"I know." She sat on the edge of the table and closed her eyes. She didn't want to panic, she had to think clearly. "Quin has to be okay."

"She is. And she's feisty."

No one, not even Hans Vigo, could predict Maggie's erratic behavior. Nora sensed that Quin was in jeopardy as soon as she spotted the pictures in Maggie's closet, but she couldn't even hazard a guess at how long it would take before Maggie called her, if ever. Dr. Vigo said within twenty-four hours, but Nora wasn't so sure. It depended on Maggie's end game.

"She's trying to wear you down," Duke told Nora. "She doesn't know that we're on to her."

Nora wasn't so sure, but had agreed to a stakeout at Maggie's apartment. "She didn't go back to her apartment."

"Because she kidnapped Quin. Hard to get her into the building. You said she'd find someplace secluded."

"If she didn't know we were on to her before she took Quin, she knows now."

"Why?"

"She left the water running in Quin's town house, for one. That's going to attract attention, probably from her next-door neighbor. We impounded Scott's truck. We were all over her apartment. And — I don't think Quin will keep quiet. I laid out the case against Maggie, trying to prove it to Quin. The only thing going for us now is that Maggie and Quin have a long-standing relationship. Maybe —" She paused. What was she hoping for? "Maybe Quin understands her. Maybe she can stay alive until we can find her."

Hooper walked in with Rachel close on his heels. Hooper announced, "The judge didn't approve our warrant for a wiretap on David O'Dell's phone. Said we didn't have enough evidence that he was involved in his daughter's alleged activities, and that the charges against Maggie O'Dell were specious."

"What?" Duke exclaimed. "This is why I'm glad I never became a cop. The evidence

452

is pretty damn clear. You didn't see her apartment, Dean."

Hooper tensed and said, "I saw the photos, and I agree that she's our killer. But knowing it and proving it are two different things. We still have evidence to process. We have fingerprints but can't prove they belong to Maggie O'Dell."

"Not necessarily," Rachel said, holding up her BlackBerry. "Donovan just emailed a preliminary report that the prints in the apartment match prints in both Edwards's truck and Teagan's town house."

"But we haven't matched them against Maggie O'Dell," Nora said. "Once we bring her into custody, we can tie up the entire case with a pretty bow, but until then, it's as if she doesn't exist."

"Agent English?" Warden Greene said over her phone.

"Yes, Warden, I'm here."

"I'm afraid I can't help you."

Nora's chest tightened. She was out of ideas. If Lorraine didn't talk, they'd have to wait for Maggie to make the next move, and Nora didn't want to cede control to a psychopathic killer.

"Why?"

"Ms. Wright said if you want that information, she'll only tell you face-to-face."

■ ■ ■ ■

The duck stood on the table and stared at Quin. The last duck from Butcher-Payne, she thought. Securely tied to the chair, hands behind her back, each ankle tied to the base, she was dressed only in her jeans and a bra. Maggie wouldn't give her a shirt to wear, didn't even seem to notice that it was freezing up here — wherever "here" was. All Quin knew was they were in the mountains — the fresh pine, the redwoods, the moist, woodsy scent. But the Sierra Nevadas were a big place, they could be almost anywhere — though it had taken less than two hours to get here.

A cat jumped onto the table next to the duck, who waddled away and hopped onto the floor. Now the cat stared at Quin, before sitting and licking his paw.

It was pitch black outside, the only light in the cabin from a naked bulb in the middle of the room. The place was cluttered but neat. Books and papers stacked tightly on a solitary bookshelf; dishes washed and dried on the sideboard; knives hung neatly on a rack.

Maggie had left three hours ago, if Quin's internal clock was working. She had no idea what Maggie had planned for her. She hadn't spoken much after Tasering Quin in her bathroom.

Quin's bottom lip quivered as she thought about Devon and what Maggie had done to him. What she wanted to do to Nora. It was clear that Maggie's goal was to kill Nora, and Quin didn't know how to save herself, let alone her sister.

Did Nora even know she was missing? Quin couldn't believe some of the things she'd said to her sister. She wished she could take them back. What if that was the last conversation she ever had with Nora? She didn't want to die with Nora thinking she hated her.

Quin didn't hear anything but the faint sounds of night outside the cabin. Tree branches rubbing against the back wall, moved by a breeze that occasionally strengthened enough to rattle one of the two windows. The call of owls, a howl of a lone coyote. The door opened and Quin jumped. "Hi, Quin! I'm back!" Maggie announced.

She put a bag down on the counter and unpacked it.

"Where were you?" Quin asked.

"Out," she said, then laughed. "Sending Super Special Federal Agent a message.

We'll see how long it takes her to find it." She put a cell phone down on the counter.

"What kind of message?"

"A fun one." She frowned. "Why all the questions?"

"I'm curious. I'm a captive audience, after all."

She shrugged. "You're not part of this anymore."

"Then let me go."

She laughed again. "Silly. I was joking. You're the *best* part."

Maggie unpacked the bag. Peanut butter. Bread. Bottled water. She proceeded to make a sandwich, then held it to Quin's mouth. "Go on, bite," she said.

Quin turned away. She didn't care how hungry she was, she wanted nothing from Maggie.

"Fine," Maggie snapped. She ate the sandwich herself and chased it down with water.

"Maggie, why did you kill all those people?"

She frowned. "Is that what she's saying? That's what she told you? That I killed someone?" Maggie sounded almost indignant, but there was a hint of pride in her voice.

"She told me everything."

"I seriously doubt that."

"You were involved in the arson, you killed Dr. Payne. You poisoned your friends."

Maggie pouted. "I'm not talking about that, and if you want to live, you'll shut up."

"Nora never hurt you."

Maggie slammed her fist on the table. The cat jumped off and ran behind the small couch. "You made me scare him," Maggie said, obviously upset. She slapped Quin. "Nora killed my father and she deserves to die for it. You don't know how long I've been planning this. *Years.* I came up here to go to Rose College just to be close to you, and you didn't want me around."

"That was because Nora might have seen you!"

"Nora doesn't even know what I look like. I walked right by her twice this week and she didn't notice. You could have introduced me as your friend Maggie."

"Nora knows what you look like now," Quin said. "She knows everything about you."

"She doesn't know *me* and she never will. Because I'll kill her the minute she walks into my trap. I could have been special. I could have been important! But she made me a nobody."

She wasn't making sense, and Quin had

little experience talking to killers. What was she supposed to say to this girl? This wasn't the Maggie she knew.

"You are special," she said quietly. "You were always special. I saw that the minute we met." And in some ways she had — she'd been enamored of having a little sister, and thrilled to have a secret she'd kept from Nora.

"You're just saying that."

"I'm not. I've always liked you, Maggie. We are so much alike." That's what Quin thought before finding out Maggie was a killer.

Maggie looked at her as if she didn't know whether to believe her or not. "I don't believe you, not after I killed your boyfriend. Why, Quin? Why did you pick him over me?"

For a moment, Quin thought Maggie was talking about a *sexual* relationship, but she quickly realized that it wasn't about sex, it was about kinship. Maggie had wanted Quin for herself.

"I liked him, but it wasn't you *or* Devon. We could have been friends forever." Now Devon was dead and Quin felt responsible. She'd befriended Maggie, never thinking she was a killer.

"No!" Maggie shouted, and began to pace

the length of the cabin. "You don't understand! You're just like everyone else. Don't placate me. Don't pretend we're friends, because we're not. The only reason I talked to you was because you gave me information I needed."

"What? I never —"

"Little things. Like Nora is allergic to peanuts." Maggie picked up the jar of peanut butter. "This might come in handy. Face it, Quin, you'll be better off without her."

Quin couldn't remember ever telling Maggie about the peanuts, but maybe she had, in conversation. She'd had a lot of talks with Maggie, mostly about growing up . . . with Nora. Missing her mother. Not understanding why Nora never let her see Lorraine. Complaining, always criticizing Nora.

It was no wonder Maggie thought Nora was to blame for everything. Quin had blamed her, too.

"Please, Maggie. Stop this right now. You can leave and disappear and it'll be over."

"No!" She kicked Quin in the stomach so hard and suddenly that the chair fell backward. "I can't stop this. I don't want to stop this. It has to be finished."

All air rushed from her lungs and Quin couldn't move, couldn't breathe, the pain spreading from her gut so fast she thought she'd pass out. She focused on taking shallow breaths.

Maggie walked past Quin on the floor and went into the bathroom. She was talking to herself and Quin made out a few words here and there: Prison. Traitor. Hopeless.

When Nora said Maggie was crazy, Quin hadn't believed her.

She shuddered. She sure as hell believed her now.

At the former Mather Air Force Base, where J. T. Caruso housed his small plane, Duke pulled Sean aside.

"Be careful, Sean. You just got your license in June, you don't have a lot of solo hours logged."

"You're doing it again, Duke."

He wasn't going to apologize for caring about his family. "I'm worried. Not just about you, but about Nora."

"You really care about her." Sean raised an eyebrow. "I'm not going to crash, Duke, I promise."

Sean was the only one Duke had confided in about being nervous when flying; ever since their parents' small-plane crash. Sending Sean and Nora in the air to fly to Victorville to talk to Lorraine Wright was hard, but it had to be done.

Duke was staying behind, because Nora had asked him to.

"Okay," Duke said.

"You're fueled and ready, Mr. Rogan," the attendant said to Sean.

Mr. Rogan. Duke didn't think he'd ever heard Sean addressed as such.

"I'll get Nora," he said.

She was talking on her phone, making arrangements with Warden Greene for landing privileges on prison property. "We just don't have a lot of time, Warden. This is the fastest way in and out. Please."

When her shoulders relaxed, Duke knew she'd gotten her way.

"Thank you." She hung up and smiled wearily at Duke. "We'll be there between four and five this morning, and he'll let me question her immediately. I will find out where Quin is."

"I know you will," he said, though he had his doubts. Sending Nora down there was a risk. If Lorraine was playing a game and didn't know where Maggie was, then Nora was going to waste precious time and suffer emotionally. She hadn't seen her mother in twenty years — Duke had wanted to go with her. To support her.

"Thank you, Duke," she said. "For stay-

461

ing. I need you here, helping find Quin. You can do more than the FBI can."

He read between the lines. And while he did have some abilities that weren't sanctioned by the government, he didn't think they would help now. But he would pull out all his resources, human and otherwise, to find Nora's sister and the killer who'd abducted her.

"Call me, okay? As soon as you leave the prison."

She nodded. Dark circles sagged her eyes. He leaned over and kissed her, then pulled her into a hug. She squeezed him back, clinging to him. He whispered, "Remember, Nora, you've overcome your past. Don't let her drag you back down there. Be strong, and know that I'm here waiting for you."

Duke reluctantly let go of Nora and helped her step into the Cessna. He closed the door and stepped away from the plane. Why was it so hard to let go? But he did. While Nora needed his support, she needed him to find Quin more.

He watched the plane under Sean's command roll toward the runway, where he stopped, waiting for the okay from air traffic control. Duke realized at that moment the two people he loved the most — his brother and Nora English — were leaving in a plane eerily similar to the plane his father had been flying when he crashed in the Cascades.

Duke couldn't protect everyone he cared about 24/7. The plane quickly picked up speed as it traveled down the runway. Then it was airborne, and disappeared into the inky black night.

Duke wasn't surprised that J. T. Caruso was in the office when he turned the key at four that morning, but he had something else to do before greeting him.

He slipped into his office and closed the door. The desk light was on, and that was all he needed. He strode across the room and sat in his executive chair and opened the bottom drawer.

His Colt was still there, its bullets boxed and waiting.

For thirteen years he hadn't needed a gun, and in that time he hadn't lost a client or a case. And though Nora was a trained FBI agent with strong instincts, and she certainly hadn't hired him, he still considered her his case. He was her consultant, and he'd promised to keep her safe.

He might need a weapon other than his brains and brawn. There was too much at stake to continue to appease his guilt.

Duke reached into the drawer, grabbed the Colt, and automatically checked the magazine and barrel. Both were empty.

He loaded a magazine with seven bullets, slammed it into the grip, chambered a round, then popped out the magazine to fit another round in and slammed it back in again, double-checking that the safety was on. It was an automatic process, something he'd done over and over until he could load and unload, clean and put together his gun in his sleep.

He cleaned this gun on the first of every month, so he knew it was in good working condition, but he hadn't held it loaded in thirteen years.

He pulled his holster from another drawer, threaded it through his belt, and holstered his gun. He filled two more seven-round magazines and pocketed them.

He only needed one bullet, but he was a Marine. Marines were always prepared.

Duke heard voices from Mitch Bianchi's office at the opposite end of the hall, but first went to talk to J.T. in his office next to Duke's. He stood in his doorway and said, "Thanks for the plane."

J.T. waved off his appreciation. "Sean knows what he's doing. He's a quick study. Someday he'll be better than me."

It wasn't an arrogant comment. J.T. had been a Navy SEAL and had flown fighter jets, landing on moving aircraft carriers at sea.

"Any luck?"

"Some," he said. "Jayne has sorted the property records and extracted those in the area Megan felt were most likely to be Maggie's home base. If anyone knows psychos, it's Megan."

They were using Rogan-Caruso equipment because it was better and faster than what the FBI had locally. The Menlo Park cybercrimes unit could match them, but they had other cases and priorities and couldn't drop everything to devote the majority of their server time to find one missing adult. Rogan-Caruso could.

"We have the best people mapping the area," J.T. said. "Then we'll pull down satellite photos and overlay in the high-target areas."

This was where it would get dicey. J.T. had high security clearance and worked extensively on top-secret projects, but he was using his clearance for nonsanctioned activities. When Duke had first asked him for help after Quin was kidnapped, J.T. said he wouldn't ask permission, because he already knew the answer. "And," he'd added, "I know you'll be able to clean up any trail we leave."

"I can't tell you how much —"

J.T. put up his hand. "Don't. You'd do the same."

"I'll see how I can help. Are they in Jayne's office?"

J.T. shook his head. "Megan wanted to see the maps printed, so they took over Mitch's office. Megan's on the phone with Hans Vigo at Quantico as they narrow down the range. Since you know a lot more about the case, you'd be invaluable. I thought you were going to Victorville with Nora."

"I need to be here to act on any information she gets from her mother. I feel like we don't have a lot of time. When Maggie O'Dell decides to kill, she does it fast. I keep thinking about the three college students — her friends. Did she plan to kill them then, or was it a reaction to the investigation? Did one of them say something and that was it? Quin Teagan is spirited; she's not going to sit meekly by and wait."

"Psychopaths aren't my area of expertise," J.T. said. "The killers I deal with are completely sane with motivations that are never personal."

Personal. That was what this was about. O'Dell's personal vendetta against Nora.

When she'd killed Russ Larkin for information, it had been quick. He wasn't made to suffer. She'd had personal reasons for wanting the others to die. She'd prolonged their agony. For Nora, the most important thing in the world was family. There was only one thing Nora cared about more than her own life: her sister.

"I think Quin's still alive," Duke said. "She's bait. And Nora will walk right into it. The million-dollar question is whether Lorraine Wright is part of setting the trap, or the key to springing it."

CHAPTER TWENTY-SIX

Nora watched as the lights of Victorville Federal Penitentiary brightened upon the plane's descent. They'd just seen the thin line of dawn on the eastern horizon before their approach; by the time they landed it had disappeared again. But Nora knew that morning would come, just as surely as she knew that Lorraine Wright would lie to her.

But Nora didn't have any other option.

Warden Greene himself met the small plane. "I have Ms. Wright waiting in a private room," he said. "I hope you're not wasting your time."

Me, too. She glanced at Sean. "Are you staying here?"

"Unless you need me."

It was a kind thing to say. Duke had done a terrific job raising his younger brother. Sean was ready for the world, whatever it held. Nora hadn't done the same for Quin. But she'd tried, damn, she tried.

"I'm okay." She walked with the warden to his open-air Jeep. They'd landed a thousand feet from the outer walls of the prison on a little-used road. The warden had a guard block it off at both ends so they'd had a safe place to land.

It was cool this morning up here in the high desert, but Nora liked the dry air and vast starry sky. The stars began to wink out as she watched, as dawn caught up with them. She'd slept under the stars many times, and that was the only thing she'd appreciated about her mother's gypsylike lifestyle.

The closer Nora got to her mother, the tighter her chest felt. She hadn't seen Lorraine since she'd been sentenced, nearly a year to the day from when she'd been arrested at Diablo Canyon. She'd sat in the courtroom and watched as her mother impassively accepted her sentence of life without the possibility of parole. She could have gotten the death penalty, but the federal prosecutor told Nora the jury wouldn't give a pregnant woman the death penalty.

And Nora had been relieved. She hadn't wanted Lorraine's death on her conscience, too. She already had too much pressure. For Quin, for herself. From Cameron Lovitz nearly killing her. From Lorraine killing Andy Keene. It was all coming down on her, and sparing her mother's life at the time had been the only thing to do. But for years she didn't know if opposing the death penalty for her mother was as much her mother's indoctrination of her, or her own beliefs. Because to this day, Nora didn't like the death penalty. It made her uncomfortable knowing someone she arrested might die at the hands of the justice system. But she still did her job. When Maggie O'Dell was apprehended, she would be eligible for the death penalty. And Nora would testify. Not just because it was her job, but because she believed in the system. The system her mother had made Nora fight against for seventeen years.

"I need you to check your weapon," Warden Greene said when they walked through the main entrance.

Nora nodded, showed her credentials and gave the correctional officer her Glock. She was cleared to go through, and the Warden escorted her through a maze of hallways, to a row of doors and windows. Every room was dark except one.

"I'll be right outside, watching, and there's video surveillance, but you have audio privacy. No one can listen in. When you want to leave, ring the bell next to the door."

"Thank you."

Nora looked through the window to the woman in orange sitting at the metal table, hands clasped in front of her. A plastic cup half full of water was next to her.

Lorraine's light brown hair had turned nearly white. Her skin, which had always been tan from living outdoors, was thin and leathery. Her hands were covered with age spots, her nails short and unpainted. Lorraine had once been a beautiful woman, and had taken quiet pride in her appearance. She'd taught Nora to give her manicures, and often shoplifted the latest fashion color for Nora to use. To see her hands so worn and unkempt seemed so very strange. Nora stared at her own hands. Her own nails short, clean, unpainted. She'd never had manicures, as they reminded her of Lorraine.

She had never wanted to see her mother again.

But she had to do this for Quin. She looked through the window, and focused on Lorraine's eyes. Her large, round brown eyes were the one feature she'd passed to all three of her daughters; otherwise, Nora, Quin, and Maggie looked nothing alike. Lorraine couldn't see her, but she sensed someone was outside the window. She straightened her back almost imperceptibly and loosened her hands.

"Okay. I'm ready." Nora wasn't, but she'd never be ready. She didn't want to talk to Lorraine. Lorraine was going to lie to her, Nora knew that. But pathological liars often told the truth. The hard part was knowing what was true, and what was not. But Nora had thirty-seven years' experience watching liars. First Lorraine, then raising a teenager, then going through Quantico, then interviewing suspects. If she didn't let her emotions interfere, her experience and instincts were going to be her advantage.

She removed her badge, which was clipped to her blazer, and pocketed it. No sense antagonizing Lorraine from the start. But still Nora stood tall and confident, knowing that you never show criminals weakness.

The guard at the end of the hall buzzed her in. She stepped over the threshold and the door closed behind her.

"Hello, Lorraine."

Lorraine smiled. "You finally came to visit."

Nora strode to the chair opposite Lorraine and sat down. "This isn't a visit. Quin is in trouble and I think you know why."

Lorraine pouted. Quin wore the identical

expression all the time, but Nora just now realized it came from their mother. The childlike frown was not appealing on a woman of sixty.

"Did you punish her because she came to visit me?" Lorraine asked.

Her tone was innocent, but Nora watched her eyes. When she'd been a child, she'd avoided Lorraine's eyes because they seemed too sharp, too all-knowing. But now — that's where the truth would be told.

Lorraine watched Nora under hooded lids. A neat trick, but Nora had learned interview techniques from the best.

"Maggie killed seven people and will kill Quin if you don't tell me where she's hiding out."

Lorraine's mouth dropped open. Her eyes were confused, glancing down at her hands, then up again. "I don't believe you."

"You know Maggie isn't right in the head. You've seen her every month — or more — for twenty years. You're far from stupid, Lorraine. You had to see that Maggie is wired differently." Nora leaned forward, keeping her face hard, her eyes cold. "Maggie killed Quin's boyfriend because he showed up while she was waiting for Quin. I know Maggie has Quin. I want her safe. It's me Maggie really wants to kill, but she'll kill Quin if she thinks that'll be the way to hurt me. So if you care at all about Quin, you'll tell me where Maggie is."

Lorraine leaned forward, her eyes as cold as Nora's. "Go to fucking hell."

Nora didn't flinch. Inside, she was petrified. Was this why Lorraine had manipulated her to come down here? To get her away from Maggie and Quin, to give her the personal satisfaction of telling her to go to hell for turning her over to the police? Maybe she didn't know anything. Maybe she was ignorant of Maggie's lunacy.

No. No one could spend that amount of time with someone like Maggie and not know the truth.

"You miss your freedom," she said.

"You stole it from me."

"You chose to commit those crimes. You had to pay the penalty."

"I did everything for you."

"You lied to me, you used me, you left me time and time again. You lied to Quin, told her that Randall Teagan was her father. You intentionally put a wedge between me and Quin because you could not stand it that we were happy."

"Happy? Quin hasn't been happy since you sent her mother away to prison."

Nora couldn't help but wonder if that was

true. Quin had troubles for years. She'd experimented with drugs, she'd cut herself in junior high, she'd slept around. She was constantly searching for something, and Nora didn't understand what, but maybe now she did. It wasn't a mother, it wasn't even Nora. It was herself. Lorraine was imperfect, horrid in many ways, and a criminal. But she was Quin's only lifeline to her identity, and nothing Nora could say was going to change that.

That's why Quin had needed to see Randall Teagan. To believe that he was her father. So she could believe, even if deep down she knew it wasn't true, she wasn't the by-product of a one-night stand.

Nora had tried to counsel Quin herself, and maybe that's where she'd gone wrong. She was too emotionally close to her sister, and to stand apart, at a distance, to compartmentalize her feelings in an attempt to help Quin overcome her problems she'd taken away the one thing her sister needed from her. Unconditional love. She couldn't be everything to Quin, but she could be a sister.

Lorraine was watching Nora closely, and suddenly said, "You killed Maggie's father and were never punished for it."

"I didn't pull the trigger."

"You might as well have."

"You told Maggie about that night," Nora prompted.

"I told her the truth."

"*Your* truth," Nora said, pushing back the waves of anger that threatened to explode. She couldn't afford to get angry. That's what Lorraine wanted. Nora saw it in her eyes, in her posture.

Nora did the opposite. She leaned back in the chair, against the instinct of every nerve and muscle in her body, and stared directly into her mother's eyes. "Let me lay it out for you, Lorraine. Either you help save Quin — your daughter — or you won't be going outside for the rest of your life."

"You can't do that."

Nora raised an eyebrow. "Oh?" She pulled out her badge. "You were right, Lorraine. Law enforcement are a bunch of fascist pigs, and I'm the biggest oinker you'll meet. You will never see the sun except through bars in the rec room. And if Quin dies? You'll be in solitary for a year. I have records that you've been meeting with Maggie regularly, and those meetings have increased in the last two years since the arson fires started in Sacramento. She used similar bomb techniques that you and Cameron Lovitz employed. You taught her everything you knew." Lorraine didn't have to know the bombs were common and generic. Nora hoped she squirmed.

"She killed three college students — people you would have liked, people who believed in your cause — because they no longer would help her," Nora continued. "She killed them with jimsonweed. Now, I remember some lessons you gave me about poison. And if you think I won't testify, you know that's not true because I testified against you before, and I will do it again."

"I don't believe you."

Nora pushed back her chair and stood. "I'll take this as a sign that you don't choose to cooperate." Nora shook her head. "And Quin thought you actually cared about her. I told her you never cared."

"You know that's a lie."

Nora put her hands on the table. "Since you won't be having any more visitors, I don't suppose you will ever convince her of that. When I find her, she'll never want to visit you again. She'll never write, she'll never visit, she'll never even think of you. And Maggie will be in prison far, far from here, so you won't even have your crazy lovechild to talk to."

"Maggie won't hurt her!" Lorraine said. "They're sisters."

"Maggie is using Quin to get to me. She has already hurt her," Nora said. She didn't have proof, but she had Maggie's history to predict her behavior. "She will kill Quin if I don't find her soon."

Lorraine said nothing.

Nora's stomach threatened to rebel, but she willed her insides to be still. Had her mother *ever* cared about her? About Quin? In the back of her heart, Nora had imagined that there was a time when Lorraine had looked at her and liked her. Wanted her. But she saw no evidence of this now, and maybe it was all a fantasy Nora had created to get through the long, long days and nights of loneliness.

I'm here waiting for you.

Now she had someone waiting for her. Someone who wanted to be with her. But any future happiness with Duke would be impossible if Quin died.

"You have sixty seconds," Nora said coldly.

"I don't know where she is." It was a lie, as automatic as the sunrise.

"Fifty-five seconds."

"You're just another drone of the Establishment."

Nora stared at her. "Fifty seconds."

"You can't take away my exercise time.

It's my right! I'll sue the prison system."

"Tell it to the judge. Forty seconds."

"Maggie won't kill Quin. I promise you. She loves Quin."

"Thirty-five."

"I love Quin. If I thought she was in danger, I'd tell you. I would! I don't want her hurt. You have to believe me. Just follow the trail and you'll find her."

The trail? What did that mean? Nora said, "Twenty-five seconds."

Lorraine froze. "You're bluffing. You won't do it."

"Twenty."

Dead silence. Stalemate. Nora was losing the battle. Had she played Lorraine wrong? Had she missed something?

"Fifteen."

Lorraine said in a low voice, "Do you remember when you were little, before Quin was born, when we had that wonderful summer with Tommy?"

Tommy Templeton. She'd been seven the summer Lorraine met Tommy. He wasn't one of her regular friends, but a sweet, older man who took Nora on long walks and taught her about flowers and trees and birds. He knew everything, Nora had thought at the time. She'd wanted to stay in his little cabin in the woods forever. He had been a Vietnam vet; some of the scars she saw, some of the scars she didn't. No one did.

"He used to visit me here. Told me he was disappointed that you'd turned on me."

That part was a lie. Nora read it as clear as if Lorraine had first said, *I'm going to lie to you.*

The next part was the truth.

"He stopped visiting five years ago. I wrote to his sister, a bitch — you'd probably like her — and she sent back a cruel letter. Told me he'd died. Just like that, no niceties. No kindness." Her voice took on a snooty tone. *"Dear Ms. Wright, I regret to inform you that my brother Thomas died last April of lung cancer. Please do not contact our family again."* She rolled her eyes. "Bitch." But her voice cracked and Nora wondered if maybe Lorraine had cared for Tommy — maybe in the same way she cared for Quin.

"Tommy's place in the mountains was owned by an army buddy who was MIA. Don't know why Derek Jackson's family never claimed it, maybe they didn't know about it. But Tommy lived there for thirty years and no one bothered him."

It was the truth. It had to be.

Nora walked to the door. "Thank you."

"I don't want Quin to die."

"Neither do I," Nora said. She took one final look at her mother.

The expression on Lorraine's face clearly said, *But I don't give a fuck what happens to you.*

CHAPTER
TWENTY-SEVEN

Duke arrived at Nora's house at six that morning. There were several sheriff's cars, and he spotted Dean Hooper talking to one of the deputies. Hooper saw Duke as he approached and met him halfway. In a low voice he said, "Nora has a silent alarm. It went off at one-fifteen a.m., but patrols didn't respond for nearly thirty minutes."

If Nora had been home . . . Duke couldn't imagine what Maggie's game was. Kidnap Quin, then head to Nora's house to do what? Kill her? Why take Quin in the first place? All Duke knew for certain was that Nora was in grave danger from that young killer, and he hated being separated from her when she was in trouble. He needed her, and Sean, back and under his watch. Only then could he relax even a little.

"What took so —"

Hooper interrupted. "They came, determined no one was home, and left. Dispatch then contacted our office when they realized that the house was flagged as belonging to a federal agent. It was a series of unfortunate events — I didn't hear about the alarm until thirty minutes ago. I called you from the road."

"What did that woman do?" There was no doubt in either of them that Maggie was responsible for the break-in.

"There's some damage."

"And they didn't notice anything when they did a drive-by?"

"There were no lights on, no broken windows or unlocked doors. You'll see."

Duke followed Hooper inside the house. "O'Dell's message is clear," Hooper said. "She didn't spend a lot of time here — in and out — but she left a note."

That Maggie had gotten into Nora's house unnerved Duke. He wanted to be with her right now. How could he make sure she was safe if he wasn't with her?

Maggie had gone straight to Nora's bedroom. She'd taken the largest of Nora's stuffed bears and gutted it. Cotton was strewn everywhere. Pinned to the bear was a note.

You for her. Call me 805-555-4509 to discuss. Any tricks? Look at Mr. Teddy

Bear. Tick tock, I'm not going to wait forever.

"Have you traced the number?"

"It's a prepaid phone, cash transaction,
no name or address."

"Dammit." Duke didn't know why he was
surprised. He'd often used prepaid phones
on covert assignments. "What if a female
agent calls the number?"

"I'm not going to risk it. O'Dell has a
hostage, I don't want to set her off. She
wants an excuse to kill Quin. And we're at a
disadvantage because we don't know where
she is."

"Why break in while Nora wasn't home?
Why not last night? The night before?" As
Duke spoke, he realized maybe Maggie had
known Nora had company all night.

"Maybe she didn't know where she lived
until she took Quin."

"I don't see Quin giving that woman
Nora's address."

"Maybe not, but she had access to Quin's
house, address book, computer — it could
have been written down."

Obviously. Duke was weary and worried.
He said, "Okay, so Nora calls and agrees to
an exchange? We need a plan."

"Agreed."

"Location is everything, but in the mean-time we need to put together a team. J.T. and I are in. Unfortunately, Jack's out of town."

"I've already given our SWAT team leader the heads-up. He's assembling his very best as we speak. O'Dell's not going to hurt Nora."

Duke wasn't so sure. "I don't think she cares about whether she lives or dies. If she goes into this with a suicide plan, it doesn't matter how strong a team we have."

Duke's cell phone rang. "It's Nora," he said, then answered. "Hey."

"I have a location, but it needs some research," she said.

"Give it to me."

"I just sent a text message to you and Hooper. But the problem is the property is extensive. It's in the mountains, probably inaccessible in the winter months. I remember helping stack wood . . ." Her voice trailed off.

"You've been there?"

"When I was little. I'd know the cabin if I saw it, but I have no idea how to get there. I sent you the name of the property owner and the squatter my mother lived with one summer. It's where she is. I know it. If I could see a map of the property, I might be able to figure it out."

"Are you okay?"

"Yes. We're about to take off. Why?"

Duke glanced at Hooper, who nodded. "I'm in your house."

"What's wrong?"

"Maggie broke in and left you a message. She wants to arrange an exchange. You for Quin."

"When and where? Can we stall her? Sean said it'll take about ninety minutes to get back to Mather Field."

"She wants you to call her to arrange the meeting."

Nora was silent and he thought he'd lost her. "Nora?"

"I'll call her. I don't want her getting antsy. She won't know I saw Lorraine. The warden agreed to deny her phone privileges for the next forty-eight hours."

"Hooper has put together a SWAT team, and J.T. and I are on board. You're not alone in this. Don't agree to anything without talking to us."

"I might have to agree to something, but I'm not going anywhere without backup. She's dangerous, I'm not jeopardizing my life or Quin's. But Quin is our number-one priority."

You're my number-one priority. But Duke

486

didn't say it. "She's a civilian," he said in-stead.

"Exactly. I'm going to call Maggie before we take off. What's her contact number?"

He told her. "Nora, I —"

"I'll call you right back." She hung up.

It was better this way. He'd tell her he loved her in person. He'd damn well make sure he had the chance.

Nora took a deep breath. "Hold off for five minutes, Sean. Maggie O'Dell made contact and wants to talk to me."

"You're the boss." Leaning back in the pilot seat, he looked at her. "Here." He handed her a bottled fruit smoothie that advertised one hundred percent of essential vitamins.

"What is it with you Rogans? Always try-ing to get me to eat." But it was cold and she was thirsty. She drank half of it in one long swallow.

"Duke gave me a cooler for the trip, told me to make sure you had something to keep your energy up."

She couldn't keep her lips from twitching into a smile.

"Thank you." She took a deep breath and dialed the number Duke had given her, notepad and pen in hand.

The phone rang. Voice mail picked up on the fourth ring. Nora frowned, then realized that it was a message only for her.

"Nora, this is Maggie. Get a pencil because I'll only say this once and then the phone will self-destruct. Ha ha. The clock has started. You have two hours from this minute to go to the end of Last Chance Road for your next order. Or Quin dies. No tricks. I know this mountain better than you or your fucking FBI friends. Don't test me, or she dies and I'll take as many fascist pigs with me as I can. You miss the deadline, she dies. Keep your phone on, I might have a special treat for you."

There was no beep, no way to leave a message. She called back. No answer.

"Start the plane," she told Sean. "Get back as fast as you can. Find a place to land near Colfax."

"Colfax?"

"Yes." She dialed Duke's number. She knew exactly where Last Chance was. That was where Tommy had lived. It came back to her now. She could picture the cabin as clearly as any of her childhood memories. But it wasn't at the end of the road, it was much farther in the mountains. From her house it would take her at least ninety minutes to get to the end of Last Chance

Road, if not longer. It was mostly a one-lane, precarious road.

From here? She didn't know if she could make it in time.

"Duke," she said breathlessly, "it was a recording. I have two hours to reach the end of Last Chance Road. It's east of Colfax up steep mountain roads. It's near the cabin I told you about, but the cabin is even farther in the mountains. I don't know that I can make it, but she'll kill Quin if I don't."

"Do not go there alone."

"I'm not." But she wasn't certain she would be able to keep that promise. "If she's watching, she'll know if someone other than me shows up. And what if it's a trap? I can't let someone else die in my place."

"You're not going up there to die," Duke said. "You stay away —"

Someone was talking in the background, but Nora couldn't make out the conversation. "Duke, Sean is going to find a place to land near Colfax. That'll bring me closer."

"Nora, don't —"

"You can't ask me to stand down, Duke. Quin is my sister. I can't let her die. Not like Leif Cole or Anya Ballard. Please."

Sean said, "I'm ready."

"We'll find the cabin," Duke said. "Let me know where you're going to land.

Hooper said he'll have backup waiting."

"I promise. Thank you, Duke. I —" What could she say? Appreciation seemed too mild. "I'll see you when we land."

She hung up. "Go," she told Sean. "As fast as you can."

"I have some ideas to get closer. When we are airborne, how'd you like to fly the plane while I look at maps?"

"I've never flown before."

"You're smart, and I'm a great teacher. Besides, once we're airborne there's nothing to do but hold her steady."

"Finally!" Maggie twirled around the room. "It's six in the morning! It's about time she called. I'll bet she wasn't expecting that." She giggled, and Quin knew Nora was in trouble.

"What are you going to do?" she asked, keeping her voice calm.

"Kill her, of course. What'd you think? I'd thank our dear sister for turning her back on the cause and working with the Establishment to put our people in prison? That's what Mom is, you know, a political prisoner."

"She killed someone."

"They were under attack! This is war! It's a revolution. My parents were the leaders of

490

a great movement and I am continuing their work. I have a list of people who are next. They'll never expect it, they think they're invincible. Leaders of the Industrial Complex. Computer giants. Car makers. They're all vulnerable because I cannot lose." She twirled around again, and Quin felt ill. Did Maggie really believe what she was saying? How could she get away with so many murders?

Then Quin realized something. All the people who'd died had been killed this week. This wasn't the culmination of years of crimes, it was a week-long killing spree. Maggie would be stopped. She was too far gone to continue to get away with it.

"Okay, next step," Maggie said, pulling out a digital video camera. It was state-of-the-art, and Quin suspected she'd stolen it from one of her victims.

"Where'd you get the camera?"

"That's for me to know and you to find out," she mocked. "Okay, this is cool. Wow, I can get you really close up here. It's totally clear. You look scared, Quin. Good. That's really good."

Quin tightened her jaw, but couldn't stop her bottom lip from quivering.

"A-O-kay." Maggie had the camera balanced on the table next to Quin. "Perfect.

Don't move. Like you can." She giggled.

Quin scooted the chair two inches to the side.

Maggie screamed and slapped her. The chair fell over. Again. Damn, maybe that had not been so smart, Quin thought as she tasted blood in her mouth.

"Fucking bitch," Maggie mumbled as she paced. She strained to upright the chair, and put her face an inch from Quin's. "Don't do that again or I'll make you really hurt. And Nora will see every second and hear every note of your screams."

Quin didn't doubt her. She sat still.

"Good girl." Maggie clapped and left the room. When she returned, Quin couldn't see what Maggie had in her hands. She pressed a button on the camera and Quin saw a small red light inside.

Maggie pointed the camera toward a knife, then put the blade to Quin's neck. Quin gasped from the shock and fear and started shaking.

"The human body is pretty incredible," Maggie said for the camera. She untied one of Quin's arms. "Quin, sweetie, turn your palm up for the nice people."

Quin held her arm out. She looked at the long-healed scars on her left arm. She'd been twelve when she first cut herself. She hadn't done it in a long time.

Maggie held the knife to her arm and sliced. The sting both hurt and felt good, the pain turning into forbidden pleasure. But it wasn't the same. When she'd cut herself, she'd felt marginally better for a while, before the pain of her life returned. The pleasure now was only in the memories.

"The blood drips and then slows," said Maggie. "Just a little pressure." She put a cloth on her arm and pressed. "It'll start healing. That's the blood clotting."

She tied her wrist back behind her and showed the camera a small vial with a needle sticking out of it. "This, dear sister, is heparin. You know what heparin does. It stops blood from clotting. It doesn't take long to take effect, either. Especially in the dose I prefer."

She drew out the needle. It was filled with the clear drug. She stuck it unceremoniously into Quin's arm. It stung worse than any bee, and Quin gasped.

"An hour, plus or minus. That's all it takes. Now, I don't know how long it takes to bleed out from one slice, and I'm afraid it won't work, so I'm going to try something different." She took a red marker and drew on Quin's body. A three-inch line across her breasts. A five-inch line down each biceps.

"Is that enough?" She looked at Quin. Quin couldn't stop shaking. She wished she could control it, but the fear was growing. She didn't want to die. She didn't want Nora to die. But she didn't see any way out of this. Maggie had the upper hand.

"One more for good measure." She marked Quin's other forearm to match the cut she'd already made. "Good. I think she'll last at least an hour before losing consciousness, then another hour before her blood pressure drops so low she won't be able to recover. This is my insurance, Nora. You bring anyone, you set your fascist pricks on me, and you'll never find her before she's dead. I promise you. In one hour I'll cut along these lines and she'll slowly bleed to death. If you do what I say, I'll come back and bandage her up, which might save her." She held up another vial. "Oh, and this will help. It's Npate, and it'll help the blood clot. I don't know what happens when the two drugs mix, but if you're a good girl we'll find out together. If you're naughty, no one will be here when Quin dies."

CHAPTER
TWENTY-EIGHT

Duke had sent J.T. all the information about Last Chance Road and the property that was owned by Derek Jackson or Tommy/Thomas Templeton. The SWAT team was headed up to the small Colfax airport where they'd stage the manhunt for Maggie O'Dell. They'd transport Nora when she landed and cover her. Duke drove in his sports car with Hooper. They were ahead of the SWAT team.

He had to make sure Nora was safe, and right now he had an edge. J.T. would find the property and they could go in dark and rescue Quin. If Maggie was there, they'd take her into custody before Nora's plane landed. If Maggie wasn't, at least the hostage would be safe. If Nora knew that Quin was safe, she would have the upper hand. But if Maggie took Quin with her to Last Chance Road . . . or set a trap, Duke would need to get to Nora fast. Maggie wasn't logical — anything could happen, which terrified Duke. Suddenly Duke felt claustrophobic. He rolled down his window as they merged onto Interstate 80.

Twenty years old, younger than Sean, Maggie O'Dell had killed at least six people. How could she be so hardened so young?

"Let's get there in one piece," Hooper said. "Cut it to about fifteen miles over the speed limit and I think we'll be fine."

"We don't have time," Duke said, but eased up a fraction on the gas, going from close to ninety to eighty-two.

"What did Sean say?" Hooper asked.

"He's planning on landing at Colfax Airport. It's a small private strip a mile off the freeway. It's a good place. But that's still twenty to thirty minutes from the meeting spot on Last Chance Road. He's not going to make it, and I sure as hell don't want him hotdogging it. The Corvalis goes nearly three hundred miles an hour, but even going maximum speed with a good tailwind is going to put them here in just under ninety minutes."

"Is there any other place he can land closer?"

"I don't know," Duke said, but he didn't want to think about Sean risking a landing in the middle of the mountains. Their

496

parents had died in the Cascades when their dad attempted to land in a valley during a mechanical emergency. Any other place and he might have made it. But the mountains had far more dangers with unexpected terrain and winds.

Sean had better not risk his life, or Nora's. They had time. Just barely, but enough.

J.T. phoned. "I got a parcel that used to be owned by Derek Jackson that fits. It's one hundred ten acres with a Weimar Zip Code, but it's way the hell in the mountains. It doesn't border Last Chance Road, but from the satellites there appears to be an old logging road that cuts through the south portion of the property."

"Used to be owned? Who owns it now?"

"The county foreclosed on it a year ago for back taxes."

"Where's the cabin?"

"I'm still looking for it. Don't go down Last Chance Road, take Weimar Road to Old Bet Road, and by then I hope to have the exact location."

"Why there?"

"I just emailed you the satellite photos and maps. If you look at Last Chance Road, there's no way to get from it to the property by car. If the information you gave me is accurate, you'll be stuck and have to back-track."

"She told Nora to pick up her next in-structions at the end of Last Chance Road."

"That doesn't change the facts, Duke. Civilians first."

He didn't need to be reminded, but he was unhappy about the turn of events.

"You're going to get spotty cell reception up there."

"I'm fine as long as I'm near my car." He had a digital booster in his dashboard.

"I'll send you the coordinates when I find the exact location."

"Thanks, J.T."

J.T. added, "I know what it's like to have someone you care about in danger. Follow your instincts, not your heart."

Nora watched the video stream Maggie had emailed to her phone. Quin would die if Duke couldn't find her. Nora felt so damn helpless, trapped in a plane, unable to stop Maggie O'Dell from hurting her sister. Hadn't she and Quin gone through Hell already? Forced to grow up too fast, doing things no child should have to do, home-less, often hungry, listening to conversations they didn't understand. No medical care, no dentists, no education . . . they might as

498

well have been growing up in a third world country for all Lorraine had cared.

And now . . . this. Dammit, Nora wanted peace in her life. Quin safe. A home. A home with people she loved.

Her sister. And Duke.

"We haven't much time, Sean."

"I heard," he said, grim. "I'm working on it."

She forwarded the link Maggie had sent her to Hooper and Duke and also to Hans Vigo in Quantico for impartial analysis. She was too close to the situation to be useful in that respect; it was her sister in jeopardy. She had to get perspective.

She focused on flying. Sean was a good instructor, and she wasn't doing anything complicated. When they hit turbulence, he simply said, "Hold the wheel with both hands and pull it slightly up. Not too hard, but enough to keep that line right there" — he tapped a gauge on the panel — "level. Watch the line, not the sky."

She did, finding the process calming.

Until Hans Vigo called her. "You sent me a bad link."

"It goes to a video of Maggie and Quin. She injected her with heparin. We don't have much time."

"There's nothing at that URL."

Hooper called her a minute later with the same response.

"How did she know I viewed it?" she asked.

It was Sean who answered. "Easy. She's watching from her computer. As soon as you hit the link, she timed how long it took to buffer the video and then took it down off the server."

"Why would she do that?"

"She doesn't want you to trace her."

"Could I? If it was streaming?"

"Yes, but not instantaneously. It takes time."

Hooper asked, "Did she say anything incriminating?"

"Yes — and she hurt Quin and threatened her." Her voice broke.

"Don't mess with your phone, we can pull the buffer from your memory. Don't turn it off, don't delete anything."

"I won't. Where are you?" she asked.

"We're passing through Auburn."

She turned to Sean. "Where are we?"

"Stockton is coming up to the west."

"How long?"

"Depends where you want to land. I think I have a place that will get us real close." He tapped the map. "It's right next to the reservoir, and at least ten minutes closer than Colfax to your final destination, plus we gain five minutes' flight time."

"I'll take it. Hooper, Sean found a landing spot. He'll give you the coordinates. I need someone to meet me there."

"Negative," he said. "SWAT is headed to Colfax Airport."

"But we may miss our window of time. You didn't see that video! Maggie injected Quin with heparin and will cut her in less than an hour. I need this time."

"We have a little time, Nora."

"No we don't!" She squeezed her eyes closed. "Hooper, the woman is on edge. I can't trust her, and the more time we have the better. Please understand that. I need to get to Last Chance Road earlier than she thinks I can make it. We need every advantage we can get at this point."

"Let me talk to Hooper," Sean said to her. She handed Sean the phone.

"Hooper, tell Duke I'm not landing anywhere I'm not one hundred percent confident that I can get both in and out without trouble." He listened, then read off the coordinates of the landing spot. "Yes, and enough for takeoff as well . . . Thanks, see you there."

He handed Nora back the phone. "Hooper cleared it."

"Your brother just worries about you, like I do Quin."

"It's a little more than that." He paused. "Our parents died in a small-plane crash."

Nora looked at Sean, her heart breaking. "I'm sorry. I didn't know."

"Duke didn't like it when I started taking flying lessons from J.T., and I just made my hours to fly solo. But I assure you I know what I'm doing," he added quickly.

"I have complete confidence in you, Sean."

"It's time, Quin." Maggie took out her knife and cut Quin on one biceps.

Quin bit her lip to keep from crying out. Her head felt fuzzy, and she wondered if Maggie had put something else in the heparin. Or maybe this was a side effect of the drug.

She turned her head and watched as her blood seeped from the long, shallow cut. She was going to die.

"I wish we could have really been sisters." Maggie cut her other arm along the mark she'd made earlier.

Quin wished she'd listened to Nora. She wished she hadn't fought with her. She wished she could tell her she was sorry.

Maggie cut the small mark on her right

forearm to match the one that was still bandaged on her left. Maggie didn't seem to notice or care about the bandage. She was focused intently on running the blade lightly along her skin, cutting the skin and barely slicing the layer of muscle underneath. Under any other circumstances, the cuts wouldn't be fatal. But today, they would be.

Maggie kissed her on the cheek. "I'm sorry."

She sounded sincere; then Quin saw the sick joy in her eyes as she cut along her chest.

It was the most painful cut of all, and Quin cried.

Maggie whispered in her ear. "Just a little advice — the more you move, the more you panic, the faster your heart pumps, and the faster you die. Maybe that is for the best — get it over quick. But it won't be as much fun for me if Nora can't watch, so I'd rather you calm down." She kissed her again. "I'll see you soon." She grabbed a backpack and left.

Quin willed her heart to slow down, she tried not to panic. But Maggie's words had been meant to terrify her, to make her heart pump, and it took every ounce of strength to control her breathing. To control her thoughts. To keep her eyes closed and not watch the blood seeping out of the cuts on her arms.

She felt the warm blood drip down her cold skin. It was pooling under her buttocks, dripping off her fingertips. Her head was heavy, and she just wanted to lie down. To lie down and sleep forever.

Duke had turned off on Weimar Road when J.T. called him with information about the cabin. "I sent you detailed maps. They're fresh, you should be good."

"You found the cabin?"

"Yes. You're ten minutes away, plus or minus. You'll have to park a quarter mile away, and there's a chance she will hear you."

"Noted. I need a footpath from the cabin to Last Chance Road."

"Give me a couple minutes."

Hooper said, "What makes you think there's a footpath?"

Duke said, "I think she plans on taking Nora out as soon as she reaches the end of Last Chance Road. Think about it — if she planned on sending Nora from place to place, she wouldn't tell her to meet this close to where she's hiding. There's no easy road, so there has to be some sort of trail."

504

"True," Hooper said. "But it's still a risk. She could hunker down in the cabin, draw out the time."

"So we go in smart. We were both Marines, we assess and act. On foot she can disappear. If she has any survival skills, which we have to assume she has, she can run parallel to us if she spots us, or simply get away. I'll bet we don't see her car. It'll be well hidden."

Duke drove as fast as he dared on the winding mountain road. He smelled something and first thought his car was burning transmission fluid, but immediately realized that wasn't it.

"Hooper, do you smell that?"

Hooper said, "Yes. A fireplace? We're close." He frowned. "No — it's not."

"It sure as hell isn't a fireplace. We have a forest fire on our hands."

"Damn weird coincidence. I'll call it in."

"It's no coincidence," Duke said. "Tell your SWAT team to step on it and get their ass to the airstrip. Sean and Nora are five minutes out, and if that fire is anywhere near the road, they could be trapped."

Sean said, "Nora, look over there — to the west. That's a fire. And there — there — I see three."

"Five," she said, and frowned. "Five fires? They're pretty small, but two are right next to the road."

"That woman is fucking crazy," Sean said as he pulled back and prepared to land on the old abandoned airstrip.

"Why would she set fires? It makes no sense — she'd be preventing me from —"

"Hold on tight." Mouth set grim, Sean fought to control the plane on the short, rocky runway. Nora held on as the tail swerved when they braked too fast. Sean eased up, then down again, and stopped with plenty of room to spare.

"I hope I didn't damage the plane too much," Sean said.

"You did great, Sean." She got out of the plane and looked around. "Brian and his team aren't here."

"Maybe that's why she set the fires," Sean said, taking off his headgear and walking around the plane for inspection. "To stop you from having backup."

"But the fire could have stopped me from making it as well."

Sean shook his head. "If you were on time, you would make it. Your backup might have as well, unless she set one closer to the highway."

"But it's September — the forest is dry.

This could set off a huge forest fire, thousands of acres. The waste —" Nora was distraught. She couldn't help but feel partly responsible. "Or she set them to trap us all. She doesn't care who dies as long as she gets what she wants."

No. She wasn't responsible in any way for Maggie O'Dell and her behavior.

She called Duke. "It's Nora. Sean and I just landed. We saw five small fires close to Last Chance Road while we were descending. But they're going to spread quickly."

"Hooper and I smell them. Is your backup there?"

"No."

"Shit. Hold on."

Nora looked around the mountainside. The smoke was beginning to rise, she saw billows heading straight up. But a wind was beginning to kick up, and that would be the worst thing for the forest. And them.

Duke got back on the phone. "SWAT couldn't get through. There's a fire on the road. Deliberately set bonfire. The fire department is on their way, but it'll be at least thirty minutes before they can get it cleared."

"I have to go."

"Drag it out with her, if possible, Nora. Hooper and I are almost to the cabin."

"Okay."

"Nora, please — I can't lose you or Sean."

"And I have no intention of getting either of us in trouble. But there's no way in hell I'm leaving anyone alone on this airstrip with that woman running around setting fires, and until I know that you have Quin, I have to head to the meeting place."

"I understand, but — just be careful."

"I promise." She wanted to say more, but what else could she say? She hung up and motioned to Sean. "We're on our own, Sean. But if she sees you, I don't know what she'll do."

"I'm pretty good in the mountains. I made myself a map —" He held it up. She couldn't read it, but he didn't seem to have that problem.

"You're a city boy."

"Looks can be deceiving," he said with a wink, reminding her of his older brother. He tossed her a walkie-talkie. "You go, I'll follow, and I won't let you out of my sight — even if you can't see me. And you can buzz me on the walkie-talkie any time."

"Let's go."

CHAPTER
TWENTY-NINE

The small roughly hewn redwood cabin
with a wide porch along two sides rested in
the center of a wide, flat knoll with a
hundred feet of open space around all sides.
Canyons dropped down on two sides, one
so steep it might as well be a sheer drop. An
idyllic setting under any other circumstances.

But the fires to the north and west were
growing, and they had no idea where Maggie O'Dell was, or whether Quin was dead
or alive. Or if there was a booby trap.

But they could find out quickly. Duke
took the thermal imager out of the sheath
in his belt and turned it on. A minute later
it began to register heat signatures in the
cabin.

"There're two people inside," Hooper
said.

Duke shook his head. "No. Just one.
Here." He pointed to the long humanlike

shape in an array of colors, from dark to light.

"Move it a bit — see! There. It moved."

"Too small. It's an animal."

"You're sure?"

"Yes. Small dog or cat."

In tacit agreement, Duke and Hooper ran low to the ground to the cabin from opposite sides. They made it without trouble, and listened, waiting for a ten count.

There was no sound from inside the cabin. Duke concentrated, bringing up all his past military training, and listened. Nothing but breathing. Gasping.

He double checked the thermal imager at closer range and identified one individual inside.

At the count of ten, Duke went around to the front door. Hooper joined him. "It's secure," he said.

Duke kicked open the door and went in low, while Hooper went in high.

Quin Teagan was tied to a chair, her torso covered in blood. She wasn't gasping, but breathing through her mouth, a low raspy sound. Her head lolled forward.

Duke went to her while Hooper checked the bathroom and closet and cabinets.

"Clear." Hooper knelt next to the chair and helped Duke untie her from the chair.

"The missing Butcher-Payne duck is in the bathroom."

It took Duke a minute to register that Hooper said *duck*. "We need sheets. Towels if there's nothing else."

Hooper ran through the cabin, found sheets on a Hide-A-Bed. "This is it."

"They'll have to do." Duke eased Quin to the floor while Hooper cut the sheets with his pocketknife.

They tied the strips of cotton tightly around all wounds. The cut on her chest was the worst, and Hooper applied firm pressure while Duke searched the cabin for any strong tape. All he found was duct tape, but it was going to have to suffice. They needed to keep firm pressure on the wound while moving her.

"Nora," Quin whispered. "Nora."

"She's fine," Duke said, hoping it was true.

"Fire. Trap."

Duke cringed. He needed to get to Nora and Sean. But Quin would die if she didn't get immediate medical attention.

"Nora said there was a vial of something to counteract the effects," Hooper said.

"I don't know that I'd trust anything O'Dell said," Duke grumbled.

Hooper looked around. Found two vials,

one nearly empty and labeled heparin, one labeled with a name he didn't recognize. He shoved them in his pocket. "I'm taking them just in case."

Duke was about to pick her up when Hooper said, "I'll do it. Save your energy for the trek to Last Chance Road. You're going to need it. Back me up to the car, then I'll take her to town where the ambulance is waiting, and you continue to the other road. If O'Dell is setting the fires to create a trap of some sort, you've got to alert them and get them the hell out of there."

The end of Last Chance Road was a loop around a mountain peak more than four thousand feet in elevation. This part of the road was used only for forest patrol and fire prevention — it was so narrow a vehicle couldn't turn around, so you literally had to drive around the peak, about a half-mile journey, in order to head back to town.

Nora caught sight of Sean only two or three times during the fifteen-minute jog along Last Chance Road until she'd gone around the entire loop. He'd stayed in the middle, on the peak, flitting in and out from behind trees, as sure-footed as a mountain goat. The smoke was getting thick coming from the south, and to the north and west were both deep ravines that were impassable.

She'd come from the east.

She pulled out the walkie-talkie Sean had the foresight to bring with him. "The fire is coming from several points south of the loop, and the other two sides are deep canyons. We need to go back."

"Roger. I'll follow your lead."

Nora looked around for any sign of Maggie. Where was she? She started back along the edge of the road, and every hair rose on her skin. She was being watched. Her phone vibrated. She glanced down.

It was a text from Duke, and he'd sent it to both her and Sean.

We have Quin and Hooper is taking her to town. She's alive, but needs medical attention. I'm on my way to you. The fire is a trap. Get back to the plane ASAP.

Quin was alive. Lorraine hadn't lied about the cabin, and for the first time Nora felt a sliver of forgiveness. Her anger and resentment toward her mother faded a bit, now that she knew Quin was safe, that Lorraine had helped to save her.

The heavy weight of fear, worry, and guilt

lifted from Nora's shoulders. Now she could focus on her suspect, Maggie O'Dell.

Sean said in the walkie-talkie, "Move it, Nora."

She started walking, then running. The sense of being followed increased as the smoke blew in her direction. The wind was increasing, which was the worst thing for the fire other than the dry needles and brush lining the forest floor.

A rock the size of a large fist fell from the hill and rolled in front of her, and she had to jump over it to avoid twisting her ankle. Another rock rolled down, and another; then one grazed her in the shoulder, this one smaller but with greater velocity. Damn, that hurt.

She pulled out her gun, unable to see her predator.

Sean asked, "What are you doing?"

"Where are you? Sean, get down here. Someone's up there!" It had to be Maggie.

They were sitting ducks here on the road. Nora couldn't see Maggie, but Maggie had sight of her enough to throw rocks.

"I'm coming — I'm on the road behind you."

Another rock hit her in the shoulder, and she dropped her gun. She dove against the mountainside, grabbing her gun on the way.

Sean rounded the corner, and rocks were flung at him. Maggie must have a slingshot, and was damn accurate with it. A good-size rock hit Sean in the side of the face, knocking him to his knees.

Maggie could stone them to death if they couldn't find cover.

Nora shouted, "Maggie! Show yourself."

"You brought someone?" A voice came from above. Nora looked, but couldn't see anyone. The air was getting thick. "It's your fault that he's going to die."

Another rock hit Sean as he rose, this one in his lower back. He fell back down.

Nora aimed her gun toward where the rocks were coming from and fired. Once. Twice. Three times, then ran to Sean as he struggled to rise from the road.

"Come on, Sean, please," she ordered.

He stood, shook his head as if to clear it, and ran unsteadily with Nora back against the cliff. "This is the safest place," she whispered. "Stay close to trees and —"

A rock hit her on the top of her head and she fell to her knees, her vision gone. She tried to shake it off, but couldn't move. Sean picked her up and sat her back against a redwood. "Nora — shit." He touched her head and she winced. "You're bleeding."

"You can sit there as long as you want,"

Maggie's voice called from above. "You'll die from the fire if you hide, or I'll pummel you to death if you move."

Nora whispered, "Fire tower. I'll bet there's a fire tower up there."

Sean tried calling Duke on his cell. "Damn, I'm not getting through. We're going to have to make a run for it. If we can get just a bit more down the road, we'll be out of her range."

"I can't. Wait a minute."

"Okay."

Nora put her head in her hands and willed herself to stand, but she couldn't. Sitting still she felt dizzy, but standing she'd pass out. She had to get over this.

"You go," she told Sean. "I'll cover you." Her hand was shaking as it held her Glock.

"You'll shoot yourself in the foot. I'm not leaving you. I'll think of something." He coughed. "If we wait ten minutes, she won't be able to see us through the smoke."

"It'll be too late. Do you hear it?"

They listened to the fire crackling on the other side of the peak. "Small consolation that she'll die in the blaze, too," Nora said.

"You're not going to die. Duke would never forgive me."

"I could say the same about you," Nora told Sean.

"Then think."

Duke heard the gunshots and followed the footpath up the south side of the mountain. Fire was to the west of him moving north, and the wind kept the worst of the smoke away from him.

And toward Sean and Nora.

He picked up his pace, faster than he should be going on the steep path, but suddenly it flattened out on Last Chance Road and he saw the trail to the fire tower J.T. had told him about. He glanced at the digital map. The trail was a steep incline all the way up for more than a hundred yards, which meant he'd be seriously winded, with Maggie well prepared for his arrival.

Or he could go toward the smoke and come up the western slope. Less steep, but harder to breathe.

He chose the path obscured with smoke.

He heard helicopters in the distance. He had to give Maggie credit — she'd set the fires in a pattern, starting closer to the interstate and moving southeast. That would keep the firefighters working first on the flare-ups closer to the population centers, leaving Maggie, him, Sean, and Nora alone on this lonely road.

A text message from Sean popped up on

his screen.

I don't know if this will get to you, but
hurry — Nora's injured and we're trapped.
If we move, that bitch will kill her.

Duke ran into the smoke.

CHAPTER THIRTY

Hooper passed Quin off to the paramedics. She had lost consciousness completely in the car, her skin extremely pale.

"She was injected with heparin," Hooper told them. He pulled the vials out of his pocket and showed the EMT. "Will one of these counteract it?"

The EMT handed the vials to the lead paramedic. "This is heparin, this is ethylene chlorohydrin."

"Can that help her?"

"It'd kill her pretty quickly if injected."

Duke had been right, Hooper thought. If Nora had found Quin she might have taken what O'Dell said on the video at face value and injected her thinking she'd save her, only to end up killing her.

"Is she going to be okay?" Hooper asked.

"She needs blood." He got a vial ready.

"What's that?"

"Vitamin K. It will counteract the effect

of the heparin, but it's going to take a while. Have you typed her?" he asked the EMT.

"A-negative."

"Ask around, we need blood now. She's not going to make it to the hospital."

Hooper was B-positive. He called his SWAT team, which was only five minutes up the road. "Anyone there have A-negative blood?"

A moment later, one of the men responded. "O-negative."

Hooper asked the medics. "Is O-negative acceptable?"

"The universal donor. Get him over here."

Duke's lungs were burning as he reached the base of the fire tower. Here, the smoke wasn't as bad, but it was getting worse every minute. He quietly climbed the ladder to the top of the tower. Maggie O'Dell was holding a slingshot and was so focused on her target that she didn't hear Duke as he stepped silently into the open-air tower.

Duke quickly assessed the situation. The tower was twenty feet square, open on all sides with three-foot-high walls. There was nothing inside, nothing to hide behind. Just him and Maggie O'Dell.

Her back was to him. Her backpack, full of rocks, at her feet. Rocks that she was pummeling Sean and Nora with below. But the smoke was growing thicker, and he could practically see her body tense in frustration. Her perfect plans were not-so-perfect, Duke thought. In a few minutes Sean and Nora would be safely away, or the smoke would be too thick to see them.

He approached cautiously, slowly, drawing his gun. He didn't want to shoot her. He didn't want to kill anyone, even someone as vile and psychotic as Maggie O'Dell.

She froze. She'd sensed him.

"Hold it right there," he said gruffly.

She didn't move.

"Put down the slingshot. I have a gun." He took another step toward her, a watchful eye on her hands.

She whipped around and fired the slingshot at him. But her aim was off. The rock barely grazed his shoulder. Damn, it still hurt, but he wasn't out. He held his gun steady on her. "Drop it."

Maggie's face twisted in anger. "You! You're not supposed to be here!"

"Hands up, Maggie."

"No. You can't make me."

"Quin is safe. We found her, she's already on her way to the hospital. She's going to live."

Duke wasn't certain that was true, but he

wanted to convince Maggie that she'd failed. He needed her compliant. He didn't have handcuffs, but he couldn't very well wait here in the tower until help arrived. Forest fires were erratic and could shift direction without warning. Right now, winds were low, but at any time that could change.

He didn't know if she had a gun, but she had a knife strapped to her belt. He watched her hands. A knife could easily kill even if thrown twenty feet, and Duke was much closer than that.

"Get your hands up now!" he ordered for the second time. He saw her calculating her options.

He approached her, finger on the trigger. He would have to shoot her if she went for the knife. She stood there, lips tight, glaring at him. "You're screwing with my plans," she snapped. "I don't like that!"

Duke put the gun to her neck and unsheathed the knife in one fluid motion. She stood perfectly still, neither helping nor hindering him. He didn't trust her. After everything she'd done, she wasn't going to come in this easy.

He had no place for the knife, and tossed it over the side of the fire tower.

"You first," he said, gesturing toward the ladder.

"I don't want to go." She crossed her arms.

"The fires you set are heading this way."

"I know. You'll just die with me I guess."

"I'm not dying today, sister, and neither are you, unless you try some dumb-ass move. Now get a move on."

She glared at him.

"Fine," he said. "Nora had a lot of questions about your handiwork, I guess you won't be able to answer them."

"Don't talk about her!"

"She's on her way to her plane right now. She'll be out of here and you'll be stuck. She can tell the media anything she wants about your activities. Your murder spree."

"I didn't kill anyone who didn't deserve it!"

"Your best friend deserved to be poisoned?" Duke shook his head. "And what did Quin ever do to you other than offer you friendship?"

Her face reddened. "She ignored me! She was so scared of what Nora would say she didn't want me anywhere near her. Well, I showed her! I will *not be ignored!*"

"Then you'd better get your ass down that ladder or Nora English will make sure you're not even a footnote in serial killer history."

Maggie laughed harshly, ending with a cough. "Sure, we're both killers. She killed my father, I just balanced the scales."

"Nora had nothing to do with your father's death."

"That's what she told you, but she's a liar. She set him up, him and our *mother.* Can you believe she testified *against* her own mother? Sent her to prison for the rest of her life?"

Duke pushed harder. He had to get the woman out of the tower and off the mountain. He didn't know how much time they had. "Do you know how we found Quin? Through Lorraine. Your mother ratted you out."

"Bull-fucking-shit. My mom didn't know about any of this. But she hates Nora as much as I do, she'd approve."

"When Nora told her you'd kidnapped Quin, Lorraine was heartbroken. Told Nora about Templeton's cabin in the woods and exactly how to get there." He'd fudged the details a bit, but saw that it was working. Maggie was shaking, her mouth open. He went on. "She picked Quin over you."

"I don't believe you!" But her expression said she did. She believed it because he was here and had told her he'd saved Quin.

"We have Quin," he said, "and your cat and the duck you stole from Butcher-Payne. It has a broken wing. You thought it might not be able to survive on its own."

Her lip quivered and tears streamed down her face. "Lorraine told you?"

"Lorraine told *Nora.*"

That did it. She practically collapsed into herself and shuffled across the floor toward the ladder.

"Hold it," he said as she was about to step down. Gun to her head, he quickly patted her down. He still didn't trust her, but he couldn't find a weapon on her.

"Okay," he said. "Go down slowly." He coughed, the smoke was thicker, and he feared they wouldn't be able to find their way to the plane. He hoped Sean knew exactly how to get there in the dark, because they might as well be blind in this smoky forest. He couldn't see any flames, but he smelled the aromatic scent of burning pine. He preferred it in his fireplace.

This high up he had a perfect cell phone signal. He called Sean. "I have her. I don't have cuffs, but she's unarmed."

"Hold on," Sean said, and Duke heard him ask Nora about handcuffs. "Nora has a pair," he said.

"Good. We'll meet you at the road. I hope you know how to get to the plane."

He watched Maggie carefully walk down the ladder. Methodically. Slowly.

"I do. Hurry."

"Maggie suddenly slid the rest of the way down the ladder, her hands tempering her fall as they loosely held the wooden sides. That had to sting, but Duke had no time to think. She was already at the bottom.

"She's running," he told Sean, stuffed his phone and Colt in his pants and followed Maggie's lead.

Nora tensed. "Did Duke just say she was running?"

"Yes." Sean stood next to her protectively. "We need cover. Can you walk?" He coughed, the smoke becoming a major problem for both of them now.

"I have to," she said.

Sean helped her up. Shoulder aching, Nora was limping and could practically feel the bruises growing on her thigh and back and head. But she no longer had the urge to vomit, and while her head throbbed, she felt marginally better.

Apprehensive, she watched the mountainside for Maggie or Duke. The smoke waffled in, hanging eerily in the air. It was nine in the morning, but it might as well have been dusk.

"Are you okay?" Sean asked quietly.

"Why?"

"You're listing to the right."

"I didn't notice," she said. "My head hurts, but —"

"I think you have a concussion. Here — this is a good place to take cover while Duke tracks her." He helped Nora over a fallen redwood tree. It was large enough that if they sat behind it, they would be mostly out of sight. She pulled her gun out. Maggie couldn't think she'd be able to get to them, not three against one, but Nora knew that Maggie didn't think logically. Maybe in her own mind it made sense, but not to Nora.

"Sit still," Sean said, "I'll keep —"

Movement to the west had them both bracing for attack. But it was Duke who emerged from the woods.

"You're both okay?" he asked, partly jogging, partly sliding down the mountainside to reach them.

"Yes," Nora said.

"Nora has a concussion," Sean said.

"We don't know that —"

Duke squatted beside her, touched her face, her head, his hand came away with sticky blood. He kissed her lightly, then helped her stand. "We need to get out of here. You need a doctor, and the smoke is getting so thick I don't know if Sean will be able to take off."

"Don't worry about that," Sean said. He glanced at Duke, concern on his face. Nora caught the exchange.

"Boys," she said, "I'm okay. Really. Do you know which way Maggie went? She obviously knows this mountain well, she can disappear and we won't be able to find her."

"Right now, getting the three of us out of the middle of this forest fire is my number one priority," Duke said. "We'll come back and search for her when it's contained."

"She could be long gone," Nora said. She wouldn't be able to rest knowing that Maggie O'Dell was free to go after the people she loved.

"We'll cross that bridge later." Duke helped Nora over the log, down to the road, and then they stayed to the side, away from the steep incline down into the deep canyon. Duke kept his gun drawn, knowing that they weren't safe from Maggie yet. "You do know how to get back, right Sean?"

"Yes. Keep to this road." He had a compass in his hand. "Where the road meets itself, we head two degrees northeast and we'll hit the plane in less than a quarter mile."

Duke was extremely worried about Nora. She insisted she was fine, but she couldn't walk in a straight line. That made her vulnerable, and Maggie was in the woods. Waiting.

Duke had watched her, listened to her, and knew Maggie wasn't going to run away. She wanted revenge on Nora for a whole host of things that had little to do with her in the first place. But in Maggie's head, Nora was to blame for everything that had gone wrong in the young girl's life. Maggie fully intended to go after her now, especially because Nora was physically nearby. Duke didn't think that Maggie would be able to help herself.

He made hand motions to direct Sean to keep his eyes forward, and Duke would scan the mountainside and rear. The smoke had him at a disadvantage, but his military training gave him an edge. He relied more on his ears than his eyes.

Nora tripped and Duke caught her before she fell to her knees. He steadied her and said, "We have to move faster."

"I know," she said.

Cough cough cough.

Duke listened. The coughing came from

the tree line right above them on the mountainside. Maggie was there, just out of sight, but he'd heard her.

"Duke —" Nora had heard her as well.

"Keep moving," he commanded. He glanced at Sean and motioned for him to flank Nora's left side. "Faster." Maggie had uneven terrain, which gave them a second advantage. He couldn't rule out that she had a weapon. He had frisked her, but not as extensively as he would have liked. And for all he knew, she could have had a hidden cache near the fire tower.

The road curved up ahead, signaling they were halfway to the plane. Helicopters in the distance told Duke that fire suppression was in full force. A far distant siren gave him additional hope. The smoke didn't seem to be thickening any more, and visibility was about twenty, twenty-five feet. He hoped it was better in the field where Sean had landed, or they'd be calling for a helicopter.

A glimpse of movement in the woods above them. Maggie was traveling parallel, and Duke suspected she was either trying to make it to the plane before them, or running to cut them off.

Duke said to Nora, "Come on, sweetheart, pick up the pace. We have company."

Though Nora was limping and in pain, he didn't have any choice. He had to push her. They needed to reach the curve first.

A sharp sting hit Duke on the side of his jaw and he stumbled and fell to his knees. He could see nothing but black and stars for several seconds. He started to shake it off, called, "Nora —"

She'd stopped when he fell. "Duke, you're bleeding!" She started toward him.

"No!" he cried as he heard a screech from the trees and saw Maggie running down the mountainside, gravity aiding her momentum as she lunged toward Nora.

Duke jumped up, Sean right behind him, as Maggie slammed her body into Nora's. Nora had only a moment of realization before she fell to the ground.

The women rolled across the road, Maggie holding Nora by the shoulders, forcing her to come with her.

Maggie was aiming them for the cliff. She planned to kill herself, and take Nora with her.

Duke sprinted, reached for Nora's shirt and caught the collar, pulling her back. Sean dove like he was sliding headlong into first base and maneuvered his body between the women and the edge of the cliff.

"Sean!" Duke shouted. He was precariously close to the edge, but he controlled his slide and his body thwarted Maggie's plan. Her head hit Sean's legs. Duke tried to pull Nora away from the deranged killer, but Maggie held on to her body tightly.

Nora screamed and Duke saw the knife in Maggie's hand. She brought up her arm, her face full of unstable rage, and Duke saw blood dripping from the blade.

She'd stabbed Nora.

Duke aimed his Colt at Maggie's hand and without hesitation, fired *one two three.*

Her hand was no longer there, only a bloody pulp from three well-placed bullets.

Maggie was on her knees, screaming in pain, inches from the edge of the precipice. Nora was beneath her. Too close to the abyss. Too close to death.

Sean scrambled to grab Nora under the arms and pull her to safety, while Maggie caught hold of her waist with her uninjured hand. On purpose, Maggie put her own legs over the edge, holding on to Nora's lower body. Nora cried out. "Duke!"

"I'm right here!" He maneuvered for a shot, but it wasn't clear. He was sweating, unable to get a lock on Maggie.

Nora pleaded with Maggie. "Let me go!" She tried to kick the woman away, but Maggie held on tight. Her grip on Nora was the only thing preventing her from free-falling hundreds of feet.

"Never! You're dead, Nora, dead!" Maggie screamed.

Duke shouted, "Sean!"

"I have her! Do it!"

Duke aimed and fired a bullet between Maggie's eyes. Time seemed to freeze. The shock on her face, the realization that she was dead right as the bullet hit. Her body fell, her weight dragging Nora farther over the edge, the dry earth crumbling, jeopardizing both Sean and Nora.

Maggie disappeared from view and Duke heard the sick thump of her body hitting a tree. Nora's legs had disappeared over the edge. Sean had her by one biceps.

"Duke! She's slipping!"

Duke crawled over and grabbed Nora's other arm. "Now!" he told Sean. They pulled Nora up and onto safe ground.

There was so much blood on her. Duke didn't know what was Maggie's and what was hers. "Nora, where are you hurt?" He had to stop the bleeding.

"My thigh," she said. "She had a knife strapped inside her thigh. When she tackled me I felt her reach for it. I'm okay."

Duke highly doubted that Nora was okay. He pulled off his shirt and found the knife wound on Nora's upper thigh. It went deep on the outside of her leg. He pulled off his shirt and tied it as tight as possible around the gash.

He then inspected the rest of her body. She winced when he found the place on her shoulder where Maggie had pummeled her with rocks. There were a myriad of scrapes and bruises and she was going to feel like shit for the next few days. But she was alive.

"God, Nora, I —" He couldn't say it out loud. He thought he was going to lose her. He pulled her into his arms, kissed her forehead, her cheeks, her lips. "I love you, Nora. Don't scare me again."

Nora rested her head against his chest. "Why did she do it?" she asked, but Duke didn't think she expected answers. He didn't think there were any that they could understand.

"I had to —"

Nora reached for his face, tears streaming down her own. "Shh. She gave you no choice. I just — I wish it was different. I wish I could have fixed it before — but I don't know. It's such a tragic waste."

Nora closed her eyes and started coughing.

Sean said, "We need to run, folks, or we'll be in serious shit."

"She's in no condition to walk." Duke picked her up. She held on to his neck. "Lead the way, brother." He looked around. "The smoke isn't getting worse. It might be improving."

"I hope so," Sean said. "I don't think I could get out if it's this bad where the plane is parked."

"I'm proud of you, Sean." They walked briskly in silence until Sean led them to an old logging road that branched off of Last Chance Road. "If you want a full-time position at Rogan-Caruso, you have it."

"Thanks, Duke. I appreciate it. Let me think about it."

Duke frowned. "What do you need to think about? I thought that's what you wanted."

"Maybe I do. But I have some other ideas I want to explore."

Nora squeezed the back of Duke's neck. He glanced down at her in his arms, still concerned, but pleased that the color was returning to her face.

"Sean will be fine in anything he does," she said.

"I know. I just want to keep my eye on him," he whispered. "And you."

"Good," Nora said with a weak smile. "I want to keep my eye on you, too. I love you."

CHAPTER
THIRTY-ONE

Nora sat next to Quin's hospital bed. She was so pale, still so weak, the cuts turning into angry red welts. She'd be scarred forever, but she was alive.

Her sister would live.

Agent Ted Bliss stepped in with a vase of yellow roses. Hooper had told her Ted saved Quin's life by giving blood in the ambulance on the way to the hospital. She smiled at him. "Come in."

"How's she doing?"

"Better."

"She has more color."

"Thanks to you. You can put those on the table."

"Thanks." He put them in a vase on the night table. "Well, I just wanted to bring those by."

"Thank you. I know she'll love them."

He looked at Quin, nodded. "Um, tell her I said hi."

"I will. Thanks, Ted." She watched him leave. Yellow roses meant friendship, but Nora bet he wanted more. He had a crush on Quin big-time.

Nora took Quin's hand and lightly rubbed it. Her skin was still cool, though she was under multiple blankets. She'd woken up several times, but not for long, and the doctors said the sleep was good for now, but in the next day they'd be working on keeping her awake more, getting her up and walking around.

Quin yawned. "Hi, Nora."

"Hey. How are you feeling?"

"Like I've been beaten to a pulp."

"That's what you said yesterday. What's new?"

"Okay, I feel like I've been beaten into partial pulp. A little better than yesterday."

Nora handed her some water. Quin sipped through the straw.

"Ted came by again."

Quin glanced at the night table. "He brought more flowers?"

Nora nodded, grinning.

"He's sweet."

"He is."

"I loved Devon and I never told him." Quin's voice cracked and her eyes welled with tears.

"Honey, you need to take one day at a time."

"I heard you talking to Duke yesterday."

Nora frowned. "When?"

"In the evening, near the end of visiting hours. I'm glad you have someone like him. He treats you like you're special. Like you're the only woman in the world for him."

Nora's stomach fluttered. "He's good that way."

"You deserve someone like him."

"So do you. Not Duke," she quickly corrected, "but someone like him. Someone who treats you special."

"I heard you say you went to see Lorraine. Did you really?"

"Yes." Nora still had mixed feelings about her experience, but she didn't regret it. Without the visit, she'd never have found Quin in time.

"You did that for me."

"You bet. I love you, Quin. I'd do anything for you."

Tears streamed down Quin's face, and Nora brushed them aside. "Don't cry." Nora's own eyes burned with unshed tears, watching the anguish on Quin's face.

"I'm so sorry for what I said. I thought I was going to die and never tell you how much I love you, how much I appreciate you, how much I need you. I don't know why I —"

"Shh. Quin, I'm not perfect. I'm a control freak, I always think I'm right, and you were right: I did follow you here to Sacramento. Not because I wanted to watch out for you — though that was probably part of it — but because I missed you. You're my family. You were my rock. You're the reason I became strong. You needed me, and back then I needed to be needed. It kept me focused. So when you didn't need me, I didn't take it too well."

"I did need you, I just didn't want to admit it. And I still do. I — I talked to my doctor about seeing a shrink. I think — I think I need to. I've got a lot of stuff in my head, and I know it's not all good stuff."

Tears rolled down Nora's cheeks now. "I'm proud of you, Quin." She kissed her.

There was a knock on the door, and Duke entered. "Hey Quin, can I borrow Nora for a minute?"

"Yeah. Nora, want to send Ted in? I want to thank him."

"I'm sure he's still out there. I'll find him."

She left and Duke asked, "Are you okay?"

"Terrific." She kissed him.

"Melanie Duncan is here. She came by to share some great news. I think you'll want to hear this."

"Okay." She saw Ted talking to Hooper. "Ted, Quin's awake. She wanted to talk to you."

He looked skeptical, but went into her room.

Melanie Duncan was in the waiting room. "Great news!" she said. "Fish and Game didn't terminate D-Eleven."

"D-Eleven?"

"The missing duck. The one Agent Hooper found in the cabin."

"Right."

"The lab in Wisconsin said none of the ducks had symptoms of the avian flu, and I'm flying with D-Eleven to the national lab there to re-create Jonah's research." She sighed heavily. "It's going to take years. But with D-Eleven, we'll be much further along."

Duke said to Nora, "Jim Butcher agreed to donate all materials to the lab, and he's taking a job with a biotech company in the Bay Area as their spokesman."

Nora smiled. "I'm happy for you, and for the project. It's good news."

"It is. I'm leaving tomorrow, so I need to pack. Ian isn't happy, but I told him I'd find him a job." She smiled. "Absence makes the heart grow fonder, and the bank account shrink — he'd already planned on flying out three times before Christmas!"

She hugged Duke and then Nora, and left.

"Come with me," Duke said, and took Nora's hand.

He led her out into the rose garden in the courtyard of the hospital. "What's wrong, Nora?"

"Nothing."

He stopped, sat her on a bench, and kissed her. "What's wrong?"

"I'm tired. I'm still worried about Quin, though she's doing better. I'm sad that fifteen thousand acres were destroyed. And — I didn't want Maggie to die."

"I know — but she tried to push you over the cliff."

"But the thing is — I don't feel guilty. And that bothers me."

"Sweetheart." Duke pulled Nora into his arms and breathed in deeply. "I love you so much. For your compassion and your determination and your honesty." And for so much more. Spending the rest of his life with Nora would make him so happy.

He kissed the top of her head. She'd had a concussion, and that first night Duke had worried greatly about her. Between the smoke in the mountains, the running, being hit with rocks, she'd been in worse shape than either of them thought at the time. It made him realize that Nora was as much a part of his family as Sean.

He kissed her again.

"I have a little surprise." He pulled an envelope from his back pocket and handed it to her.

"What?"

He smirked. "Open it, or don't you like presents?"

She stared at the envelope for a long minute. He pushed her chin up. "Don't you dare cry on me Nora, it's good news."

"I know — I just don't — nothing," she ended abruptly.

"You don't get a lot of presents, do you?"

She shook her head. "I'm being silly."

"Open it."

She did, and she stared with wide eyes. "What?"

"You can read."

"It's an airline confirmation receipt. Florida?"

"Look at page two."

She flipped it over. "Hotel confirmation. The Disneyland Hotel?"

"Just a monorail ride from the park."

"We're going to Disneyland? When?"

"We leave in two days. Don't tell me you can't leave on the spur of the moment, because —"

"I wouldn't. I can't believe — I'm excited."

"You are? Do you want to smile then? Because I can't tell that you're excited."

She threw her arms around his neck and squeezed him tightly.

"Better?"

"Much."

She sighed contently and rested her head on his shoulder. Duke smiled over her head, promising himself that he would give Nora presents and trips to fun places every chance he got.

"I learned something this week," Nora said.

"That you love me?"

"Yeah, that too." She kissed his neck.

"What else?"

"Home isn't my house or your house or my things," she said. "My entire life, I was looking for a place to be home. And it's not a place at all. It's a person. You're my home, Duke. Wherever you are, I will be happy as long as I'm with you."